THE SINNER KING:
BOOK OF EARTH

A novel by D. R. Crislip

PUBLISHED BY DONALD RAY CRISLIP

All of the characters and events in this book are fictitious, and any resemblance to actual persons, living or dead, is purely coincidental.

ISBN 978-0615927664

First Edition:
December 2013

Also by D. R. Crislip

The Sinner King: Book of Fire

For my wife, Nici . . . always.

ACKNOWLEDGEMENTS

A big thank you to my editor, J Keirn-Swanson, for his work on this book and his patience with my excessive deployment of colons. His keen eye and literary sense was invaluable, and he undoubtedly made this book far better than it would have been without his editorial comments.

Another big thank you to my wife, who pushed me to stay focused on finishing this book in a year's time (unlike the first book which took six). As always, her sense of what's right and wrong serves as navigational stars to my completion of these novels.

And last but not least, a big thank you to YOU for purchasing this book as well as the first one (assuming you did) and fueling me with encouragement to continue to write.

THE SINNER KING:
BOOK OF EARTH

PROLOGUE

District 11, Sector 20 – 3529 AFT

He was told not to move. If he kept still—absolutely still—they wouldn't see him; the suit he and the rest of his squad were wearing would shield him. It was hard for Garret to trust his life to what he classified as an assumption. He knew next to nothing about the suit. It was supposedly captured during a raid on a Ministry Security Force warehouse two months ago. "It's one of their Thermo-G camouflage," Carlsberg had told him. "Top-secret stuff. They've yet to put them into production. The boys on the Western Border discovered the warehouse on one of their recon trips. They had no idea what they had stumbled upon. They raided the place, and this suit"— Carlsberg had thrust the suit into Garret's hands—"is what they came back with." What the boys on the Western Border had actually found was an entire platoon worth of suits, still in testing phase.

The test is over, Garret told himself. Any minute now they would discover whether the suits actually worked. Garret looked down at the bizarre sight covering his body. The suit was shiny and yet gave no reflection. It made no sense. It felt like plastic against his skin, and bore swirly patterns that changed in shape and color when light touched its surface, what supposedly made them invisible to MSF radar. How Carlsberg or anyone else knew that piece of information was beyond Garret's knowledge. All he had of substance to trust was Carlsberg's word, which wasn't comforting considering that Carlsberg was an MSF reject who had bad personal hygiene and picked his nose. But times were tough and winning battles was crucial to their survival, especially when the battle he was about to face involved rescuing one of the most important men in modern era. So trust he must.

The moment when news of Corbin Byrne's capture had reached his ears, Garret almost gave up his life within the Free People's Society. Life was certainly not as glamorous as he had hoped. As a boy, he had heard all of the utopic stories told by his friends, how the Heretique could do whatever they liked, whenever they liked, and however they liked; that no one governing body ruled them and that each man and woman was responsible for him and herself; that the members looked out for each other and gave a helping hand when another struggled; and that each person could decide his or her own fate. Those stories were radically different from the life of his mother and father, of the life he was going to live, once he was of age. Garret's father had come home each day after spending ten hours in the mines, covered in dirt, soot, sweat, and who knows what else; and each day his father would stumble—literally stumble from exhaustion—over to the only set of table and chairs they owned, and collapse down in a heap of rugged skin and bones wrapped inside one of two thick canvased uniforms he wore. Either his helmet would tumble off and onto the table or floor, or he would pull it off and spin it onto the table as sweat and sometimes blood made vertical streaks along his forehead and face. Garret's mother was very aware of her husband's pain and would always have a glass of "clean" water waiting for him. "Clean" being the key, since getting uncontaminated water from the village well was a task of its own; nonetheless, she had made it a daily duty of making sure he had at least one glass of dirt-free water to enjoy after slaving to the point of death. Garret had witnessed this hideous routine his entire adolescent life, and when he had received the results of his Cognitive Examination, he knew that his fate would be no better, and that was the day he had decided to run. But as already mentioned, life amongst the Free People wasn't candy and cake. His skill with the axe and hammer was all he had brought with him; his life in manual labor was inevitable; but doing it because he *could* was somehow different from doing it because he *had to*. As the Cognitive Examination showed, Garret was not the sharpest tool in the mine, but he didn't have to be in order to understand that there was a difference between "can do" and "must do." But all of that was before. Now things were different. Once again, Garret was using his manual strength to survive; however, this time it was in arms and not in mines. Over thirty some odd years had passed since he took up life within the Free People, and inside those years he had grown externally strong, even though he still felt internally weak. It wasn't until volunteering to rescue Corbin Byrne that Garret had finally found the strength deep within his heart. They had said it would be a one-way ticket for most involved, and yet it was that promise that gave him the power he so desperately needed. Never in his life had he truly felt like he had made a difference—even after joining the Free People—until he had stood at the gathering and tossed his hat into the ring. This was finally going to be his moment to "shine"—as long as the damned suits did not.

"You hear that?" asked a nervous voice from behind. Garret didn't recognize exactly whose it belonged to nor could he look back to see; they were all face-first on the ground, weapons underneath them. Garret had the privilege of lying on top of what was known as the Equalizer: a weapon used to bring down MSF hovercrafts. It was a bulky, metallic tube that unleashed the most menacing beam of energy he had ever seen, capable of destroying or damaging almost all of the MSF light and medium-armored vehicles—thus the title. "It brings the MSF to our level," as they say. The Equalizer came to exist in the Free People's Society by some helping hands working within the Ministry, people who were sympathetic to the Free People's cause but concluded that they were more useful staying within the Collective instead of leaving it.

Garret tilted his head slightly to listen for any out-of-place sounds.

There was nothing.

Garret could feel his heart pounding through his chest and against the Equalizer. Sporting that large cannon was a hell of a job; it typically took two people to hold and fire it, but Garret, being the strong manual labor type, was capable of handling it alone, which was crucial for their mission.

Garret knew that once the hovercraft carrying Corbin passed overhead (and as long as the suits protected them against the MSF radar) they would have a few seconds of total surprise to act. Every man had a place he needed to be, and no two men could be spared to carry out a single task.

The challenge with operating the Equalizer, outside of its enormous bulk, was prepping it to fire inside such a short window. Like all laser weapons, it needed to charge. But none of the weapons could be charged prior to attack without alerting the MSF. So, again, once they passed overhead, Garret was tasked with not only lugging the cannon into firing position and accurately aiming it, but he was also burdened with getting it ready for use—a minimum of seven seconds—which in actuality wasn't a long amount of time; but in battle, seven seconds could seem like forever.

"Did you hear that?" asked the nervous voice again.

Garret listened closer but only heard the wind cutting through the wild grass surrounding them. "Stay quiet," ordered another, calmer voice.

The men behind Garret were there for fire support. Their weapons charged faster and could unleash a barrage of attacks while he prepared the Equalizer. Far out in front of him, lying in the grass, were three teams of six, forming a rudimentary triangle. The idea was to down the hovercraft in the middle of the triangle, making it prone for a three-sided attack. The plan sounded great; the problem was that almost nothing went as planned.

Garret took a deep breath and blew it out against the metallic tube pressed against his lips. *Relax*, he told himself. *Relax. There's no use getting upset. Everyone dies. It has to happen sometime. Today may be your day or may not be—just relax.* His mind flashed visuals of his father sagging at the family table, eyes drooping from exhaustion, rough stubble poking through his face, his father's scraped knuckles and dirt filled fingernails. *You're fighting for him, for men like your father. You're fighting for something better.*

Garret considered their situation for a moment. Code Zero was absolutely dependent upon the success of their mission, and Garret played a key role in either its achievement or its failure.

Code Zero was Corbin Byrne's brilliant conception. He understood that a time would come when his capture was inevitable. He also understood that dead leaders were more powerful than living leaders. The problem, however, with dead leaders is that they are dead and can no longer lead, yet Corbin conceived of a way to have both the power of being a martyr but still retain the ability to lead.

When Garret first heard of the plan he thought there was no way it would work. "People will never believe it," he told Hugh Townsend, his squad leader.

"Of course they will," Hugh said boldly. "A rescue mission gone awry; everyone will believe it, especially when we broadcast it across the planet."

"The MSF will know the truth."

"Will they? I think not."

"How can you be so sure?"

"Because . . . we will annihilate everything. By the time the MSF arrives there will be nothing to find but smoldering ashes."

"But what if I . . . I mean . . . what if *we* fail? What if he dies in the attack?"

Hugh laughed. "That is the brilliance of this plan; if we shoot them down and Corbin dies, then we still win: Corbin will be the martyr he desires."

Garret didn't look too convinced. Hugh wrapped a long arm around the broad man and said, "Relax. The only way we fail is if we don't shoot them down and the MSF changes their minds about Corbin's execution. All we have to do to win is shoot the hovercraft down; that's not too hard, right? Just try not to kill the big man, aye?"

Garret took in a deep breath and released it. "Aye."

A breeze blew in around Garret, pushing against the suit protecting him; the air tickled his nose. He heard birds sing their peaceful songs, and for an unprotected moment, Garret's mind was allowed to wander from the upcoming doom and bring forth a wistful memory of his youth, when things had yet to become too complicated . . . back before he understood the world and his meager place within it.

A low murmur was heard way off in the distance, and the memory vanished.

The murmur was accompanied by several higher pitched whines.

Garret knew the hovercraft would be escorted—but by how many? The answer was coming quicker than Garret was prepared for. *They're moving fast.* He wanted to turn and look in order to gauge what they were up against, but that would have only granted him death, which he figured was coming along just fine on its own.

Garret slid his hand down the Equalizer and placed his fingers overtop the Power Save button. The smaller, light-armored hovercrafts were above him now and moving at a very high velocity. The sound of the hovercrafts' engines ripped through his ear canals. It was very loud—*too loud*. Garret struggled against the instinct to cover his ears.

"*NOW!*" screamed one of the men from behind.

There was no time for fear. Garret pushed the Energy Save button and popped to his knees. He looked down at the Equalizer and saw the charge light blinking. His eyes looked up to the hovercrafts high above; they were quickly flying into the distance. Garret realized that they had waited too long. He gripped the Equalizer and threw it up to his shoulder like it was made of cardboard. His right eye trained through the electronic sight that automatically focused in on the central subject: the medium sized hovercraft reportedly carrying Corbin Byrne. Certain that seven seconds had passed, Garret's right index finger closed on the trigger . . . but nothing happened.

"*FIRE!*" shouted a voice from behind.

At once, the sky zipped to life with beams of light, cutting through the white cotton clouds separating them from the hovercrafts. Almost simultaneously, the three teams making up the triangle in the distance began to fire as well. But no one was supposed to fire before Garret, and everyone was exposed now. . . .

The plan was quickly falling apart—*I'm supposed to be the first to fire*—but nothing happened when he squeezed the trigger again. *Shoot, damnit!*

Seven seconds was the difference between life and death.

Shoot!

And then it did.

A brilliant red beam blinked out of the Equalizer and severed the medium hovercraft's right mounted engine. Garret loosened the trigger just before the beam slashed into the cargo hold.

Through the viewfinder, sparks, flames, and smoke began pouring out of the right engine. The hovercraft turned onto its right side as the left mounted engine over compensated. The hovercraft immediately began to lose altitude and continued to turn sharply to its right. It was coming down.

There was an explosion of cheers from behind.

The two lighter hovercrafts turned in unison, departing from their damaged comrade.

And then reality hit.

Complete loss of the right mounted engine proved too much for the crippled hovercraft and it came down a lot faster than anticipated. It splashed into the field right were one of the attack squads was positioned. Upon impact, the entire hovercraft rippled and bent. The tail swung overhead and then slammed into the ground. A guttural roar followed as pieces and parts exploded off. Garret watched this scene in utter horror.

Burnbeams scorched a patch of grass next to Garret and his attention snapped to the light hovercraft bearing down on him. His support team returned fire but the beams from their burnboxes did little damage to the tough exterior of the hovercraft. Garret dropped to his knees and blindly aimed the Equalizer up at the hovercraft. He squeezed the trigger but nothing happened. It needed to finish charging again.

Screams bellowed out from behind. Garret looked back just in time to see his entire support team cut in half by a second burnbeam attack. All four men toppled to the ground in pieces.

Some were still alive.

Garret pulled the trigger again and the Equalizer blew out a beam of red light directly above the attacking hovercraft. He then slashed down with it, severing the cockpit through the middle and heavily damaging the hull. The hovercraft began to slowly spin and drop downward. Flames shot out of where the cockpit was located before crashing into a heap in the field about a hundred yards in front of him.

Off in the distance, the second light hovercraft was in battle with the surviving two attacking squads. Garret looked back at the medium hovercraft and saw several injured MSF agents tending to each other. There was little hope that Corbin had survived the crash. Regardless, Garret needed to try and find him.

He lowered the Equalizer from his shoulder and began recharging it again before breaking into a jog toward the crash site. To his left he heard cries coming from the burning hovercraft he had just shot down.

An explosion erupted from the light hovercraft battling the two attacking squads, followed by a billow of heavy grey smoke. The hovercraft lowered to the ground and attempted to land. The survivors of the attacking squads charged in and surrounded the craft, concentrating their firepower on its main hull. Garret turned his attention to the downed medium hovercraft. There were more survivors gathering at the spot, armed with laser rifles—

about eight at this point. He considered stopping and firing the Equalizer at them but he knew that the beam would cut through them and into the hovercraft behind, further risking the death of Corbin Byrne, if he was even alive.

One of the agents amassing at the downed hovercraft noticed Garret through the swaying weeds. He limped behind a chunk of the wrecked hull and called out something inaudible. Three other agents looked in Garret's direction and raised their laser rifles. Garret was a sitting duck.

Without thinking, Garret aimed the Equalizer at the closest of the three agents and pulled the trigger. In a flash, the beam hit the agent dead center and released a poof of red carbon matter that used to be his body. Garret then slashed the laser across the other two agents, killing them instantaneously, before painting the remaining men, which included the piece of hull insufficiently protecting the agent with a limp.

After three seconds, it was all over.

Garret cautiously jogged toward the hovercraft while checking on the other downed hovercraft, which seemed completely overtaken by his comrades.

When Garret arrived at the wreckage, he clearly saw all of the damage he had single handedly done. The sight was beyond gruesome. It took him several seconds to connect what he was seeing to what he had done. He then began to vomit.

Two of his fellow attacking squad members came running onto the scene, battle ready. They stumbled to where Garret was trying to recover, and one of them said, "*Jumpin Ginger-shit,* what happened here?!"

The other man walked over to Garret and patted him on the shoulder; it was Hugh. "It's alright, son. Better them than you."

"You used the *Equalizer* on them?" asked the other agent, Jack *something* (Garret had not learned his last name).

"*I . . . I had no choice,*" Garret stammered out.

"Shit-on-a-stick, I guess not. Damn. Is there anybody alive?"

The question fell hard on Garret's ears.

Hugh said, "We better take a look."

Garret nodded and stood on shaky legs.

"Why don't you wait here, son. Just take a breather."

Jack went around the hull and found a hole leading inside. "Hello?

Anyone alive?" He flipped on a light and shone it inside. "Damn. What a mess."

"*It came down too fast,*" Garret said through shaky breaths. "*It wasn't supposed to happen this way.*"

Hugh continued to pat him on the shoulder. "It's not your fault."

Jack shouted out again, "Damn! What a mess!"

"*We were supposed to save him.*"

"Nothing could be done, son. We tried our best."

"Damn!"

"*He can't be dead . . . he can't be.*"

"He's just a man. We all tried. Nothing can be done. May God have his soul."

"Crap-on-a-branch, you guys need to get in here!"

CHAPTER ONE

District 9, Sector 2

The room was silent. Rebecca chose it because of its silence. Everywhere else inside the compound, there was noise . . . all of the time . . . night and day . . . but inside this room, there was only a hint of life outside a faint murmur of voices and footsteps, doors opening and closing. This room was Rebecca's only reprieve. Its walls, a golden yellow; its floor, a royal red with gold damask patterns; its curvy Calliver chairs, upholstered in royal red fabric; and its Vastino sofas, upholstered in dyed red leather, beaded with gold; these things were her only friends. They never passed judgment on her. They never talked down to her. When Rebecca was with them—these inanimate objects—she felt the faint spirit of family lift her soul. The misty memory of her youth billowed inside her mind and she could almost hear her father, Francis, in the neighboring room, chatting with her mother in an inaudible tone, just loud enough so that their voices could be heard. It was a form of silence, obviously not total silence, but a comforting silence. This room was the closest thing she had to this silence. And sadly, whenever she had to accompany Simon to a dinner, or to some kind of political Ministry function, she would greatly miss this room and its silence.

Six months had passed since Rebecca's return to the Collective, since her translation of William Coulee's manuscript, since the betrayal of her biological father, Corbin Byrne, and the botched rescue attempt that left him dead inside an MSF hovercraft bound for Sector 1, where he was to be publicly executed for his crimes against the Collective and its Ministry.

Five months had passed since the ripple effect of Corbin Byrne's martyrdom ignited global uprisings that have turned nearly one half of the Collective's Sectors into a war zone between the united rebel factions known as the Free People's Society (or as the Heretique) and the Ministry.

Four months had passed since her ceremonious marriage to Simon, which was projected in every public square across each sector of the Collective, inviting the whole world to participate in the event—except for Rebecca's mother; she was now hiding somewhere within the folds of the Free People's Society.

Corbin Byrne's death was viewed by the Ministry as an incredible victory against their rebellious foe, but the reality of the situation was that the Heretique had gained in strength, far more so than when Corbin was alive. Because of this, the MSF took a more prominent presence within the Collective.

Security Chief Jonas Lundquist was silently becoming more powerful. With the growing number of MSF agents meddling within the Collective, Jonas's control over its people was growing too. Rebecca could literally see the conflict of who was really in charge on the faces of the MSF agents who were placed within the Wylde's compound by Jonas, but then ordered by Simon—the future Director of Social Affairs—to stay out of sight. The growing impression was that Jonas was the real power within the Ministry and for a good reason too.

Rebecca had heard whisperings concerning Jonas's ability to influence whoever he desired, whispers that told of a horrific gift he had for torturing people by simply using his mind. None of this was news to her; Rebecca had long known of a speculated division of the MSF known as the Thought Police. They were supposedly comprised of men and women who were capable of reading and manipulating a person's thoughts. However, no evidence of this group had ever been brought to light. Rebecca had believed the stories to be nothing but legend used to frighten outlaws. But the past few months had seen some dark changes within the Collective, and rumors of this mind control practice being used on suspected Heretique members were growing.

Rebecca walked slowly over to one of the Calliver chairs and placed her hand onto its armrest. The fabric was wonderful to touch, as were many things within the compound. The chair looked comfortable as well; it was obviously designed that way. But when she sat down on it, the chair forced her back slightly inward, the seat cushion wasn't as padded as its plush appearance, and over a matter of a few minutes, Rebecca would have to stand again, leaving the majestic beauty of the chair and its unconformable stiffness. She would look back at it, feel its allure, and wish the chair to be more suitable for sitting. Rebecca realized that the same could be said for her feelings toward the Collective and the Ministry.

While briefly living as a fugitive six months ago, Rebecca desired nothing more than to be back within the Collective . . . so much so that she concocted a plan to locate her biological father and to use him as a bargaining chip to secure a safe return. But as things progressed, the man she had perceived as an evil terrorist was far from it, and the governing body she had so desperately wanted to return to have proven to be sadistic and terrible. Unfortunately, the latter was discovered too late, and now Corbin Byrne was dead. The whole ordeal was a harsh lesson in reality. Nothing was as it seemed. Her marriage to Simon was a fraud; she loved him no more than he loved her. Rebecca was positive that his plan to marry only continued because he felt it was his duty to take her as his wife, per the Ministry approved Cognitive Examination. It would have been an awful catalyst for the uprising had Simon refused to go through with the engagement; it would have been like throwing gasoline on a small fire raging at the base of the Ministry ideals. No, the marriage had to continue, and it did. They faked their way through it, smiling and holding each other's hand, kissing on cue, dancing, and boarding the luxury hovercar that swept them away from the ceremony and into what the audience believed to be a wonderful retreat. But that was hardly the reality. As soon as the door closed, Simon ripped his hand free and began brooding out the side window. Rebecca had hoped that his contempt for her would lessen as time wore on, that he would regain the infatuation he once had for her, and that he would move past the malevolent whispers that followed them everywhere, but it eventually became apparent that he would never forgive her for being the daughter of a "villain." She embarrassed him, and apparently there was no worse crime.

They spent their entire retreat separated. Their marriage was never consummated; apparently his body could not forgive her either, not that Rebecca wanted their consummation to be shadowed by such disdain. She did all that she could to move beyond the ordeal, but nothing appeared to have an effect. It wasn't until a month and a half into their sham of a marriage that Rebecca finally tossed in the towel and accepted reality: She was utterly alone.

There was no word from her mother. Rebecca had no idea if Francesca was safe or not. With MSF agents crawling all over the compound, there was no way anyone could send a message to her regarding Francesca's condition or location. And Rebecca was strictly forbidden to go anywhere without Simon. All was not forgiven by anyone within the Ministry, no matter how many smiles and greetings they extended toward her.

As for William's manuscript, Rebecca did her best not to think about it. As far as she knew, it was destroyed during the fighting down in the Vriezen. She made the mistake of asking about it once, and Simon immediately accused her of being under its spell. "Do you still believe it to be true?! It's Heretique propaganda! Your accepting of this book is a damnation of all that we swore to uphold! I demand of you, Rebecca, to never speak of it again!" And so Rebecca has done just that—not because Simon demanded it of her but because she didn't want it ruining her life any further. She had done all she could to try and forget its message. But how could anyone truly forget reading about how they supposedly once lived and died in a completely different time, and that they are supposed to have some sort of mysterious power?

Rebecca sat on the Calliver chair. She pressed the fabric of her gown down around her legs. No more uniforms for her and no more Duties; she was no longer an active member of the Ministry, just a mascot now, Simon's toy to show off to the Collective. She was a wife, yes, but was more of a possession. Rebecca could finally grow her hair out, if she chose so; that was about the only freedom she had. But even growing her hair out was expected, and she didn't dare do anything unexpected; so she grew her hair out.

****

It was almost an hour after Rebecca had entered the room that the door swung open. Simon, dressed in full Ministry garb, stood inside its frame. He didn't look at her, choosing instead to focus his attention on his uniform sleeve. "It's time to get going."

Another dinner. Rebecca stood up from the beautiful, uncomfortable chair and straightened her dress. At some point in time, she had slid her feet out of her shoes. Rebecca carefully bent over, so not to reveal too much of her legs, afraid to further embarrass Simon, and slid both shoes back on. He turned from the door and left her behind. An MSF agent filled his void. "I'm coming," Rebecca breathed out. The agent stepped aside while she left through the door. He then followed closely behind. Rebecca looked back to the agent and said, "I'm not going to run off; you don't have to follow so closely."

The agent said nothing in return.

There were people littered all throughout the main entertainment space: officials she recognized, officials she didn't recognize, maintenance workers, MSF agents, and even a few children who obviously belonged to some of the Ministry socialites. A few of these people, the ones not engaged in conversation, nodded and smiled at the beautiful bride of Simon Wylde. Rebecca continued the charade, smiling back and returning nods. These people were always there; if not these specific people in the room, then there were others, but basically they were all the same: desperate individuals trying to leech or further their good standing within the higher echelon of the Ministry. Every so often Rebecca would pass Simon's father, Director of Social Affairs Arthur Wylde, or his wife, standing amongst these admirers, and witness just how phony the leeches could truly be, with their fake laughter, false interests, and over-complimentary declarations. It was sickening. But that was the real world, Rebecca realized, and she often wondered if she would have been so repulsed had her circumstances been different.

Outside, the luxury hovercar built for long distance travelling waited. The driver stood beside the opened passenger door and inside sat Simon, looking at his digital notepad. "You look beautiful, Mrs. Wylde," the driver said with a smile.

Mrs. Wylde. Rebecca was sure she would never get used to it. "Thank you," she said, not knowing his name; he was new. Rebecca bent down and slid into the hovercar. Simon pretended not to notice. The driver closed the door and went around to take his seat behind the steering console. *Mrs. Wylde,* she thought again. Had Rebecca been higher ranked or even of the same rank as Simon, she would have maintained her mother's last name. *How Mrs. Wylde used to sound so good,* wistful thoughts of a once guileless little girl.

"Where are we going?" asked Rebecca. Simon hardly informed her of anything other than to get dressed for dinner tonight.

"We're going to the Ministry Palace in Sector 4," he said without looking up.

"*Sector 4?* Why are we going there tonight?" Sector 4 was hardly a casual drive. It was 800 hundred miles away.

"Sector 4 has been the most heavily hit with uprisings. My father felt that our presence at a Ministry dinner would help boost local moral." He looked up at her, finally; his eyes were dry and slightly red. "Especially considering that rumors have you as the daughter of their slain hero. Your loyalty and presence will help assure that the Ministry is right and the Heretique is wrong." His eyes returned to the notepad.

"Someday"—Rebecca's voice trembled—"you'll have to forgive me."

Simon said nothing in return.

"Okay," said the driver as he climbed inside. "We're off."

"Please do not speak," ordered Simon.

Rebecca cringed at his callousness and looked at the driver's eyes through the rearview mirror. Expecting to see embarrassment, Rebecca saw something curious: The man's eyes almost seemed to be smiling at her.

CHAPTER TWO

The Dead Sands – OP6

The land was a craggy dust bowl sprinkled with rocks; why the MSF had an outpost there was beyond William Coulee's comprehension. He kicked a jagged chunk of granite and watched dust clouds puff each time it made contact with the ground. The wind ripped through the barren landscape, fierce and unchallenged; there was nothing out there beside sand, sun, and the tiny steel outpost that was usually occupied by a disgraced agent. Everyone posted there since its construction had understood that it was a punishment, including William. The difference between all of the post's previous occupants and William was that they knew why they were there— William did not. Even after spending a week in this solitude, William was incapable of figuring out why Jonas was punishing him.

It had all begun six months ago, when William orchestrated the capture of Heretique leader Corbin Byrne. His agents failed to locate the secondary target, some ancient manuscript Corbin's illegitimate daughter had brought him, but that was hardly ground for demerit. They achieved their primary objective; they captured one of the most dangerous men threatening the Collective. How could anyone fault him for not locating what he considered a meaningless book?

When word reached the Minister that the book had not been gained, William was sent back with a small task force. William was directly ordered by the Security Chief not to return until he located the book or discovered where it had gone. William had tried telling everyone—meaning his superior, the Security Chief, and even Director Wylde—what Rebecca Badeau had confessed the day he captured her, that the book was destroyed during the fighting, but Director Wylde and the Security Chief were unmoved. "We can't take risks on assumptions," Director Wylde had said. William struggled with why the book was so important. Director Wylde said, "It's misleading propaganda. What more is needed? Look at what it did to this young woman, she risked everything, including her marriage to my son, just to take the book to the Heretique. That should be enough evidence to warrant concern. We simply cannot risk it further confusing naïve minds." That last statement troubled William the most. From everything recorded in the dossier on Rebecca Badeau, her mind was far from naïve or easily impressionable. She was a brilliant individual who appeared to be strong-willed and very dedicated to her work. It would take quite a lot to make her turn away from the Ministry and enter the dark world of the Heretique. William didn't know what it was, but he was certain Rebecca was motivated by more than ancient propaganda.

The thing William found most shocking, however, was how forgiving the Minister was with her. It was law that anyone born illegitimately would be condemned to a death sentence. It was an ancient, crude law but it was the law nonetheless, and up to that moment, and as far as William knew, it was always followed. He did have a theory as to why she was spared: When Corbin was turned martyr, it made sense to spare his daughter and bring her back into the Collective—to reform her—because executing Corbin's only daughter would have ignited the dangerous situation that was rapidly forming in the outskirts of the Collective. The uprising already had one martyr; the Ministry didn't need it to have a second. Plus, Rebecca was beautiful. History had shown that martyring a beautiful girl only made matters worse. When the fourth Minister executed Abraham's wife, there were small uprisings all over the Sumer, which was a microcosmic representation of what was happening that moment in the Collective. No, the Minister was right for not executing Rebecca.

William sighed and sat down on a small granite boulder. Sweat dripped off his brow as his soaked brown hair stuck against his forehead. His body was a swimming pool inside his uniform. He didn't understand why he was there nor did he know why he continued to dress in full uniform. He chalked it up to habit, but that didn't explain why he hadn't stripped it off. It must have been a hundred and ten degrees that day. The desert was dry heat but ridiculously hot nonetheless. The MSF uniform only contributed to his discomfort. If he took the uniform off, there would be no one there to report his infraction. But William took pride in his position; he wasn't going to let some discomfort tarnish his appearance.

After a few minutes of drowning in sweat, William left the boulder and went back inside the outpost. The building had plenty of fans running off the solar powered generator on the roof, but the building wasn't outfitted with a cooling unit and so it was hot inside as well. William couldn't complain too much, the building provided shade and therefore it was better than being outside.

He walked over to the steel desk he kept immaculately clean by dusting it twice a day—more out of boredom than duty—and sat down on the steel swivel chair behind it. William and boredom were becoming good friends. Normally when William was bored he would turn to his notepad or watch the Ministry Monitor, but he could only activate those things when he was off duty; and since William was the only person at the outpost, he was never off duty, so his notepad was incapable channeling anything considered "entertainment." So, instead, William had developed several humorous games in order to keep himself entertained: He took a pair of his socks and balled them up together, and then threw the sock ball at objects placed on his desk; and when that became boring, William worked on doing handstands. He also became quite good at memorizing things and estimating numbers based on visual measurements—he would basically look at a paragraph of text, guess how many words were inside it, and then count them out. He became so good that he rarely missed by two words. . . .

So yes, William was bored.

However, his isolation gave him one good thing: He became quite the crack shot with his laser rifle. All agents were good shots; it was a requirement, but William had become better. The isolation also gave him time to think about what he truly wanted out of life, to meditate truly on himself, which was something he hardly had time for before his posting in the desert.

As an MSF agent, the Ministry forbade William to marry. The restriction wasn't for life but it was required during his active duty years. William contemplated this for the first time since taking the oath and surprisingly found a desire to make a change. Something happened to him during the course of the previous six months—something beyond getting posted in the desert—he had become curious as to who he would have been paired with had he not tested into the MSF through the Cognitive Examination. William would never outwardly confess what stirred this wonderment, but a betting man would probably guess Rebecca Badeau. Reading her dossier and seeing recorded images of her had caused something deep within him to twist and turn. She was smart, beautiful, and clearly cunning. The manner in which she outsmarted several of his agents, survived a Stalker attack, made her way to the Vriezen without using her Identity Imprint, and infiltrated the most secretive organization outside the Ministry, was beyond his expectations. One could say any woman like that could make a man yearn for her, and William was no exception. However, William also understood that there was no use in coveting another man's wife. If he made his feelings known, he would be placed on the fast track to corporal punishment. An MSF flogging wasn't desirable. He had witnessed several of them in his lifetime, and each ended with the criminal left unconscious on the ground, drowning in a pool of his own blood. They would beat him until he fell; that was the rule. Six months ago, he risked having his feelings exposed on the hovercraft, where he met her for the first time, and vowed never to make that mistake again. But at the time, he found it difficult to hide his desire to stare at her in total infatuation. She was beautiful. William assumed that every man felt attracted to her; *how could they not?* But again, it was pointless to dwell on; Rebecca was paired and possibly married now.

William found a sock ball on the ground and picked it up. Over on the wall was a framed picture of Minister Theoman, grinning. William imagined that the Minister was smiling at his inner turmoil. William chucked the sock ball at the picture; it hit the wall just above it. *Just as well*, he thought; it was dumb to risk another infraction. With all of the hidden MSF recorders throughout various outposts, William had no idea if someone was watching. Yet, then again. . . .

William spun the chair away from the desk and stood up, stretching his back and groaning loudly. His voice echoed through the empty space. "Here I am," he said loudly. "Bored to bits. Thank you for this assignment; I think this is a *great* allocation of my skills." The worst part was that a month prior to his assignment to the outpost, Amon Walkure was promoted to Director of Cognitive Services, which was completely baffling. William had done a couple of operations with Walkure and quickly drew the opinion that he was a man not to be trifled with; Walkure's ruthlessness could rival the Security Chief's. Assigning him the responsibility of overlooking all of Cognitive Services seemed to be completely unfit. But what was far more perplexing was how the Security Chief gained approval from Director Wylde for the promotion. William even contemplated whether the approval was ever given, *not that it's any of my business*. He hadn't seen Walkure since their joint pursuit of the Cognitive Services caretaker and alleged Heretique member, Jillian Heddington. That awful day still haunted William's memory.

Again, six months ago, word was sent to William via one of Walkure's agents that a man living in Cognitive Services, Benjamin Vermil, was suspected of being a member of the Heretique and possibly connected to Corbin Byrne. Walkure had mentioned that his team had reason to believe that Vermil was attempting to send a coded message to Byrne through one of Vermil's caretakers: Jillian Heddington. One of Walkure's agents tailed Jillian to a cave where she retrieved a safebox allegedly planted by another member of the Heretique. This agent then contacted Walkure and informed him that Jillian was heading toward District 2, Sectory 27 in order to deliver the safebox to a woman named Rebecca Badeau. At that time, neither William nor Walkure knew what role Rebecca was to play. This information was sent to the Security Chief who then scrambled a reconnaissance team, including William, to rendezvous with Walkure in District 2. The Security Chief also declared that he was taking over the operation, which William found shocking. The Security Chief's direct involvement meant that this operation was very sensitive.

After William arrived, the Security Chief ordered everyone to stay back and allow the exchange to unfold. William and Walkure were sent to the next station in District 9 and were told to wait there until the railway made its stop with Jillian, post exchange.

The plan was to flush Jillian into an empty car where the Security Chief would be waiting for her. William didn't see the exchange between Jillian and Rebecca but he later learned that it was very peculiar; Rebecca didn't appear to know Jillian, nor did she seem to want the safebox. It wasn't until after some convincing that Rebecca finally agreed.

When the railway arrived, William and Walkure boarded it and immediately found Jillian. They did as ordered and quietly forced Jillian to the last car where the Security Chief was waiting. They watched the interaction between the Chief and Jillian, and Walkure said quietly, "We should push her out of the train and rid the world of her treachery." William found Walkure's words to be a bit harsh considering that they didn't know for sure if Jillian was Heretique or not. "Of course she is," Walkure said coldly, "we wouldn't be here if she weren't. The Security Chief is wasting his breath. He should end it." And it did end. Jillian walked toward the back of the car, clearly panicked, and tried to open the door. William and Walkure entered the car in order to stop her escape, but they quickly realized she wasn't going anywhere alive. Walkure began to laugh as she flung open the door and fell backward from the railway, three hundred feet through the air. Jillian screamed all the way down.

Her scream was still in William's mind.

It wasn't until later that William was informed that Jillian was indeed a Heretique, but even then, his conversation with Walkure left him sour. *And now he is in charge of Cognitive Services.* Walkure partook in the raid down in the Vriezen and supposedly lost an eye in the process. William heard that Walkure chose to wear an eye patch instead of having the commonplace surgery that would have fitted him with a false eye. *It suits him,* thought William.

An alarm went off on William's notepad. It was time for another patrol in the great desert. He picked up a thin towel off a cabinet against the near wall and wiped his face. This was going to be his third patrol of the day. So far, in his previous patrols, William had spotted a lizard playing dead, a couple of dust tornadoes, a few twisted cactuses, rocks—lots of rocks—and a small mountain range not too far off in the horizon but outside his patrol radius. *There's nothing out there; the heat scanners would show something if there were.* The MSF did infrequent satellite flyovers with heat reading radars that were designed to pickup human heat signatures. Not once in recent memory had they read anything out of the ordinary.

William left the outpost and walked over to a standalone garage that held the outpost's only means of transportation, an outdated hoverbike. His laser rifle was still in the holster since the last patrol; he didn't see a need to extract it. He then noticed that his shovel was missing, which was sometimes needed if the bike slipped into a sand dune.

I left it in the holding cells, he suddenly remembered. The desert heat was making him unusually forgetful.

William climbed on board the dusty hoverbike and pushed the cracked, green ignition button. The engine roared, blowing out smoke and dust. William coughed and fanned the air in front of his face. The hoverbike choked and stalled. "Yup," he said and then cranked the reset lever in order to try again. The outdated hoverbike usually took four attempts before maintaining a steady run. This time it took William an alarming seven tries. The engine roared loudly before settling into its normal state of gyrating. William was able to lift off the ground and pull out of the garage. There were a couple of moments where the hoverbike felt as if it was going to stall, but it maintained. *My luck will be that it stalls in the middle of the desert*, which would be a grievous situation.

Like the three patrols earlier in the day, this patrol rendered the same results: dust tornadoes, cactus, lizards, rocks, and the mountain range in the distance. William pulled around his final patrol marker and hovered steadily as he looked out into the distance. There were no clouds in sight. The rich blue sky became white as it touched the horizon and for the first time in three days there was something of a breeze. William removed his dust mask and ran his fingers through his sopping wet hair dripping salty sweat into his already burning eyes. *This is my future: sitting out here in the sun, sweating, alone, and terribly bored, with no foreseeable end. What did I do to deserve this?* The horizon danced in the heat of the day, which was known for creating illusions that something existed out in the nothing. William watched the waves of light entangle the landscape when something out of the ordinary did occur: there was something moving. *What is that?*

Through the haze of the midday heat and the dust clouds kicked up by the breeze, William could see something foreign. He reached down, grabbed his binoculars, and focused them on the grey spot. It was definitely moving and it was definitely not native to the desert. *What in the Minister's name?*

CHAPTER THREE

District 1, Sector 4

The banquet hall in the Ministry Palace of Sector 4 was no different than the palace in Sector 2. The arched ceiling had alternating rows of light and dark stained marble tiles; there were twelve marble columns running parallel to one another, dividing the floor, which was polished to a fine sheen; Eastern rugs were laid out along the perimeter walls where there were sofa furniture squared off from another, forming what was referred to as conversational chambers; and circular dining tables clothed in pearly white satin were strategically placed all through the main space of the hall so that the view of the head seating table, where Rebecca and Simon joined Sector 4's high officials, was not obstructed. There was a mouth-watering scent of roasted turkey wafting from the kitchen, which caused Rebecca's stomach to grumble. She had not eaten a thing since breakfast, thirteen hours ago. She looked to Simon, who sat next to her, and saw that he was expertly downing his third glass of vintage Shorbourne Wine. She asked over the roar of conversations and dining utensils, "How much longer until dinner will be served?"

Simon dripped some wine from his lip and onto the lapel of his dress uniform. "Damnit. . . . Can you not wait longer before fattening those hips of yours?"

Rebecca's hips had become his point of attack since most admirers of the couple tended to make comments regarding her ripeness for child bearing, drawing unwanted attention to the fact that she and Simon had yet to consummate their marriage. Rebecca knew that if Simon had it his way her body would be stick thin so that the fault for lack of children would fall entirely on her. "You should be happy to know that I haven't eaten since breakfast."

Simon gave up on wiping clean the stain on his lapel. "Well, that is a bit of good news, now isn't it? Maybe we should take that approach every day."

"I'm starving, Simon."

"Then drink some water, for *Minister's* sake."

"I have been doing that—about as much as you've been drinking wine."

He shot her a glare that warned: *don't push me.* But Rebecca didn't care anymore. Her life had become devoid of meaning. She would have said more but at that moment a waiter passed through the doublewide door of the kitchen with a cart full of dishes stacked with turkey and trimmings. It was custom to serve the Head Seating Table first, which Rebecca was very thankful for this evening. "Oh, thank God."

"*God*?" Simon repeated.

Rebecca hadn't realized she used that word.

"What is *God*?" asked Simon.

She didn't know how to explain. ". . . I don't . . . wait, where are they going?"

The servers weren't heading to the Head Seating Table but toward the rear of the room, where the lower status guests were sitting.

Simon observed what Rebecca was looking at. "Oh, did I not mention the changes in the serving order for this evening?"

"*No*, you didn't."

"Yes, well, the Minister has decreed that we serve the less fortunate first. He feels that with all of the uprisings, showing small levels of appreciation for the lower echelon will go far in winning hearts and minds."

Rebecca saw waiters delivering deliciousness to the back row of tables.

Several of the fortunate receivers of food stood and bowed toward the Head Seating Table in appreciation. "See," Simon said while raising his glass of wine in acknowledgement, "winning hearts and minds."

"What else has the Minister decreed?"

Simon took a long drink before saying, "He revoked Decree 493: the mandated surrender of seats to higher officials"—he tapped his left temple with his glass—"let's see . . . oh, this is a big one, he lowered the tier level for hovercar ownership to six—"

"To *six*? Are you kidding me? Sixth Tiers can have hovercars now?" She used to be a Sixth Tier.

"Yes, well, many at our level aren't happy about this, but the decree seems to be working"—he gestured toward the back few rows—"just look at them, happy as clams before a bake."

"What do you mean?"

"They don't know what's coming, that's all."

Rebecca didn't like the subtext of his message. "What's coming?"

Simon took another drink and shook his head. "Don't worry your pretty little head about it." He reached over and glided two fingers along a handful of her hair. "Your hair sure is getting long." His touch was tender for once and almost endearing, but it didn't last long. He pulled his hand away and adjusted his collar. "Changes are coming; this is only the beginning."

Rebecca's stomach grumbled again. "Well, I wish he would have waited one more day before decreeing that we eat last."

A man's voice bellowed out from the right, "Mr. Wylde, how is your evening thus far?" It was Gordon Lowell, Director of Social Affairs – Sector 4, one of Simon's soon to be subordinates once Arthur Wylde finally resigned. "Are you enjoying our festivities?"

"I'm enjoying your wine—yes."

The man's double chin grew obnoxiously large as he smiled and laughed. "Continue on then! And just wait until you have our chef's trademark dish; you will enjoy much more, I'm sure of it."

"Inevitably, we'll see."

Rebecca sighed quietly. "Not soon enough."

Simon rolled his eyes and reached into his pocket. He pulled out a standard issued Ministry snack: a small granola packet. "Here, eat this and be quiet."

Rebecca was shocked. She reached over and took the pack and cautiously said, "Thank you." She wanted to ask why the sudden gesture of kindness but then realized why; Simon was on his fourth glass of wine. Unlike most drunks, Simon actually became nicer with each spirit. "Drink up, honey."

Simon said, "I don't need the encouragement, thank you."

The wrinkly wife of Sector 4's Director of Technology walked up to Simon and said, "Mr. Wylde, I haven't had the chance to thank you for attending tonight's feast. It is an absolute honor to have you."

Simon smiled and said, "The honor is mine. I'm sorry my father couldn't attend; he had business elsewhere and couldn't be released."

"Well, that is a shame, no doubt, but having you here instead is as much of an honor."

"Thank you."

Rebecca filled her role of smiling and nodding but the woman didn't acknowledge it; *I'm a ghost.*

For the next forty minutes, servers pushing carts full of food served the remaining tables in the room, including the Head Seating Table. Rebecca finally had her dinner and it was as good as it smelled. Simon, on the other hand, barely touched his plate, choosing to drink instead. When everyone finished, there was a lull before serving desert that was to be filled with news from the sector.

Here we go, Rebecca thought, *always bad news before fattening up on cakes and pies.*

A man wearing a higher-leveled MSF uniform walked to the middle-front of the Head Seating Table while carrying his digital notepad. He nodded toward Simon and company and then spun to face outward, toward the crowd. In a booming voice he announced, "Here is the status of the realm. In the North: Several villages in Districts 17 and 19 are in the recovery stage after being ravaged by the vortex storm that struck earlier this week. MSF resources aiding the redevelopment have been allocated from Districts 13, 22, 29, and 31. Also, there was a small protest situated outside the recovery operation that was successfully suppressed, peacefully. Here, in the East: There is still an operation carrying out the search for three Heretique members suspected of plotting a strike against the Ministry Commons. Four other suspects have already been apprehended and are currently under interrogation. In the South: Floodwaters from last week's typhoon have decreased, allowing emergency workers access to several neighborhoods that the floodwaters isolated from receiving aid. Airlift supplies will continue until safe passage has been restored. And in the West: Skirmishes involving several tribes of Heretique fighters continue. The fighting has been sporadic thus making a full out assault difficult, but MSF agents are making headway and it is estimated that the overall suppression of these groups will be achieved in three months' time."

There were several cheers and a wave of applause to that bit of news. Sector 4's Director of Social Affairs stood and said, "I'll toast to that estimate." He then turned to Simon, who was growing flush in the face, and said, "To the elimination of our enemies and to our soon-to-be Director of Social Affairs: cheers!" Everyone in the room lifted their glasses and said, "Cheers!" including Rebecca, who pushed out a practiced smile. Simon stood and nodded to the crowd and then sat back down. He leaned over to Rebecca and said, "Everyone is paying attention to you, now."

Rebecca looked about the room to the crowd of drinking and clapping guests, and saw that Simon was right. "Why?"

"Because you're their enemy's daughter." He then placed and awkward hand onto hers, intertwined their fingers, and raised their hands together. The applause grew louder. He quietly said to her, "And you've converted into one of them."

"I was always one of them."

"Clearly, they don't know that."

Simon lowered their hands but kept his fingers interlocked within hers. She looked down at their hands together and thought, *So this is how it's supposed to feel.* Simon was still smiling, either because he was drunk or because he truly enjoyed this moment, being the hero of the room, without having to do anything other than *converting* the enemy.

Several dings sounded out from Simon's tucked away notepad. He released Rebecca's hand and reached inside his jacket to extract it. His brow furrowed when he saw who was calling.

"Who is it?" Rebecca asked.

"It's the Security Chief." Simon stood and wobbled a bit. "*Whoa—*I stood too quickly."

"Or you drank too much."

Simon held a finger toward her and grinned before stepping away from the table with his notepad and glass of wine in hand. Rebecca watched as he left the main room and then saw a waiter pushing a cart full of different deserts, each looking as inviting as the next. Rebecca knew she shouldn't have any—Simon would not accept it—but Simon was drunk, and getting drunker by the glass. *He probably won't notice.*

Simon left her alone at the table for twenty minutes as Sector 4 officials intermingled with the crowd. Simon had been disappearing a lot recently, and it hasn't gone unnoticed—at least not by Rebecca. *Something is going on.* What exactly, she has no idea, but Simon has spoken to Jonas Lundquist a lot in the past month. *They're acting like a couple of Academy-aged kids with all of these communications.* And Jonas Lundquist acting like an Academy-aged kid was warrant enough to be suspicious.

Simon finally returned from his call and had a new glass of wine in hand. He was all smiles. "Is everything okay?" Rebecca asked.

"Ah . . . yes. Nothing too important."

"*Nothing too important?* That doesn't sound like Jonas."

A younger woman in a black formal dress approached them at the table. "Excuse me, Mr. Wylde," she said with a semi-sexy smile, "but do you remember me? From the banquet we both attended at the Ministry Capitol last month?"

Simon wobbled a bit and pretended to be thinking. "Ah . . . Joya—is it?"

"You do remember!"

"Of course I remember; you're the assistant to Mrs. Hommet over there"—he pointed to a larger woman sitting at one of the round tables in the front row.

"That's right. My, I'm quite flattered that someone of your importance could remember a little person like me."

Simon looked down toward her chest and then nodded. Rebecca sighed and turned away. Had their marriage been anything other than what it was, she would have been jealous with rage.

"Is this your wife?" Joya asked in an unflattering tone.

"Ah . . . yes, this is my Rebecca"—he wobbled some more—"who . . . well, introduce your*selve.*"

Rebecca sighed again, making it very clear she wasn't interested, and then turned toward the young woman—but as she did, Simon lost his balance and spilled his wine glass onto Rebecca's lap. She sprung up as the liquid puddled all over her dress and dripped down her legs. "Damnit!" she said a little too loudly. It seemed the entire room took notice and grew suddenly quiet. Rebecca grabbed some napkins to soak up what she could and caught sight of Joya grinning slightly. "Don't just stand there, get some more napkins."

Joya gave a little huff and walked toward the kitchen. Simon took what napkins he could find and passed them over to Rebecca and then smiled to the crowd. "My wive is quite the klutz. Please, return to yours convzations."

"*Klutz!* You're talking about me?" Rebecca spat out and then hushed her tone. "How about not getting so *damn* drunk."

"Yesss . . . well . . ."

Rebecca took the last of the napkins and scrubbed frustratingly at her dress before throwing it onto the table. "Forget it. I have to use the restroom."

Simon didn't say anything. He stumbled into his chair and waved for a waiter.

Rebecca hissed, "You're embarrassing yourself, by the way," and then left.

Inside the restroom, she took a handful of paper towels and soaked them in the sink, but it was no use; her silver dress was ruined. Outside, in the main banquet hall, Rebecca could hear a male voice speaking through the loudspeaker. He was addressing the Heretique situation. She went over to the restroom door and pushed it open to see who was doing the talking. Her suspicion was that the voice belonged to Gordon Lowell, and she was right.

". . . we'll soon rid our great realm of the Heretique scum plaguing our people's minds, and then we'll focus our efforts on aiding the surrounding sectors so that they too can be Heretique free." There was applause from the audience. "The tide has turned, my friends, and their great leader is dead." He looked over to Simon and extended a hand. "And we have this fine patriot and the people of the Ministry Security Force to thank for it." Another applause erupted, louder this time. Simon looked like he was on the verge of passing out. Lowell continued, "Please, join me once more, and raise your glass to the death of Corbin Byrne." Everyone in the room raised a glass. "Long live the Minister, and keep the Collective free!" There was a barrage of *Cheers* and *Long live the Minister*.

Rebecca slowly closed the door as her eyes filled with tears. She couldn't show her face out there again. They hated her, and she knew it. *I was never one of them*, she realized. *It was all a charade.* She tried, oh so desperately, to be an exemplary member of the Ministry. she executed her role as Director of Historical Events – Sector 27 with impeccable professionalism, she upheld all of the Minister's decrees, she fully and wholly participated in all of the duties, and she hated the Heretique with all of her heart. But in the end, none of that mattered; Rebecca was born illegitimately and she was the daughter of a Heretique hero; therefore, she was the enemy. There was no conversion that could take those two realities away. *It is no wonder why Simon hates me so much.* She took another paper towel and wiped her eyes. *I have to get out of here.* Rebecca went back to the door and walked out.

The people in the banquet hall had returned to their conversations and didn't notice the glum girl in the heavily stained silver dress. She walked past rows of guests and out through the front doors that she first entered earlier that evening.

Outside, there were several agents in civilian clothes serving as escorts and valets as well as providing security. Normally, a guest would present themselves to one of the agents and he or she would contact the guest's driver. Tonight, however, Rebecca didn't want to be seen by them. She quickly went around the main series of stairs leading down to the front walkway and took a side channel that led to the hovercar allotment. She wandered aimlessly for a few minutes before deciding that it would probably be best if she found her and Simon's ride.

"Mrs. Wylde?" called a voice off to her right.

Rebecca looked over but didn't immediately see whom it was. "Yes, hello?"

A man maneuvered around several hover cars and gave a friendly wave. "Mrs. Wylde, I thought that was you." It was her driver. "Are you looking for the hovercar? I parked it . . ." he noticed her dress. "Looks like you're having a rough night."

Rebecca looked down at the large stain and faked a laugh. "Yeah, you know what they say when you party hard."

"I guess so. Come on, I'll take you over."

Rebecca followed the driver to Simon's hovercar, which was parked deep within the field of other officials' hovercars. "Where is Mr. Wylde?" the driver asked.

"Oh, he's still inside, enjoying the festivities. I'm sure he'll be calling soon"—*and will be drunker than a shipman.*

They reached the hovercar and the driver opened the door for her. As soon as Rebecca sat down, her prophecy rang true; the driver pulled out his notepad and said, "Oh, here's Mr. Wylde now."

The exchange was brief, and Simon's words were barely comprehensible. "We better get going," the driver said.

Rebecca slumped slightly and simply nodded her head.

"Are you okay, Mrs. Wylde?"

She was tired of continuing the lies. "No . . . I'm not okay."

The driver looked into the rearview mirror with concern. "May I ask what the problem is?"

Rebecca sighed and thought, *Of course not; what would my darling husband think?* "It's too long and complicated of a story to tell."

The driver seemed to understand and said, "Well, with all sad stories there is the opportunity to write a happy ending."

Rebecca laughed slightly at the driver's naïveté. "Unfortunately, this story has no possibility of a happy ending."

"Are you sure of that?"

"Oh, I'm very sure."

The driver stopped the hovercar in midflight and turned in his seat to look at her. "It's true that some happy endings can't be written alone; they need help from another."

Rebecca looked sullenly out her window and said, "Yeah, well, who's going to help me?"

The driver grinned and said, "Maybe you should ask your father."

Rebecca snapped her gaze back to the driver. "My father? He's dead."

The driver didn't flinch. "No, Rebecca, he's not."

"What do you mean, *he's not*?"

The driver turned back to facing the windshield and started the hovercar moving again. He looked into the rearview mirror and said quite assuredly, "Rebecca, your father is not dead—Corbin Byrne is alive."

CHAPTER FOUR

The Dead Sands – OP6

Sweat dripped off William Coulee's face as he idled in the desert. He was in the spot where he thought he saw a man or woman walking, and yet there was no one around, nor a single track. *I must be losing my mind*, he thought. *But the vision was so real.* He had heard of mirages and of people believing they saw water in sand, but this was far different; William saw someone, or some *thing*, walking around. He figured it could have been an animal but the lack of tracks was absolutely perplexing. He had circled the entire area twice, and found nothing to support what he initially thought: a man or a woman dressed in grey, walking northwest. There was a mountain range far off in the distance but nothing that was remotely reachable on foot in the time frame allowed; William was hardly a mile away. *How could he have gone so far?* The answer was that they couldn't have.

William checked the time and knew he needed to report in; he was already late. He pulled out his notepad and brought up the global tracking system in order to mark his location. The hoverbike coughed a few times and sounded unhealthy. William returned his notepad and accelerated away.

The sun was no longer full overhead. It took almost ten minutes to return to the outpost. William left the bike outside the door where it coughed again and stalled. The temperature had risen another miserable ten degrees. He walked inside the outpost and was smashed by a wall of heat. William looked up and saw that all of the ceiling fans were not operating. "What in the world"—but he knew what had happened: the generator had overheated again. "*Damnit!*" He had enough of this. William stormed through the unbearable inferno and began stripping off layers of uniform until he was shirtless and pantless and purely in his underwear. He crossed the room and began climbing up the ladder leading to the roof hatch. The heat was twice as bad by the ceiling. He unlatched the hatch and swung it outward. He reached his hands onto the roof for leverage and felt the searing heat coming off the metal surface. "Damnit!" He didn't care, though; he needed to get the generator working again. William wiggled his way onto the hotplate of a roof and stood up as fast as he could. Anyone watching from outside would have seen quite an interesting sight: a nearly naked man in his skivvies and military boots, cursing, and whacking away at some piece of junk generator that was easily ten years past its retirement age.

After an hour of hopeless tinkering, William managed to do something right and the generator kicked back to life. The machine gargled and clanked, spewed a plume of black smoke, and then resumed its operational status quo. "Thank the Minister," William said, relieved, and then began checking the solar panels for any damage that might have accrued through the weeks of grueling heat and sand abuse. Everything looked in order— as far as his limited knowledge allowed—and he climbed back down the ladder. All of the ceiling fans were running again, and the heat had subsided slightly.

At the post's impeccably dusted desk, William called up MSF HQ – Sector 1 in order to give his patrol report. A woman with a dull-eyed expression appeared on the monitor and said, "HQ1: give your status, Dead Sands – OP 6."

William, dressed only from the waist up, said, "Points 1-4 are clear. I observed a UIB between points 5 and 6 but was unable to verify."

The woman's eyes gained some life. "A UIB? You're certain?"

"Yeah, pretty certain."

The woman began to concentrate on something off screen and then returned her attention. "Your report is late, Agent Coulee. Do you care to give a defense for the record?"

"Yes." William explained his search and then the discovery of the decommissioned generator.

"Your defense has been recorded. You should receive a ruling from the MSDA within twenty-four hours."

"Wonderful."

The woman concentrated off screen again and then said, "You're due for patrol in less than an hour. I have created a new objective for this patrol that includes locating the UIB and creating an Observation Report."

"Great, thank you."

"This way, if you're late at reporting in again, you will be excused."

"Thank you."

"Anything else?"

William shook his head. "That's all."

"Have a good day, Agent Coulee."

They signed off. William sat back in his chair and yawned, raising both hands to his face. He had another patrol to do in less than an hour. That left him with little time to eat and rest. *What a day*, he thought.

William spent the next thirty minutes cramming food into his body and examining a map linking points 5 and 6 of his patrol route. The problem with reporting an Unidentifiable Intelligent Being (UIB) is that you have to provide proof, which in this particular instance, was going to be tough to gather, especially since there was nothing remotely identifiable around the area he marked as the position of the UIB. It was like the person he saw was a ghost, one of them Desert Demons the locals liked to talk about in the neighboring sectors. William never took their stories seriously—nomadic people living in the desert, kidnapping children in the middle of the night, and killing cattle—but at this particular point, he realized that he might just have to, despite what the MSF satellite reports have stated.

Outside, William was fully dressed again and dusting off the tired looking hoverbike. Sweat streamed as he mounted the hoverbike and pushed the cracked, green ignition button—but nothing happened.

He pushed it again. Nothing happened.

And again.

Again.

Again.

. . . .

"Really?" William said.

He pushed it again, and again. "Damnit!"

The hoverbike was dead. William took in a deep breath of air, felt his body shake slightly from the lack of rest, food, and patience, and then let it all out with a guttural roar, "YYYAAAAAAAAWWWWWW."

After a moment of just sitting on the hoverbike—gathering himself—William realized he still needed to patrol for the UIB, regardless of his situation. It was his duty, after all.

He dismounted and pulled out his laser rifle, slinging it over his shoulder. He checked the time and calculated how far he had to walk in order to get to the position marked on the global tracking system; it was going to take him roughly an hour. He would have about another hour to search around and then he would have to get walking back; the sun would be set not too long after, and it was very dangerous to be walking around inside the Dead Sands after nightfall; it contained too many pitfalls: creatures looking for blood, plants that poisoned, quicksand, and other dastardly ways for a man to die. William went back inside the outpost and collected a couple of bags of small Ministry-distributed granola bites and nuts, and then headed out into the sandy abyss.

CHAPTER FIVE

District 9, Sector 2

The entire drive back to the Wylde's compound in Sector 2 was painful for Rebecca; there was so much she wanted to know, so much she wanted to ask the driver, but right after he told her that Corbin Byrne was alive, he landed the hovercar and picked up Simon, which ended any opportunity she had to learn more. Instead, she had to quietly sit the entire two-hour drive next to a drunken mess who eventually passed out an hour or so into the trip. But even though Simon was snoring on her shoulder, Rebecca felt it unwise to try and ask questions about her father. The driver, who clearly was anything but a typical driver, remained silent as well. She did, however, learn that his name was Giles Stoykich.

Simon woke just as they parked and he immediately grabbed his head in agony. "Where are we?"

"We're home," informed Rebecca.

Simon struggled out of the hovercar and leaned against its side. Two MSF agents, the night watch, walked over and offered assistance. "No,"

Simon said, trying to straighten up. "I can manage just fine. Rebecca?"

Rebecca was lingering inside the hovercar. Giles only looked at her through the mirror, smiling. She said, "Yes, Simon?"

"Aren't you going to join me?" It wasn't a question.

Giles gave a subtle nod in the mirror as if to say, *We'll have our chance to talk*—and Rebecca sighed. "Yes, of course." She opened her door and slid out of the hovercar. Simon was blinking with some level of intensity and looked as if he was on the brink of losing his composure. "Alright, let's get inside and go to bed." She took Simon by the arm and together they walked inside the massive home. Simon did his best to play the part of a sober man but he was losing his grip the closer they came to their bedroom. "We're almost there," Rebecca assured him.

Simon said in a quiet and strained voice, "Yes . . . thank you."

Thank you? thought Rebecca with much disdain. *How dare you thank me after the way I was treated tonight?* But Rebecca kept the thought to herself. She closed the door behind them and allowed Simon to fall onto the bed. "If you're going to be sick, I would prefer that you move your body to the bathroom instead."

Simon was already asleep.

Rebecca sighed and turned back toward the door. The answer to all of her questions was just two hundred feet away. All she had to do was walk out the door, find Giles Stoykich—if that was indeed his real name—and ask him, "What do you mean Corbin Byrne is alive?" But it wouldn't be that simple; agents patrolled the ground at night, and Rebecca was supposed to be in bed. If any of them spotted her trying to talk to him, they would most certainly report it to Simon, Arthur, or Jonas; they trusted her that little. *And for good reason too*, thought Rebecca. She was done with the Wyldes, with the Ministry and its terrible leader. *My father is alive*, she kept saying to herself. It was unbelievable. It was her second chance—a shot at redemption. If she could only learn what had really happened, where her father had been, and how she could get to him, Rebecca would give up this life with Simon and continue the journey she began six months ago; *It's my only option now*, which reminded her that she had completely forgotten about the manuscript—the one thing motivating everything—and if she was to be truly useful to her father, to the Free People's Society, then she would need to get another copy of it. *But how?*

Simon rolled over on the bed and curled up into the fetal position.

Getting another copy of the manuscript would prove to be absolutely impossible, and she knew it. She was no longer a Director of Historical Events, she was not allowed out of the compound without Simon, and she did not have any kind of security clearance. *Ugh*, she thought. *What use am I? Think!* As far as she was aware, the original copy of the manuscript was either destroyed or still lying amongst the rubble inside the Vriezen, so regaining it was not a possibility.

Rebecca walked over to the large triple window with its curtains drawn. She looked out into the inky blackness of night and tried to figure out what else she could do, what else she could provide the Free People's Society . . . some sort of information that could serve as an olive branch for all that she had caused. Unfortunately, nothing reasonable came to mind. She contemplated killing Simon, and possibly his father, but Rebecca was no assassin and she was no murderer; those were senseless thoughts.

Eventually, Rebecca grew tired and began to yawn. She had been at it for almost two hours. Her mind had spun through one ridiculous scenario after another, each more outlandish than the last. When it came down to it, Rebecca had no cards to play. The only thing she could do was hope that she could find Giles in the morning and ask him all that he knows about her father. Anything else was just . . .

Footsteps came to the bedroom door and then stopped, blocking what little light that leaked underneath. Rebecca held her breath and listened intently, but no sound was made.

After a few seconds, Rebecca exhaled and realized that it was probably an agent assigned to her bedroom door while she and Simon slept—not Giles Stoykich.

Security was ridiculously tight. *What are they afraid of?* wondered Rebecca. The Ministry pretended that the security was for protection against the Heretique, but Rebecca thought otherwise—*but for what?* The only thing she could think was that their fear had something to do with the manuscript . . . *William Coulee's* manuscript.

It had been six months since she had read it and it took her just as long to try and forget it, *but I can't.* As far as she could tell, William Coulee was not aware that he supposedly wrote the manuscript. Rebecca did her best to poke around about it and it seemed that no one knew what it contained, including Simon. Rebecca developed a knack for detecting when Simon was lying; he would adjust his collar frequently, look around the room, or excessively clear his throat and lick his lips. And if Simon didn't know what the manuscript contained then surely William Coulee didn't know, which meant that Jonas and the Minister were keeping a tight lid on it. *And the only reason they would keep a lid on it*, Rebecca figured, *is because there is something authentic about it, which scares them . . . and me.*

The shadow moved away from the door and Rebecca could hear someone's footsteps leaving.

I have to get to bed. Rebecca changed out of her stained, silver dress and into a nightgown. She crawled into the cold bed and looked at Simon's incapacitated face. He looked so peaceful lying there, so handsome, as he took in deep breaths through his nose, snoring slightly. *Why can't you accept me?* He was all she ever wanted—and *nothing* she ever wanted—wrapped into a single conflicted man. Rebecca rolled away from him, pulled the blankets up tight and closed her eyes. It was going to be a long night of wonder.

CHAPTER SIX

The Dead Sands – OP6

William trekked for close to an hour without spotting anything out of the ordinary. He spent most of the time inside his head, thinking about many different topics, including his parents, who he had not seen since his assignment to hunting Corbin Byrne, which took up all of his time and resources.

William's father, James Coulee, had been a pilot for the shuttles that taxied workers to and from the space station orbiting Earth. After thirty-two years of service, he was placed at a desk position due to his failing eyesight. James looked into having a medical procedure done in order to correct his vision but discovered that the procedure was only available to Third Tiers and above. . . . From then on, he seemed pretty miserable; James was born to fly. He told William a couple of days after his disappointing news, "Having my wings clipped is like taking the legs off a runner. I don't know if I'll ever be the same." This confession had always bothered William. He wished there was something his father could do that still involved flying, even if it meant driving a hovercar for an official. James Coulee was a Sixth Tier member of the Ministry and so he was higher ranked than those who typically drove hovercars, *but if it would be enjoyable for him*. William spent a little time—just before his assignment to hunt Corbin Byrne—looking into whether his father could take a demotion in rank and work as a driver. Nothing he found supported whether it was possible or not. He had since hoped that his father had found peace with his new role in life. William desperately wanted to reconnect with his father in order to find out how things were going; however, he would not have that opportunity for another three months; it was an MSF rule. Just like the rule that forbid marriage, the Ministry forbade an MSF agent to speak to family and friends while on special assignment. Family and friends could compromise an agent's position and risk the success of the operation—not to mention the lives of the agents involved. William's assignment to hunt Corbin Byrne was a special assignment—as was his assignment to the Dead Sands outpost, which didn't make sense considering that there was nothing *special* about the post. William simply took it as part of the punishment, and punishment it was; William had always been a mother's boy. They had a close bond, and so it was tough on both of them after his placing into the MSF through the Cognitive Examination. William was just thankful that she had his father— especially now since he couldn't make contact with them anymore. That was the one good thing about his father's grounding: he was with William's mother a lot more than ever before.

William stopped walking and sat down on the sand. The sun was still above the horizon, but it was getting late. He pulled out his water jug and drank from it before checking the global tracking system. He was nearly there.

A gazelle came into view on William's right—then came two more— walking over a dune. William knew gazelles lived in the desert but had not seen one. They were beautiful creatures. He watched as they dipped their heads to the sand, eat the sparse desert grass, and then rise back up, looking around for potential predators. William stayed very still, not wanting the gazelles to misread him as a threat. The gazelles went back to eating and slowly walked along. William removed his binoculars from around his neck and raised it to his eyes. He focused in on the three gazelles and saw just how amazing they truly were. It was one thing to see these animals in a

Ministry Menagerie but a completely different thing to see them in their natural habitat. For the first time that day, William smiled.

The gazelle in the back of the group suddenly stopped and snapped its head toward William, as if it was looking directly at him. The animal remained completely still. Then its mouth opened, making a low murmur and the other two gazelles looked over; all three of them began sprinting away at an incredible speed.

What on Earth? William wondered. He had barely moved at all. *They couldn't have seen me.* The gazelles ran out of view and William lowered his binoculars. It was just as well; he needed to get moving. William replaced his binoculars around his neck and stood up.

A voice called out from behind, "Well, well, well, well, there!"

William dropped to his knee and spun around while simultaneously pulling at his laser rifle.

"NAH, NAH, NAH, NAH!" cried out a skinny, sun-beaten man holding a crude looking rifle. "Put yo hands away, boy! Get em away!"

William was beat, and he knew it. He stopped reaching for his rifle and moved his hands outward.

"Oh yeah, boy . . . oh yeah, Mista Iceman. Go head an' stand, Mr. Man wit a bad ass rifle."

William watched him carefully and stood slowly. The desert man was bald and sandy; he had small beady eyes, a gap between his front teeth, and veins popping out of his neck. He was wearing a mishmash of different pieces of clothing that were sun-beaten to the point of colorless—hence the grey looking clothing William saw through the binoculars on his earlier patrol. "Why don't you lower that rifle, mister?"

"Aw, yeah, Mista Iceman;" he said with a lisp, "I'll lower this piece jus' as soon as you decide notta use yours."

It wasn't easy for William to determine if this man was a threat or not. "I have no plans to hurt you, sir. You were the one who approached me."

"Aw, yeah; you were lookin' for me tha . . . wernchya?"

"Yes, you're right. I saw you earlier. I wanted to see who was living out here. I wanted to know how you could survive out in this desolate place."

"Deslate? My home? Yah not know shit, Mista Iceman. There ain't no survivn . . . jus' livin, boy."

Shit, William thought. *This guy is crazy.* "So, you live out here? Where's your home? I looked around for you; I wanted to say hello, but I couldn't find you."

The desert man didn't answer.

"What's your name?"

The desert man said, "Yuz not gonna try anyfing funny, Mista Iceman? Yuz gonna play nice?"

"I'm not here to start a fight."

"Alright, Mista Iceman; I believe yuz." The desert man lowered his rifle and shouldered it.

William released a sigh of relief.

Now. He dropped to the ground and rolled to his right, coming up with his rifle in hand and the desert man in direct sight. The desert man had barely reacted, choosing instead to raise his hands to surrender. "Yuz, gots me, son."

"Let the rifle slide from your arm to the ground. Do not touch it with your hand or I will put a hole in you—got it?"

The desert man smiled and did as told. "Yuz win, Mista Iceman." The rifle had hit the ground.

"Thank you. Now take ten steps back. You can count to ten, right?"

"Ah, shit. Mista Iceman finks I dumb-ass stupid. I'z count: one . . . two . . ." he continued counting while taking steps.

William took matching steps and retrieved the rifle, which he shouldered. "Thank you, again. Now, what is your name?"

The desert man, completely relaxed, said, "I'z got thousands of names; which one ya wanna call me?"

"How about just giving me one?"

The desert man laughed. "Yeah, son. Yuz can call me One, or Two, or Three, or—"

"*Alright*, enough."

William tried to relax his frustration and smiled at the man. *Now what?* In the midst of his frustration back at the outpost, William hadn't considered what he would do if he took a prisoner. "Are there more of you out here?"

"Jus' me, Mista Iceman."

"My name isn't Iceman, it's—"

"I'z knows yuz name, son. Yuz the Iceman cuz you soooo like ice; yuz sooo cool, right? Yuz the Cool Man . . . the Cooley Man. God willed ya hear and yuz so cooley like. God willed me cooley—he willed cooley—yuz Willed Cooley—yes, son; yuz William Coulee."

CHAPTER SEVEN

District 9, Sector 2

For Rebecca, the next morning came quickly; and yet despite how tired she was, Rebecca sprung out of bed with great energy and vigor.

Simon had barely moved the entire night; he was still lying in bed, dressed in his formal uniform.

Rebecca quickly dressed and hurried out of the bedroom.

As usual, a silent agent was standing guard outside the bedroom door. Rebecca said, "Good morning," to him but he didn't respond—as usual. She walked into the main lounge room on her way to the parking garage and saw Florence Wylde, Simon's mother, sitting on a sofa chair reading her notepad. Rebecca tried to pass through without drawing attention but failed.

"Is my son still resting off his evening, or did you wake him before leaving?"

Rebecca slowed her pace and thought, *Good morning to you too.* "He's still asleep. We had quite an . . . *extensive* . . . night last night."

Florence's lips formed a line as she hummed. "Yes, so I've heard. Are you planning to break your fast without my son this morning?"

Rebecca hated how she used old terminology. "No, I was merely going to the garage. I think I left my handbag in the backseat."

Florence scoffed, "How on Earth did you manage *that*? Outside of your husband, a lady's priority is to *always* manage their personals."

Rebecca sighed. "Yes, I know. Unfortunately, your son required all of my *managing* last night."

"Oh," Florence said, slightly surprised. "I hope your management will someday produce a son for us."

It wasn't that kind of management, Rebecca wanted to say. "Hopefully." She then took leave.

When Rebecca finally made it to the garage, she found no one inside; just the fleet of hovercars the Wyldes kept on hand. Rebecca paced around, keeping her disappointment to herself. *Had he left already?* she wondered. *Was he here only to let me know that my father is alive?* Neither thought was comforting. *Did I blow my only chance?* Rebecca lightly kicked the side of a hovercar's landing gear. She didn't know what to do. Her hope was quickly obliterating. Rebecca walked out of the garage and saw two mechanics chatting beside a hovercar lifted for repairs. Beyond the mechanics and all around were green fields and trees, enclosing the complex. She decided to take a stroll; *maybe some fresh air will help.*

One of the only good things about living at the complex was all of the nature she was exposed to. Rebecca didn't get to stroll through wooded areas while living in Sector 27. Lake Callidas was the closest she came to any real nature experience. But there, in Sector 2, Rebecca saw it every day.

She stopped to listen to the sounds of nature, to the birds in the trees overhead. It was peaceful. *I could stay out here forever.* The wood was a far cry from the hustle and bustle of the Wylde's compound.

Suddenly, a voice drifted to her through the foliage, "Rebecca?"

She turned and saw Giles Stoykich walking near. "There you are!"

"We don't have much time," he said hastily. The man was clearly nervous. "I saw you in the garage but I didn't want to talk to you there. People watch, you know?"

"Of course I know; no one knows more than me."

"Well—then—you probably know that they're watching you in

particular."

"Of course I know! I can't go anywhere without someone following me."

"Which is why I must leave in a moment's time."

"Wait," Rebecca said quickly. She walked over to him and lowered her voice. "You have to tell me about my father. Is he really alive? Where is he? Do you know about my mother?"

The man looked around and said, "Your father is alive, but I don't know where he is, and I don't know anything about your mother."

"But you're a member, right? You're—"

"Of course I'm a member."

"But you don't know where my father is?"

"I told you that."

"But you can take me to him—to the Free People—right?"

Giles took a step closer. "That's why I'm here. I'm on orders to get you out."

Rebecca was so happy she could have kissed him. "When? Right now?"

Giles shook his head. "No . . . in two days."

"Why two days?"

"Because, Simon will be leaving for a security meeting in Sector 1. It will be the only time you'll be away from him for a long stretch."

Rebecca had completely forgotten about it. He was right. Fleeing while Simon was away would be best for her. But that didn't make her anxiety lessen. "Okay, in two days."

"Take care, daughter of Byrne. We cannot speak again until then." He bowed his head and swiftly left her alone.

Rebecca wanted to stop him, to continue their conversation, to pry every last bit of knowledge he had of her father, but Giles was gone . . . and he was right, the less they talked the better. Two days was only two days, after all. Rebecca smiled and continued her stroll; life suddenly seemed more precious than she could ever remember.

CHAPTER EIGHT

District 9, Sector 2

Back inside the compound, the others had wakened and they were now having their informal breakfast in the main lounge. Rebecca spotted Simon slouched on a sofa in front of the Ministry Monitor with a bowl of bacon and scrambled eggs on his lap. He was dressed for the day, *somehow*, but she could tell he hadn't showered yet. Arthur Wylde was pacing on the other side of the room and talking heatedly to another man whose name had slipped Rebecca's memory. Arthur was in full Ministry garb; he had a meeting that afternoon at the Ministry Capitol in Sector 1. He was holding his famous paper notebook (Arthur was notorious for forgetting mundane things, so he wrote everything on paper instead of using his digital notepad; Rebecca had no idea why).

There was something peculiar about Arthur's demeanor that really grabbed Rebecca's attention. She wanted to eavesdrop on his conversation. Rebecca formulated a plan and walked into the main dining room, where a buffet style breakfast lay, and quickly took a plate loaded with eggs, two slices of bacon and toasted bread, and then headed back into the lounge. She found an empty sofa chair semi-close to the conversation and eased in.

". . . the gall of him!" Arthur grumbled. "He has grown too big, too powerful, and now he thinks he can just override any decree the Minister orders? The gall!"

The man sitting casually on the formal décor chair, with his legs crossed, nodded and said, "It's the Minister's doing; he empowered the Security Chief, having private meetings with him, bypassing you and giving direct orders to him—"

"*That's my point!* Why have the Director of Social Affairs in charge of the MSF if the Minister is going directly to the Security Chief without my knowledge?"

"And that is why we now have this ordeal."

"Well," Arthur said with an ironic laugh, "this will end today, that I promise. I've called a meeting with Lundquist; we're going to settle this matter once and for all. It is time he understands who is really in charge." Arthur Wylde huffed and puffed for a moment before he continued, "How could he think slaughtering those people was a good idea?"

Slaughtering? thought Rebecca.

"A march poses no real threat! The District was in no real danger!"

"Yes, but others have fallen," the other man said.

"*Hogwash!* The other Districts were poorly led and were attacked by an organized army, not some march of women and children! This was not an apple-to-apple situation! The Minister made Decree 517 in order to prevent the growth of our enemies—to prevent this very thing from happening! All that idiot did—and I'm talking about that damned Security Chief of ours—all that idiot did was rally more supporters to those forsaken Heretique! And now our jobs will be a whole lot harder!" Arthur readjusted his uniform jacket and said, "Mark my words, next time it won't be just a march; next time it will be a damned militia they will have to face. . . ."

"May I give a suggestion?" the other man asked.

Arthur Wylde nodded his head swiftly and said, "Of course!"

"Keep yourself armed when meeting with the Security Chief. Jonas has developed quite the *reputation*—"

"Do you think that man threatens me? I know how to handle my subordinate, Mr. Cassell."

Cassell—Rebecca realized—*Officer Yarman Cassell—that's his name.* Rebecca had heard of him through random chains of conversation. Officer Cassell was in charge of Sector 2's security force and was a direct subordinate of Jonas Lundquist. *Why on Earth is Arthur talking about such things with him?*

Arthur Wylde continued, "Jonas will bend or else he'll break; that much I can guarantee." But there was fear in Arthur's voice.

This is very suspicious. Is Officer Cassell feeding Arthur inside information regarding Jonas Lundquist's doings? I wonder if Arthur knows how much his own son corresponds with Lundquist.

Without notice, someone stood directly in front of Rebecca.

"Where did you go this morning?"

Rebecca looked up and saw Simon; his usual air of arrogance had returned.

Rebecca's mind scampered for an answer. "I thought I had left my handbag in the car last night. I went to the garage to find it."

"Yes, and did you retrieve it?"

"No . . . I had mistaken."

Simon's face contorted into a curious expression. "Oh . . . *well*, where do you think it is?"

"I don't know; somewhere in our room, I suppose."

"Yes, I agree; it quite possibly could be lying on top of your dresser."

That was a little too specific for Rebecca's liking. "I take it that you have seen it there?"

Simon didn't answer.

"Okay, thank you."

Simon looked down at his uniform and brushed off a piece of lint. "What were you really doing this morning?"

He's on to me, but Rebecca didn't care anymore. She sighed and said, "I already told you. Stop being so paranoid. I didn't see—"

Simon reached down with one hand and grabbed her face, pinching her cheeks. "*Watch your tone.* I know you were up to something, now spill it!"

Arthur Wylde bellowed from behind, "Simon!"

Simon released her cheeks and looked over to his father.

"That is quite enough! Go get some air for the Minister's sake! You look absolutely deplorable."

Simon grew a scowl that matched his behavior and then marched off.

Rebecca remained in her seat. Some eggs were spilled onto her clothes and onto the chair. Her heart was beating out of control and she could feel her face flushed—initially from outrage and then from embarrassment. As she started to pick up the little bits of egg from her clothes, she noticed someone standing next to her. She looked up, half expecting to see Arthur Wylde, but saw Yarman Cassell instead.

"Deplorable is hardly the word. I hope he didn't offend you too much."

Rebecca wanted to scream out of rage but contained herself to a quick, "No."

"Not even a daughter of the enemy deserves to be humiliated in front of others." He then walked away. Rebecca was left uncertain on how to translate his words. She looked around, for other faces, but no one was paying her any further attention. Rebecca was alone.

She finished picking up the eggs and took them to the kitchen where several men and women worked diligently to clean dishes, pots, pans, and counters, while others were prepping for the lunch service. Rebecca saw finer china, folded linens, and unboxed crystal glassware sitting out in columns and rows. One of the female kitchen aids walked over to Rebecca and said, "I'll take that for you, ma'am." Rebecca handed the dish over and thanked her with whatever dignity she had left. From there, Rebecca went to her safe haven.

She closed the door behind her, shutting out the noise, Simon, and her humiliation. *Two days,* she repeated to herself. *Just two more days and I'm free of this nightmare*—a nightmare she brought on herself. A nagging voice in the back of her mind continually reminded her that she *chose* to return to the Collective and to the Wyldes. She had the option to stay with her biological father, but her pent-up resentment spoiled it.

A knock came from the door. Simon slowly entered, looking no better than he did in the main lounge. "May I come in?"

"It's your house."

Simon closed the door behind him. "It's our house."

His sudden sentiment toward their marriage made her laugh. "Right, of course."

Simon took her sarcasm in stride and said, "I'm sorry about lashing out at you." He didn't look her in the eyes. "It's just that . . . I mean to say . . . I'm under a lot of pressure and I tend to not handle it . . . *well.*"

"Yeah, no kidding. What do you think I was up to this morning? Do you think I was trying to escape? Trying to formulate some plan to aid the Heretique?"

Simon calmly and quietly said, "Were you?"

"OF COURSE NOT! Why would I do that?" The answer was simple to her but she wanted to see his response.

Simon shook his head and slowly walked through the room. "I haven't been the best husband; that's why."

What is this, Rebecca wondered.

"I don't think you can possibly understand what it is like to know that the woman you wished for is the daughter of your enemy."

Rebecca wanted to laugh at him again, but her anger couldn't fake it. "Gee, is it something like discovering that your biological father is the enemy of all that you believe?"

Simon arched his eyebrows and looked toward the floor. "Possibly."

Rebecca didn't buy what he was trying to sell. "Listen, Simon, you haven't exactly been all that I dreamt of either. I came into this marriage with the highest level of excitement only to learn just how big of an arrogant ass you truly are."

"That's not me."

"*Sure it is.* You've got your image to look after and when I stopped fitting the portrait painted in your mind you stopped caring about me. *Aren't I right?* You once told me that you didn't want to be the next Director of Social Affairs . . . well, I now know—"

"*You know nothing!*" Simon's face reddened as he drew near her. "You have no idea what kind of pressure I'm under! My father is a louse! He says he's preparing me to take over the DSA but then makes no plans to resign—instead—forcing me to be his little puppet that goes everywhere he demands, kisses the asses of those he despises, and then belittles me in front of the Minister with every given chance! My marriage to you was supposed to be the one thing he couldn't plan for me, but then . . ." Simon's eyes danced as he held his tongue.

"Then what?" Rebecca almost feared what else he had to say.

Simon wiped some saliva from his lips and turned away. "I was going to say, then you turned out to be Corbin Byrne's daughter. He has made me the laughing stock of the High Officials."

Rebecca thought he might have said something else. She took in a deep breath and sighed. "Simon, we can't help who our fathers are. You have to stop hating me for mine, or else you will never be able to stop hating yourself for yours."

Simon, still looking away from her, laughed. "Yeah, easier said than done." He then spun back around, his face returned to its normal color. "Anyway, I have some business to attend. I'll probably be back tomorrow or in a couple of days . . ."

"Where are you going?"

Simon shook his head. "Let's not continue the charade; I know you don't care." He then walked immediately out the door.

Rebecca remained inside the room, utterly stunned. *He's acting as if I'm the one shunning him.* Simon was a man who had never ceased to surprise her.

Rebecca struggled with Simon's odd behavior for some time after he had left. Simon was a complicated man, yes, but there was a level of confliction in him that she had not noticed before. However, the thing that crippled her ability to move beyond was the unexpected, undisclosed journey he had embarked upon that morning. *Is he attending the Ministry meeting with his father?* Rebecca soon learned the answer to that question when she left her hideaway and saw Arthur Wylde eating lunch with his wife, Florence. Rebecca considered approaching them to ask if they knew of Simon's travels. *I should have the right to know where my husband is going.*

She walked over to the round dining table the Wylde's were sitting at and paused, making her presence known but not interrupting the conversation. Florence looked toward Rebecca and then to Arthur, hinting that she was annoyed. Arthur placed his fork down and wiped his mouth with a linen cloth. "Yes?"

"Excuse me," Rebecca said quietly, "I was wondering if you knew where my husband has gone? He told me he was leaving for a couple of days but did not say where."

Arthur cleared his throat and took a sip of water. "Then he clearly doesn't want you to know."

Rebecca nodded her head but wanted to say, *I have a right!*

"Regardless," continued Arthur, "I haven't a clue where the boy has gone; he didn't disclose his plans to me. He told you he was leaving for a couple of days? Well, he had better make himself visible at the officials' meeting tomorrow if he has any hope of earning the respect of the Minister." Arthur checked the time and turned in his seat so that he was facing Rebecca full on. "Your husband thinks he can just exist and life's rewards will be placed on his lap. One could argue that we"—he gestured to himself and Florence—"haven't done an adequate job of raising him with a proper work ethic—"

"*Ehm*," Florence interjected; her face was contorted with disbelief.

Arthur looked to his wife and appeared to want to say something, but no further words came out of his mouth. He wiped his lips again, checked the time again, and then stood. "So, no, I do not know where my son is. If you'll excuse me—"

Rebecca stepped aside as Arthur Wylde walked away from the round table and toward the stairwell leading to his suite.

"You haven't learned anything, have you?" Florence said to Rebecca in a seething tone.

Confused by the accusation, Rebecca said, "What do you mean?"

"You have no place here. Your marriage to my son is a crime."

"Excuse me?"

Florence was shaking with fury. "Honestly, do you really think you have the right to interrupt our lunch? To agitate my husband like so? Ever since you came into our son's life, you've been a burden on this family. You drove a wedge between Arthur and Simon's relationship."

Rebecca had no idea where all the hostility was coming from.

"I sure hope you see just how much a nuisance you are." Florence slammed her napkin onto the table with all the might her frail arms could muster and stormed off toward her suite. Rebecca remained at the table; she was utterly stunned. This was the second time today that she had been publicly reprimanded—*and the day is only halfway done*. Rebecca looked around to see who had witnessed Florence's outburst and happened to lock eyes with Yarman Cassell, who gave a sardonic grin and nodded.

Rebecca felt the need to explain what had just happened, but she didn't know where to begin. Cassell slowly walked over and stood at her side. "It seems you have developed a talent for getting yelled at."

"I don't know what I've done."

Cassell seemed somewhat surprised by her reaction. "You exist, my dear. Plain and simple."

Rebecca looked into his eyes and saw he was not jesting.

"You're The Daughter of Abraham—at least that is the name given to you."

"What are you talking about?"

Cassell nodded his head; he understood her confusion. "No one has told you—of course. People in the Collective, officials in the Ministry, the Wylde's—everyone—refers to you as The Daughter of Abraham. It's meant to be—"

"Insulting, yes, I get it."

According to the Ministry approved history, Abraham was the founder of the Heretique. It wasn't difficult for Rebecca to understand the name's venom.

"Of course you get it; I was told you are sharp as a whip. And so I assume there is no need for me to explain why having a daughter-in-law with this derogatory nickname is troubling."

She got it all right. "But that's not what set Florence off. She was angered by how Arthur reacted to my mentioning of Simon's disappearance."

"Ah, yes, the other point of contention." Cassell looked around at the people passing by, in and out of the room, and said, "Let us walk, shall we?"

Sensing he was about to divulge something considered *sensitive*, Rebecca agreed. They walked through the main lounge and out the front door.

"Your husband is developing a rather raw reputation for being a little too blasé with his role as the upcoming Director of Social Affairs. Arthur feels that Simon should be exercising more of his leadership qualities rather than his rebellious qualities."

"*Rebellious*, Simon?" Rebecca wanted to laugh.

"Yes, well . . . rebellious in the sense that he hasn't been demonstrating his acceptance of the gift bestowed onto him, being the heir of the DSA."

If only you know how much Simon talked to your boss, you might not think he is being blasé. "Okay, but what does that have to do with me? That's not my fault."

"Florence seems to think so. It's her impression that you are the catalyst for Simon's unrest. She has connected the dots between his rebellious behavior to his appointed marriage."

"*That's ludicrous!*" Rebecca said a little too loud. "I'm sorry, but that's insane. I *want* Simon to be happy with his appointments. I'm not trying to get him upset."

"Surely, but what can I say; a mother sees what she wants to see. And when your biological background was discovered . . ."

He didn't need to finish. "So she hates me."

Cassell nodded. "Increasingly so with each passing minute."

"Why are you telling me this?"

Cassell stopped walking. "Because I feel that you've been dealt an unfair hand. Your life was never your own. Believe me when I tell you, you should have never been born."

Rebecca didn't know how to take that statement.

"Allow me to clarify. Your parents had you illegally, and no one caught this act of deceit. You've lived your life upon a lie served to you by them—a lie that has tainted anyone who has ever known you. You see, your existence has brought joy to some, pain to others, and has bound people that would have never been bound otherwise. If you were born legitimately, Simon's appointment to you would be a glorious thing; there would be none of this resentment. And had you never been born, Simon would have been appointed another wife, who is legitimate, and he and his family would be rejoicing for that reason. So what I'm getting at is that you are the true victim here; you never had a say. You were born, unknowingly, into a world that doesn't want you, thus, negatively affecting others and making them into victims."

No words had ever made Rebecca feel more alone than those uttered by Yarman Cassell. "You're telling me that everyone will be better off if I just die."

"If that is the conclusion you are drawing, then so be it."

"Are you stating something otherwise?"

"I'm simply stating my observations, Mrs. Wylde, not conclusions."

Rebecca felt her stomach turn. "Please don't call me that."

"That is your appointed name."

"As you just suggested, it was never mine."

Cassell was silent for a moment. "That is true."

Rebecca knew right then that Yarman Cassell was no friend, but he was also no foe. "With my assessment of your observations, it is clear that I don't belong here."

"Yes, that's what I'm saying."

"Dying would then be a resolution."

"Yes; you have no place within the Collective. Dying is a solution, as is being committed to Cognitive Services or being exiled from the Collective."

It was laughably clear. "I don't belong. So why am I here?"

Cassell continued to walk. "All three of those options are viable, yes? The Wyldes could execute each one of those, yes?"

The thought was chilling. "Of course."

"And would you agree that getting rid of you is what they would like to do the most?" Rebecca had never considered that question before, but it was an extremely viable one. Deep down, she had thought that Simon secretly loved her and that was why she was still around, *but he doesn't. He wouldn't treat me this way if he did.* "Yes, I guess so."

Cassell smiled. "I can see whatever hope you have clung to these past six months is evaporating into oblivion."

A lump had formed in her throat; Rebecca couldn't respond without crying.

"Don't let it get you down; there is a reason to rejoice. . . . Someone wants you alive."

Rebecca wanted to ask, *who might that be?* but there was no reason to—deep within, she knew whom: the Minister.

She turned away and saw at the front door Arthur Wylde hurriedly walking to an idling hovercar with Florence close behind. Arthur stopped abruptly and turned back. He patted his pockets and said something Rebecca could not hear. Florence replied to him but Arthur waved her off, clearly frustrated, and climbed inside the vehicle.

Cassell gazed up as the hovercar rose into the clouds above. He said, "All you have to do is figure out why the Minister wants you alive. From there, the answer to your existence will come flowing like Assada's River."

Rebecca knew that to be true—possibly more so than ever before. Just as she had learned six months ago, her fate would forever be tied to William Coulee's manuscript and whatever secrets it held. The Minister was aware of this too. That was why she was being kept alive, and a prisoner to the Wyldes. *He needs me for something . . . or is afraid to lose me.* Both thoughts seemed the same, but she knew there was a difference, somehow. *I have to get another copy of the translation; I have to find out more.*

"Can I give you a final word of advice?" Yarmen Cassell asked.

Rebecca simply shrugged.

"Watch your back."

"*Watch my back?* I thought you just said that the Minister wants me alive?"

Yarmen Cassell pointed toward Arthur Wylde's hovercar disappearing into the horizon. "Change is afoot, Rebecca. The Director of Social Affairs is leaving to confront the most powerful man in the world."

Is he talking about Minister Theoman or is he talking about Jonas Lundquist?

Yarmen Cassell continued, "And I'm afraid things will not end well."

Rebecca was at a loss for words. *Should I tell him about Simon?* She twisted for a resolution but found none. "So, what are you trying to say?"

"Change is coming, whether we like it or not. And with change, usually comes . . . well . . ."

CHAPTER NINE

The Dead Sands – OP6

William woke with a start. He had a terrible dream about creatures rising out of the desert and attacking the small outpost. He never actually saw the creatures; he just heard their growls and cries. The creatures had beat on the building's walls and collapsed them. The ceiling had fallen too, revealing the terrible nighttime sky and its horrible master, the moon—but this was no ordinary moon, it had the face of some sadistic looking human, taking pleasure from the destruction it was witnessing. And all the while, William had heard the skinny, desert man laughing in hysterics and saying, "God willz it! God willz it!"

Now awake and still recalling the events of his dream, William rubbed his left hand through his sweaty hair and then sat up on the cot. The details of the dream faded fast except for one: the desert man. William remembered that the desert man was in the outpost's holding cell and then quickly recalled every bizarre detail concerning his walk back with the new prisoner:

"How do you know my name?" William had asked eight hours ago while standing in the desert where they had first met; he had been pointing his laser rifle at the desert man.

The man had smiled and started bobbing his head to an inaudible beat. "Thatz be a damn goo question with the damnest damn anzer yuz ain't prepared to hear."

"What's your name?"

"I'z already told yuz. Yuz can call me whatevaz yuz like, Mista Iceman."

"It's not my responsibility to name you. Give me your name."

The man had begun to suck on his bottom lip, apparently in contemplation. "Alright, I'z toss yuz a bone this time—but only once, yuz hear? Call me Saño." He had looked at William with a curious expression.

"Saño? Okay, Saño."

"Ringz a bell?" Saño had asked, still curious.

There was something about the man's name and face that rang some sort of deep seeded memory, but William wasn't about to admit it. "I have no idea who you are. Now, if you will please answer my question, we can get on our way."

"God willz it; God willz it."

"Who is God?"

"Ah man, Mista Iceman, yuz not know? Seriousness? Ah man, Mista Iceman, yuz know nothin!"

Fed up, William said, "*Alright*, enough. Let's go."

"Goez? Goez where?"

"Until you can answer my questions, I will be detaining you under Ministry Decree 477."

"Minnisty *what?*"

"Ministry Decree 477."

"That mean nothin."

"Let's go."

"Alright, alright, I'z go-wen, I'z go-wen."

The two of them had finally started walking. Sweat caused from the extreme heat and the encounter had poured off William's face. They had a long trek in front of them. Nearly the entire time, Saño had babbled: "I'z knew yuz be comin for me. . . . I'z knew it. . . . We'z got great thingz, yuz and I'z. Great damn thingz! We'z go way back Mista Iceman, way back! I'z still see it all: steel treez and jungle streetz, terrible facez of old and new . . . o the thingz they had uz do . . . terrible, shameful thingz."

"We don't know each other, Saño."

"Wez don't? Well I'z be damned screwed then! My'z mind iz damn screwed! Well I'z don't know then . . . maybe I'z got thingz wrong, all so wrong. Yuz okay with that?"

"Okay with what?"

"That I'z got so much wrong. Yuz okay?"

"I don't care."

"So yuz okay."

"*Yes*, I'm okay."

"Cool, I'z not want to pizz yuz off, Mista Iceman. Yuz have that nasty rifle andz all."

"Then don't give me any reason."

"I'z don't plan on it. I'z plan on uz being friendz. We'z gotz the same goalz, yuz and I'z. We'z both want to get out of herez, right?"

"I don't know what you're talking about."

"Yuz coy? Yuz coy? Okay then. My'z mind been enslaved fo-so long by them terrible demonz sent by The Man Himself that thingz getz a bit confuzin, yuz know?"

"No, I don't. Are you referring to the Desert Demons?"

"Hellz naw! Yuz gotz it all wrong, Mista Iceman. Hellz naw! I'z a Dezert Demon! I'z not talkin about myself; I'z talkin about The Man Himself. He controlz evathing, boy . . . or so he'z likez to think . . . and boy doez he do that! He'z big goddamn thinker; it'z hiz job, ya know? Thinkin. It'z the mind the createz the world; haz yuz ever thought about that? The mind makez the world a wonderful place, or it makez the world a livin hell that ain't worth LIVIN IN . . . boom!"

After William had watched Saño flail his hands around while trying to make his point, he silently thought, *Can we just get back?* There were several moments when William considered releasing the man into the desert, just to shut him up.

"The mind iz a terrible mazta when you let he be. We'z all—and I'z mean ALL—give that bad boy too much control. We'z gotz to make a stand againz that terrible mazta. We'z gotz to get hiz butt under control, becuz the mind will ruin life, take ourz awezomous away and leave uz hollower than moszy log in a termite infezted zwamp."

For some reason, William had decided to comment, "Without our minds, how will we be able to function?"

"Ah, seez, thatz the kinda bullshit thinkin thatz got uz herez in the first place! We'z say, 'Take control mind and tellz uz what to do,' and thatz all wrong!"

"But the mind's job is to think and control our functionality."

"Yuz so wrong yuz not knowz whatz right! The mind thinkz, yez sir! But we'z can controlz what it thinkz about. We'z control function. The mind by itself iz nazty little bugger. The mind under control iz a wonderful thing full of wonderful pozibilitiez. We'z control ourz destiniez! The mind jut leadz uz there. Yuz think that the mindz iz yuz, when actuality, yuz iz the mind!"

"Alright, I see your point," but William hadn't seen his point; he had just wanted the guy to shut up. But Saño had not stopped talking all the way back to the outpost. He had rambled on and on about the mind and its dangerous power.

When they had arrived, William had locked him up in the outpost's only cell and had told Saño that he would be back in the morning.

And now it's morning. William stood up from his cot, stretched his arms upward and then folded them behind his head, grunting. His world in the desert had come further into focus and he realized that food would need to be prepared for both him and his prisoner.

Saño's voice echoed down the corridor: "*Yuz up!*"

William chose to ignore him and walked into the makeshift kitchen area that utilized outdated filing cabinets as countertops and a steel tub as a sink. He extracted a couple of dehydrated dishes and put them into the hydration machine. Within a few minutes, and after a few more calls from Saño, the food was ready. William took one dish with him and walked down the corridor and to the cell.

"I'z been callin for yuz," Saño said in a disappointed tone.

"I was getting your breakfast ready."

"Beckfast . . . ? Whatcha got?"

William went to turn over the tray to the prisoner but then decided to take a better approach. "Here's a deal, for every meal I give you, you have to give me an answer to a question. And once I feel that you've told me everything I need to know, I'll set you free. Deal?"

Saño looked like a caged hungry animal pacing back and forth behind the bars. "Yuz play some gamez with me Mista Iceman? Yuz wantz to play gamez? Alright, I play a bit."

"Alright," William said and then heavily considered what his first question would be. "Where are you from? And be more specific than the desert."

"Shootz . . . I'm from the land o Free! From the land of no new taxes, yellow ribbons and Saturday night pardoy!"

William squinted and said, "*What?*"

"Yuz knowz just as I, bears and pistons, Jordan and jokes. The land o Free! But it turnz out we weren't-zo free."

"Give me the name of this land," William demanded.

"Yuz-es-eh, Sucka!"

"Yuz-es-eh?" William repeated.

Saño smiled and said, "Land o Free."

Yuz-es-eh? William repeated in his mind. The name was completely unfamiliar. *Either he' is feeding me a lie or he's truly crazy.* William handed the dish though the bars to Saño and said, "Thank you. I'll look into this Yuz-es-eh."

Saño immediately unwrapped the dish and began fingering the food into his mouth. "Yuz have a tough time, Mista Iceman."

"And why is that? Did you lie to me?"

"Hellz naw! I'z never lie! But the answer yuz lookin for ain't on no nifty device yuz carry. It'z in yuz brain . . . in yuz mind."

"Terrific. So what you're telling me is that you're from my mind?"

Saño winked. "Now thatz be somefin. Yuz a smart fella, Mista Iceman; yuz figure it out."

CHAPTER TEN

District 9, Sector 2

For the entire day, Yarman Cassell's message haunted Rebecca: she needed to watch her back; she didn't belong within the Collective; Minister Theoman has plans for her. . . . Rebecca counted the seconds until Giles returned and she could make her escape. But even that thought came with a taxing price: Rebecca knew she needed to get another translation of William Coulee's manuscript, and she knew that it would be impossible to do so once she left, which meant her time to act was fleeting. *But how am I supposed to do this?* Going to a sector's Department of Historical Events and pulling down a translation was no longer an option. Plus, Rebecca was quite positive that the second translation results she created in Sector 28 had long been erased. The only way to get another copy was to pull it directly from whatever vault the Minister had stashed it inside. Rebecca had not forgotten Simon's admission that he didn't have high enough clearance to read the translation—*but his father was a whole different story.* Surely the Director of Social Affairs had sufficient clearance. Rebecca knew that Arthur Wylde had a secure portal inside his suite on the second floor. And both Simon and Arthur were still away on business. *Now is my best option.* But getting inside the Wylde's guarded suite, and past Florence Wylde, would not be easy. *I have to try.* Rebecca had been in dire situations before. *I can do this.*

Over the course of the following hour, Rebecca scrutinized the complexity of the situation she would be facing: The Wylde's suite was constantly guarded by two MSF agents that changed guard every three hours, and Florence Wylde hardly left the suite whenever Arthur was away, so getting inside was going to be extremely tricky. Also, there was the challenge of getting into the portal. Rebecca would need Arthur Wylde's security clearance, which was a random alphanumeric code that changed every seven days. *He has such a bad memory*, thought Rebecca. *How does he keep the ever-changing code memorized?* She realized that the answer could be that he doesn't memorize the code; *he could be keeping them inside that notepad of his.*

The memory of Arthur Wylde cursing because he had forgot to grab his notepad came immediately back. *It's inside the suite.* Where, however, was a whole different story, so was whether the code was actually written inside the notepad.

Rebecca checked the time and saw it was getting late. *Tomorrow, I'll be leaving this place forever, with the translation.* The question was when to act. *Sooner than later*, she supposed.

Rebecca left her bedroom where she had been held up all day—avoiding everyone—and went into the main lounge. It was nearly empty. An MSF agent was posted by the hall that led to Rebecca's bedroom; a housekeeper was vacuuming a rug by the main seating area, where Simon frequently watched the Ministry Monitor; and there was a kitchen aid clearing a few used glasses and linens from a dining table in the back of the room. Rebecca looked at the grand staircase that led to the second floor and to the Wylde's suite. It was empty. She walked casually through the lounge and to the stairs, ascending them. She was conscious of every step she took, desiring to be as normal acting as possible. *What was it that William wrote? If you act like you belong, then people will believe you belong.* She reached the top of the steps and the arched double doors to the Wylde's suite were directly in front of her as were two MSF agents. Both men looked directly at her. *Remember, you belong up here.* She walked and stopped confidently in front of the guards and said the only thing that came into her mind: "I need to speak with Mrs. Wylde."

The agents stared at her for a moment and then toward each other before looking at her again. The one on the left asked, "Is she expecting you?"

"No. But it's an important matter . . . a private matter."

The agent said, "Mrs. Wylde requires us to clarify the reason for all unexpected visitors."

Of course, thought Rebecca. "Tell her I need to speak with her about my husband."

If that doesn't get her to the door then I don't know what will.

The agent on the left contemplated before clicking the communiqué on his uniform. "Mrs. Wylde, I'm sorry to disturb you but I have Rebecca Wylde at your suite door requesting to speak with you about her husband." He released the communiqué. "If she wants to speak with you, she'll come—"

The double doors clicked and one of them slowly opened. Florence was standing before Rebecca, half hidden behind the door, in a robe with her hair pulled back. "What is it?" she said impatiently.

Rebecca really didn't have a response prepared. "I was hoping we could speak in private, ma'am."

"Do you know where my son is?" she asked, sounding accusatory, as if Rebecca had been keeping Simon's whereabouts from her.

"No, I told you before: Simon didn't tell me where he was going."

Florence sighed and said, "Can't we talk tomorrow? I have a terrible headache."

Not wanting to push it, but having little choice, Rebecca said, "This really can't wait until tomorrow. If you could just give me fifteen minutes—"

"I can't *give you* fifteen minutes," Florence said harshly. "My head throbs, I haven't heard from either Arthur or Simon all day, and . . . no, I won't speak with you tonight. I'll make time for you tomorrow." And with that, she closed the door, hard.

The agent on the right cracked a smile.

Rebecca wanted to ask him, *what's so funny?* but refrained. Something in his eyes told her to just leave. As she turned away, Rebecca thought she heard the faint sound of a sob coming from behind the double doors. She continued down the stairs and thought, *What's wrong with that wretched woman? Has something happened? Surely she cannot be this upset because her husband hasn't called.* It was very clear that it was unusual for Arthur to go a day without checking in with Florence. *Being gone for only a day is hardly a reason to be in hysterics.* Rebecca could care less if Simon left for a week, month, or year; but their relationship was nothing like Arthur's and Florence, they truly loved each other, which was something Rebecca couldn't relate.

Rebecca returned to her bedroom and locked the door. Her plan to get a copy of the translation had quickly failed. *Maybe tomorrow,* she thought. *Tomorrow is going to bring good things . . .* or so Rebecca had hoped.

CHAPTER ELEVEN

The Dead Sands – OP6

Shortly after breakfast, William had left the outpost to go on a patrol, and when he returned, he found a supplies delivery had just arrived. The MSF Supply Unit stationed thirteen miles away delivered goods once every week; the only thing, however, was that it had come a day earlier than usual.

William, walking in from the vast desert with a cooling scarf over his head, called out and waved to the deliveryman. The man opened the door to the large hovertruck and stepped out of its comfortable air-conditioned cabin. "Are you Agent Coulee?"

"Yeah, you're a day early."

The man, who seemed very distracted, said, "Oh . . . I don't know. With everything going on, I was told to deliver here today."

William didn't care, he was just happy to see another face other than Saño's. "What do you have?"

"The usual, I'm assuming." He walked around to the back of the hovertruck and opened the cargo hold. William assisted in the unloading.

The deliveryman said, "It looks like food rations, restroom supplies, and . . . did you request a new hoverbike?"

That was pleasing news. "Yeah, I sure did. This is a good surprise for once."

"Has it been pretty tough out here?"

"Not a moment's reprieve . . . until now. Here, I'll help."

The deliveryman had a lift already attached to the supplies bundle and was rolling it out but told William he could help by getting the hoverbike out. William went inside the hovertruck and found it still inside its protective wrapping, which was another pleasant surprise: *It's new.* He was convinced that the Ministry would issue him another used hoverbike. *Maybe I'm coming back into favor.*

"That's a nice one," the deliveryman said with forced enthusiasm. He dropped the large supply package off inside the storage shed. "Looks like you will be back in business."

"That's good news indeed," William said with a smile, which was not returned by the deliveryman. *What's this guy's problem?*

The deliveryman brought over a digital notepad and asked William to scan his identification chip, acknowledging that he received the delivery. "Sir, if you don't mind me asking," the deliveryman said a bit sullenly, "what do you make of everything that's been happening? I mean, we've been told to carry on with our duties as usual, but I have to say—"

"What are you talking about?" William said, confused by the man's question and demeanor.

The deliveryman seemed a bit unsure of how to answer. "Well, you know, the takeover and all. I know that—"

"What takeover?" William said suddenly.

The man looked even more taken aback. "Sir, are you saying that you haven't heard about the coup?"

"The coup? I have no idea of what you are talking about. People tell me nothing out here! *What coup!*"

The deliveryman looked as if he felt guilty for being the one to deliver the news. "I'm sorry, sir; I don't know all of the details, but the Security Chief, Jonas Lundquist, has detained the Minister."

The words fell like anvils.

"Jonas Lundquist did *what?*"

The deliveryman looked upset now. "He detained the Minister! . . . And I thought we were late in hearing the news."

William grabbed the man's arms and said, "Tell me *everything*."

The deliveryman nodded nervously and said, "Obviously I don't know everything—they haven't told us much . . . our superiors, that is—but I guess this whole thing started a couple of days ago, when there was an uprising in Sector 16's Capitol. About five hundred protestors took the southern section of the city under its control. The rebels were met by security forces, and supposedly the Security Chief personally ordered the slaughter of two hundred or so of the civilians."

"He *what?!*"

"Yeah! He broke Ministry Decree 5—*something*."

"517," William finished.

"Right." The deliveryman looked agitated. "He . . . he ordered the agents to fire onto the crowd. About two hundred were killed, sir."

William ran a hand through his sweaty hair and thought, *What in the Minister's name was he thinking?* He looked at the nervous deliveryman and said, "Continue."

"The Minister was reportedly not happy about this and ordered the Security Chief to stand down . . . but he didn't. He . . . I feel terrible saying this . . . he had the Minister detained."

William shook his head in total disbelief.

The deliveryman licked his lips several times before saying, "Just three hours ago, The Security Chief announced the indefinite suspension of the Ministry and declared martial law. He has the power of the MSF on his side . . . I thought you—"

"Let me get this straight," William said to the man, stopping him mid-sentence, "Jonas Lundquist has detained the Minister and declared himself the new leader of the Collective?"

"In less direct words, yes, sir."

"*What in the Minister's name is going on?!* I've heard none of this! Who is running the DSA? I can't believe Director Wylde would allow Jonas to take such extreme measures."

A grim expression formed on the deliveryman's face. "Director Wylde is dead."

"He's *dead?*" William felt a tingling chill run all through his body. He felt light-headed. "I need to sit down."

The two men sat on the loading lift of the hovertruck. The deliveryman seemed almost pleased by William's reactions. "Trust me, sir; we all felt similarly when word made its way around. We were all told to carry on with our duties while our supervisors, I think, are trying to sort it all out."

"What was said about the Director's death?"

"The report on the Ministry Monitor stated that he had a brain aneurism and died in his office late yesterday—or early this morning, I guess—just before the Security Chief detained the Minister."

"A brain aneurism? *Right.*" The coincidence was a bit too convenient.

At that moment, a loud holler came from inside the outpost.

The deliveryman looked at the building and said, "What in the Minister's name?"

William could barely process it. "Now what?" William shook his head and sighed.

The hollering continued.

"Is he all right?" the deliveryman asked, clearly bothered.

"I have no idea. Probably not." William ignored the hollering. "What's the mood within the Ministry? How is everyone handling it?"

The deliveryman tore his eyes away from the outpost and tried to answer William's question. "Like I said, everyone is in shock. I don't think anyone knows how to handle it. I mean, we're all loyal to the Security Chief, but of course we're all loyal to the Minister. . . ."

More screaming came from the outpost.

"Is there any indication of retaliation?"

"I . . . I don't know, sir." The deliveryman was obviously bothered, either by the hollering and screaming from within the building or by the line of questioning William was following.

Another scream made its way through the outpost walls: "MIIIISTAAAA COOOOULEEEEE!"

Damn that man! William shook his head and said, "I need to check on this guy."

Without further words, William ran into outpost and the deliveryman wasted no time climbing back inside the hovertruck.

The screaming was made clearer once inside: "MISTA ICEMAN! YUZ NEED TO GET HERE QUICK! HEY! ICEMAN! WILLIAM! COME ON!

GET IN HERE QUICK!"

When William arrived at the cell he was startled to see just how frazzled Saño looked. *"What in the Minister's name is the problem?"*

"Yuz okay? . . . Yuz not hurt?" Saño said quickly.

The questions were both alarming and curious. "I'm fine! why would I be hurt?"

Saño seemed to have calmed himself for the moment before saying, "I'z not one to interfere. I'z let life happen. But yuz need to know that somefin serious is on the horizon, Mista Iceman."

More chills ran down William's spine. "What are you talking about?"

"I'z got eyes beyond the two on my head. Some say it be second sight. I think itz morez than that—but that make no difference thiz moment. Yuz need to watch out, Mista Iceman. I'z think you get too comfortable, and so now I'z think I did my job."

Could he hear our conversation outside? William tried to sort the madness and said, "Are your people coming for me? Who do I need to watch out for?"

"My'z people are waitin, Mista Iceman. Yuz people are a takin. I say nothin else cuz I'z know yuz listen to nothin else. So no I'z just sit, and wait, and see what yuz do."

"Did you hear us talking?"

"I hearz nothin yuz said, but I'z fink we be talkin about the same."

William gave a frustrated sigh and said, "What do you know?!"

"Yuz be warned, Mista Iceman. Now I'z wait and watch."

"Fine. You do that." William then left the room.

As he stood in the hallway he shook his head again and wondered what he did to deserve all of this. He felt a strong desire to cut Saño loose. With everything that was happening within the Ministry, William saw little need to keep Saño around. *I need to think.* So much was running through his mind that it was nearly impossible to concentrate on one thought. *Jonas arrested the Minister . . . on what basis?* Nothing he heard made sense. I need answers. He then thought of the Ministry Monitor.

Quickly, William walked into the main office of the outpost and turned the Ministry Monitor on . . . but there was no broadcast. He fiddled with the dials for a moment before realizing that it may have never worked. *But then why have it in here?* Even though he had never used the Ministry Monitor he always assumed it worked. *Maybe it does work and there isn't a broadcast right now.* That was an unwelcoming thought. Never in his life had William known of a time when the Ministry Monitor was not broadcasting.

He muttered a curse and turned the machine off. *Now what?* William thought of his parents. *Shit, I hope they're okay.* He had no reason to think otherwise. *But then again, I would have never guessed Jonas would do this.*

Saño's words returned to his mind. William was convinced that Saño was truly mad; however, the crazy man's warning remained inside William's heart for no other reason than *what if he isn't crazy.*

With knowing little else, and having nothing better to do, William walked back to the supply shed to begin breaking down the newly arrived package. He did it mindlessly while taking stock of his own situation in light of recent events. William wondered where he stood with Jonas Lundquist. *He sent me here . . . didn't he? Or was that Director Wylde?* Truth be told, William was never a fan of Director Wylde, and now the man was dead, and William did just receive a new hoverbike. *Maybe I am back in favor.* The thought gave him a fleeting moment of hope. *But still, I can't agree with what Jonas did to so many defenseless people. Is he mad? And overthrowing the Minister . . . what is he thinking?* To date, there had been no sustaining attempts at overthrowing the Ministry. *Ziusudra always returns.* He looked out over the vast desert and then shook his head again. He would have been lying to himself if he had declared that his quick scan of the horizon had nothing behind it other than a desire to see the barren landscape.

William returned his attention to the supply package, which had thirty food ration items, ten restroom items, several new uniform and underclothing items, and several miscellaneous items that revealed to be new parts for the rooftop solar panels and a couple of requested tools. He put each item into its predetermined location and then sat down to take a break just outside the supply shed. William's mind wandered through many topics, many of which dealt with his future within the Ministry and whether it would be favorable. But mostly, William wondered how much longer he would have to endure this outpost. He spent a decent chunk of time thinking about different scenarios that revolved around his eventual reassignment and what would be required to make it happen, but basically each ended with him just doing what he has been doing and continuing to endure.

There was, however, one possible scenario he came up with that involved Saño and using him to hunt down the Desert Demons. He considered that that scenario might end his tenure at the Dead Sands outpost . . . one way or another. Capturing Desert Demons single-handed would not be an easy task. This was their home. They knew it far better than William ever could. It was luck that he ever crossed paths with Saño in the first place . . . William paused on that thought. *Luck . . . or was it?* Until that very moment, William had not considered their encounter anything more than coincidental. But as he considered it further, William realized that Saño should have not been seen; William had *never* encountered a Desert Demon before, so why now? *Either Saño is an outcast and so utterly crazy that his own people allowed him to be seen or . . . this is a set up.* William thought back to their encounter. Saño was waiting for him on the return trip, so he must have known William was out there at some point, which in itself was an unsettling thought. *What would they want with me?* There was no easy answer to that question either. The Desert Demons could be looking to get Ministry supplies, they could be looking for revenge for something William was not a part of, or they could simply want to extract information out of him so they could better understand their enemy . . . *or it is none of these answers.* William knew there was only one way to find out. He stood up and went back inside the outpost.

Saño was lying on his side, pretending to be sleeping. William said to him, "What are you doing here?"

Saño pretended to be waking from William's words. "Wha'z that? Wha'z yuz want to know?"

William shrugged, pointed around the room, and said, "Why are you here? Desert Demons don't get caught."

"Yuz caught me, Mista Iceman."

"You caught yourself; why?"

"I see yuz been a thinkin. Thatz dangerous buziness."

"Yeah, I know, trust me. I've also been thinking about turning you loose, but I need answers."

"And anzwers yuz shall find."

"Why did you approach me?"

"I think I'z already toldz yuz."

"What did you tell me?"

"We'z gotz great thingz to do, yuz and I."

"Are your people coming for me?"

And it seemed that the timing could not have been more perfect.

There was a startling loud rattle at the outpost door. . . .

Saño quieted down. "Not my'z people."

William looked at him and then to the doorway leading out toward the direction of the sound. "What was that?"

"I'z think we'z not want to find out."

William's heartbeat quickened. He had no weapons on him and there were none in the room.

Another bang and rattle sounded out as if the door had broke free from its lock.

Saño was standing now at his cell door. "I'z think we need to get out of here, Mista Coulee."

William looked at him for just enough time to quickly consider Saño's change in demeanor and then returned his attention to the noise. "I think you're right."

CHAPTER TWELVE

District 9, Sector 2

There is nothing quite like being shook awake in the middle of the night, as Rebecca discovered. A hand was held over her mouth by a silhouette of a figure. "*Whhhhht rrrrr dddnnn?*" she tried to say.

The figure shushed her and said, "*Be quiet.*"

It was Simon.

Rebecca peeled his hand from her mouth and said quietly, "What are you doing? Where have you been?"

He sat next to her and said, "Your boyfriend, *Roland*, just tried to kill me."

It took her a second or two to register what he had said. "*Roland, what?*"

"You heard me, that son of a bitch tried to kill me yesterday."

"*How* . . . where were you? Why would he do that?"

"You tell me."

Rebecca had no idea what to say. "I haven't talked to Roland since . . ."

"Yeah? Since when?"

"Since he helped me get to Sector 28."

Simon's face became more and more visible as Rebecca's eyes adjusted. There was some swelling along the right side of his mouth. He had been in a fight. "Be truthful with me," he said in a serious tone, "what is your relationship with that man?"

"I don't have one."

"Well, he seems to think so." Simon rubbed the side of his mouth.

Rebecca sat up in bed and examined Simon's jaw. "What happened?"

"I told you. He attacked me and tried to kill me."

"But *WHY?*"

"Keep your voice low, damnit. I told you why. He thinks you two have a relationship. This fool is in love with you."

Rebecca's heart sank. *Oh, Roland, what did you do?* "How did he find you? Where were you yesterday?"

Simon opened and closed his mouth, flexing his bruising jaw. "Actually, I found him."

"You were looking for him? *Why?*"

Simon looked like he was choosing his words with care. "Roland is suspected of being a Heretique. Jonas wants him brought in for questioning but fears that he will run if approached by MSF agents. He thinks Roland has valuable information and doesn't want him . . . spoiled. . . . So, instead of agents, he sent me to talk to him. I think—Jonas thought—that I might be able to reach him easier."

"Why you?"

Simon scoffed. "Isn't it obvious? He's in love with you. Jonas thought I could proposition him. I would bring him to meet you and he would come willingly. But as you can see"—Simon pointed to his swollen, bruising face—"he wasn't willing."

Roland is a Heretique? "And so he attacked you? That doesn't sound like him."

"Apparently you don't know him very well."

Maybe I don't. Still, though, something wasn't right. "What makes Jonas think that Roland is a Heretique?"

"Truly, Rebecca? You are truly asking this question? He helped you reach them. He took you in a Ministry hovercar to Sector 28 and aided you in stealing information from a TRNSLTR machine."

"Because I made him; not because he wanted to, or because he is a member of the Heretique."

"*Don't be foolish!*"

Rebecca's eyes widened from his sudden outburst; Simon was growing angry.

"Do you always expect every member of the Heretique to jump up and down, shouting proclamations of their rebellion? *Hmmm?* Do you think locating a member is that clear-cut; that all one has to do is ask? You are a *fool* if you do."

Rebecca slapped Simon across his face. She was trembling with anger. "I will not be talked to this way! You think you married a fool, do you? If so, then you are no wiser. Unless everything that happened six months ago was one GIGANTIC conspiracy designed to guide me into the lair of the Heretique, then Roland is no more a member than you. I manipulated him into taking me there. I led him to—"

Simon grabbed her face, like he did in the lounge before, and said, "You used your sexuality to lure him, *didn't you?* All while engaged to me? How DARE you!"

Rebecca smacked his hand away just as the bedroom doorknob began to rattle and a voice from outside ordered, "Open up!"

Both Simon and Rebecca stood, looking at the door. Simon said, "Now look what you've done." He readjusted his uniform and prepared to address the agent outside when suddenly the door crashed open from a fierce blow.

Standing before them were two MSF agents with their weapons drawn. Rebecca instinctively raised her hands, but Simon stood angrily defiant. "Lower your weapons, for Minister's sake!"

The lead agent stepped inside the room and said, "The Minister isn't in charge anymore," and targeted Simon's chest.

Simon stepped aside and said, "Lower that weapon, you fool! I know the Minister isn't in charge, I am!"

Rebecca couldn't believe her ears. "*What?!*"

The agent followed Simon's movements and said, "Not according to the Security Chief."

Simon looked a little loss for words.

Rebecca's eyes danced back and forth between Simon and the threatening agent. Her hands worked on their own. Grasping the decorative jewelry box on the bedside table and flinging it at the agent with surprising strength and accuracy.

The agent jerked his burn rifle in reaction and blasted a beam right past Simon's head, taking off part of his right ear, and into the wall beyond. The jewelry box hit the agent in the face and sent him staggering a few steps back.

Simon yelled out in pain and bent down, clutching his ear.

The second agent advanced into the room—only temporarily, though—before being pulled back from behind by an unseen force. He gasped and fell to the ground; there was something wrapped around his throat . . . an arm.

Rebecca grabbed her bedside lamp and yanked it free from the wall, but it was too late; the agent she had hit with the jewelry box was raising his weapon toward her.

Simon lunged forward and slammed the laser rifle up against the agent's chest, causing a second beam to slice through the room and out the exterior wall, severing the glass of the triple window.

The two men struggled for control as Rebecca swung the lamp down onto the head of the agent, crunching his skull. The agent gave up the struggle and Simon rolled off him.

Outside the room, and in the hall, another struggle continued. Rebecca saw a man, whose face was hidden, choking the other agent into unconsciousness.

Simon grabbed the burn rifle from the limp hands of the agent on the ground and pointed it at the two struggling men. Rebecca placed a hand on Simon's trigger finger and said, "Wait."

The unknown man rolled the incapacitated agent off of him and stood up.

Rebecca couldn't believe her eyes. "*Roland?!*"

Roland was out of breath and noticeably perspiring. He stepped over the knocked out agent and said, "We have to get out of here."

Simon kept the rifle pointed at him and said, "Don't take another step."

Roland paused and held out his hands in submission. Rebecca grabbed the burn rifle in Simon's hands and the two struggled for control. Rebecca shouted at him, "Stop it! He saved us!"

Simon yanked and pulled the rifle, saying, "He tried to kill me earlier!"

Roland took a small step forward and said, "No I didn't! You tried—"

Simon jerked the rifle free and aimed it at Roland's face. But before he could pull the trigger, the power inside the house went completely out. All three of them were standing in total darkness. Rebecca felt chills run the course of her body. *Stalkers*, she thought. Visions of their menacing shapes entered her mind. "Stop it, Simon . . . We're all in danger."

Roland, invisible in the darkness, said, "I have a car. Please, let's get out of here."

Rebecca couldn't see Simon, nor could she see his finger was still on the trigger, all Rebecca could hear was his heavy breathing.

"Fine," Simon said. "Get moving, both of you."

Rebecca felt for the doorway and slid her hands along the frame and to the left wall of the hall as she walked. She kept her right hand out in front of her just in case she ran into Roland.

Once down the hall, moonlight could be seen spilling into the main lounge. The room was alien looking in the darkness. The furniture subtly reflected the moonlight and took unrecognizable form. Rebecca could see Roland once again, swiftly walking toward the front door. She wanted to ask him, *How did you get here? How did you get inside?* but knew better than to make a peep. She could sense Simon walking closely behind her, ever so often feeling the barrel of the rifle nudging her back.

A beam of laser light passed between Roland and Rebecca, slicing the floor and nearby wall. Both of them dropped to the ground and looked for the source.

An MSF agent was standing on the grand stairwell.

Simon shouted out, "Don't shoot! It's me, Simon Wylde!"

A beam nearly severed him in half. He spun and fell to the ground, somehow unscathed. Simon rose to his knees and fired a beam of his own, cutting straight up the stairwell. There was a grunt and then the sound of a body falling down the stairs . . . actually, the sound of two bodies falling down the stairs.

Simon said, sounding completely unnerved, "Why are they shooting at us?"

"Come on!" Roland called back, already at the front door.

Rebecca wanted to go but then thought, *Florence*. "Simon, your mother."

It was as if he had totally forgotten about her. "My God!"

Simon rushed away from Rebecca and toward the stairwell. Rebecca looked back to Roland, who was crouched at the door and cautiously looking around outside, and then to Simon. "Wait," she called faintly.

"What are you doing?!" Roland called after her.

Rebecca caught up to Simon at the stairwell and saw half of a man lying in a bloody heap. She tried not to look at it. Simon was hurriedly running up the stairs. Rebecca followed close behind.

A snap and a sizzle could be heard from behind. Roland cried out.

Rebecca looked back but couldn't see him.

"Mother!" Simon called out; the suite doors were wide open.

Rebecca saw him run inside the suite. She crouched down at the top of the stairs, paralyzed with indecision: She didn't know if she should continue following Simon or go back down the stairs and look for Roland. Several burn beams carved up the room below, making the decision easy for her. Rebecca ran into the suite.

Like the rest of the house, the suite was completely dark. Rebecca stepped to the side of the door and crouched down, almost afraid to make too much noise. She called out quietly, "Simon? Where are you?"

The zapping of laser fire continued outside the room.

Rebecca crawled further inside. The suite was massive in comparison to hers and Simon's. She reached a sofa and peeked over it. "Simon?"

There was a faint sound—maybe of a sob—coming from another room to her right. Rebecca held her breath so that she could hear it more closely. It was a man's muffled cry.

Rebecca feared the worst.

She made her way over to the doorway and then stopped when she saw Simon on his knees in front of an immobile body. "Simon . . ."

His shoulders raised and lowered in a single quivery motion. He appeared to be stroking his mother's hair.

Rebecca didn't know what to say; their lives were still very much in danger. "Simon . . . we have to leave."

"She's dead," was all he said in return; his voice was completely under control and emotionless.

Rebecca went further in but kept her distance, too afraid of what she might see. "Simon, we have to leave. Please."

"This wasn't supposed to happen," he said quietly. "She wasn't supposed to die."

Rebecca reached out to him. "We need to leave."

Simon turned and looked at her; just a faint glimpse of his swollen jaw could be seen by the moonlight coming through the window on the far wall. He stared at her for a moment before nodding his head.

Rebecca considered a plan to escape . . . but then her mind froze.

Simon walked past her and stopped at the door. "What are you doing? Come on."

The notebook.

"Simon, I need to find your father's notebook."

"My fa—*why?*"

Rebecca walked over to him and said, "I need a copy of the translation . . . from the manuscript I translated six months ago."

The contortion of Simon's face could be seen, even in the dark. "You need to get *what?*"

"The Minister fears the manuscript, Simon. And he obviously no longer wants us alive, so I—"

Simon took her by the arm and said, "Listen to me. The Minister is no longer in charge. This isn't his doing, *damnit*; this is Jonas's work."

"I don't care! I need the translation—*we* need the translation."

Rebecca could tell that Simon wanted to argue further but time was of the essence.

"Where does he keep it?"

Simon held the burn rifle in one hand and wiped his face with the other. "I don't know. Probably by the portal."

"Where is that? I've never been in here before."

Several snaps of laser fire were heard outside the suite.

A man cried out in pain.

Please don't be Roland, thought Rebecca.

Simon led her over to the opposite side of the room and to a desk placed against the wall. He leaned in close in order to examine it in the low light. Rebecca looked at the monitor on the desk and noticed that there were three little dots blinking, one at a time, in the center of the screen. "The power is still on?"

Simon glanced at the screen and said, "The portals don't lose power."

Rebecca went to the desk and began looking for the mind sensor and found it at the base of the monitor. She placed it on and the screen flashed to life, creating a glow that filled the corner of the room.

"Found it," Simon said, holding the notebook.

"Look for your father's security clearance code."

Simon quickly flipped through the pages and found the last entry. He angled the notebook so that he could read what was written inside. "Here—ready?"

"Go."

"Z7-tsRE8-KU:90"

Rebecca suddenly realized why Arthur Wylde wrote them down. "Give it here." She took the notebook and read Z7-tsRE8-KU:90.

The screen showed little black circles for every character she thought and then flashed a new screen, which was the Ministry database.

"What should I search for?" she asked.

"How should I know?"

The possibilities seemed endless.

The surrounding noise fell to an eerie silence.

Rebecca thought, *William Coulee's Manuscript.* The screen displayed 0 results.

She thought, *Manuscript translation.* The screen displayed 4,391 results. "That's too many," she said.

Rebecca thought, *William Coulee translation.* The screen displayed 0 results.

She thought, *Coulee's Manuscript.* The screen displayed 0 results.

"Come on, Rebecca," Simon breathed, frustrated.

William's Manuscript. The screen displayed 0 results.

Top Secret translation. The screen displayed 0 results.

Outside the compound, a voice called out, "Rebecca!"

Both Rebecca and Simon looked toward the windows in the suite. Simon said, "Is that *idiot* really screaming your name?"

That isn't Roland's voice, Rebecca knew. She returned her attention to the screen. *It has to be something more cryptic . . . but what?*

Rebecca thought, *Book of Thoth.* The screen displayed 0 results.

She thought, *Logos.* The screen displayed 0 results.

Simon said, "Damnit, Rebecca; this is taking too long."

"I need just a few more seconds."

"We don't have a few more seconds."

Outside, the voice called again, "Rebecca, where are you?"

Simon looked to the window and then back to Rebecca. "He's going to attract everyone."

Rebecca was now panicking. "*Just a few seconds.*"

Simon said in a rush of words, "It won't be long before Jonas sends Stalkers after us."

The terror of Stalkers filled Rebecca's mind.

The screen displayed 4 results.

"What is this?" asked Rebecca.

Simon looked at the screen and said, "I don't know."

Rebecca reached out her hand. "Give me your notepad—*now.*"

Simon pulled it out from inside his uniform pocket and handed it over. Rebecca pressed it next to the Monitor and used her index finger to swipe all four files over to the notepad.

"Are you done?" Simon asked.

"No. One more second."

Rebecca cleared the search field and thought, *Forbidden Translation.* The screen displayed 0 results.

The voice outside called once more, but further away this time, "Rebecca!"

Simon gripped his laser rifle and said, "I'm going to shut him up."

"No," was all she could get out. *It has to be something similar to what William wrote about.* She thought back to what was written inside the manuscript, to when William went inside the Bosnian pyramid, to when he found the fake wall and what was painted on it: *a snake in front of a fruit tree.* Her mind focused on fruit tree. The screen displayed 0 results.

Rebecca thought, *Forbidden Fruit.* The screen displayed 1 result.

"Oh my! I think I found it!"

Simon looked at the screen and said, "*Let's go.*"

Rebecca dragged the file over to his notepad and then removed the headset. *But is this file it?* She had to know for sure.

Simon was already at the suite's double doors, aiming the rifle outside.

Rebecca located the file on the notepad and opened it.

Simon called out, "*Come on.* What are you doing?"

Rebecca opened the file and saw that it read:

****

The following are the results for TRN—1152393—DEO—1123h

****

My dearest reader:

Within your grasp is a chronicle written many years ago, possibly well before your time. The author has long passed, but the importance of his message holds truer today than it did back then. This man, who will identify himself through his writing . . .

****

"This is it!" cried Rebecca.

"LET'S GO," demanded Simon.

Rebecca closed the file and ran toward the door. Simon turned the corner and went for the stairs, aiming the laser rifle at everything in front of him. Rebecca slowed to a stop behind him and thought, *Roland, please be alive.* They walked past half of an agent's body Simon slewed earlier and then came to the other half at the bottom of the stairs.

The main lounge was ravished; laser burns had sliced through the furniture, walls, and doors. Rebecca wanted to call out for Roland but she kept her silence. There were several bodies scattered about the room. Rebecca's eyes bounced from each while looking for anything identifiable, to see if any of them were Roland.

Outside, and by the garage, a voice could be heard. "Rebecca, are you here?!"

"Is that Roland?" she asked Simon quietly. The voice didn't sound like Roland's.

"No," he said flatly and continued to the front door.

When they crossed its threshold, Rebecca felt the prickly coolness of the grass against her bare feet and could see several trees flaming like candles from an obvious laser attack.

Over by the garage, a man was carefully walking from shadow to shadow, searching for something. Rebecca assumed it was the person calling her name. Simon kept the rifle pointed at the person, unwilling to let his guard down again. Rebecca placed a hand on Simon's arm and said, "Wait a second; I might know this person."

"Yeah," Simon said softly, "me too."

"It's not Roland." Rebecca found herself thinking. *It's Giles!*

"I know."

Simon started making his way closer to the silhouette of a person. Rebecca followed him closely, feeling uncertain about what was to come.

The person in shadow stopped and bent down to one knee. "Who is that?" he called out.

Simon stopped and said, "You first."

The man raised his hands into the air and said, "My name is Giles Stoykich. I'm a chauffer for the Wyldes."

Rebecca's heart skipped. "Simon, lower the rifle, it's okay, he's—"

A blast of light formed a straight line right through the silhouette in front of them. There was a sizzle and then the beam disappeared.

Giles Stoykich fell limp to the ground. A faint cloud of smoke billowed into the air.

"WHY DID YOU DO THAT?" Rebecca cried out and started running toward the body.

Simon reached out a hand and grabbed her arm, which swung wildly. "Stop—stop it—he was going to kill you."

Rebecca looked at Simon with horror all over her face. "You killed him! You killed him and you didn't even wait to hear him explain—"

"Rebecca, listen to me! He was going to kill you"—Simon dropped the laser rifle and pulled her closer with both hands—"He was going to kill you. I know him."

"*He was your driver*, of course you knew him."

"No—he wasn't a driver, damnit; Giles worked for Jonas. He was pretending to be Heretique in order to lure you into escaping. Jonas wants you dead. He wanted you to give him an excuse to kill you. The Minister was protecting you, and Jonas wanted you dead."

Rebecca stopped fighting. Tears streamed down her cheeks. "I don't know what to believe anymore."

"Believe me, at least for this; Jonas wants you gone. I don't know why; he just wants you dead. I tried to protect you, I told him that you are trustworthy, but he didn't believe me. He told me that he wanted to plant Giles in here, in order to test your loyalty. I knew that you would fall for the trap, but what was I to do?"

"If he was going to kill me," argued Rebecca, "then why didn't he do it two days ago, in the woods?"

"He wasn't going to kill you then; he was just setting you up to be arrested. Tonight—this moment—he was going to kill you. Jonas has betrayed me. He wants both of us dead. Giles would have killed both of us."

"*You don't know that.*"

Simon pulled her in for a hug—their first *real* hug. Rebecca wanted to push him away. She hated him, but she had no control . . . over anything, it seemed.

A whining noise became clearly audible as a hovercar swung around the house and lowered to the ground. Both Simon and Rebecca watched. Simon released her and bent down to the ground, retrieving the laser rifle. Rebecca looked hard at the car and recognized the driver. "It's Roland!" She then looked at Simon and said, "You better not hurt him, or I swear . . ."

Simon was hiding something sinister behind his eyes, but he agreed. "I won't do anything."

The two of them ran over to the hovercar and climbed inside. Roland didn't wait for Simon to close the door; he fired the engines and ascended up into the sky. "We're out of here!"

Rebecca leaned forward and kissed Roland on the cheek. "Thank you! Thank you so much!"

Simon was less enthusiastic. "Yeah, thank you—*friend*."

CHAPTER THIRTEEN

The Dead Sands – OP6

William quietly eased the barred door open; he was careful not to make more noise than necessary. With no hesitation, Sańo slipped out and stood next to William. He whispered, "Iz there another way out?"

"Not from this room." William looked around and saw the shovel he used the day before. He picked it up and said, "We have to go into the main office to get out."

"Yuz lead the way, boss man."

William passed through the doorway with the shovel clutched like a club and listened to the sounds of whoever—or whatever—walking around inside the office space. *They aren't too cautious*, he thought. William remembered where he left the laser rifle, on top of the desk, and silently pleaded that the decision would not be a fatal one.

As they passed out of the hall and into the office, William looked hastily around for the source of the sound that had just fallen silent. He could now see the laser rifle still sitting on top of the desk. He was a bit hesitant on whether he should make a go for it. *Do I call out? Maybe it's another agent.*

"I'z be quiet," Saño whispered, as if hearing William's thoughts.

William pointed toward the door with his free hand. Saño nodded and slowly crept toward it. William listened as intently as possible; all he could hear was the humming of the generator on the roof, the whooshing of the ceiling fans, and his own heartbeat thumping in his chest. His attention to the stillness was reaching a maddening level. Saño placed a hand on the battered door, which William turned to see and observed the level of damage; *the door was busted open. So much for the intruder being an agent.*

Saño gently placed a hand on the metal façade of the door and gave it a slow shove forward. A creaking sound followed.

Surprised by the noise, William looked back toward Saño.

With a sudden rush of sound and force, the metal desk holding the laser rifle flipped up and over in a resounding crash. A black figure emerged from its hiding place, standing tall.

William instantly recognized it: a stalker.

There was not time to scream, run, or even panic; the stalker charged William with its limbs flailing. William instinctively jabbed the edge of the shovel into the stalker's chest and caught it square in the sternum. The weight of the beast was too much for William, and the two of them collided into the door and Saño. The force swung the door wide and shoved Saño onto the sandy ground beyond, while William and the stalker wrestled in the doorway.

The beast was overbearing. William tried to roll it off, but it had gained too much leverage. The stalker's hands found their grip around William's neck. The constricting power was immense.

Saño witnessed William's impending doom and acted. He ran up and kicked the beast in its featureless face.

This act only managed to redirect the stalker's attention.

Saño kicked and caught it in the face again, but this time it grabbed his leg with its right hand and yanked Saño off his feet.

William unleashed a powerful blow to the stalker's left hand, knocking it from his neck, along with some of William's flesh, and the stalker came down onto him. This opened a very small window for William to maneuver his body out from underneath.

Saño repeatedly kicked at the beast, continuing the distraction.

William tried to get to his feet, but the stalker took a hold of William's shirt and yanked him toward the ground, using William as a counter balance for it to stand.

"Get the rifle!" William shouted out, while he futilely struggled against the beast.

Saño scampered to his feet, courageously leaped over the stalker, and landed half on its legs and half on the ground.

Realizing what Saño was attempting, the beast relinquished its fight with William and turned all of its attention toward the receding desert man.

Saño fumbled with the rifle before finding the charge button.

The stalker lunged for him, but William grabbed its legs, causing the beast to fall to the ground a few feet short of Saño.

Saño ran away from the stalker and toward the outpost's kitchen; he needed to buy more time for the rifle to charge.

The stalker sprung up and charged toward the desert man.

The fight ended in a flash.

The stalker crumbled in two pieces, spilling a shallow pool of blood and wires.

"Hit it again!" William cried out from the doorway.

Saño didn't hesitate; he slashed the laser beam through the stalker's head this time, charring bone and gray matter. The sizzling sound it made quickly faded as the heat from the beam dissipated.

William cautiously walked over to the carcass. "I think it's dead."

"I'z sure hope so," Saño said through heavy breaths.

Feeling mentally numb from the attack, William leaned over the head of the beast and further examined its makeup. "I've never seen one this close up," he confessed. "It's known as a stalker, but that's about it. A special division that reports directly to the security chief controls these things."

"That'z yuz people, right? Why'z it here?"

"That's a good question; why did it come here?" *Someone wants me dead,* was the obvious answer.

Saño, still holding the rifle, said, "I'z think it be best we'z gets out of herez."

William understood his trepidation but wasn't prepared to abandon his post just yet. "Hold on, I need to think about this for a moment. Something is clearly wrong, but it might be some kind of mishap . . . or something"—

he stood up—"I don't think it's prudent that we leave." How a stalker could accidentally attack him was beyond his ability to rationalize, but William tried anyway.

"I'z think you makin a big mistake, Mista Iceman. Yuz need to leave too."

William looked toward Saño, who was walking to the battered doorway, pointing the laser rifle in William's general direction. "What are you doing?"

"We'z need to leave, Mista Iceman. I'z askin now, but I'z won't be askin for long."

"So this is my repayment for defending you?"

"Yez, sir. I'z payin you back. Yourz life for my'z life. Yuz comin?"

"Do I have a choice?"

"Yez, sir. Yuz can stay, but I'z be taken this here rifle."

"Well, then we have a problem; I can't let you do that."

"Then I'z suggest yuz come on with me."

William was in no mood for a fight. He glanced down at the dead stalker and then back to Saño. "You win. I would rather take my chances with you and the Desert Demons than be here without a rifle."

"Yuz makin a wize decision, Mista Iceman. Now letz get."

CHAPTER FOURTEEN

District 9, Sector 2

Rebecca watched the Wylde's mansion disappear below as Roland pulled the hovercar into the cloudy nighttime sky. Turbulence tossed them around, making Rebecca's stomach turn . . . or maybe she was feeling nauseous from everything that had just transpired.

"What happened back there?" Roland said excitedly.

Rebecca was the first to answer. "I have no idea! Simon?!"

Simon was still breathing heavily, like the rest of them, and said, "They tried to kill us. What more needs said?"

"WHY, SIMON?!" Rebecca had no more patience for his attitude.

"I don't know *WHY!* Jonas ordered them to kill us, plain and simple."

"And did he send you to kill me?" said Roland.

Rebecca looked at Simon. "Well . . . ?"

"No. . . . He sent me to talk to you, to find out if you are Heretique."

"So killing me was your own idea."

There was an intense level of embarrassment and frustration on Simon's face, but what could he say or do?

Rebecca stared at him with an incredulous look and then reached over and smacked Simon across the face. He caught her hand afterward and held it tight. Rebecca wrenched it away and said, "You make me sick."

The three of them sat in silence for a few minutes before Simon finally said, "So where are you taking us?"

Roland looked into the rear view mirror and said, "I have no idea."

"You need to take us to the Here"—Rebecca caught herself—"to the Free People's Society. They're the only ones who can help us now."

"That's suicide for me," said Simon.

"I think it's a good idea," affirmed Roland.

"Look," Simon said quickly, "I did what I did because I thought you were a threat."

Roland turned back and said, "A threat? To who?"

"To me! To Rebecca!"

"Why would I *ever* be a threat to either of you?"

"I thought you were Heretique! And you're obviously in love with *my wife* . . ."

Rebecca raised her hands, clearly tense from the accusations.

"She's your wife because of that bullshit Ministry test," said Roland.

"Stop it!" shouted Rebecca. "Don't do this right now! We have to figure out what we're going to do!"

Simon opened his mouth to say something, but nothing came out; there was nothing for him to say.

"How can I find them . . ." asked Roland, unsure of what exactly to call them. "The Free People's Society?"

"I don't know," confessed Rebecca. "I haven't been in contact with them in over six months." She paused for a moment. "I thought I had a new contact, a guy who was going to take me to them . . . but—"

"He was a plant," grumbled Simon. "I told you this."

"But what?" asked Roland.

"But, Simon killed him."

Roland cursed quietly and looked out his side window.

"He would have killed you, Rebecca! Why won't you listen to me?!"

Roland snapped his head back around and said to Rebecca, "We should leave him behind. We should drop his ass off right here."

Rebecca began to massage her temples.

"Shut your mouth," ordered Simon. "You don't know what you're talking about. Rebecca, listen to me. I was trying to protect you. I couldn't let that guy get near you. I was—"

"You're so full of lies, Simon! I don't believe anything you say! If you were so concerned about me then why did you allow those people at Ministry dinner to humiliate me? Why did you act like a complete jerk to me and treat me like I was some burden chained to your ankle?"

Simon ran both of his hands through his hair and said, "Look—"

"I'm tired of listening to this guy," interjected Roland. "No one wants him around; that is more obvious than ever. And if he doesn't want to go to the Free People then so be it! I'm dropping him off down there." Roland put the car into a dive.

Rebecca reached out and braced herself against the dashboard.

Simon called out, "Wait a second! There are other options!"

"Roland," said Rebecca, "take it easy."

Simon held onto an emergency handle above his seat and said, "You're right, I have no place to go. I'm in deep trouble. But if you drop me off down there, then I'll die for sure. Do you want that on your hands?"

Roland didn't answer.

Rebecca looked over to Roland and said, "We'll find the Free People and we'll let them decide on how to handle Simon. Maybe they can use him as trade bait, or maybe—"

"They will kill me!" Simon leaned forward and said, "You have to know this; they will kill me without a single thought."

"Not my father. He's not like you. He will show mercy."

"You're assuming that I will make it that far. Others aren't as merciful."

"Then we'll protect you."

Roland shook his head and said sharply, "I will not protect him! He tried to kill me!"

Simon's face turned red, and he clenched the seats tightly. "Damn you! Is that all you can say? Do you have no other value other than reminding everyone about our history? You're right! I tried to kill you! And I should have succeeded!" With that, Simon reached over and began to choke Roland—his left arm wrapped around Roland's neck.

Rebecca screamed for him to quit and pulled on his arm, but he had it wrapped tight.

Roland had let go of the steering wheel with one hand while he tried to break Simon's hold; he reached around and clawed at Simon's face.

"IF I'M GOING TO DIE"—Simon bellowed—"THEN WE SHALL ALL GO!"

Roland released the steering wheel entirely as his ability to fight back diminished.

Rebecca reached over and took the wheel, trying to level them out, but the hovercar was becoming out of control: rolling onto its side and angling deeper toward the ground. The speed of the descent added gravitational force that made pulling out of the dive nearly impossible.

Rebecca looked at the crazed-eyed Simon and said, "STOP IT! WE DON'T HAVE TO DIE! WE'LL FIND A WAY! I PROMISE, WE'LL FIND A WAY!"

Simon looked at her and released his grip on Roland.

Roland coughed and took a hold of the steering wheel, but control was lost. He fought against the controls with all of his might, screaming for mercy.

The ground came zooming toward them in a rush of sight and sound.

The hovercar lifted slightly. They snaked between trees, and then they crashed.

The car flipped forward seven times, smashing the windshield upon first impact and then the rest of the hood and trunk with each contact. Rebecca saw herself hit the dashboard and then the roof, seat, dashboard again, roof again, seat again, over and over again before falling into complete darkness.

CHAPTER FIFTEEN

District 4, Sector 2

The wind woke her. Rebecca could feel it tease the skin on her face. She could hear its whistle in her ears. She opened her eyes and the daytime light blinded her. Everything was red and fuzzy. She tried moving the fingers of her right hand: each one moved successfully. She tried the left and discovered that she was laying on her left hand. She could feel her fingers wiggling against her ribs but couldn't actually feel them moving alone. There was no feeling at all in her left arm. Rebecca struggled to free it from under her body. It was completely numb. Her legs ached as she moved them and she wiggling her toes too.

It then occurred to her that she was no longer inside the hovercar.

Rebecca was sure that all of her limbs were still intact despite the numbness, and she rolled onto her back. The sky above was clear of clouds but odd looking; it wasn't blue, but orange. Rebecca wiped her eyes and saw traces of dried blood on the back of her hands. She wiped them again and discovered wet blood. Her eyes began to itch. *My eyes are bleeding?* This was a first for her.

Rebecca braced her elbows against the ground and pushed her way up. Her body suddenly made its aches known. Her clothes were dirtied, torn, and bloodied. She looked around and saw where the hovercar had ended up: about twenty yards away and against a pair of trees. It was in a twisted heap.

Wow, was all she could think.

She rubbed her eyes again and noticed that the blood was lessening. She then realized where it was coming from—the blood, that is. It was coming from little cuts along her forehead, undoubtedly caused by the windshield shattering. The blood had been running into her eyes. Rebecca found a clean section on her gown and pulled it up to wipe her eyes.

And then it finally struck her: *Roland? Simon?*

Rebecca cried out, "Hello?!"

There was no response.

"Hello? Roland? Simon?"

There was nothing still. . . .

And then a man's voice whimpered out, "*I need help.*"

"Who is that? Where are you?"

The man said, "*I'm still in the car. I'm Simon.*"

Reality was biting at her. *Oh no. Where's Roland? How hurt is everyone?*

Rebecca stood on shaky legs; her bare feet felt the harshness of the dry soil while her eyes swept the area again. There was a lump of something inside the foliage to her left. Rebecca held her breath as she walked toward it. "Roland?"

Simon cried out, "*Please, Rebecca . . . help! I'm completely stuck!*"

The body didn't move, but it was indeed Roland. Rebecca stopped a few feet from him and said his name again, "Roland?"

He was breathing; she could see it now. "Roland!" She went to his side and knelt down beside him. There was dirt caked to one side of his face and dried blood all around his nose and left eye. Rebecca rolled him cautiously over and observed his body. His left arm had several nasty gashes in it. It was apparent that he was tossed from the car too. "Roland . . . can you hear me?"

He stirred and tried to roll back over. Rebecca held him in place and pulled open his eyelids. "Hey! Hello! Wake up!"

Simon continued to call out, "*Please, don't leave me here!*"

Roland grabbed both of her hands and pulled them away. "Stop it."

His voice was dry and low but he was alive. Rebecca began to laugh. "Are you okay?" It wasn't funny but her happiness to see him alive bubbled over.

"Yes . . . I'm okay . . . I think."

"Simon is stuck in the car," she told him.

"Good," was all he said.

"I have to help him."

". . . Okay, fine."

"Are you really okay?"

Roland tried to sit up. "Yeah, I think so." He then grimaced with pain. "My arm; it burns."

Rebecca gently ran her fingers through his hair and then left him. She walked to the wrecked hovercar. It was incredibly mangled. How Simon was still alive, she realized, had to be a miracle—however, when she finally saw him, she realized no miracle had occurred.

Simon was twisted inside the vehicle like a rubber toy.

"*Thank you,*" he said, "thank you for not leaving me."

Rebecca was terrified by what she saw. Simon should have been dead. "Oh, no . . . Simon."

"I'm bad, right? I can't feel my legs. I can move my fingers on my right hand, but I can't feel anything below."

". . . Okay . . ." Rebecca pulled out of her shock. "Okay, I'm going to get you out." *He's going to die*, thought Rebecca. *You can't help him.* "Okay, I'll figure this out."

"Is it that bad?"

"It's bad, Simon."

She heard Roland staggering behind her. He called out, "Is he okay?"

"No—he's alive but he's hurt pretty bad."

"Great . . ." muttered Roland.

Rebecca saw a chunk of bent metal covering Simon's right arm and tried to pull it back without success. She tried repeatedly; her hands bled from the sharp metal. "Ah! Damnit! I can't move it."

Roland stood beside her now and reluctantly reached down to try and help. The two of them pulled again but it was so difficult finding leverage inside the heap of wreckage.

"It's not moving," gasped Roland.

Rebecca looked down at Simon's face; his eyes were glossy and his skin was deathly pale. "How are we going to get him out?"

"We aren't," said Roland.

"*What?*" Simon was a scared child.

Rebecca looked into Roland's uncaring eyes and said, "We have to try."

Roland said nothing in return.

She reached over and forcefully took him by the arm and away from the wreck. "Hey, I'm serious. We have to try."

"I know you're serious. He's stuck, Rebecca. What can we do? I don't have tools to pry the car apart and we need some heavy duty stuff."

"Maybe we can pull him out."

Roland didn't have to say anything; his stare said enough.

"Well . . . what then? *Leave* him?"

Again, silence.

"No . . . no, that's not an option."

"He's dead, Rebecca. If we stay, then we're dead too."

"You don't know that."

"What do you think is going to happen if we stay?"

She had no good answer.

"Exactly." Roland took a few steps away from her and looked around, clearly frustrated with everything. "He did this, you know. We are here because of him."

"He saved me at the house," Rebecca muttered.

"You wouldn't have needed saved if it wasn't for him."

The words were hitting hard. "Do you honestly think there is no way to save him? Honestly—do you think he's done for, no matter what we do?"

Roland took her questions as serious as he was able; he hated this man. "All feelings aside, I don't see how we can help him."

She had hoped he would have given her something. "I can't leave him in there, Roland. I can't just walk away. I don't care about what he did—or has done—he is still a person."

"Oh yeah? Prove it."

Rebecca sighed and threw her hands into the air before walking away from him.

"*Guys?*" called Simon. "*Are you still here?*"

"Yes," Rebecca responded, her words shaky. So much was pumping through her system at that moment: adrenaline, emotion, pain. . . .

"Does anyone have water? I'm so thirsty."

Rebecca's heart sank further. "I'll go look for some."

"Okay. Please, hurry. I'm so thirsty."

As Rebecca walked away from the wreckage she saw Roland sorting through chunks of the wrecked vehicle that had broken off. It was a surreal moment. There she was, essentially unharmed, as was Roland, walking around in her sleeping gown, bare foot, inside a field of wreckage, while Simon was alive and mangled inside the vehicle. It was amazing to her how much had changed in a blink of an eye. Only moments earlier—or what appeared to be moments according to her mind—Simon was viciously attacking Roland inside the hovercar, still full of his pride and entitlement, and now he was struggling to live, completely lost of his rage and begging for aid.

Her mind left that thought for a moment as she looked down at her dirty feet. *Am I really going to be trekking through the wilderness in my bare feet?*

Rebecca spotted something in the grass, right by an impact mark from one of the hovercar's tumbles. She walked up to it and saw that it was a digital notepad. *I had completely forgotten about Simon's notepad!* Thrill rushed through her once again as she bent down and picked it up. The notepad seemed wholly intact. There was a crack in the screen and some scratches, but when she powered it up, the screen functioned correctly. The only hang-up was that she needed Simon's password . . . *and he's dying behind me.* This gave birth to an incredible conflict within her: *Do I go back and ask him for the password, or do I try to find water and risk him dying before my return?*

Nothing was simple.

Rebecca saw Roland far off to her right. She knew she needed his help but wasn't sure what to ask him to do. *I could see if he will look for water while I try and pry the password from Simon.* Something about the idea reeked in her soul, but she needed access to the translation and Simon was the only person who could give it. *Just do it.*

Rebecca ran over to Roland, waiving the notepad in the air. Roland saw it and gave a curious expression. "What is that?"

"It's Simon's notepad."

"So . . . we can't use it to help us."

"I downloaded the translation of William's manuscript onto it."

It took Roland a moment to comprehend what she was saying. "Are you talking about the manuscript from when . . . you know . . . from when I last helped you—get into Sector 28's Department of—"

"Yes, Roland—yes!"

He wasn't giving her the satisfaction she was hoping for. Roland took in a deep breath and said, "Why do you want it? That thing is bad news. It almost got you killed last time. . . . It almost got us *both* killed."

"That's because the Ministry wants it! It's not bad news—it's my only hope! *Our* only hope!"

Roland released a deep, frustrated sigh. "That thing isn't going to get us out of this mess. That translation can't conjure a hovercar, or food, or supplies. It's a black hole that keeps sucking you into some bizarre, alternate reality. Instead of wasting your time reading this thing, you should spend it trying to find a way to get us out of here."

"I'll do that. But having this translation for when we're safe will only help us. You have to understand, this thing is powerful, and the people trying to kill us fear that power."

Roland didn't look ready to give up the argument, so Rebecca made a deal: "Look, help me find some water for Simon while I ask him for the password. I'm afraid that he might die if I leave him alone for too long; we need his password."

Roland gave her a curious look. "Where's your sentiment for his well-being?"

His words punctured a new hole of guilt inside her heart. "That's why I'm asking you for help. Please, go and find some water to bring back. If we can't save him . . ."

"He tried to kill me, Becca."

"I know . . . but wronging him isn't right."

Roland's shoulders slumped. "Okay, Becca, you win. I'll go, but only because we will need water too."

Rebecca hugged him and said, "Thank you."

"Yeah . . . just hope there is something close by."

She hoped for that all right, for all of their sakes. Rebecca also hoped that Simon's guard was low enough that he would be willing to give her his password. *Maybe Simon will be willing to share more than his password*, she thought. Or maybe he wouldn't share anything at all; dying or not, he was Simon Wylde after all.

CHAPTER SIXTEEN

District 4, Sector 2

Rebecca and Roland parted ways and she returned to the wrecked hovercar. "Simon?" she called out as she drew near. "Are you still with us?"

"*I'm here. . . .*" he said weakly. "Do you have water? I'm so thirsty."

Rebecca climbed over parts of the wreck and peered inside. He was just as she last saw him, except now he was licking his parched lips.

"Do you have it?" he asked.

"No, but Roland is out looking for water right now."

Simon grew agitated. "Please, please, not him; he won't bring anything back. I need you to help me, Rebecca. You have a heart. *Please.*"

"Calm down. He will bring water back, I promise."

"He hates me, Rebecca. He would sooner see me die."

"You've given him lots of reasons, haven't you?"

"The more it should be you."

"Do you think I love you? Have you forgotten how you've treated me?" She stopped there, realizing she needed to be careful not to agitate him further.

"I have wronged you, I know. But I have also loved you."

It was an opening; Rebecca didn't want to look at it that way, but it was an opening. "I had loved you too. . . . Simon, Roland will bring you water, I promise, but in the meantime, I need your help."

Simon laughed lightly and then grimaced in pain. "*My help? How can I help you?*"

Rebecca held up his notepad and said, "I found this."

Simon seemed to struggle to see what she was talking about and then said, "A notepad?"

"It's your notepad. I need your password so that I can open the translation we downloaded."

Simon stared at her blankly for a moment and then something familiar returned inside his eyes. "Now I see your plan."

"My plan?"

"*Oh, yes . . .* your plan to leave me."

Rebecca's pulse quickened. "What are you talking about? I have no plan."

"Oh, I'm sure—the cunning Rebecca has no plan of escape?"

"Simon, you're getting delusional. I have no plan."

"Right . . . right . . . and I have no password."

Rebecca was afraid of this. "Simon, I'm not going anywhere. Roland is—"

"Why do you want my password, Rebecca? Don't feed me some lie about wanting to read that pointless translation. I know what you really want it for."

She would have admitted, she was curious to know what he was thinking. "Tell me, then, what am I going to do with it?"

"You're going to contact those Heretique bastards."

That was ludicrous. "How am I to do that? I have no one to contact, and I'm beyond certain that all communications with your notepad are being scrutinized this very moment. If I tried contacting anyone, MSF agents will be all over this place within minutes."

Simon simply smiled at her. "Okay then, that's not what you want to do." His words dripped with sarcasm.

"You're hurt, Simon. You aren't thinking straight."

He tried to adjust, grunting and wincing, before settling with a gasp of pain. "Oh . . . this pain is becoming unbearable." His eyes danced all around. ". . . My mother . . . she wasn't supposed to die. That wasn't in the plan." Tears formed in his eyes. "This is my punishment for her death. She didn't deserve to die. Only men who seek power deserve death. And I'm getting it, boy . . . oh how I'm getting it."

Rebecca wanted to put him at ease, somehow. "Simon, I'm not going to leave you. *Know that.* I'm here, despite everything, I'm here. I am your wife, after all."

Simon's eyes found hers again. His cheek muscles trembled.

"What happened last night? What *was* the plan? If you won't tell me your password then at least tell me why we're in this position; what did you do?"

Simon stared at her for a long moment before saying, "*I killed my father.*"

Rebecca expected just about anything but that.

"I hated him. He . . . he was never going to let me be the Director of Social Affairs; he told me this a month or so ago. That's why he hasn't retired . . . hadn't retired. It's a funny thing—past tense and present tense. I've become so used to speaking of him in present tense, and now, for a short while at least, I get to speak of him in past tense." Simon laughed a sad, sadistic laugh. "My father is dead. I had Jonas kill him. It's a bit of a long story . . . but the plan was supposed to end with us overthrowing the Minister and taking control. You should be proud—with your rebel blood and all— because it was all my idea. Once my father made his intentions clear, I was so angry with him, with everything, that I approached Jonas on the subject of taking over. The uprisings were really taking form at that point, and Jonas was unhappy with the measures the Minister was taking—Jonas thought he was being entirely too soft and forgiving"—Simon laughed again and winced—"I have to stop doing that. . . . Anyhow, once my father was dead, I was to take his authority; and together with Jonas, we were supposed to overthrow the Minister. Jonas would have been named the new Minister of the Collective, and I would have had the power to ensure the transition."

Rebecca couldn't believe her ears: such malevolent ambition. "Your plan was flawed."

Simon looked like he wanted to laugh. "*Clearly.*"

"I mean, even if you had succeeded, you would have failed."

"How so?"

"If there is any truth to our history—to the Ministry's and the Collective's history—it would be that a Minister can't be self-made, he has to be ordained. Every time men take power over the Collective and declare themselves Minister, that power consumes them and their control is lost. This happened with the poisoning of the thirteenth Minister. Ziusudria was governed by power-seeking men who didn't want to lose that power, instead choosing to take more. They killed the young heir and proclaimed themselves rulers. And over time, these former allies became enemies, and Ziusudria became divided and weak. They were eventually attacked by the Titans of Titanus and dominated, which led to the second coming of Ziusudra and his reuniting of Ziusudria . . . our Collective."

Simon remained silent.

"You and Jonas didn't accomplish anything; already you're divided. He might have power now, but he'll lose it."

"I think you rely too heavily on the history you study; Jonas has all of the power. There is no one to stand up to him."

"Did you not here what I just said? Ziusudra will return. Not even Jonas Lundquist is powerful enough to stop that."

Simon laughed and winced. "You can't *really* believe that, can you? Those are fairy tales created by the Ministry to keep fools in line—they aren't reality. . . . No, reality is that Jonas is now the ruler of the world, and he doesn't share power."

"Then our only hope is the Heretique."

"They're too small. . . . A nuisance, yes, but too small to cause any real damage."

"I guess time will tell."

"Not for me, I'm afraid. My time is up. The longer I lay here, the more evident it becomes. I know I'll never escape these woods . . . and the funny thing is, I'm okay with it. My family is dead, my inheritance is ruined, I have no children or legacy to carry on . . . I don't have you . . . I have nothing. So bring death along; I think I'm ready."

"No, Simon, you can't die now. You still have one more thing to do. . . ."

"*What? Giving you the password? Aid the enemy of my beloved Ministry?*"

"Call it revenge, then; an act of defiance against the enemy of all of us; one last stab at the man who put you here."

Simon laughed without wincing this time. "You truly think that translation will save you and the Heretique." It wasn't a question. "Tell me, Rebecca, who wrote this thing that you so dearly covet?"

"You don't know?"

"I've told you—haven't I—I know nothing about this book. I never cared to know . . . except for now. Who wrote this book? Where did it come from? What is so special about it?"

Rebecca wasn't sure what was the right thing to say. "It was written by William Coulee some 3,500 years ago."

Simon's face morphed from sardonic to perplexed. "*William Coulee,* did you say? Like the MSF agent?"

"I don't think it is *like* William Coulee, the MSF agent; I think it is meant to *be* William Coulee, the MSF agent."

Simon held his perplexed stare for a moment longer before erupting into a laughing and coughing fit. "*You . . . have truly . . . been had!*"

"I should have expected you to react this way."

Simon began wincing again and continued to cough. A little bit of blood trickled down his cheek. "It's over, Rebecca."

"Simon, please, give me your password."

"You're too smart for this, Rebecca. They've made a fool out of you. Just stop now. Go away and try to live out your days in peace. Just go and hide. . . ." He started taking short, labored breaths.

"Simon! Stop that! Hang in there!" Rebecca reached down and inside the wreckage, and touched his face. "Don't go yet. I'm not a fool! This thing—this translation—is real! Jonas fears it! The Minister fears it! I'm going to do something great! But not if you don't help me . . . please!"

Simon's eyes looked off, beyond hers, and trembled terribly. "*Re . . . bec . . . it . . . ss . . . you . . . har . . . t . . .*"

"I can't hear you! Stay here with me! Try to say it again! Shout out, damnit!"

It happened so quickly: his breaths became deep rattles and gurgles, his eyes wouldn't look into hers, they moved all over and then settled on something in the sky . . . and then he settled.

"Are you okay?" she said, happy that the fit was over. "Simon? . . . Simon?"

And then she realized it:

Simon Wylde was dead.

CHAPTER SEVENTEEN

The Dead Sands

William and Saño had walked for many hours before finally stopping. They were at the base of the mountain range that William seldom traveled to during his patrols.

There was little talking during the hike, and Saño forced William to walk out in front the entire time, unwilling to trust that William wouldn't try some crafty trick to disarm him, which William was very much looking to do. *I have to get out of here.* The stalker attack really had William on edge. He spent most of the time trying to figure out why someone would send a stalker after him. There were rumors, again in the surrounding sectors, that Desert Demons had control over some stalkers. But William had never taken that very seriously—*Maybe I should.*

"Okay, Mista Iceman, we'z take a fillin and then we get a treken."

William interpreted that statement as it was time to eat. He had wisely packed as many rations as possible before they left the outpost. Saño seemed less than interested in having the food. William unpacked two meals and handed one over, but Saño refused. "You're not hungry?"

"I'z eat once a day, O yes. And I'z already had my'z meal."

William knew that he was referring to the breakfast William served hours before the attack. "Fine. More for me." He placed the ration back in its pack and opened his own. "Are you ever going to tell me where we're heading?"

Saño found a large rock and dropped it across from William before using it as a seat. "A little way'z more; thatz be it."

"They're going to come for me; you realize that, don't you?"

"They'z be commin already, I'z certain of that; I'z seen it with my own two blue."

"So what's your plan? We're on foot and you can bet that they won't be."

"We'z be fine as long as we'z keep on movin."

"But then what? What are your plans for me?"

Saño spat out a bit of sand that collected in his mouth during the trek and said, "Nothin comin yuz way but yuz own destiny. Plain and simple, sucka."

"What's my destiny, Saño?"

"If I'z told yuz that, yuz wouldn't believe me."

"Try me."

Saño laughed out, "Yuz think I'z a real chinken brain, don't yuz? Good . . . good. Allz the better when lifez revealed."

"Life? What do you mean by that?"

"Life, my brotha! From beginnin to end and end to beginnin"—he pointed at the Ministry emblem on William's chest—"just like that beast on yuz garm. We'z but in the belly of that there serpent, and we'z don't get out until she say so, and she ain't sayin shit until yuz say so . . . yuz want destiny, yuz got it, boy."

It was all nonsense to William; but, for the time being, Saño was in control and William needed to play along. "Who is she?"

"Thatz be the great mystery; we'z know but we'ze don't know. Right?"

"No, not right. I have not an inkling of what you're saying."

"No? Come on, Mista Iceman. Yuz know all about her. Yuz two been together since the beginnin."

William sighed. "No, I don't know."

"She'z yuz mother, boy! She my'z mother! She birthed them there rocks, them mountains, them sand, them sky!"

William had never heard of such a person. "I come from my mother, Valerie Coulee. She comes from her mother, Katterly Roche. Neither of them, as far as I know, had ever birthed rocks, mountains, sand or sky, and I'm pretty positive they didn't birth you, Saño."

Saño laughed. "Yuz not ready to believe, Mista Iceman."

"No, I guess not."

"Yuz destiny comes when yuz ready, and when yuz destiny comes, yuz understand."

William didn't know what else to say other than, "I believe you."

This caused Saño to laugh some more. "Yuz finish with that meal? We'z need to be movin. I'z got a feelin we'z won't be alone for long."

William was learning not to like Saño's feelings. "All right, let's go."

CHAPTER EIGHTEEN

District 4, Sector 2

Now what? Rebecca remained at the wrecked hovercar the entire time it took for Roland to return empty handed. Simon was dead—as was her chance to access the translation one last time. Rebecca looked down into his drying, open eyes, and thought about how different life could have been . . . how their life together could have been so much more.

"Is he dead?" Roland asked.

Rebecca stared blankly at Simon. "Yeah. . . ."

Roland walked over and put his arm around her. He gave a heartfelt apology.

"It doesn't matter," she said, almost devoid of emotion. "It's all over. He didn't give me the password."

"Defiant until the end. . . ."

"Loyal," said Rebecca, correcting him. "Simon was always loyal to the Ministry and to the Collective. He might have been disloyal to his father and to the Minister, but he was never disloyal to the Ministry. He was doing what he thought was right . . . in his own deluded way."

Had Rebecca looked at Roland, she would have seen that he wore a confused expression. But he didn't press her to explain; instead, he left in silence, because Rebecca was in a strange kind of mourning. She didn't understand it, nor could she have explained it. Seeing Simon's face lose all sign of life stirred a sentiment for what kind of man he could have been, not for what kind of man he was. She mourned for her dream of him, for her hope that he would someday be who she thought he could be. *And it's all over now.*

Eventually, she left the wreckage and walked over to Roland who was sitting in the grass, fiddling with a stick, looking as depressed as she felt; his injured left arm was tucked close to his body. She sat down next to him and said, "We should probably start walking."

Roland looked at her and said, "Yeah? Where?"

"North," she said matter-of-factly. "That was where we were heading anyway."

"I was just driving, I had no idea where I was going."

"That doesn't make it wrong."

"It doesn't make it right either."

"Well, we won't know until we try."

Roland nodded his head. "So, what did he tell you when you asked for the password?"

Rebecca looked down at the notepad in her hand and said, "Not much; he was paranoid that we were going to call the Heretique."

Roland chuckled a tiny bit and said, "Oh, yeah? Why did it matter?"

"I don't know; it's like I said, he was loyal to the Ministry. He wanted to make a difference . . . no matter who he hurt along the way."

Roland nodded his head again and then stood. "I know it's too soon, but he wasn't a good person."

"You're right; it is too soon."

". . . . I'm sorry."

Rebecca shook her head, wiped two tears from her eyes, and stood up too. "I guess it doesn't matter."

Roland looked at her bare feet and said, "We have to do something about that."

Rebecca looked down too and said, "What? I don't have anything."

"Simon does. . . ."

Rebecca looked into Roland's eyes and then over to the wrecked hovercar that now contained Simon's corpse. "I guess he does."

"I'll get them for you," offered Roland and then walked away.

He climbed through the wreckage, and with some hesitation, he bent down and began doing something that Rebecca couldn't see. Roland grunted and cursed a few times before flinging one of Simon's boots out of the wreckage. His head popped up briefly as he moved toward what Rebecca suspected was the other foot and then dipped back down.

"This one is stuck. . . ."

Rebecca started to call out, "Do you need my—"

"I got it!"

A second boot came flipping out of the wreckage and onto the grass. Roland then followed, wiping his hands on his shirt and picking booth boots up. He walked over to Rebecca and handed them out. She took them and said, "Thank you."

The boots were several sizes too big, and a bit rough against her bare skin, but they were better than walking on the ground.

And so they began to walk slowly through the tall grass and into the foliage beyond. The sun was high overhead and the day was heating up. Neither Rebecca nor Roland spoke of how dire their situation was becoming; they just kept walking until one of them declared a need for rest. Every so often, Rebecca would steal a glance at the notepad and wonder what Simon's password was and whether or not she could guess it.

"You don't have an inkling?" asked Roland after spotting her looking at it.

She stopped walking for a moment and leaned against a nearby tree. "Not really."

Earlier, she had tried entering in POWER, MINISTER, WYLDE, SIMON WYLDE and SIMON IS THE MINISTER, but each one failed.

"Guessing it has to be one in a billion," she declared.

Roland walked over to the tree as well and sat on the ground. "That's too bad. We could use that thing to call someone. It's a terrible tease to have something that could literally save us and not be able to use it."

"It can't save us," Rebecca declared. "If we used it to call someone, we would be found, but by the wrong people."

"Even then . . ." Roland said.

"Are you that ready to throw in the towel?"

"No, but I don't like our chances otherwise."

Neither do I, she thought.

"There isn't anything he might have said to you . . . anything over the past six months that might lead to a possible answer?"

"No!" exploded Rebecca, unexpectedly. "I'm sorry . . . but there isn't anything. Simon wasn't kind to me, and he didn't let me in to his personal affairs." *I barely knew him*, she realized.

Roland sighed and changed the subject: "I'm getting hungry."

Me too, she thought, but said nothing. "Let's keep going. If we don't find something soon, we will have to start looking for shelter, and figure out how we're going to eat."

Roland slowly stood up and they continued.

Rebecca looked over at him as they passed through the foliage and into another clearing. Something was different with Roland. He seemed much more a man than she had noticed before. Maybe it was the fight at the compound, or that he came looking for her in the first place, or maybe it was how he stood up to Simon . . .

"Where were you when Simon found you?"

Roland glanced at her before saying, "Well, after our little journey six months ago, my status was demoted and I lost my driving privileges. They reassigned me to hover car maintenance in District 5. I had to move and everything."

Rebecca could see a glimpse of sadness and regret in Roland's eyes. "I'm sorry."

"I know, but don't be; I'm glad I helped you. I've been a Ministry stooge my entire life; helping you was the first real decision I had ever made. . . . I care about you, Rebecca . . ." his face blushed.

So it's true, thought Rebecca. She didn't know what to say. "Roland . . . I . . ."

"It's all right; I understand. All I'm trying to say is that I couldn't fathom leaving you to get hurt . . . or killed. Helping you was the best decision I've ever made."

Rebecca wanted to smile and say thank you but for some reason felt it would have been inappropriate; Roland could very well die because of his decision.

She tried redirecting the conversation: "What did Simon tell you that he wanted?"

Roland looked a bit lost in thought. "It was at the end of the day. Simon walked into the garage and called out my name. He was trying so hard to be friendly . . . you know, the politician side of him."

Rebecca knew it well.

"He asked me how I was doing and tried apologizing for my demotion. But I could see the insincerity in his eyes." Roland lightly touched one of the gashes on his arm before continuing, "Anyhow, he offered to take me to see you, if I wanted."

Simon's plan seemed so foolish. "And you told him no?"

"Of course. I knew he was up to something. I told him to shove off. It pissed him off a bit, but he tried once again to convince me to go and meet with me. This time, however, he said that you had been doing nothing but talking about me, wondering how I was, and worried about my well-being. I could see how much it pained Simon to say those things . . . he nearly had me convinced." Roland's cheeks blushed again. "But I told him that you were too good for me, and for him, and that he should be thankful for the compatibility test, otherwise he would have some whore for a wife instead of a dove."

Rebecca remained speechless.

"That's when Simon attacked me. He first threw a wrench at my head, which I dodged, and then he started to charge at me, but then thought better of it, choosing instead to pull out a laser tube from inside his uniform jacket. He fired two shots and then fled. I waited a moment before following him outside of the garage. I could see his hovercar rising into the sky. I then thought about you . . . I was worried he would lash out at you for the things I said . . . for the feelings I showed." Roland glanced at Rebecca and then looked down at the ground. "I took one of the hovercars we had repaired and followed behind him. I don't think he ever suspected I would do such a thing."

I would have never suspected, thought Rebecca.

"I had landed in a small clearing just outside of the Wylde's compound and had found the gate unguarded, which at the time I thought was curious . . . and now I know why. The guards must have been amassing somewhere else, getting their orders to attack you and the Wyldes. . . . I carefully walked up to the house and found the front door open. I don't know why I continued onward; I guess . . . well . . . I just needed to make sure you were okay. But I went inside and . . . well . . . you know the rest from there."

Rebecca still didn't know what to say; Roland was not the man she took him for. His confession was confusing and unexpected. She tried to form words of gratitude but didn't want to expose her feelings at that moment; she didn't really understand what she was feeling. "Roland . . . I just . . . I don't understand why they went after you like that. Simon said that Jonas had sent him to find you, but . . . I'm so sorry."

"I don't think the Security Chief sent Simon after me. . . ."

Roland didn't need to finish his thought. *Simon was jealous.* The image of his dead face reentered her mind. Their final moment together replayed: *"You're too smart for this, Rebecca,"* He had told her. *"They've made a fool out of you. Just stop now. Go away and try to live out your days in peace. Just go and hide. . . ."* His coughing fit and gurgling noises echoed in her ears. *"Re . . . bec . . . it . . . ss . . . you . . . har . . . t . . ."* he had said.

And that was it.

Was he just saying my name, Rebecca? But there were distinguishable other sounds that followed. She didn't know if they were substantial or not; they could have been caused by his struggle to speak. She decided to include Roland. "There was something that Simon did say just before he died, but I can't quite figure out what." She then told him all that was said.

Roland scratched his head and asked her to repeat it.

"It was something like, 'Re—bec—it—is—har—t.' "

"Well, he was obviously saying your name."

"Yeah, but was there something else?"

Roland repeated it back to himself, inflecting the sounds in different ways: "Rebecca it is hard . . . Rebecca it is heart . . . Rebecca it is cart?"

"My cart?" she said. "I doubt it."

"Maybe he was trying to say car—like 'Rebecca get a car'—and the t sound was just extra."

The joke made her smile despite everything.

"Joking aside, I think it makes some sense; he was telling you to go and hide."

"Yeah. . . . But I'm certain I heard an 'h' in there before the end: 'Rebec har-t.' "

"So, Rebecca it is heart? . . . I mean, Rebecca's heart? Your heart?"

"That doesn't make . . ." she stopped herself.

Roland observed her pause and said, "What?"

He said he didn't have me. He said he had loved me.

"What?" repeated Roland.

"Is it that simple?"

"What?"

Rebecca turned on the notepad and typed into the password field—one simple word: REBECCA.

The screen unlocked.

CHAPTER NINETEEN

District 4, Sector 2

Neither Rebecca nor Roland could believe that the password was Rebecca's name. It was so unlike Simon, *and yet he actually loved me*, she realized. Not that it changed her feelings for him much, but Rebecca did realize that he was not full of lies.

After walking for another forty minutes, and having not found any civilized life, Rebecca and Roland decided to take a break. Roland wandered off to relieve himself while Rebecca sat down against a fallen tree and eagerly opened Simon's notepad. It had taken everything within her power to keep walking after unlocking the notepad earlier. She and Roland had decided that it would be best to keep walking and looking for civilization before resorting to use the notepad to call for help. But now that they were stopped . . .

Rebecca keyed in *REBECCA* and the screen unlocked, giving her access to the files she had downloaded back at the Wylde's compound—an act that felt like a lifetime ago at this point. She located file *TRN—1152393—*

DEO—1123h and opened it. The familiar sight of the translation she made six months ago filled the screen. Rebecca could feel her pulse race as she paged through—her eyes stopping on familiar sections of text:

****

. . . Charles had a unique outlook on mankind's development. He believed archeologists were merely scratching the surface of what was buried in our long forgotten past. My involvement spawned from a question he once proposed: How historically accurate is history?" Mr. Vermil directed the question toward me, "Can you answer that William?"

****

She stopped on another section.

****

. . . . I tried pushing on the wall and felt it give slightly. Then an explanation suddenly dawned on me: The snake was protecting the tree. It didn't want anyone to have access to its fruit. The snake was protecting something behind the wall. . . .

****

And then she found where she had left off, like it was just yesterday.

****

. . . Professor Haggins thought about it for a second and

then said, "In the 1970s: the NSA, CIA and FBI all took stabs at trying to crack the Voynich language. They didn't consider it a language but a masterful cipher that could prove monumental in their espionage war with Russia. Only one man in those agencies ever came close. He had claimed he had deciphered an entire section of the book— before retracting his statement. . . He might be a person we want to speak with."

"Who is it?" I asked.

"His name is Jonas Lundquist."

"Jonas Lundquist?" I said.

"Yes;" confirmed Professor Haggins "he knows far more about the Voynich manuscript than any of us."

Great, I thought, another bookworm to talk my ear off about the historical importance of his work. I looked down at my filthy hands, bloodstained shirt, and scuffed up pants, and thought, *I need a vacation*. As interesting and exciting as all of it was, I was exhausted. "Where does this Lundquist guy live?"

Only Professor Haggins was paying attention to me. "I believe his office is in D.C. The last I knew, he was retired from the NSA and owns a rare bookstore. But I could be wrong. I haven't thought about him for many years, but his work on Voynich still holds up today. We should contact him and see if he can help us."

"Hold on there," Mr. Vermil said suddenly. "Who are you talking about contacting: Lundquist?"

"Yes," I said.

"Let's not be hasty," Mr. Vermil warned. "We need to be careful about whom we inform of our secrets."

"I agree," Iah added. "We know so little about Jonas Lundquist. It might be wise to err on the cautious side of things."

****

"What are you doing?" asked Roland upon his return.

Rebecca looked away from the notepad and said, "I opened the translation. William Coulee is learning about Jonas Lundquist for the first time."

"Too bad for him," said Roland. He bent over and stretched his hamstrings. "Is Jonas a warmonger in that world just as he is in ours?"

"I don't know, he was just introduced."

Roland finished stretching and then looked up at the sky, searching for the sun. "We should probably keep walking, don't you think?"

He's right, she knew, of course, but she didn't want to walk that moment—she wanted to read more. "Okay, let's go."

"Can you pull up a map on that notepad, so we can see what's around us?" asked Roland.

"Only if Simon had one saved locally, which he didn't."

Maps were constantly provided through the Ministry network, but Rebecca would have to connect in order to access them, which would have meant risking their being discovered by the MSF.

"How much longer should we go before stopping for the night?" asked Rebecca.

Roland shrugged. "I don't know, another couple of hours?"

The sun was past midday at that point, a couple of hours might be right. "Okay."

And so they continued. . . .

CHAPTER TWENTY

The Dead Sands

The climb through the mountains was not an easy one, even for William, who kept himself in top condition. Sańo, however, was more nimble than he looked; he scaled the mountain with great ease and often had to wait for William to catch up. Sańo hummed some kind of song the entire hike, which added to William's frustration with the difficulty. *I trip and fall, slide on my hands and knees, while this moron gracefully leaps from one foothold to the next, humming a tune. If the other agents could see me now, the great hunter of the Heretique.*

Sańo had let out a sharp whistle and pointed over William's head.

William turned around and saw a black dot in the sky. The average person would have mistaken the dot for some bird far away, but William had not seen a single bird his entire stay at the Dead Sands outpost, and he knew that maybe his little jape about the other agents seeing him now might actually be a reality. "We need to find cover!"

Sańo was already on the mission. He had reached the mountain's summit and was hurriedly looking around.

On hands and knees, William reached the summit and joined the desert man. "We just need a simple cover. A rock or an edge, something like that."

Saño ran behind a bolder and called out, "Here! Here! Come on!"

William sprinted over to Saño and saw that the boulder had an indention that created a ledge large enough to cover three. "This might work."

"I'z hope so."

Saño was sweating for the first time, William noticed, and breathing a bit heavily. *He's afraid.* Saño had the laser rifle slung over his right shoulder and had left it unprotected. *I can get it if I'm fast enough.*

Saño's eyes found William's and he said, "I'z know what yuz thinkin."

William covered his thoughts by saying, "They might be overhead now."

"That's not whatz runnin through yuz mind." Saño placed both hands on the rifle. "Yuz take this, and yuz take off, yuz die."

I'll die if I stay with you.

Saño went to say something else but William snapped a hand out and gripped the barrel of the rifle; his other hand reached the strap. "*No!*" Saño ordered as the two of them began to struggle. "*You're mistaken!*"

William swung Saño's light body against the boulder wall and ground the rifle into his chest.

"*They've come to kill you!*"

William positioned his right foot next to Saño's right side and pivoted with all of his weight, trying to wrench the rifle free.

"*It's been ordered!*"

Saño fell half over William's side and the rifle came away clean. William took a step out of the boulder's cover and pointed the laser rifle at Saño. "It's done!"

"*We've seen it! We've seen what they're planning! That's why I was out there yesterday! I was looking for you!*"

William realized that Saño's lisp and language had completely changed. "You've been lying to me!"

"I had to, damnit! You don't believe anything unless it's right in front of your damn face! You've always been that way!"

"What are you, an assassin?" The words came out of his mouth before he had the chance to realize how stupid of a question it was.

"You know I'm not!"

William quickly glanced around for the hovercraft and saw it overhead. "It's too late now! You should have told me who you were!"

Ropes hit the craggy surface thirty or so feet away. William looked up and saw four agents repelling down, weapons ready.

Saño cried out, "Shoot them, William! You're dead if you don't!"

William looked at him and then to the agents, who had just landed on the surface. *I can't shoot them; they're my brothers!*

"Agent Coulee!" one of the agents shouted out. "Drop the weapon!"

All four agents raised their rifles in William's direction.

"SHOOT THEM!" Saño cried.

William was in indecision.

And then he heard the familiar MSF call for open fire.

William tried to swing his laser rifle toward the agents, but he was too late. A beam shot out and through the side of his thigh. A sound thundered nearby, and the heads of all four agents burst open. Their bodies folded to the ground.

William dropped the rifle and slapped both hands onto his wounded leg. He looked at the four dead agents in total bewilderment.

William looked up and saw that the hovercraft overhead was floating away from its original position. *They're getting into firing position.*

Saño shouted, "Take cover!"

William didn't hesitate. He retrieved the rifle and limped over to the boulder. As he turned around and placed his back against it, he saw the impossible. The ground around the edges of the summit rose upward and took human form. *Desert Demons.*

The figure on the outside edge aimed a large cylindrical weapon at the hovercraft. A roar ripped out of the weapon along with a smoke trail that coursed upward and into the hovercraft. Its hull exploded into fire and shrapnel, and the hovercraft spiraled out of control toward the summit. The Desert Demons vanished down the side of the mountain. Saño took William by the arm and pulled him away from the boulder. William hobbled to the edge of the summit as the hovercraft crashed into its surface. Shrapnel sprayed all around and a piece ripped into Saño before he disappeared over the edge of the mountain. William tumbled down the rock face and landed against a ridge. He clung to it so as not to follow Saño down.

Dust, sand, smoke, and fire billowed and sprayed off the mountain.

William curled up into a ball and covered his face.

The echoes of the crash still sounded out even after the hovercraft dropped to its final resting place.

Cautiously, William uncurled his legs and struggled to stand. He could see the wreckage of the hovercraft through the pillar of smoke and fire that consumed it. He looked around for Saño but didn't see him anywhere. Climbing the summit, he found the laser rifle. It only took him a few seconds to realize that there were no survivors. "Saño!" William called out.

There was no response.

William went back to the edge where he and Saño tumbled down, and that was when he saw him. Saño was lying far below.

"Saño!" he called out again.

There was no response.

William knew what had happened, why Saño wasn't responding. He heard footsteps from behind and quickly turned around, rifle ready. Standing before him were the Desert Demons, all five of them, each wearing some kind of cover that resembled the desert land and holding strange rifles.

Knowing that he had no chance of survival alone, William immediately dropped his rifle and raised his hands in surrender.

CHAPTER TWENTY-ONE

District 4, Sector 2

The sun was three hours from setting when they finally stopped again. Rebecca's feet ached inside Simon's large shoes. "I can't go any longer," she had told Roland.

He didn't argue; instead, he looked thankful for her admission—clearly he was tired and hurting too. "We should try and find shelter."

"Yes, definitely."

"Have a seat," he offered. "I'll look around."

Rebecca sat gladly onto the ground and watched as Roland went into the dense foliage. The sounds of the wild surrounded her, which created an eerie reminder that they were not alone.

Rebecca tried to visualize where they were geographically. She was positive that they were north of District 9 and that they were still in Sector 2, however, she wasn't sure if they were in District 4 or in District 16; neither had human habitats and neither were where she wanted to be. *District 4 is where the Coctavians once lived*, she remembered. The Coctavians were a deeply spiritual and superstitious people that thrived a thousand years before Rebecca's time. While the early Ministries were expanding the Collective (which at the time was known as Ziusudria), the Coctavians flourished and were unknown to the rest of the world. However, they had never reached the technological achievements of the power amassing in the east; *the Minister's will conquers all.* The power in the east, led by the 32nd Minister, eventually located and conquered Coctavia.

Rebecca looked around at the sights and listened to the sounds and wondered if much had changed since the time of the Coctavians. She imagined the tribesmen and tried to visualize their normal everyday life: women and children gathering water from a nearby stream, men hunting and constructing huts for their family and their tribesmen families. She remembered a Coctavian tradition, which was based on a certain breed of bird whose name she could not recall. The tradition was that every new pair of Coctavians that mated were required to leave the village and travel into a new area in order to breed. This practice helped the Coctavians spread their numbers and strengthen their hold over the land.

Rebecca remembered another tradition of theirs, which involved the ritualistic sacrifices of virgin boys and girls, and the rolling of their lifeless bodies down Coctavia's tall stone temple steps. The Coctavians believed that sacrificing the innocent would give them the power to fight off invading evil, all the while not realizing it was their evil that was bringing the invading forces . . . or so Rebecca was taught.

Rebecca sighed, looked around for Roland, and opened the notepad again. She found where she left off in the translation.

****

"True, true," Professor Haggins acknowledged.

"Guys," I said, "I agree, wholeheartedly. The last thing I want to do is sprint out of town and go on another perilous adventure where my ass could end up on a pole. I definitely agree that haste is unnecessary, and that we should take time to thoroughly examine our options. Plus, we have to decide how to handle Simon and Dr. Thatcher."

"Again, true, true."

"It won't be easy," Iah said, "Simon is wily and Dr. Thatcher is so thoroughly plugged into the historical community that it would be difficult to discern whether or not she was aiding Bertók. Any evidence of contact between the two of them can easily be written off as everyday work talk—catch my drift?"

We all nodded and then I asked, "What do you mean that Simon is wily?"

"He's a billion-dollar businessman, Mr. Coulee. I think that is explanation enough."

We all looked toward the other billion-dollar businessman. Mr. Vermil smiled at us and nodded his head. "Indeed."

"Okay," I said and then gestured to my ruined self. "As you can see, I need a few days to collect myself. Take a shower, sleep, eat, and heal. Afterward, I'll look into this Jonas Lundquist and see what I can dig up. But in the meantime, what about Bertók? Do we just sit back and hope that the authorities will arrest him? I mean, crazy or not, this guy is extremely cunning and dangerous."

No one immediately answered. It was Mr. Vermil that finally said, "I fear that there is not much we can do at the present but keep our eyes and ears open. Leave Simon to me, I will find out what his involvement, if any, is and inform everyone of my discoveries. It could be that the answer to our Bertók problem might come from Simon. As for Dr. Thatcher, we need to at least warn her of Bertók's treachery, just in case she isn't involved in any malicious way, but that should be the extent of it."

Everyone agreed.

Our meeting ended shortly after. Mr. Vermil had the book

from Instanbul (I call it that because we still had no con-
firming evidence stating otherwise) placed inside a secured
vault there at his house, but not before Professor Haggins
took several photographs of the first few pages and made
hard copies of them for each of us to have. He also took a
couple of samples from one of the pages in order to have
them tested and authenticated. He told us it would take a
couple of weeks to get the results. I was fine with that; my
initial excitement had quickly vanished after exhaustion
settled in and I was ready to go home, to whatever home
was at that point. Mr. Vermil offered to have his helicopter
fly me back to the Time Warner Center and I accepted.

The flight gave me a chance to let things settle further in
my mind. It was a very weird feeling going home. When I
initially left the Iraq war—after your murder, Rebecca, and
the incident outside the Dora Killing fields—I felt like I was
leaving something foul behind and entering a safe haven
where evil couldn't touch me. But when I left Tarrytown
and was flown back to the City—back to "home"—the feeling I had deep inside was something similar to false security. My mind kept trying to feed me the lie that everything
was fine now, that I was safe, but my heart and soul knew
that wasn't true. I guess the best way to describe it is when
you do something wrong and then act as if you had nothing
to do with it but know that it might come back to get you—
have you ever felt that way before? It's a sickening feeling
deep within your stomach. The thing ulcers are made from.
Well, I had that feeling and I wanted it to go away. So, yes,
my excitement for what we (Vermil, Iah, Haggins, and I)
had just learned was sourly gone.

After the helicopter touched down on the building roof,
and I passed the four Platonic Solids, I crossed paths with
Dohlman who was waiting for me in the *Time* lobby, and
boy did he have questions for me. He wanted to know *everything*. And why shouldn't he? I did owe him a story, after

all. Mr. Vermil and I had discussed what to tell Dohlman just before I left. We both felt it best to stick to the basic facts: there is a cover up occurring in Visoko, the hill is a pyramid, and all of the evidence was destroyed.

"Are you kidding me?" he said shocked, and then angrily, "Are you *fucking* kidding me?" The news of my photographic evidence being lost was devastating. "How in the hell are we supposed to run a story that is *so* goddamn condemning without a single shred of evidence? *How?*" I had nothing reassuring to tell him. "I'm getting The Old Man on the phone. We can't run this story. We just can't. We need something else. I'm getting him on the phone." I just nodded my head, agreed, and silently slipped out of the lobby and into the elevator. The sun was already set.

My stop came at the corner of 42nd and W 8th.

As I exited the train, I could hear the crude singing of some wino up ahead. It sounded like he was singing some kind of psalm, or better yet, he was taking what I referred to as a "subway sermon" and putting it to song.

The catz, yeah boy, the catz, are coming my dear.
Watch out—o'z watch out—for they'z knowz no fear.
The manz in the beard,
o that Goddamn manz in the beard,
he'll takez your mind
he'll keepz it bind.
Don't everz let his catz in.
O no, never let his catz in.
It will take evything you holdz dear
and leave yuz in a mez of fear.
Oh that Goddamn manz in the beard.

As I walked past him, I could now see that he was indeed a homeless man. He was an old African American wearing what looked like Vietnam War Army fatigues. His blue jeans were dusty and torn and his shoes had no laces. His dark scalp showed through the thinning hair desperately trying to fill his skull. His icy blue eyes followed me as I nodded and passed. *Poor bastard*, I thought.

At last, when I reached my apartment I had planned on taking a shower, making something to eat, and then hitting the sack. And of course, none of that happened. Instead, when I arrived inside the narrow hallway leading to my shoebox apartment, seven New York Police Department Officers greeted me.

****

Footsteps could be heard coming through the brush. Rebecca looked over and saw Roland. He looked slightly uplifted. "Did you find something?" she asked.

"Yeah, I found a cave that we can use. But what's better, I found water!"

Thank goodness. Rebecca stood slowly, truly feeling the pain in her feet now, and said, "That's wonderful news. How far away is it?"

"I don't know, a couple of minutes. Come on."

Roland turned back and led her through the tall grass and trees. The thought of sleeping in a cave wasn't exciting but it was a whole lot better than sleeping out in the open, where the wild things prowled amidst the moonlight. *I just hope we can find something to eat, or at least get some sleep.*

Unfortunately, in a few hours time, food would be the last thing on their minds, including sleep. There would be no rest that night.

CHAPTER TWENTY-TWO

The Dead Sands

The mountain range where Saño fell was barely visible in the distance. William had just finished replacing the wrapping around his right thigh; it seemed sand could find its way into anything. However, the good thing about laser burns was that they sealed wounds when they burned through, leaving little blood loss, if one was lucky . . . and William was lucky; the beam had burned a groove into his thigh but did not slash all the way through.

Saño, on the other hand, was not so lucky.

After the foreign speaking Desert Demons detained William, the five warriors went down the side of the mountain and buried their fallen comrade. William could only watch for they had bound both of his hands behind his back. Saño's burial was careful but swift. William tried to be respectful and yet he warned them that four more hovercrafts would be coming. The Desert Demons, whose faces bore unusual painted symbols, seemed uninterested in what he had to say. William wasn't surprised by their reaction, nor was he surprised to see that the warriors had sun-beaten skin, were much younger than Saño had been, and didn't speak a lick of William's native tongue.

When the men finished their burial ceremony, they dressed William in an extra camouflage covering, and led him away from the mountain. It wasn't long after that, William's warning about the hovercrafts proved to be true. Four hovercrafts came into view behind them and over the mountains. They broke apart and swept the area but didn't find William and the warriors; the camouflage coverings did a sufficient job at hiding them from the hovercraft scanners.

The Desert Demons led him a little further before stopping and allowing him to change the wrapping around his leg. One of the warriors gave him some water, but they almost never spoke. And when they did, it was quiet and strictly to each other. William took their caution as a sign that they truly did not trust him, but they were respectful toward him; and for that, he was thankful.

"I'm finished," he said after tying the wrapping. A warrior William identified by the wide nose on the man's face walked over and bound William's hands again. The men recovered themselves in the camouflage, including William, and continued walking.

Eventually, the mountains were swallowed by the hazy horizon, leaving nothing but rolling sand dunes to be seen for miles, and the sky took on an orange hue. William couldn't fathom traveling any farther on foot; his leg was burning with pain and he was exhausted. At one point, he had called out, "How much farther?" And to his lack of surprise, the warriors said nothing.

William spent a large amount of time thinking about his parents and their safety. *I don't know what this coup means for them, but if Jonas—or whoever—is willing to kill me then they are willing to kill my parents. I have to get back to them.* But no plan seemed like a good plan.

Nighttime came quickly; it was then that the warriors stopped the trek. They did not build a fire nor did they eat any meal. William felt as if he was starving. He asked if he could eat something, but the warriors ignored him. Fortunately, William was utterly exhausted and fell asleep with little effort.

He awoke the next morning to the five warriors eating some kind of flaky concoction they had produced from the bags strapped to their bodies.

One of the warriors, a skinny-faced man, brought William's ration bag over to him and took one out. The man untied William's hands so he could eat.

William's hands trembled as he tried not to eat the whole ration inside a single minute. His leg was tenderer than before and his feet were blistered and achy.

William examined his companions' weapons a little closer. The rifles were long, each had a hefty scope mounted on top, and each had camouflage that made them resemble pieces of sandy debris. William had also recognized that they were old ballistic rifles retired long ago by the Ministry. William had seen a few in the MSF Archive in Sector 1 when he was a newly appointed agent. He now understood why the warrior's weapons had made such an explosive sound when fired; it was one of the reasons why the Ministry went away from ballistic weapons and focused on laser technology. Another reason was the accuracy of laser technology over ballistic. William considered that while assessing the skill of the warriors. *They must be excellent marksmen.*

The warrior with the wide nose noticed that William was finished with his ration. He walked over and began retying William's hands behind his back. William said, "I'm not going to cause problems," but it was a futile attempt. The warrior finished and then helped William to his feet. William grimaced as the blisters shot sharp pains through the balls of his feet; his wounded thigh muscle screamed with sourness. The warriors exchanged a few words, broke camp, and began to walk again.

The sun was just above the horizon when the lead warrior stumbled to a sudden halt and shouted, "*Revelity! Revelity!*"

Everyone stopped. A spot of sand next to the lead warrior erupted in a tiny explosion of air. The sand beneath the warrior swallowed his feet and shins. He fell to his side, using his hands to break his fall. The desert consumed both hands before the warrior ripped them free while crying out, "*Kipi ta mossa! Fleez rosta da errosi!*"

William and the other warriors had sprung away from the scene before assessing the situation. William shouted, "Pull him out!"

The lead warrior didn't struggle but continued to sink slowly. His shouts were more commands than cries or pleas.

The four free warriors formed a human chain. The man in front went toward his sinking companion and fell waist deep into the sand, which unsettled the sand around the lead warrior, who sank further and was now chest deep. The other three warriors kept a tight yet careful grip on the man trying to reach the lead warrior.

With his arms still tied behind his back, William was incapable of helping. *I have to get my arms free.*

The lead warrior shouted more commands. The man trying to reach him was about four feet too far away. William witnessed this and then looked for another way around. *Maybe the other side is safer.* "Try going around! The ground looks steadier there. Go around him!"

The warriors appeared to be ignoring William as they continued to fight the sinking sand.

William shouted curses and dropped to his butt. He wedged his hands underneath and then rolled onto his back. His body was compact enough so that he could get his hands past his rear and underneath his hamstrings. He rocked forward into a sitting position, brought his chin toward his knees, slipped one foot through the ring his bound hands created, and then the other.

With his hands in front of him, William quickly stood and worked the route he had suggested to the warriors.

The lead warrior was in it up to his neck with both arms overhead, waiting for someone to take a hold.

William found that the ground was sturdier on the lead warrior's flank and cautiously moved closer. The other warriors took notice and cried out incoherent words of either support or opposition. William had lain on the ground and was inching closer to the sinking warrior. He crawled within a few feet of the warrior before shouting at the others, "Someone grab my legs! I can reach him!"

There was another small explosion of air; William felt the ground quickly drop below him. The sand swallowed his arms first, his head, and then his upper body. *You fool!* He thought as he continued to plummet. Sand went up his nose, into his mouth and ears.

Someone took a hold of William's feet as he clawed for something to support his weight. Everywhere he placed his hands, the sand broke free and sank through an invisible hole.

William felt the hands on his legs tug, and he started to move in the reverse direction. His lungs burned from the shallow breath of air he sealed while plummeting. He could feel all of the sand shifting around on his bare skin and inside his uniform. When he broke through the surface, the sound of the world returned. The warriors pulled him completely free from the sandpit and laid him onto his stomach.

William took breaths of air in-between spats of sand. He pushed himself up and onto his knees and tried to wipe the sand from his hands onto his uniform, also covered in sand. He kept his eyes closed; William was fearful of the sand on his face getting inside his eyes.

After a minute or so, and after continually wiping his face with every semi-clean surface he could find, William thanked the men who pulled him free. He opened his eyelids just enough to see that the warriors were all sitting a few feet around him; their heads were draped. William counted four of them. He then looked around for the fifth, the one that was sinking, and realized he had not made it out.

The gratitude William had felt for the warriors saving his life was replaced with the horrifying realization that the fifth man was suffocating to death that very moment. And what was quite possibly worse, William realized that the warriors had left their sinking companion to save him instead.

William and the four warriors remained silent and still for a long time before three gazelles came up over a dune. The men watched the gazelles walk safely past where they assumed the sandpit stretched. William saw one of the warriors rise up to his feet, as did the other three. William stood too. The warrior muttered something to his companions, and they all geared up.

The warrior with the wide nose walked over to William, the sadness that was in his eyes evaporated as he unbound William's hands. He said, "*Kepcha-usaline.*"

William looked down at his free hands and then said, "Thank you."

The warrior turned abruptly and joined his three remaining companions trekking up the dune. William sighed and followed behind. The pain that was once so noticeable in his feet and leg was no longer noticeable.

CHAPTER TWENTY-THREE

District 4, Sector 2

The enclave Roland had found inside the wall of a cliff was hardly worthy of being called a cave. It did lead inside and away from the surrounding jungle, but it was very shallow and was only large enough for several people. *Which might make it good*, thought Rebecca. But when she saw that just about anything could walk inside it, she thought, *Or maybe not.*

"There's a waterfall just a little ways over there," said Roland, pointing through the cave wall. "Come on, I'll show you."

"Hang on"—Rebecca braced herself against the uneven stonewall—"my feet are killing me. You go ahead, I have to sit and rest." She plopped onto the ground and pulled off Simon's shoes, revealing three blisters on her right foot and two on her left.

"Damn, are you okay?" asked Roland, suddenly realizing her problem.

"Yeah, I think so . . . I'm just done with walking today."

Roland observed her feet a little longer before saying, "I'm going to see if I can find something to carry the water back to us."

Rebecca gave the best smile she could offer under the circumstance. "Be careful."

"I'll be back soon." Then he left.

Rebecca sighed and massaged her feet some while looking around the cave. She never thought she would be on the run again—especially with Roland. This was the second time he had saved her skin. The first time she had purposefully involved him in order to get where she needed to go, but this time he had willingly interjected himself into her mess, following Simon back to the Wylde's compound and attacking the MSF agent aiming his rifle at her. Rebecca was very thankful for his interference, but at the same time she felt sorry that his life was now on the brink of ending alongside her own. *Simon is already dead*, she told herself, *and we're likely to be next.*

Rebecca shook her head and thought, *Stop thinking that way. You'll surely die if you don't.*

Rebecca looked around at the rigid and shadowy cave walls. She spotted some peculiar looking bugs crawling about, which of course made her skin crawl. *Great, these things will make our stay lovely.* One bug in particular was very curious looking. It was about the size of her palm and its exoskeleton was very dark and had white dots all over it. Rebecca drew a little closer to it and noticed that it was an arachnid. She stepped away from it out of mixture of fear and respect and then examined the wall surrounding her to make sure there weren't any other arachnids creeping their way towards her.

That's when she noticed the faint remnants of what could be considered cave art—*Coctavian cave art?* Rebecca stood up and examined it closer but had a hard time making out what she was seeing; the lighting was too poor. She then had the idea of using Simon's notepad to take a photo of it—the flash would light it and make the image clearer.

Rebecca positioned the notepad in front of the painting and pressed the photo button. The cave lit up for a split second and the image of the cave art appeared on the digital screen. Rebecca turned around and looked for her new arachnid friend—it was right where she had left it—and then sat back down.

The image on the notepad was clearer, just as she expected, but it was still tough to make out. The focus of the crude rendering was a busty female with her disproportionate legs spread open, mirroring the disproportionate arms spread wide overhead. Between the female's arms were what looked like celestial objects: the stars, the sun, and the moon. Between the female's legs were what appeared to be animals, trees, and water. Rebecca then realized that painting was of a creator being—a female creator—Coctavian or not.

She sat looking at the photo a little longer and felt nostalgic about the life she once lived as the Director of Historic Events – Sector 27, a time when a cave painting such as the one she had just photographed would have been a wondrous discovery. Rebecca closed the photo and thought, *This means nothing now.* The tinge of excitement she had momentarily felt quickly evaporated. *What's going to happen to us,* she wondered. As hard as she tried to suppress her thoughts of death, Rebecca couldn't push them fully out of her mind. *Will we starve to death? Will we die during an animal attack*—she looked at the immobile arachnid—*or by a venomous bug bite?* Rebecca sighed and fought her thoughts. *You will live. Roland will live. You will find a way and you will survive.*

Rebecca felt a compulsion to reopen the translation and find where she had left off. It only took her a few seconds and already the dreadful thoughts of death disappeared. Rebecca reread about how William had just returned to his flat and was greeted by a security force.

****

"Hold on, sir," said the nearest one, a tall man with a bit of a belly. "Are you William Coulee?"

At that point, I could only sigh. "Yes. What's the problem?"

He asked me for my ID and then appeared to be somewhat relieved. "We've been waiting for you for about three hours now. We weren't sure if you were alive or not." His radio squawked with something indistinguishable. The officer— Miles, according to his badge—turned his head toward the radio mounted on his chest and said, "William Coulee just arrived." Another squawk. "I checked his ID." And another. "Yeah, I'm sending him through." He turned back to me.

"Follow me, please. You had a break-in while you were away."

Officer Miles led me down the hall to where another officer was interviewing my next-door neighbor, Mrs. Steinberg, and a couple of other officers were leaning against the hall wall and chatting about the local sports team. I could see that my front door was fully open as well as my mail strewn across the floor. Officer Miles took me inside and loosely explained everything. He spoke with a low grumble and his breath stunk of stale coffee. "Your neighbor, Mrs. Steinberg, said she heard some wrestling at your door a few minutes past six this evening. She was in her bedroom at the time and was about to use the bathroom when she heard your door get kicked open. She then went over to the viewing hole and saw two men dressed in all black forcefully entering your apartment. Mrs. Steinberg said she watched one of the men go into your bedroom and the other shut the busted apartment door. She then called us."

I looked around my bare apartment and saw whatever things I did have tossed and turned upside down. Officer Miles continued, "When we got here the perpetrators were already gone. This is how we found the place. There was some concern that you were either injured or taken hostage; but clearly—you know—that's not the case. We need you to go through and see if there is anything missing or damaged."

I could only nod at that point.

"But first," Officer Miles continued, "I need you to see something. Follow me, please." He took me into the living room where I saw my couch half pulled out and away from the wall as well as my nineteen-inch television lying on the floor. One of the officers in the room pressed the on switch and the picture filled the screen. "Hey, it works," the officer said gleefully.

I looked around the rest of the room but didn't see what Officer Miles was referring. He then pointed to the wall behind me. I turned around and suddenly understood. On the wall was a piece of paper that I had never seen before. "That's not mine."

"We didn't think so. As you can probably see, this is why we were a little concerned for your safety."

I could definitely see. On the piece of paper, which was a single sheet of white printer paper, was an archaic etching of a man skewered from his ass to his throat—impaled. But that wasn't what startled me. What gave me chills was what else was on the paper.

"Are you familiar with that photo?" Officer Miles asked, a notepad and pen in hand.

"Yeah, that's the photo *Time* magazine uses for my profile."

"And the knife?" He was referring to the twelve-inch chopping knife sticking through my face and into the wall. I looked at it closely and recognized its long curved black plastic handle with a wavy design etched into its surface. "That's mine." It looked as if someone might have taped or glued my picture on the head of the impaled man and then held it against the wall and stabbed at it with the knife. It was also clear that whoever did this was a big man because the knife was about four inches into the wall.

Officer Miles held down the curled end of the paper. "Do you know what this is referring to?"

I didn't know how to answer. How does one explain going to Bosnia on an assignment to investigate what turned out to be a bizarre murder of an archeologist by another who claimed to be Zeus and Dracula, reincarnated, and having to escape being murdered by impaling, only to be nearly blown apart and shot to death in Istanbul by the same group while trying to steal an ancient book that may or may not be a mystical text that teaches men how to be Gods?

"Mr. Coulee, do you know what this is about?"

It was like an atomic bomb exploding in my head.

"Mr. Coulee?"

Knowing I should talk to Mr. Vermil before admitting to anything, I quickly said, "I have no idea."

Officer Miles eyed me suspiciously for a few seconds. "You're sure? You seemed to be contemplating something just now."

"I'm just in shock," I told him. "I can't figure out what this is all about." My act was earnest.

He nodded and then led me back down the hall. "Okay Mr. Coulee, take a moment and look around to see if anything is missing and then I need you to come down to the station to fill out some paper work."

There wasn't much to look at and I was pretty sure nothing was missing; besides, I knew what they were really after. I walked around my apartment and did a quick inspection. To my lack of surprise everything seemed to be there despite being displaced. The bedroom had my clothes tossed about—on the bed, on the closet floor and on the room floor. My nightstand was emptied out; a few notes and pens lay discarded on the ground, each broken. The bathroom was much of the same. My medicine cabinet was open, although nothing was taken out, and there were a few miscellaneous items on the floor from under the sink. The kitchen had its drawers opened and dumped as well. A few utensils lay on the ground and several post-it notes and potholders. I'm actually quite embarrassed to say that my apartment didn't look too different from before.

I walked into the building hallway in search of Officer Miles; I wanted to tell him that everything seemed to still be inside, but instead I came across my short, Jewish, widowed neighbor, Mrs. Steinberg. "*Mr. Coulee*, Mr. Coulee, thank heavens you're okay!" she shouted in her thick Long Island accent.

"Are you okay, Mrs. Steinberg? I'm sure all of this has given you quite a fright."

"Good heavens, yes, my dear!" she said in a shaken voice. I could see in her eyes that she was still not settled in the slightest. "They were monsters, I tell you, *monsters!*" She nodded her head and attempted to swallow. "They were black as night . . . their eyes were cold and soulless."

I thought she was being a little dramatic. "Did you give the officers a good description?"

"I tried, but I couldn't really make out any facial features. Simply awful they were. I felt like they could kill me just by looking at me."

"They saw you?" I asked.

"Not entirely. I was behind my door, see, and I was watching through the peep hole," she pointed over to her door and the tiny viewing hole each of our apartments had. "I stood there quietly and held my breath so they couldn't tell I was there but somehow they did!"

I tried to assure Mrs. Steinberg that it was just her imagination.

"Oh no, they could see me," she said insistently. "One of them stopped in front of my door and started to smile right at me! Right at me Mr. Coulee! He gave a big old grin and then put his finger up to his lips to tell me to stay quiet." She imitated what the man did, the universal *sshh* gesture. "But

I had already called the police, nothing stopping that, and besides I thought you were in danger."

"Well I wasn't, Mrs. Steinberg, no need to worry anymore. I'm sure they won't be back."

She started to breathe a little easier but then went back into it again. "Soulless. I've never seen men with such blankness before. I felt like the devil had just arrived right here," she said exaggeratedly. "Right here where we're standing. Right here! The devil, Mr. Coulee!"

I spent the next several minutes trying to convince her the devil didn't break into my apartment. Mrs. Steinberg was a pretty eccentric woman. Eventually I was able to sign off that nothing was missing with Officer Miles. I then went back into my disaster of a home.

Mrs. Steinberg was still standing at her door, watching me.

"Are you going to be all right, Mrs. Steinberg?"

She nodded her head. "If only Harold was still here. He would have confronted those beasts; I'm sure of it." Harold was the name of her late husband. "Harold was a warrior he was. Did I ever tell you he fought in the Korean War?"

I shook my head.

"You would have liked him. Everyone loved Harold. If he were here he would have chased those hooligans right out of this building. He would have taught them a lesson. The nerve of them, breaking in during the day, tossing your things around."

She didn't know the half of it. What alarmed me the most was how fast they acted. It had not been twenty-four hours since I left Istanbul. I told Mrs. Steinberg not to worry about a thing. If she heard something else out there to just call the police like before.

"Where are you going to be?" she asked, sensing I was about to leave again.

I stumbled mentally while trying to give her an answer. "I have some things to take care of. I'll be gone for a little while." I then went into my apartment and wrote my cell on a notebook piece of paper and handed it to her. "Call me if something else happens."

A motherly side of Mrs. Steinberg suddenly showed. "You be careful out there. I don't know your business, Mr. Coulee, but I fear bad things lie ahead. You be careful."

I nodded and tried to give her a comforting smile. She waddled back into her doorway and waved. I remained in the hall for a while, contemplating exactly what to do next. I called Mr. Vermil and told him what I found waiting for me. He considered having me come back to his house in Tarrytown, but I told him it was probably best that I stayed away; if Bertók wasn't already aware of how closely I was working with Mr. Vermil then there was no need to tip him off about it. Mr. Vermil agreed and assured me that he would beef up security around his property. But that still left me with the problem of where to go, and I still had to visit the police station. Realizing that I wouldn't be coming back to my apartment any time in the near future, I decided to gather a few things for the road—wherever it led.

I had hoped my backup camera wasn't busted. It was a graduation gift from my mother. I kept it in a special case along with some extra lenses. I found it lying on the floor of my bathtub—of all places. Luckily it was still in the hard plastic case, which was open. I checked it out and all seemed well. I gathered a few other things and loaded them into my shoulder bag including an extra memory stick, a notepad and a couple of those snapped pencils. I grabbed an extra change of clothes but that was about it. I didn't want to be too loaded down; I had a feeling that a long, winding road lay before me.

CHAPTER TWENTY-FOUR

District 4, Sector 2

Roland returned with his hands cupping a loose basket of leaves. Rebecca had set aside the notepad and observed him as he quickly, yet carefully, walked over and offered them to her. "Here, drink it quickly. I don't know how much longer I can contain it."

Rebecca smiled and stood in a crouched position, placing her lips on the leaves and allowing the water to slowly flow into her mouth. There wasn't much but enough to quench her dried lips and throat. Roland tipped the leaves all the way until every last drop was either consumed or spilled. "Of course, if we need more, there is plenty not too far from here . . . I would say about two or three hundred yards."

Rebecca sat back down and said, "Thank you. You're too good to me. I should have gone with you, my feet aren't so bad—"

"Forget about it. Your feet are done. It was no problem. I just wish I could have found something more suitable to carry the water back." Roland slipped down along the cave wall and sat, exhaling an exhausted sigh of relief. "Now, if we can just figure out what to eat. That's going to be a lot trickier than bringing water back."

"We may not eat for a little while," declared Rebecca. "Unless I'm mistaken, neither of us is versed in locating and trapping animals or which plants are safe to eat and which are not."

"I know. That's what worries me. My stomach aches for food and it has only been a day."

I understand, completely. Rebecca noticed the wounds on Roland's arms were inflamed and seeping a bit. "Are you okay?"

Roland looked down at his left arm and then nodded. "I think so. It hurts pretty bad but I'll live."

Rebecca slid next to him and said, "Don't worry too much; if it gets really bad, then I'll call for help."

They sat in silence for a moment. Rebecca then remembered the arachnid. She looked up at the cave wall but didn't see it. "Oh no."

"What?"

Rebecca explained the spider.

Roland looked around for it and then sighed; he was clearly unsettled. "I'm sure it will turn up at an inconvenient time."

"It's more afraid of us than we are of it."

Roland muttered, "Speak for yourself." He then looked at the notepad in Rebecca's hands and said, "How much battery power does it have left?"

Rebecca hadn't checked recently. "I don't know." She logged in and saw that it was already down to 51%. "We have around four more hours unless I go outside right now."

Rebecca had thought that the walk from the wreckage to the cave would have been sufficient for the solar panels to give the battery a decent charge, but she was wrong.

"We don't have a whole lot of time before the sun goes down."

Rebecca nodded her head. "I know."

Roland looked at the translation up on the screen. "Are you planning on reading it still? If you don't use the notepad then it will probably last until morning."

"I know." But Rebecca hadn't planned on not reading. *I have to read it.* "I'll go outside then, and find a place where it can charge and I can read while it does."

Roland looked like he wanted to object, preferring her to stay inside and simply not read. "Okay, I guess . . . if you must."

She felt guilty about it but said, "I must. I'm sorry, but I . . ."

"You have to, I know. Do you want me to come with you? You know, so you're not alone?"

Rebecca smiled. "Of course, if you don't mind and want to."

Roland was already on his feet. "I know where you can go—where the notepad will have the most exposure."

"Okay," Rebecca said while standing up, "show me."

Roland led her out of the cave. She had decided to leave Simon's shoes behind, thinking it would be best to let her feet breathe. They walked to the left of the cave and to a rocky slant in the cliff wall that wasn't as steep as the rest. The slant led over the cave entrance and continued all the way up the side of the cliff until it reached the top. Rebecca had noticed it earlier, when they first arrived, so it didn't surprise her that Roland wanted to go in that direction. He told her to lead the way, since she was barefoot and all, so that he could catch her if she slipped or stumbled. The climb up probably would have been better if she had used Simon's shoes; she felt every stone and pebble on the bottom of her feet, but the blisters that had formed from rubbing on the sides of the shoes were unaffected, which was the point.

At the top of the cliff, Rebecca could see more clearly why Roland had chosen this place. The view looked out and over the trees, revealing the vast forest covering the rolling hill terrain they'd been walking through all day. To her left, Rebecca spotted the small river running down the side of the cliff and into a roaring pool below. The sun was almost directly behind them, illuminating and shimmering off the wind blown trees. "It's beautiful up here."

Roland stood next to her. "Yeah, I thought you would think so."

Rebecca turned and faced the sun with the notepad out; she could see the charging meter grow in size. "It's working."

Roland bent down to the ground and sat. "Make yourself comfortable."

Rebecca did the same and maximized the translation on the screen. "Do you want to read too?" she offered, despite knowing that no one else was supposed to read it; but she felt it was the polite thing to do.

"I'm okay. I probably won't understand anyway. I'm just going to relax here for a little while . . . you know . . . try and enjoy the view. This may be the only chance I'll have to experience this place."

"We're going to be fine," assured Rebecca. "I promise."

"I know," he said, not sounding convinced.

Rebecca gave him a smile but didn't know what else to say. She turned her attention back to the notepad and found where she had left off.

William was preparing to go to the police station after discovering that masked men had ransacked his apartment.

****

The trip to the police station took about an hour and a half. The boys downtown wanted to know all about my visit to Bosnia and whom I might have pissed off along the way. It was difficult to dance around their direct questions, but all-and-all I managed to satisfy their need for information without getting myself tied down. They did, however, ask one question that I didn't have an answer for: "Where are you going to stay, if not in your apartment?" The police wanted to do a small sting operation just in case the perpetrators returned. I told them that I might check into a hotel room for the immediate time, or until they thought it was safe to go home. And I actually started going toward a Westin when I thought it might be best that I got out of New York City all together. I wasn't planning on looking up Jonas Lundquist for a few days but the current situation changed my mind.

Professor Haggins was right about him (by the way); Jonas Lundquist owned a rare bookstore down in Alexandria, Virginia—just out of Washington, D.C. It was called The Alexandria Rare Book Company. He had a rather robust and sterile looking website detailing his inventory of exceptionally rare and *expensive* books. Very uppity. I felt that maybe now was the time to pay him a visit. The question was how to get there. I contacted Mr. Vermil and told him my plans. He told me that he planned on keeping his helicopter close by in case there was a need to make an unexpected trip out of town. He offered to pay for a rental car and I took him up on it. But because of the late hour all of these events took place, I ended up staying the night in a hotel. I was finally able to take the shower I so desperately needed and slept rather comfortably considering all that I had just been through and the paranoia dancing around inside my mind every time I heard a footfall in the outside hall. When morning came, I didn't get out of bed until closer to ten. I ate a cheap breakfast, went to the car rental, and around noon, I was on my way to Alexandria.

It was some time around five o' clock when I pulled over at a rest stop to get something quick to eat and top off the tank. It had rained nearly the entire day and it seemed the further I drove the harsher the weather became. By the time I stopped the storm was full overhead with rain coming down like bullets.

The rest stop was a large modern one with all of the accommodations a person could need. There were signs promoting several fast food joints as well as a gift shop, a bank, and a twelve-pump gas station.

All around me was a rainy version of Armageddon. Luckily there was a metal awning overhead.

Lightning struck about every thirty seconds or so, immediately followed by the crack of thunder. The experience took me back to Iraq—the feeling of old familiarity—and I had visions of lying low on my balcony at the Palestine Hotel with bombs and missiles raining down on Baghdad, spraying up yellow star-bursts of falling, flaming, metal confetti. The memories were as real as the moment—the stillness of the night, a gentle cool breeze blowing across the hotel balcony. There was an electric tinge in the air, like the kind felt during a major thunderstorm—like the one I was feeling at the rest stop. I recalled how hard it was to believe that the war was finally upon Iraq.

Just a couple of weeks prior, I was walking the happy streets of what felt like an Islamic Miami. That's the best way to describe prewar Baghdad. There were people all over the streets, going about their lives, completely unconcerned about the impending doom of their city. There were tons of street vendors selling fruits, vegetables, electronics—you name it. There were street performers playing traditional music while people cheerfully danced past on their way to wherever. The town felt like one big party, everyone smiling and throwing up peace signs at us foreigners. At one point in time, I saw what looked like a pristine 1957 blue Chevy come driving past. At another time, there were several guys hanging out the windows of a bus, whistling and cheering like students on spring break. Only a few weeks later, these smiling, dancing, cheerful people would be cannibalizing each other for whatever petty differences. But at that moment, before the bombs dropped, they were living a fool's hope that this thing would pass by them like the storm cloud blotting out the sky high above the gas station. They hoped the rain would hold off for another day, for another place.

That hope ended at 5:30am on March 20, 2003 when forty cruise missiles came thundering down from the sky at a location the United States President referred to as "a target of opportunity." Two days later, I was standing at my hotel balcony with my helmet and flak suit on, camera in hand . . . waiting. It was impossible to sleep anymore. Everyone knew that it was only a matter of minutes before the feared "Shock and Awe" campaign would begin, which it did with a roar overhead and a series of explosions that were entirely too close for comfort. I dropped to the balcony floor and peered through the bars at the orange glow just on the horizon. The awesome reverb of the anti-aircraft guns echoed as the night sky filled with brilliant dashes of light and flash bursts. In a matter of seconds, the entire horizon looked like a raging wild fire. The noise was absolutely unreal. There were eerie silences in-between cracks of gunfire and heavy explosions—remnants of peace before another ripple of war. I sat on the balcony, taking photos, for five straight hours. A more seasoned journalist might have ventured out, got into the thick of things, but I was green and terrified.

The next day, I went back down to the streets; every ounce of joy that town had once displayed was dried up. The people were still there, but the energy was gone. The Iraqis pretended nothing had happened. There were cars everywhere, people eating in cafes, and food stands up and running; however, there were no more street performers, no more dancing, no more smiles or peace signs, no more guys cheering and whistling from bus windows. That aspect of Baghdad was gone. Never to be seen again with my eyes. But I've digressed.

Another crack of thunder a little ways off and the gas pump jarred to a stop. As I closed the gas cap, I noticed a black SUV exiting the highway. I don't know exactly what drew my attention to it or what necessarily caused my senses to heighten—it could have been the storm, or my memories of the war, or all that I had gone through the past few days—but whatever it was told me that something was off. I suddenly felt cold and uneasy. Gregory Hansen was dead, yes, but clearly there were more of them—mercenaries hired by Bertók—and I felt it best to get out of there in a hurry. I returned the gas nozzle to its holster and looked toward the rest stop rotunda where the SUV disappeared behind the building. With little hesitation, I hurried over to the driver side door and hopped inside. I don't have a problem admitting it: I was truly afraid.

I started the car and sped out from under the gas pump

awning, swerving dangerously past a car pulling in to take the vacant pump.

The rain blasted against the car windshield like pellets instead of water. The wipers strained to keep the window clear, but I didn't care; I had to get out of there.

Once I merged onto the highway, I looked back and saw that no one was following me. But it wasn't until I was about three miles away, and still free from any headlights in the rear-view mirror, that I finally felt safe enough to slow to a more practical speed.

I had felt stupid for reacting in such a way; there was no indication that the SUV was anything sinister, and yet I allowed my fear to consume me, which was a dangerous thing. Fear causes blindness, blindness causes chaos, and chaos causes your fear to come true. Like the ouroboros: fear is an endless cycle of self-consumption.

****

Rebecca lowered Simon's notepad and considered what she had just read: *Like the ouroboros, fear is an endless cycle of self-consumption.* She knew there was truth to those words; her worst fear was that someone would find out about her illegitimacy, which inadvertently caused her to expose that secret, which then birthed a new group of fears that managed to come to fruition as well, and so on. . . .

"The sun is almost down," Roland said suddenly, squinting toward the distant horizon.

Rebecca looked at him and then to the horizon and saw that they had maybe a half hour left before nightfall. "We should get back."

Roland sat up and nodded. "Yeah, I agree. There's no telling what will come out after dark."

Roland had no idea how right he truly was.

CHAPTER TWENTY-FIVE

District 4, Sector 2

A fire would be nice, thought Rebecca. Neither she nor Roland had the skill to create one, which was just another reminder of how out of their element they truly were. The two of them sat on the dirty, stone floor, huddled close together and talking quietly. Roland revealed to Rebecca that Director of Technology – Sector 27, Thomas Heckert—the man Roland used to drive a hovercar for—had horrible gas. Rebecca snickered and told Roland about a girl she knew at the Academy who used to obsess over her toe-jam before bed.

"You know," Roland said, "toe-jam isn't something one should take lightly. It can really ruin your walking experience if it gets too built up."

Rebecca laughed. "I guess she was very concerned about her 'walking experience.'"

Roland laughed a little and then he grew quiet. "How much longer are we going to stay out here? I know we're in trouble—in more ways than one—but eventually we'll have to make a decision on what will be worse:

the Ministry or the wilderness."

"I know," Rebecca said, "and either will probably have a bad ending. If we can somehow find our way to the Free People, or contact them in some way, then we will have a strong chance of getting out of this thing alive."

"Alive is good."

Yeah, thought Rebecca, *alive is good.* Her body was tired but her eyes were very much awake. Roland huddled further and closed his eyes. "Are you going to sleep?" she asked.

"Yeah. I'm tired, Becca. Is that alright?"

"Of course. Do you mind if I read? The battery is charged enough for another seven hours. I promise I won't wear it down too far; I just need to get my mind relaxed so I can sleep."

Roland yawned. "I don't care. Goodnight."

"Goodnight," she said and then turned on Simon's notepad. The light filled the dark void and Roland rolled slightly onto his side; he turned his face away from the source. Rebecca paged through the translation and found where she had left off.

William had just escaped a possible attack at a rest stop and was on his way to Alexandria, Virginia to locate Jonas Lundquist, who was supposedly an expert on the Voynich manuscript.

****

There were signs with Washington D.C. printed on them. "Just 60 more miles." Then 30, 15, 7, and eventually, "2 more miles." It was only my second time visiting Washington D.C., not counting my return trip from Jordan. The first time was with my sixth grade class.

We took a bus from Zionsville, Pennsylvania—which in hindsight, for the teachers, was a terrible idea; a couple of hundred kids jammed in school buses made for a stressful ride.

I still remember thinking that Washington, D.C., was what I imagined Rome looked like: large, wide buildings with ornate columns and marble facades, stone statues marking geographical points on the city grid. I remember my teacher, Mrs. Sudomire, talking to us over the bus's loudspeaker like some sort of tour guide; she had pointed out Kingman Lake, the Capitol building, the Washington Monument, and of course the White House, where the President lived.

That was eighteen years prior to my return to the great city. This time, however, the romantic awe I felt when I was twelve was gone and I found the city under siege by armies of contractors, chain-link fences, and equipment. There should have been a "City Under Construction" sign along the border. It seemed that every road and building was under some sort of work or repair.

I had the address for The Alexandria Rare Book Company plugged into the GPS and it guided me into Alexandria, which was just south of the great city and on the west bank of the Potomac River.

My palms were sweating all the way.

I pulled up to the little red destination. The time was around 5:30pm.

The Alexandria Rare Book Company was on the corner of South Fairfax and King Street—(go figure). Its building was classic-style brick and mortar, as was the sidewalk with throwback colonial-era lampposts, but the building windows looked relatively new and the frames were painted a bright blue with white trim. There was a fancy wood sign above the King Street entrance that read The Alexandria Rare Book Company, in an elegant script font.

I peeked in through the large main window but saw only rows and columns of midsized bookshelves making up the body of the floor—being perused by a few customers—and floor to ceiling bookshelves on the far wall. I looked down at the print out Professor Haggins had made of the book from Istanbul and at the bizarre language handwritten on its pages and thought, *It's now or never.*

The interior of the bookstore smelled like a bakery, particularly like cinnamon rolls—I'll never forget that. On top of a corner-side table was a lamp with a green glass shade and a little candle plate burning, making up the pleasant scent. The customers inside the store—a middle-aged man with dark hair and wire thin glasses, an older woman with several books tucked under an arm, a younger woman who insistently tucked her hair behind her ears, and an older crippled man in an electric wheelchair paging through a book from the wall shelf—paid no attention to me entering the store. I looked around the room for a counter or a register, somewhere signifying a place where an employee would be stationed, and I saw a man about my own age noting something into a tablet computer. He looked like he was taking inventory. I assumed he worked there and I walked over to the shelf he was concentrating on. "Excuse me, do you work here?" I asked.

The man didn't hesitate in his work. "I do."

"Great, I'm looking for the store owner, Mr. Lundquist."

The man pointed his finger curiously at a red cloth-covered book, still not looking at me, and said, "He's busy right now, can I help you with something?"

"I don't believe so," I said and then held up the print out, "not unless you can read this writing."

After a moment of watching his lips silently read the names of the books before him, he looked at the print out. . . . His brow furrowed. "What is this?"

"I was hoping Mr. Lundquist could tell me; can you please see if he has a few minutes?"

"Who are you?"

The man's tone wasn't exactly curt. I told him my name and that I was a journalist with *Time* magazine. "I've been told that Mr. Lundquist is an expert on exotic languages and was hoping he could help me with some research I'm conducting."

"Mr. Lundquist just returned from a long trip and is quite busy with work at the moment"—the man reached out for the print out—"but I could see if he can make time for you." He studied the sheet a little longer before forcing a smile and leaving through a narrow doorway that led into a back hall, taking the print out with him. He returned after a brief period, his demeanor altered for the better, and said, "Mr. Coulee, will you please follow me? Mr. Lundquist will see you."

I followed the clerk through the narrow passage, up a flight of stairs, and into a very well decorated office space that looked over King Street. Seated at a desk with only his profile exposed to me was a very old and yet strong looking man who appeared to be examining my print out.

The clerk left my side and returned to the main floor.

"Mr. Lundquist?" I said.

The old man lowered the page and turned his head to look at me. A strange, slithery smile creased his face. "You are *Time* magazine journalist William Coulee, I presume?"

"That's right. May I come in?"

"But of course"—he gestured toward a set of upholstered leather chairs. I knew the man's smile was meant to be friendly, but for a reason I didn't understand, I found it alarming.

****

That's because he's a snake, thought Rebecca.

****

I walked over to one of the chairs and sat down.

Jonas's eyes followed my every movement. "Comfortable, isn't it?"

"Yeah," I said, "quite comfortable."

"Those are antique Thomas Chippendales. I found them during a trip to Europe." He placed the print out onto his desk. "They were sitting in a Nottingham antique shop, collecting dust and stacks of worthless newspapers from the 1970s. The owner of the shop had no idea what she had, just a couple of old wooden chairs that needed some restoration, she thought. I bought the set for £12; in auction, they are worth around $700."

"Wow," I said, not really interested.

Jonas grinned and nodded his head, clearly proud of his purchase. "But you didn't come here to hear about my escapades in English antique shops"—he picked up the print out—"you want to know if this writing is Voynich."

It took me a second to respond; I was caught off guard by the accuracy of his statement, which shouldn't have been so shocking to me. Why else would I have been there? "Yes, actually, that is exactly why I am here. I was told by several scholars that you are the premiere expert on Voynich; that you—"

"Yes, Mr. Coulee, I'm well aware of my history with the language." He looked at the print out again and said, "There are similarities; where did you find this?"

Easy question to ask but not so easy to answer. "Unfortunately, I can't disclose that information at this time; it's part of my on going investigation, and my sources asked for anonymity."

"Oh, yes . . . I know all about anonymity, Mr. Coulee. But, unfortunately for you, without knowing where it came from, I cannot give you an accurate assessment."

"You can't look at it and tell me whether or not it is Voynich?"

"It has similarities—as I already told you—but that means almost nothing when it comes to authenticating—anyone could have written this at anytime, which means I can absolutely not rule out forgery."

"What if I tell you that I know it came from an antique source, possibly over six hundred years ago; would that make a difference?"

Jonas pursed his lips and nodded his head. "You may or may not be aware of this, but Voynich is considered an unreadable language. A hoax by many. . . . I spent a career twisting my mind inside its script—its characters—and I can tell you that each time I thought I had a possible solution, I discovered that something wasn't quite right; a grouping or a single word failed to fit the translation, like the extra parts to an electronic you disassembled and then reassembled, careful not to miss anything, and yet there they are, several screws and doohickeys sitting in a lonely pile. You want to tell yourself that the electronic will work without them, that they are unnecessary, but deep inside you know that they serve a purpose." He sighed.

"What exactly is Voynich?" I asked. "I know it hasn't been deciphered and that it is named after Voynich, the man who rediscovered it in recent history, but that is all."

"Wilfrid Voynich," said Jonas. "He was an interesting fellow. Born in Telshiai, a part of the Russian Empire during the mid-late 19th century, he joined a revolutionary organization and had some unfortunate run-ins with the Tsarist police. Eventually he moved to London, took the name Voynich, and opened a bookshop. Sixteen years later he opened another in New York. He was particularly interested in rare books. In 1912, Voynich acquired some thirty manuscripts from the Roman College, in Italy, and came upon the curse-of-a-manuscript that now bears his name."

"A curse?"—I said, surprised—"Why do you say that?"

"Because, the manuscript tormented him 'til the end of his days. He spent far too many hours trying to unlock its secrets: who wrote it, where it came from, what language it was written in, how to read it, and—ultimately—its purpose. He died in 1930 and the manuscript was inherited by his wife, who left it to a close friend, who sold it to another book dealer, who eventually donated it to Yale University in 1969. No one then, or since, has come close to unlocking its secrets."

"I heard you did."

Jonas pressed both hands' fingertips together and said, "The level of success I achieved has been exaggerated."

"I heard you were part of the joint CIA, NSA, and FBI operation tasked with cracking the cipher."

Whatever level of friendliness his face strained to display quickly left. "Unfortunately for you, Mr. Coulee, I'm not at liberty to speak of such things, nor do I know of *any* collaboration. My efforts with Voynich were driven strictly by my own desire to punish my mind. . . . At no point was I in collaboration with the United States Intelligence Community."

Clearly he was lying. "Then why aren't you at liberty to speak of such things? Who cares—if none of it's true?"

It was then, inside my head (there really is no other way to explain it) that I felt the compulsion to leave. My anxiety level skyrocketed. My palms began to sweat puddles and I found it difficult to breathe.

Jonas just stared at me, his fingers still pressed tightly together, his eyes poking holes through my head. "Mr. Coulee, are you okay?" he asked quite calmly.

I wanted to talk but I almost vomited instead. I wiped my hands on my pants and looked toward the hardwood floor; trying to regain my composure. "Yes, I'm fine," was all I could muster.

****

Thought Police, was what passed through Rebecca's mind.

****

Jonas looked back at the print out. "It resembles Voynich, Mr. Coulee, but that is all. I can't give you more and I have much to do today. So, if you don't mind. . . ."

I didn't. I wanted out of there, and fast. I was scared I was going to pass out right in front of him. I stood up and felt my head balloon. I reached over to Jonas's desk and grabbed the print out. That was when my eyes caught sight of something peculiar:

Lying on his desk, but covered with random papers, was a document titled 'PARDUS – GIZA.'

"Good day, Mr. Coulee," Jonas said. "I hope you find what you're looking for."

"Thank you for your time," I said and then quickly left.

****

A howl came bouncing off the cave walls. Rebecca was startled half-to-death. She hastily lowered the translation and turned off its screen. Her eyes were consumed by the darkness. It took them several seconds to adjust to the low light.

There was another howl further off in the distance—it was a mortifying sound, much like an old woman moaning in pain. *What is that?* wondered Rebecca with angst. It was similar to the sound the HOUNDS made but it wasn't the same. This sound was organic. Alive.

Roland popped up suddenly after another howl ripped through the small cave.

"What is that?" he said.

"I think they're coyotes," Rebecca told him, yet having never heard one before. "I think they are talking to each other," she whispered.

There were some wrestling sounds outside the cave entrance, some sniffing and a snort, before another howl bellowed out. Rebecca and Roland instinctively covered their ears. As the howl dissipated, they heard growls and saw a reflection of light flash between a pair of eyes.

CHAPTER TWENTY-SIX

District 4, Sector 2

Roland felt around the ground for something, a stick or a rock—anything. Rebecca stood up and banged her head on the cave ceiling as she backed into a corner. The coyote slowly approached them, growling.

More howls were heard outside.

Roland found a stone about seven inches in diameter and backed up toward Rebecca, bumping into her. Neither one of them spoke.

The coyote took further, cautious steps, bearing its teeth.

"GO ON! GET OUT OF HERE!" shouted Roland. He kicked some dirt at it but the coyote only hunkered lower to the ground and prepared to attack.

There was nothing for Rebecca and Roland to do. . . .

The attack came swiftly and violently.

Roland stood his ground in front of Rebecca. The coyote lunged and latched onto Roland's left arm, which he used to deflect his chest. Roland cried out in pain as the coyote thrashed around, trying to rip his arm free.

Roland swung his right arm and smashed the stone against the coyote's head, freeing his mauled arm.

The coyote yelped and fell onto its side briefly before staggering back to its feet.

Roland crumbled backwards and against the cave wall, cradling his seriously injured arm.

Rebecca didn't hesitate when she saw her only opportunity to strike; she kicked the coyote in the ribs while it was still dazed.

There was a crunch and another yelp as the animal staggered backward. The coyote struggled out of the cave while whining and slowly walked away. Two more coyotes came past the cave entrance; both of them looked inside, with their eyes reflecting the moonlight, but continued on behind their wounded leader.

"I think it was the alpha male," said Rebecca through heavy breathing. "I think I broke its ribs."

Roland was still huddled on the ground, trying to wrap his wounded arm in his shirt. "I'm hurting, Becca."

Rebecca's stomach plummeted as she stepped around him and pulled out his arm. "Let me look at it."

Roland grimaced and relinquished, revealing several more deep gashes in his skin, exposed muscle and something that looked like bone, and lots of blood streaming out.

"*Oh no*," Rebecca said, "we need to stop the bleeding."

Roland was visibly trembling now; his eyes were fixed on the wound. "How?"

"I need something to apply pressure." She looked down at her nightgown and considered ripping a strand of cloth off, but then she saw Roland's socks and said, "I need one of your socks. I can tie it around the wound in order to stop the bleeding."

Roland looked at his feet and nodded. "Okay," he said through chattering teeth.

Rebecca removed the shoe from his left foot, and then the sock. She wrapped it around his wound and tied it.

Roland cried out in pain.

Rebecca tried using her hands to wipe the blood away from the rest of his arm so she could get a better look. She considered using his other sock as a cloth but then realized that she would probably need it as a bandage at a later time. So, instead, Rebecca used her dress and wiped Roland's arm clean. "I don't know. These cuts are deep, Roland. We might have to call for help."

"Not yet," he said after calming a bit. "I can't let this be the reason we allow ourselves to be captured."

"What choice do we have? We're in a lot of trouble, and now you're hurt pretty bad. How much longer can we wait?"

"At least until sunrise," he said. "Let's just wait until then to see how I'm doing. If things look bad, then we call. But if I'm doing okay, then maybe we can continue on, and hopefully find a small village. . . . I just don't want to give up yet, Becca. I don't want to die knowing that we didn't try everything."

"I don't want to die either," Rebecca said, "but we have to be realistic, if your arm gets infected, then you're as good as dead."

"That's why I say we wait until morning. Let's see if I get an infection. What does it matter at this point?"

Rebecca realized that she was still holding on to hope that someone would rescue them and not turn them into the Ministry; or that maybe the Ministry would come and arrest them, but they would be in a detention center for a few days, which would allow for a rescue attempt to be planned. Rebecca was holding onto hope for anything, no matter how unrealistic. "Okay, we'll wait until sunrise."

"Good," Roland said. He slid his body back down to the ground, still clutching the rock in his good hand. "If those damn beasts come back, they'll get another dose of stone fury."

"If they come back, Roland, we're dead."

"We'll see," he said, shifting his arm on his stomach and closing his eyes. "We'll see."

CHAPTER TWENTY-SEVEN

District 4, Sector 2

The two of them sat there for a length of time before Rebecca realized that Roland was asleep. She, on the other hand, was wide-awake. Her mind twisted and tormented her. Every sound she heard caused paranoia. *How worse can our luck get?*

At one point, Rebecca tried looking at Roland's arm to see if it had slowed or stopped bleeding, but she couldn't get a good angle on it. *This is very bad.* There was no doubt in her mind that they would have to call for help the next day. The wound would surely become infected, which meant that their freedom was fleeting, and soon they would be detained, stripped of everything in their possession—meaning Simon's notepad and the translation—and then taken to a detention hall where they would wait for their execution.

Another hour or so passed and Rebecca gave up trying to sleep and turned on Simon's notepad; she opened the translation. There was nothing else she could do for Roland except wait for morning.

Rebecca found where she had left off. This moment was possibly her last moment with William's manuscript, and so she was going to make the most of it. Undeniably, her destiny was tied to the manuscript, which meant her destiny was in her hands. *If we're going to be saved, reading this will play some part; I know it.*

William had just met with Jonas Lundquist and learned very little about whether or not the book he found in Istanbul was related to the Voynich manuscript. Furthermore, William had begun to feel extremely uneasy within Jonas's presence and felt it best to leave—in a hurry.

****

I couldn't have left that bookstore fast enough. It wasn't until I was outside, and by the rental, that I finally felt normal again. I was never the one to have panic attacks, so that really startled me. I sat down in the driver seat of the car and just took it easy, looking back at the The Alexandria Rare Book Company and thought about just how curious of a meeting I just had. Other than a brief history on Voynich, the man, I didn't learn anything new. I was more concerned with how uncomfortable I was within Jonas's presence. I'm sorry Rebecca, I wish I could explain it better, but no words seem capable of describing how that man made me feel. There was something terrible about him.

****

No explanation needed, thought Rebecca. Jonas had that effect on everyone.

****

Anyway, I drove away from the bookstore—just because—

and parked in a grocery parking lot. I gained nothing, I had nowhere to go, and I still needed answers.

I considered looking for a local library so I could do some research, and then I remembered that my old college roommate, Daniel Carr, lived either in Washington, D.C. or nearby. I looked him up on my cellphone and saw that he actually lived in the capitol. It was just past 6pm at that point and so I assumed he was done with work for the day.

When Daniel answered his phone he was pretty surprised to hear my voice. I had asked him if he was home. He told me that he was just leaving the office. I gave him the news that I was in the area and that I needed a place to crash. Daniel was more than willing to accommodate me. "You should have told me you were coming to town," he said cheerfully. "I would have given you a royal welcome."

His royal welcome would have included a night full of booze and women. Even though Daniel was a complete awkward nerd in college, he grew into his own shortly thereafter and found confidence in his appearance, once he lost the parted hair and glasses, grew a goatee, and began working out. Daniel discovered that women were actually drawn to him—despite the fact he still ran a conspiracy website and had the largest comic book collection I had ever seen.

"I'll be home in fifteen," he informed. "Come on over!"

Daniel's home was a condominium high rise just northeast of the White House. I'm not sure how much he paid for the place, but I know it wasn't cheap—not that it mattered; Daniel was well off. After college, he had started writing software and patenting them. He sold the patented programs to large Fortune 500 companies at top dollar. He once told me that the trick to developing a successful software company was to know what people were going to need before they realized they needed it; this way you would always be ahead of the game. So when he saw companies going on hiring sprees for personnel that can handle complex databases, Daniel wrote a program that intelligently handled the data so the "man" wasn't needed. The program was self-sustaining and only needed queued each day. The downside, of course, was that Daniel was putting those data managers out of work. But he didn't care. Daniel figured it was their fault for not coming up with the program first. That's how he was—logical to a fault. But that was only when it came to business. There were plenty of other things Daniel was completely illogical about . . . or so I thought.

His conspiracy website MakerOfTheMan.com was chalked full of those illogical moments. I always figured the website was an extension of his brain—the place where he stored delusions that had no business meddling around where his moments of brilliance resided. Like a wizard with the ability to extract memories from his mind and lock them in a jar, Daniel pulled his crazed hair-brain ideas out of his exceptional consciousness and locked them away on this website. If you were ever in the need for research material on say . . . UFOs . . . you could find it on MakerOfTheMan.com. Let's also say you were in the need to read firsthand accounts of supernatural encounters, Daniel had them on there as well. There was a section dedicated to the shadow government running our country, a detailed autopsy of Big Foot as well as the Loch Ness Monster, a list of all the secret societies the world had to offer and the powerful men running them, and last but certainly not least, a complete detailed breakdown of every major Presidential assassination and national tragedy. MakerOfTheMan.com was a paranoid nut's wildest wet dream—or complete and utter terrifying nightmare—I'm not sure which one was more accurate.

"What's going on, brother?" Daniel said warmly as I entered his condo.

I told him that more was going on than I wanted to share. I asked how he had been and he said, "Same as always—busy as hell, tired as shit, and lonelier than a bastard."

That was Daniel's way of telling me he was happy and well.

"But what's going on with you?" he said curiously. "Why don't you want to share, and what brought you to D.C.?"

I sighed and laid it all out for him. I figured there was little use in hiding it, and I knew Daniel would get a kick out of the conspiracy aspect of the story, especially the part about the *Book of Thoth*. . . . And to my lack of surprise, I was right. I told him about my meetings with Mr. Vermil, the bizarre murders in Bosnia, the incident in Istanbul, my terrible fight with Gregory Hansen, and the uncovering of the book from inside the Suleiman Mosque. I basically told him everything short of my relationship with you in Iraq; he didn't need to know about that.

"All of that mess in Istanbul: the terrorist attack, the bomb, the gun fight on the street . . . that was you? . . . And you literally killed someone?" His tone was more amazed sounding than disgusted or accusatory.

I asked him if he had some liquor.

"*Damn*. . . . Who would have guessed that Willy C could be so bad ass." I think he was actually proud of me.

Daniel got up from his chair and went into the kitchen, returning with a bottle of Jack Daniels and couple of shot glasses with the words *Platinum* on them. He poured both of us a shot and then toasted: "To the coolest mother fucker I have ever met."

"To being alive," I thought was more appropriate.

We drank the shots and then Daniel went over to his shiny

new IKEA desk and opened a drawer, retrieving a small glass pipe as well as a clear sandwich baggie half-full of weed. "Can you imagine getting impaled?" he said nonchalantly. "Having a stake driven through your body?" He shook his head in disbelief as he packed a pinch of weed into the concave portion of the glass bowl.

Part of me believed that he simply couldn't comprehend everything I just told him, which is probably more than partially why he was having so much fun with it; had he seen the bodies dangling from the poles at that Bosnian house, he may not have had such an insensitive interest. But that was also how Daniel kind of worked; he hadn't really experienced anything outside of the silicon world he was so thoroughly immersed. He thought about death and horror like a middle school kid; it was like he lacked the ability to empathize, or lacked the ability to imagine life in someone else's shoes. I believe my story was nothing more to him than a movie he just watched or a video game he had yet to play—it was all just fun and games.

Daniel lifted the glass bowl to his mouth and proceeded to light the weed with an orange lighter. It crackled and smoked as he took long drags, eventually stopping to choke it out into huge clouds of marijuana smoke. "I bet being impaled sucks."

"That's the understatement of the century."

"So, you haven't told me why you're here."

"I came here in order to find someone who knows something about the Voynich manuscript. Have you ever—"

"No shit!" he choked out with several bursts of smoke. Apparently he had heard of it. "Are you telling me that crazy-ass book has something to do with the one you're looking for . . . the *Book of Thoth*?"

"We think there might be a connection, yes." I then pulled out the print out and showed it to him.

Daniel took the print out and looked at it a short moment before saying, "Yeah, that's it."

"What do you mean *that's it*?"

"That's Voynich"—he handed the print out back—"that's the same thing, or at least the same language."

"You're an expert now?"

"Did your expert disagree?"

"No, he was less cooperative than I had hoped. He thought it looked similar, but without me giving him all of the background, he wouldn't commit to an opinion."

"Why didn't you give him more info?"

I didn't know how to explain to Daniel my feelings inside the bookstore. "There was something about him that I didn't trust. The guy unnerved me a little."

Daniel offered me his bowl, which I declined. "I imagine your nerves are a little more than shot, my friend. You really should hit this; it might make you feel better."

"No thank you; the last thing I need is more paranoia."

He shrugged and took another go at it. The marijuana crackled and burned. "So . . . who is this guy anyway? Your expert."

"His name is Jonas Lundquist. He owns—"

"DUDE, WHAT? Did you just say Jonas Lundquist?!"

I had a feeling he had heard of him.

"Holy shit, holy shit, *holy shit!*" Daniel got up from his chair and began to pace around the room—his face was twisted in astonishment.

I asked what his deal was, and he said, "Dude . . . Jonas Lundquist is a fucking legend, man—a goddamn legend! Are you kidding me? You met with this guy today? He lives here in D.C.? . . . I should have known . . . of course he lives here. . . ."

I was dumbfounded. Only moments earlier I had told him about the terrible ordeal I had survived in Bosnia and Istanbul, about the mangled bodies impaled on poles, about the gun fight between mercenaries and police, and about killing a guy inside a speeding car—and this was what cranked his engine. . . ?

"Jonas Lundquist is literally a fucking legend . . . he's like the modern conspiracy theorists' version of Santa Claus—I shit you not. He was in charge of a little organization you may have heard of—PARDUS."

"PARDUS, yeah—I've never heard of it, but I did see a document on his desk that had the title 'PARDUS—GIZA.' "

"*You . . . you . . . you what?*"—Daniel almost fell to the ground—"you *actually* saw a document titled 'PARDUS'?"

The level of significance of what I saw on Jonas's desk was becoming evident. I asked, "Why is he conspiracy theorists' version of Santa Claus?"

"*Because* . . . he has brought them so many gifts. Jonas Lundquist has single-handedly fueled about a dozen different conspiracies over the past fifty years. . . . I can't believe you met him—*today!*"

"Well what are these conspiracies? Do they have something to do with the Voynich manuscript or his work with the intelligence community?"

"What do you think? . . . Of course! More so with the latter, but yes." Daniel took another hit on his bowl before explaining. "PARDUS, it's everything man."

"Yeah, right, but what is it?"

Daniel offered the bowl to me again. "It's an acronym for Paranormal Activities Research Division of the United States—or possibly of United Sciences—no one is certain which one it is, but regardless, they both make up PARDUS."

I couldn't say I had ever heard of it.

"I mention them on my website. PARDUS was once a branch of the National Science Foundation. Congress pumps about 7 billion dollars a year into NSF research. The NSF, in return, has funded some one hundred and eighty Nobel Prize winning projects. You can look up all of this online. PARDUS eventually splintered from the NSF sometime around the 1960s or 70s . . . again, speculated but everyone agrees that PARDUS runs solo now, even though they are funded by the NSF."

"How are they solo if the NSF funds them?"

"Think of the NSF as a government money launderer."

"A *government* money launderer?"

"Yeah."

"The United States *Federal* Government?"

Daniel nodded.

I held in my sigh of pain. "Okay, continue."

"The NSF was founded so the government could hide and

expand their spending on controversial technologies."

"Why do they need to hide their spending? It's the government's job to be developing the newest and greatest things."

Daniel took a long uncomfortable moment before answering. "Some things are better left unknown. Some things need to be hidden."

I knew what would come next; it was the moment when Daniel would go off on some UFO conspiracy tirade.

"The general public can't handle the truths of our world. They can't handle our true reality."

"And what's that?" I asked disconcertingly.

He picked up his bowl and lit the ashy pot for another hit. The smoke oozed out his nose and blasted out his mouth when he spoke. "Extra-Terrestrials."

I couldn't hold my sigh in any longer and checked the time. "Okay, man."

"No, seriously—it all makes sense to me. Everything you told me tonight, this *Book of Thoth*, this supposed power it holds which gives the user incredible psychic abilities. . . . I would bet my left nut that the Paranormal Activities Research Division is somehow responsible for what happened in Bosnia."

"How so? I thought psychic powers gave a person the ability to see into the future."

Daniel waved his hand in disgust. "That's all bullshit. The future hasn't been written, man. No one can read an unwritten book. Psychic powers allow a person to see, feel, and speak beyond the conventional means we all use. A person with true psychic powers can alter the world around them and communicate with the beyond—like telepathy, or speaking to animals."

"Hang on, hang on," I said, "you think that this PARDUS wants the *Book of Thoth* because of the psychic powers that legend promises?"

"Yeah, sure—why not?"

"Are you forgetting what I told you about Dr. Bertók Horvath? I'm pretty sure that psychopath isn't working for our government."

"Are you?" said Daniel while leaning in closer. "You told me about some big operation at the Bosnian pyramid . . . how you came across American workers and what looked like a military operation. . . ."

"Okay, okay, I see where you're going with this but let me clarify something: I didn't *see* the United States military, and the equipment I saw isn't solely produced by the U.S.— there are large manufacturing companies that make that kind of equipment, like Aeronyte."

"Aeronyte, the company owned by the Wyldes?"

"Yeah, exactly. Simon Wylde has more money than he can spend, and he is very interested in the *Book of Thoth*. He has strong connections with the Bosnian government and could have easily organized the operation at Visoko."

****

The vision of Simon's dead eyes reentered Rebecca's mind.

****

Daniel thought about what I said for a long moment before

saying, "I don't like it."

"Yeah, neither do I."

"No, that's not what I mean—I don't like the theory. Why would Simon work with Dr. Bertók Horvath?"

"Because, Dr. Bertók Horvath is an expert on the region. Who else has the ability to locate the *Book of Thoth* than him?"

"Yeah, okay, but . . . I don't know. . . . What about the soldiers who tried to kill you?"

"I told you. They were mercenaries. Anyone with lots of money can hire mercenaries."

Daniel looked like he was contemplating my argument.

"Besides, psychic powers and all of that bullshit is nothing more than tricks—an elaborate magic show."

"An elaborate *magic* show?" Daniel said almost sounding as if he was hurt by the statement.

"You know what I mean. There is no scientific evidence that any of this psychic shit is for real."

He almost choked on that proclamation. "*No evidence?* Are you fucking kidding me? No evidence? How the hell do you know?"

I didn't.

"No evidence? How's this for evidence?" Daniel popped up from the recliner and hurried over to a bookshelf. He pulled out several books that had decent thickness and then tossed them to me. "Take a look at those. Tell me if you actually see them or if they are imaginary."

I looked at the titles. One book was titled *Psi Spies*, written by Jim Marrs; another was *Psychic Wars*, written by a man named Gruber; and the third was titled *Psychic Battlefield*, written by a man named Mandlebad. All three of them promised to give insight into the government's secret fascination with human psychic abilities.

"Those books are just the tip of the iceberg, my friend. Secret government psychic programs have been going on for over fifty years. There have been hundreds of books written about them—" He then quickly raised a hand, "And I know what you're about to say, 'They're probably written by a bunch of quacks,' but that's far from the truth. Some of them might be quacks but most of them are not."

"Name one that's not," I challenged.

He pointed to the ones in my hands. "Those ones aren't."

I reread the authors but I had never heard of any of them.

"Have you ever heard of Dr. Saño Wining, Ingo Swann, or Dr. Harold Puthoff?"

"Nope."

Daniel looked disappointed. "Ingo Swann and Dr. Puthoff both worked out of the Stanford Research Institute. I'm sure you've heard of that."

In fact I had. SRI was a new technology think tank filled with some of the brightest minds this world had to offer. "Okay, so what did they do?"

"Ingo Swann and Dr. Puthoff are the founding fathers of 'Remote Viewing.'"

I had no idea what he was talking about.

"Remote Viewing is a psychic process where the mind travels to a specified location and views the area, sending visions back. Usually the Remote Viewer can verbally describe what they saw or draw the visions on paper."

"Sounds absurd."

"Well how's this for absurd, Ingo Swann became so good at it that he developed an eighty percent accuracy rating under tough scrutinized testing."

"Who did the testing?"

"Dr. Puthoff and SRI."

It still sounded far-fetched. "Okay, if this is true then how come no one ever talks about it?"

"Because it's powerful," Daniel responded. "The government doesn't want people to know how powerful the human brain is."

"And that's what PARDUS does? They're experimenting with Remote Viewing?"

"Oh, way more than that!" he announced excitedly. "The first guy I mentioned, Dr. Saño Wining, took this new science much further than Remote Viewing. The shit he was capable of doing . . . well . . . it's pretty frightening."

"So who's Dr. Saño Wining? Did he write a book?"

Daniel shook his head. "He's dead now, and so is his entire team, I think."

"How do you know about him then?"

"Back in 2001, an alleged former CIA Officer named Thomas Kinsella gave an interview in regards to the Psi Spy programs the CIA were running. The story was an exposé on the government's early interest in psychic power, and it covered the foundation of the Psi Spies through their demise in the mid-90s. The article was published in *Psychology Today*. Kinsella claimed to have once been the head of the Office of Strategic Intelligence and in charge of developing men with psychic abilities in order to help National Security. That's how he met Dr. Wining. According to him, Dr. Saño Wining was the most developed psychic he had ever met. He told the journalist that Saño was light years beyond Ingo Swann and SRI. He said when remote viewing was still trying to figure out its use, Saño was already executing operations for his department."

"What kind of operations?" I asked.

"Well, Kinsella never actually said but there are plenty of others that have since come forward. According to them, Saño was an expert at mind control. They said that he had developed the ability to get inside a target's head and alter his thought pattern."

"How do you mean?"

Daniel lit up his dying pinch of marijuana and blew out a thin cloud of smoke. "I mean Saño was able to make someone think something . . . different." Daniel leaned forward in his chair. "I've looked pretty deep into this. Saño supposedly had the ability to make you think you had to do something. Like he had the power to speak directly to your mind." Daniel's voice grew somewhat quieter but more serious. "One guy said he was the target in a training mission and that Saño convinced him that he needed to try dog food. The guy said he felt overwhelmingly compelled to go to the grocery and buy dog food, just to try it out. He said it just sounded so delicious all of a sudden."

"Did he?" I asked.

Daniel grew a smirk and shook his head. "I guess he got all the way to the cashier before he finally regained his senses.

Can you imagine that, though?"

I had once tried dog food when I was seven. It wasn't good. "So he was able to influence people?"

"Pretty much. Saño basically became the voice in your head."

"So what operations did he conduct?"

Daniel's demeanor stiffened a bit. "You wouldn't believe me if I told you."

"Try me anyway."

Daniel looked down at his bowl and realized it was cashed. He hammered out the ash onto his palm and scraped it into the trash. "Well, you know how I said he became the voice in your head? Well I started looking around and did some searches on people claiming to hear voices and I found some startling revelations."

"And?"

Daniel almost appeared nervous. "I think Saño was involved in several assassination attempts. And I think he succeeded in a few."

"Who? Which ones?"

"Well I had to narrow my search to the time period Saño would have been in operation and that took me to the 1970's and early 80's."

I considered who might have been killed during those years—political figures, military personnel, etc. But I came up short. "Who?"

Daniel hesitated before saying the name. "John Lennon."

At first the name sounded foreign to me. My mind was

swishing through banks of political figures and John Lennon didn't ring a bell. However, with that being said, it probably only took me half a second to understand who he was talking about. "John Lennon? From *The Beatles?*"

Daniel only nodded.

"Why the hell would the CIA want John Lennon dead?"

"Seriously?" he said in such disbelief as if implying that John Lennon was the equivalent to some worldwide terrorist. "John Lennon was the figurehead of a forthcoming revolution. He was the Chairman of Reform. He was asking questions that challenged the relevance of religion. John Lennon was dangerous."

I hardly saw John Lennon as a threat to the national security of the United States. "You really think this Saño guy killed John Lennon?"

"I don't think he physically did it, no. But John Lennon's assassin claimed that the voices in his head told him to do it. I think Saño was that voice."

Whatever legitimacy this conversation had was quickly fleeting. "Saño was the voice in this guy's head?" My tone was a bit sarcastic.

"Believe what you want, man," Daniel said defensively. "I said you wouldn't believe it."

He was right. I should have just listened to his warning. "Fine, and who were the others? *Elvis?*"

Daniel didn't find it funny. "Forget it, man. Figure it out on your own."

"Come on now, I'll be serious. Who was another?"

He hesitated again and looked as if he really doubted

whether he should name another. "Fine. I think Saño *tried* to kill President Ronald Reagan."

The name-dropping had only gotten better. "You think that John Hinckley, Jr. was controlled by this Saño guy?"

"Reagan was throwing gasoline on an already volatile fire known as the Cold War. I think it's very possible that the CIA wanted him out of there in the name of national security. You have to remember what they did to JFK."

Right, I thought. Of course I had to buy into the CIA assassination of the former President John F. Kennedy in order to *remember what they did*. "You think Saño controlled Lee Harvey Oswald as well?"

"Of course not. The timeline is all wrong. . . ." he then realized I wasn't serious. "Forget you, man."

I couldn't help but to laugh. "I'm sorry, the past couple of days have been one long string of conspiracy theories. It's hard to believe this is how my life is ending up."

"You talk as if you're dying," Daniel pointed out.

Oh I was dying all right; I'd been dying since the day I decided to go to Iraq. "Speaking of dying, how did this Saño guy die?"

Daniel simply shrugged as if it was never mentioned before. "I'm not sure. I think he had cancer or something."

It was always hard to sort the bullshit from the truth with Daniel. Most things that came out of his mouth were poorly researched, harebrained ideas, but inside some of those ideas laid a certain level of truth—and sometimes facts. "So how does Jonas Lundquist fit in with all of this?"

"He's the founder of PARDUS. He was an original member of the NSF and led smaller, less significant experiments in paranormal science. No one seems to know anything about his earlier career or how he got involved with the NSF; though some speculate he was initially involved with the original CIA: the Office of Strategic Services, particularly the Psychological Warfare Division, before the OSS was broken up by President Truman. The NSF was formed five years later and Lundquist popped up on the public radar for the first time.

"Anyway, it was within the NSF that he met Dr. Saño Wining. His supervisor was a guy named Thomas Kinsella from the Office of Strategic Intelligence. Kinsella put Lundquist and Dr. Wining together because he thought the two of them would grow the field of mind control. It was the collaboration of these two as well as the NSF with the CIA's OSI that brought about the need for a specialized division: PARDUS. The NSF funded and covered their research and Kinsella from the OSI gave them their objectives. There was a twenty-year period, 1960s-1980s, that Jonas Lundquist grew the team and the amount of substantial progress in the field of mind control. That experiment I told you about—where Dr. Wining convinced a guy to buy and eat dog food—that was led by Lundquist. He built an entire team of men who could do these things. And it wasn't long before we—the public—started to see its terrible power."

"The assassinations?" I said dryly.

"Right; exactly."

"And so what about his research into Voynich? How does that tie in? I don't know the legitimacy of these other things you're talking about, but I do know people believe he was an expert on the language. How does Voynich tie in to PARDUS?"

Daniel thought about that for a moment before admitting, "I don't know. But it has to have something to do with the

Book of Thoth."

"But that's not possible; no one knew there was a link until, like, yesterday! If Jonas Lundquist was interested in Voynich, it had to be because of some other reason."

Daniel thought on that for a moment before saying, "Well, it was an unknown language. . . . I don't know. . . . I mean, I do know that the intelligence community wanted it cracked for their own encoding purposes—because no one else knew how to read it—but why Jonas Lundquist took so much interest in it . . . ?"

And that was pretty much where our conversation ended. We got off the subject for a little while but my brain never stopped processing everything. Even a few hours or so later when I made my bed on his couch—Daniel was gracious enough to let me stay at his apartment for the night—I still considered everything he told me and wondered which part of it was the "truth." Daniel swore all of it was but I knew better then to take everything he said at face value. But how much needed to be taken seriously, I wouldn't know until much later.

CHAPTER TWENTY-EIGHT

The Dead Sands

It was past midday when William and the four warriors arrived at the Desert Demon camp, if one could call it a camp. There were eight gigantic elephants forming an octagonal shape fitted with harnesses made of an unidentifiable wood with tall poles connected to a canvas covering that greatly resembled the camouflage covers William and the four warriors wore. Each elephant was amply spaced from the other, which created roughly four hundred square feet of cover. Underneath the canvas were seven camels with riders as well as a sparse group of men and women. There were four men carrying a platform that held a stone cauldron as well as some unrecognizable types of vegetables.

As William drew closer to the table, he saw that there was actually a small fire heating the cauldron and a liquid bubbling deep inside. There was no longer a wonder why it took William and the warriors so long to find the camp. *It's a traveling caravan.*

The wide-nosed warrior led William away from the three others and deep into the slow moving caravan to an older woman riding on a camel. The warrior said, "*Potrizza bella deshonn ilk. Ida borressello da muncianno.*"

The old woman mumbled something back to the warrior and then said to William, "I hear you cost much."

Shocked to hear a familiar language, William said, "I'm sorry?"

The woman did not look kind. "You cost us much."

It was an awkward statement to hear. "I'm sorry. . . ."

The woman was not impressed.

"I didn't ask to come along, just so you know. Saño forced me to leave my post. And then—"

"The post that would kill you," interrupted the woman. "Saño saved you, no?"

William considered his response before giving it. "In hindsight, yes."

"Five of our brave left to find you and Saño, and four return. You cost us much."

"I didn't ask to be saved."

"But you could not save yourself."

"I didn't need saved until Saño came into my life."

"Saño found you because he knew you would die elsewise."

"How could he know that?"

"Saño was a *siedo-vas*—in your words, a *seeker of men*. He saw you and he saw others. He knew what was coming, even if you did not."

"How?"

"He used his third eye."

"His third eye?"

"Yes. Saño had an ability that many of us do not. He saw things that we cannot. He could see you, William Coulee, as you sat in your post. He could see you sweating on the roof. He could see you on your journeys through the sands. And when time came, he knew he needed to interfere, and the Kaa granted him this act."

"The Kaa?"

"Kaa is our chosen leader. My people have been led by Kaa since the days of Nugia, a thousand lifetimes ago."

"Why was Saño watching me?"

"Kaa can explain. Kaa is wise in many ways that I am not. Kaa knows your importance; that is why you lived and Saño died."

"How far do we have to travel?"

"As far as it takes to find *Kaacital*, the *city of Kaa.*"

"You don't know where it is?"

"*Kaacital* is never in the same place. This is how my people live."

"Do your people ever rest?"

"We rest when we can travel no further."

William was at the point where he could travel no further.

The old woman whistled and waved for a lone camel rider to join her. When the young man arrived, she said something to him in their native tongue and the man halted his camel and climbed down. The old woman then said to William, "You ride and rest. You are not one of us. You rest and learn how to travel."

"I don't know how to ride a camel."

"You will learn." The old woman pulled away from them, as did much of the camp. William went over to the young man who said not a word but tapped the camel on its front left leg with a stick. He camel knelt on all four limbs. William walked to the side of the camel and considered how to climb onto its back. The young man gave a demonstration on how to climb onto the animal, and William tried to do as instructed. His legs were very tired and sore; he had a difficult time getting one leg over the cloth saddle and situating himself. Once he was immediately on top, the young man clicked his tongue three times and the camel stood up. William felt his back muscles pull in several directions before the animal eased into a steady walk. The young man hurriedly led the camel back to the traveling caravan and under the cover. *Great*, William thought, more *traveling*. His stomach grumbled angrily and he felt very weak, but he was thankful for the rest, even if it was on top of a lumpy animal. *To Kaacital we go.*

CHAPTER TWENTY-NINE

District 4, Sector 2

Rebecca had not slept well. The ground was horribly uncomfortable. It seemed Roland tossed and turned every minute or so, jarring her to consciousness, and her legs were sore from all that had transpired during the day. Rebecca wasn't sure how long she had read for, but she knew it wasn't much; her eyes bothered her to the point of needing to stop, but her mind wouldn't quit. William's words ran circles in her head, the memory of Simon's death was on constant replay, and those damned coyotes, as well as Roland's injury, haunted her every second. So there was no sleep for the weary Rebecca. She eventually gave up trying; the sun had risen and a new day had begun.

Rebecca stood up on achy legs and stepped outside the cave. Roland was still huddled on the ground; his arm was tucked in a way that would not allow her to examine his wound without the risk of waking him, so she stepped over top of him and hobbled into the bright morning sun.

Overhead, there were birds flying about, chirping their odd calls. The sky was partially covered with clouds, and the sun was hot on Rebecca's skin. The air was extra-heavy; there was a lot of moisture that day. Rebecca noticed that the leaves on the neighboring trees were dripping with morning dew. She also noticed that she had developed an odd rash on both arms: tiny bumps that neither itched nor burned, they just existed. She ran her hands through her tangled hair and felt several knots. *Great,* she thought. It was a silly, mundane thing to be upset about, but even when in dire survival situations, people still tend to focus on the unimportant.

It was not long after Rebecca left the cave that Roland awoke and joined her outside. He had his arms crossed and was a bit hunched over; he was showing signs of having a fever.

"Are you okay?" asked Rebecca; she was sitting on a large rock. "Let me see your arm." She slid off the boulder and walked up to him. Roland stretched out his left arm. Rebecca took it with both hands and examined the sock dressing—which was caked in dry blood—before unknotting it and tossing it to the ground. The wounds were scabby and open in many areas. The wounds were seeping with some kind of ooze, and the skin around it was yellow and ill looking. Rebecca also noticed that his arm was mighty warm feeling. She placed a hand onto Roland's forehead; it was warm too. "I think you have a fever."

"I'm pretty cold," he confessed.

"There's no knowing what kind of disease or germs those coyotes carry. We're going to need to call for help."

Roland pulled his arm away and said, "No, not yet. I'm fine . . . at least I'll be fine for a little while. I don't want to give up just yet."

"I don't want you to die either."

"If you call, then I'll be dead for sure—and so will you."

"We don't know that. But what I do know is that an infection will certainly kill you."

"So die now or later; I choose later."

Rebecca realized it was an argument she could not win. If she wanted to call for help, she would have to do it without Roland knowing.

Roland removed his other sock and said, "Can you please tie this one around my arm?"

Rebecca nodded and took the sock from him; she tied it tight and then pulled him in for a hug. "You aren't going to die."

"Everyone dies, Becca," he said quietly.

There was a moment during the embrace that a kiss might have been in order, but it quickly passed, and they pulled away. Roland didn't know it at the time, and neither did Rebecca, but that moment would never come again.

Rebecca's stomach grumbled with hunger pains, and she said, "We should get going."

Roland nodded and agreed.

The two of them embarked on another hike after Rebecca put Simon's shoes back on. The day's travel was a lot slower than the previous, mainly because Rebecca and Roland were exhausted and unfed. Roland's infection played a part as well, but only after several hours of walking in the humid heat.

"How far are you in the translation?" he asked during one of their many rest breaks.

"Not far enough. There is so much to read. Do you want to hear about it?"

Roland usually refused, preferring ignorance for safety sake, but this time he accepted her invitation.

Rebecca filled him in on everything that had happened in William's manuscript, and then she gave him her assessment. "I think William is indicating that the *Book of Thoth* is what gives our Ministry its power. All of this stuff about mind control, death, and power, is essentially what we know about our own past."

"What do you mean? I don't recall there being anything about mind control and killing people to take their bodies in our history."

"Our history is full of it, Roland. Just think about Ziusudra. He supposedly never dies, and he supposedly has power over all of Earth's creatures. The *Book of Thoth* reminds me of Ziusudra."

"But what does that have to do with mind control?"

"Haven't you ever heard of the Ministry's Thought Police? Men who can get inside a person's head and interrogate them? All of this stuff that Daniel tells William inside the translation deals with mind control. It is a lot like what I've heard about the Thought Police."

Roland considered her point for a moment. He was noticeably shivering, but it wasn't due to the things Rebecca had told him. "I guess you have a good point. I just want to know what you're supposed to do with this information. I'm worried that none of it will be useful."

Rebecca fully understood his concern; it was the same concern she carried. "Its meaning will become more clear the further I read. . . . It has to."

"I hope so, Becca."

Sharp pains returned to Rebecca's stomach and she felt a bit light headed. She gave a tired sigh and said, "We have to keep walking. Are you ready?"

Roland didn't move; he sat there staring at the ground with his injured arm tucked into his stomach. "I know we haven't mentioned it yet—or really talked about it at all—but I'm surprised that we haven't been caught. I mean, how hard is it to find two people walking through the jungle? The MSF have so many tools to use; they should have found us by now."

Rebecca had been so preoccupied with surviving that the thought of being found by the MSF was really never in the forefront of her mind. "You have a point. Why haven't they caught us?"

"Does it mean that they aren't looking for us?"

"I don't know." *Does it mean that?* "Simon was so convinced that Jonas wanted us dead, but does he though?"

"Maybe Jonas just wanted Simon dead."

"The soldiers weren't very choosy. They attacked me just as much as him."

"That doesn't mean that they were trying to kill you specifically."

"I guess that's true." *Where are we going with this?* "Are you thinking about turning us in?"

Roland was hesitant to respond; his face dripped with sweat. "No . . . I just . . . I'm just thinking about our options . . . just thinking." He wiped his face with his one good hand and then changed the subject. "You should probably keep reading, Becca. You have to, right? You have to if we're to ever get out of this situation."

Rebecca sighed. "I don't know how it will save us from this jungle."

Roland shook his head. "That isn't what I meant. I mean overall, for everyone in the Collective."

Rebecca decided not to respond; she was afraid of her answer. "We should get walking."

"You should get reading."

"You want me to read while we walk?"

"For all of our sakes—yes."

Rebecca was shocked by Roland's support. She nodded her head and said, "Okay. Let's go."

Rebecca turned on Simon's notepad and the two of them continued onward. She found where she had left off.

William had just finished his conversation with Daniel about PARDUS and he was trying to decide how much of what Daniel said was factual and how much of it was fiction.

****

The following day, after Daniel left to go into the office, he allowed me to hang around his place and use the computer for research. I needed to know more about the Voynich manuscript and Jonas Lundquist's involvement with it over the years. If one thing came out of my brief meeting with the man, and my conversation with Daniel, it was that something was extremely fishy. So I decided to start with the beginning.

Where did the manuscript come from, who wrote it, when was it written, and what was its purpose? And of course, none of those questions had definitive answers.

—The following is the result of my struggle with how much to share with you, Rebecca. I don't presently know how much information you need to know, but I also don't want to vomit everything upon you because of how confusing it all can become. So please know that the following is an abridged version of what I learned that day, and I apologize if any of it seems worthless or nonsensical—

A quick Internet search told me that the Voynich manuscript was extremely mysterious and carried many different theories as to when it was written and by whom. Its first record in known history was in a letter written in 1666 AD, claiming that Emperor Rudolf II bought the manuscript sometime during the years of 1552 AD and 1612 AD. It was then given to a man, Jacobus Horcicky de Tepenecz, who was head of the emperor's botanical gardens. This is known because Tepenecz was known for writing his name in all of his books, and it was discovered that his name was written on the first page of the manuscript.

From there it ended up in the library of a man named Georg Baresch who, like all before and after him, failed to unlock the manuscript's secrets. He sent a request for help in 1639 AD to a scholar named Kircher asking for help regarding the script. Kircher came up empty but was fascinated by the book and eventually acquired it through several exchanges in 1666 AD, which the aforementioned letter accompanied it.

The manuscript then disappeared for the next 200 years but more than likely remained in Kircher's library, which was acquired by the Roman College, until it was purchased by Wilfrid Voynich in 1912 AD—as Jonas Lundquist had already told me.

What I found interesting, and worth further pursuit, was that inside the 1666 letter Kircher's friend had mentioned that Emperor Rudolph believed that the manuscript was written by an English man named Roger Bacon, who lived between the years 1214 AD- 1294 AD—a little over a hundred years before the estimated date of the manuscript. This was important to me because—if you recall from what I wrote much earlier, during my initial meeting with Mr. Vermil, Simon Wylde, Professor Haggins, Iah Vadimas, and Dr. Thatcher—the Albigensian Crusade, which eradicated the Cathars, the people supposedly hiding the *Book of Thoth*, took place between the years 1209 AD and 1229 AD. It was this latter couple of years, when the *Book of Thoth* was broken into fourths and carried away from

France, when Roger Bacon was fifteen years old and living in Paris, France. He was attending the University of Paris in 1228 AD when an uprising occurred and he was sent back to England.

What you are about to read next, like so many things, there was no substantial evidence of, just an instinctual connection of the dots, but it was easy for me to see a Cathar in hiding, carrying one quarter of the *Book of Thoth* in Paris, seeking out a young impressionable mind who might take the piece of book with him back to his home country for safe keeping. And of course I saw Roger Bacon as that impressionable mind. Here's why:

He was extremely talented in the fields of science and mathematics. He was a strong proponent for experimental science and research, and he opposed those who insisted on closing their minds to these things.

Around the time he was in Paris, and during the time of the fleeing Cathars, a newly established order had grown in strength, known as the Order of the Friars Minor (or the Franciscan Friars). Francis of Assisi was the founder. They were much like the Cathars but loyal to the Pope. And here is something I found quite curious about Francis, he was known for his wisdom and his *uncanny ability to speak with animals.*

I read that his order was very successful in converting many Cathars, and that the two groups were essentially one. So it was easy for me to see how a Cathar fleeing persecution, and hiding a quarter of the *Book of Thoth,* would seek refuge within this group ordained by the Cathar's single most terrifying enemy. And maybe this Cathar was at the end of his life, or maybe he was worried that his possession of the book would be discovered (since Franciscan Friars were forbidden to have possessions or write books), and that was why he entrusted it to Roger Bacon. I guess I could speculate forever on this, but the point I'm trying to make is that Bacon eventually became a Franciscan Friar too! So he was clearly impressed by them; and like his predecessors, the Cathars, he was persecuted for his ideas and spent many years imprisoned.

But then you might be thinking, "What about the Voynich manuscript dating to a hundred years after his death?" To that, I say: It was rewritten—or copied down.

As I had already learned, books were copied and recopied. It was a common method used for preservation. Texts back then fell apart very easily. I guess it would be silly to assume otherwise. So, with that stated, it was quite possible that Roger Bacon wrote his own copy of the quarter of manuscript entrusted to him, and then it passed on to another, and to another, before being copied again and passed on again, until it eventually ended up in Emperor Rudolph's court.

But with all of this, I was still no closer to knowing whether the Voynich manuscript was a brother of the manuscript I had located in Istanbul, nor had I come closer to why Jonas Lundquist became so infatuated with it.

I decided that I needed to present these findings to Mr. Vermil and company in order to see if anything resonated.

****

"I have to stop," Roland announced.

"What's wrong?" Rebecca asked.

Roland looked very pale, and he was trembling. "I can't continue. I need to stop and rest."

Rebecca found a place for Roland to lie down. There was a small creek nearby, and she was able to transport a little bit of water over to him. His fever was like wildfire; it was consuming his entire body. And Rebecca knew that the worst part was that neither of them would survive if they didn't keep moving, and yet Roland was completely incapable at this point, *which means that if I want to survive then I need to leave him behind.* But that wasn't going to happen.

"You should go," Roland said, as if he had read her mind.

"Go where," she said, playing dumb.

"Keep walking. You should keep walking and leave me behind. I'll be okay."

"We'll both be okay," she told him confidently. "You just need to rest and save up your strength. We'll *both* continue when you're ready."

"I don't think I'll be ready. . . ."

Rebecca shushed him. "Rest."

True horror entered Rebecca's heart for the first time since she fled the Collective six months ago.

Roland was dying.

CHAPTER THIRTY

District 4, Sector 2

Rebecca sat on the ground next to Roland as he slept. He had been asleep for nearly ten minutes, and was trembling from the fever. She tried to make a blanket out of sticks and leaves, but it was useless; Roland's fever was more than she could help.

You have to get help, she told herself. *Roland will die if you don't do something. And then you'll die.* Rebecca was scared, truly scared. She didn't know what was more frightening, Roland's death or her own impending doom. And she felt terrible about it.

She wondered, *Should I leave him to see if there is anything further out? I wouldn't be abandoning him; I would be looking for help. Would he be okay—will he be okay?* There was no answer to comfort her. *I have to do something other than sitting.* Rebecca stood up and looked at Simon's notepad lying on the ground. *No, I can't call for help. That was never an option, no matter how much he pretended it to be.* She walked away from Roland and into the foliage, glancing back once to see if he noticed; he didn't. *I'll be right back.*

I promise.

Rebecca walked on; her head was light and her legs were wobbly, but she continued the journey. *It's so peaceful out here*, she thought. *I guess there could be worse places to die.* Rebecca looked up at the exotic trees and saw some kind of animal, *a bird*, she thought, perched upon a branch. *Dying in Cognitive Services would be worse. Or getting impaled like the Free People down in the Vriezen; that would be much worse.* She walked and she walked. Every so often, she turned back to see if she could see Roland; she never did.

Rebecca stopped and leaned against a mossy green tree. Her stomach was hurting like nothing she had felt before. *It's eating itself*, she thought. "I'm eating myself," she laughed out, even though it wasn't funny. *There's no one out here to hear me. I can say what I want.* "I hate you, Minister Theoman! I hate you with all that is left of me!" She laughed some more. "Oh mom, if you could see me now. Dad—Corbin—whoever you are—if you could see your daughter now. I'm dying! And this is how it ends. I'm nothing special. I'm no great savior. I'm nothing! This damned book has begun the end of me, nothing more. And now it's almost complete!"

Rebecca was trembling horribly. Her strength was gone. Her ears were ringing. *Is this it? Am I going to die right here? This can't be the time. I'm still standing.*

There was a rustling sound coming from somewhere indiscernible. *The animals are coming to eat me*, she thought. *The coyotes are back.*

Weary and sick, Rebecca stumbled away from the tree and looked all around.

"Don't move!" shouted a voice.

Did I just hear that? she wondered. Rebecca stood still. "Hello?"

The rustling noise became louder. Rebecca turned her head to the left and literally saw the jungle moving!

Now she was really immobile; just her eyes blinked and her lungs breathed.

The moving jungle took human form. There were five—now six—now ten—now fifteen! The numbers continued. The lead figure was next to Rebecca at this point. He had no face, it was hidden inside some kind of special helmet, and his clothes were not clothes at all but some kind of special suit that reflected the world around it; and it was presently reflecting Rebecca, which created a truly surreal shroud of her own image.

"Are you real?" asked Rebecca.

The figure reached up and lifted its mask off; it was a woman with light skin, dark eyebrows, a couple of small scars on her forehead and right cheek, dark brown eyes, and a dimple in the middle of her chin.

Rebecca blinked hard and said, "Hello?"

The woman looked at her curiously. "What are you doing out here? Are you alone?"

Relief washed all over Rebecca as she began to realize what she was looking at. *This is my rescue!* "My name is Rebecca Badeau! I was being rescued from the Ministry when my hovercar crashed! We've been wandering out here for two days with no food or water!"

"We? Who else is with you?" The woman guided Rebecca to the ground, so she could sit. The woman produced a canteen of water and handed it to Rebecca.

"There were three of us; one died. The other, Roland, the one who rescued me, he's . . ." but she had no idea which direction she had come from. "Oh no! He's . . . he's really hurt. Coyotes attacked us, and he was bitten. He has a fever. I left him to find help. But now . . . I can't remember which way I walked!"

"Take a drink, ma'am. Relax." The woman looked over her right shoulder and said, "Garret—"

"I'm already looking into it," Garret said. He had apparently listened to everything Rebecca said, as did nearly all of the other camouflaged soldiers.

The woman looked to Rebecca and said, "Why were you being rescued?"

Rebecca found it difficult to concentrate. Her mind was fully occupied by Roland's safety; but despite that, she told them everything. She told them about Simon, about the attempt to have them murdered, and about Roland's rescue attempt. She even told them about being the daughter of Corbin Byrne, throwing all caution into the wind.

This grabbed everyone's attention.

"You're the daughter of Corbin Byrne?" asked the woman, her eyes wide.

Garret took a step forward, removed his mask, and said, "You're *Rebecca*?"

Rebecca nodded, looking from Garret to the woman. "Can you see him—Roland? We have to find him; he saved my life!"

Garret eyed her curiously before finally saying, "I'll find him." He then stepped away and returned to looking at some kind of digital device hanging from a strap around his neck.

The woman kneeling next to Rebecca tapped the canteen and said, "Drink." She then stood up and walked over to another person in full gear. They tried to have a quiet conversation but Rebecca could hear what they were saying, "Do you believe her?"

"I don't know. I don't think she's lying."

"So you believe her."

"I said I don't know. Just because she believes she's telling the truth, doesn't mean she is."

"Well, what are we going to do with her? We can't take her on the raid—especially if we find the other one. And we can't spare any soldiers to escort them back to base. . . ."

"I agree. But what other option do we have?"

"We could leave them. . . ."

"Come on, that's not an option."

"We could give them supplies, some aid for the wounded one, and then leave them behind—go on the raid—and then pick them up on the way back."

The man considered it for a moment and said, "If she is who she claims . . . do you really want to risk leaving Corbin Byrne's daughter alone in the jungle? What if we fail?"

"Failure isn't an option."

"Right—but what if?"

The woman sighed. She looked at Rebecca, noticed that Rebecca was listening, and then guided the man away so they could talk in private. *Don't leave us here*, thought Rebecca.

"I found him," Garret said, returning. "He's about a mile away northeast of here."

Rebecca looked up at him with hopeful eyes. "Is he alive?"

"I don't know. This reads heat signals, and he's producing heat."

Garret walked away from her and went to the woman and the other man to deliver the news. The three of them stood chatting for a moment, or two, and then all three returned. The woman looked a bit unhappy. "Garret will escort you to your injured friend. He will have medicine to help him. Then the three of you will go back to our base so that they can verify your identity."

Rebecca gushed a sigh of relief and said, "*Thank you.*"

"Don't thank me yet," the woman said. "Your friend might be too far gone, and you have a long walk still ahead of you. And, if you aren't who you say you are . . ."

"I'm not worried about that; I know who I am."

The woman nodded to Garret and then looked at Rebecca. "We'll see. . . . Good luck."

CHAPTER THIRTY-ONE

District 4, Sector 2

The Free People Fighters didn't waste time. Garret gathered the resources needed in a matter of minutes, just before the rest of the platoon began trekking through the jungle again. "We should get going too," he told Rebecca.

"Where are they heading?"

"There is a Ministry depot buried deep within the mountains over there"—Garret pointed behind them.

Rebecca looked and realized that was the direction she was heading before their encounter. "Are there MSF agents at the depot?"

"Yup."

"How many?"

"Enough," he said.

Rebecca felt her stomach turn; she realized, *I would have been captured.* "How far away is your base?"

"From your friend? About seven miles."

Rebecca thought dreadfully, *Seven miles. . . .*

"Do you have something I can eat?" asked Rebecca.

Garret slipped off a pack slung on his back and dug a hand inside. "I have several rations—here," he pulled a round package out and handed it to Rebecca. "Pull the tab on the side and the lid will open."

Rebecca thanked him and located the tab. She pulled on it, breaking the seal of the ration, and then pried open the lid. Inside were chalky dehydrated food-squares. Normally, a person applied water to Ministry produced dehydrated food before consumption. "Do I eat this as is?"

Garret nodded. "It tastes like it looks, but you'll get used to it."

Rebecca was so hungry that it didn't matter how it tasted. She picked out a square—a brown pockmarked one—and took a bite out of it. The piece crumbled in her mouth and melted on her tongue. It tasted like pudding.

"That's your dessert," Garret informed her.

Rebecca made noises of pleasure as she continued eating. The meal consisted of pudding, oranges, beans, and some kind of protein supplement that neither Rebecca nor Garret could identify.

Rebecca finished it quickly. A little too fast, actually. Her stomach felt like it was going to rip. She needed to take her mind off the discomfort; she asked Garret, "How long have you been fighting for the Free People?"

He was hesitant to answer. "Almost a year now, but it feels longer, like I've been doing this my entire life."

Rebecca could relate; that was how she would describe her life over the past six months, since being married to Simon.

Garret looked at her, and said, "I met your father, by the way."

Rebecca's mind immediately thought of Francis—her default—but then she realized Garret was talking about Corbin.

Garret continued, "I was part of the team that freed him." He explained how he used the Equalizer to bring down the MSF transport, and how he nearly killed Corbin in the fighting afterward. "I thought he was dead. The beam from the Equalizer cuts through everything. But it turned out that I had missed his head by a few feet. . . . Thank God for that. . ."

"God?" Rebecca said, surprised to hear him use that name. "What do you mean?"

Garret seemed surprised by her question. "You don't know who God is?"

"I have an idea." God was a name she was becoming more and more familiar with, but she wanted to hear Garret's take on him. Rebecca said. "He's The Creator, right?"

"That's what they say. . . . Your father talks about God, and how he will free everyone from tyranny. God is supposed to return to Earth—"

"Right . . . I know that part. God is like Ziusudra."

"No, I think God is different from Ziusudra. Ziusudra walks the Earth, pretending to be God, but God is something else . . . or maybe something more. But I'm no expert."

"I am," declared Rebecca, "and I think my father is confusing God with Ziusudra. I think they are the same person but with different names. Ziusudra is immortal. He created the first Collective—meaning he created civilized man—which could be confused with creating man, making him The Creator."

Garret listened to her argument and didn't give a fight. "Like I said, I'm no expert. I just trust your father and hope that he leads us to victory."

"Why do you trust him so?" asked Rebecca; not that she needed an explanation for why Garret joined the Free People's Society.

Garret wasn't hesitant with his answer. "He says the right things. His ideas are hard to dispute. He has led our society for many years now, and we have never been stronger. It has led us out of obscurity and into the face of the world. The Ministry fears us because they know their time will end."

The Free People had definitely stirred up the Collective with their sporadic attacks on Ministry institutes, but Rebecca didn't see any indication that the Ministry was going to lose the war. She made those thoughts verbal and Garret said, "I'm not blind, and I'm not going to pretend that what we've done is all that is needed; we need more help—that is clear—and your father has a plan. I don't know the specifics, but he says he has a big card to play, and when the time is right, he'll play it."

What on Earth is that? thought Rebecca. *Is he talking about William's Book of Thoth . . . or Logos?* Rebecca sighed. *Is he really putting the lives of the Free People's Society in jeopardy because he believes a myth about a powerful book that will bring the world's savior?*

Rebecca noticed Garret staring at her; he said, "Are you okay?"

"Yes, sorry. I was just wondering what this Big Card could be. It's hard for me to imagine what secret weapon exists that could bring the Ministry down."

Garret stared at her with an uncertain expression. "I suppose your father doesn't share everything."

"I barely know my father. I had only met him for the first time six months ago."

Garret nodded his head. "I didn't know that."

"Why should you? Everyone assumes that I've had a secret relationship with him my entire life; the truth couldn't be more different. There is another man I know as my father, and he isn't a great leader or highly respected, but he raised me and took care of me, which is more than what Corbin did."

Garret didn't respond to her confession; the two of them walked in silence. The sinking feeling in Rebecca's stomach told her that she revealed too much. *Why did I tell him that?* She obviously still had anger toward her biological father, issues that time could not easily clear up.

Rebecca switched Simon's notepad from her right hand to her left. William's manuscript returned to her thoughts, Corbin's certainty that the manuscript will help bring about the savior also returned to her thoughts. Rebecca reflected on how lucky she was to download another copy. *I may never get that opportunity again.* She also realized that the odds of her getting the copy residing inside Simon's notepad were insurmountable. So many things—crucial, necessary things—had happened simultaneously, which opened the opportunity to download the translation. Was it all a coincidence, or was there something *more . . . ?*

"We're coming up on your friend," Garret announced while looking at the tracking device hanging around his neck. "He should be right past these—"

Rebecca didn't wait for him to finish. She rushed out ahead and tore through the brush blocking her way. She wanted to cry out Roland's name . . . but didn't.

Roland was lying there, just as she had left him. He looked like he was sleeping. . . .

He was sleeping.

"He's still alive," Rebecca called out.

Garret came over and knelt down next to him. He checked Roland's pulse and then retrieved the medical supplies he had stuffed inside a hip sack. "I'm no doctor, but I think his arm is very infected. I'm giving him the antibiotics the platoon medic suggested, and hopefully he will recover in the coming days. In the meantime, we have to figure out how we're going to transport him. I can't carry him for seven miles, and we can't call in for an airlift while the operation is being carried out. I can try to make a stretcher out of tree branches. . . ."

Rebecca said, "I'll help gather branches."

"No," Garret said before standing, "you rest. I'll handle it. I'm going to need your strength to help me carry him out of here."

Rebecca sighed and agreed. He was right. She was weak and needed to recover whatever energy possible before they tried to carry Roland through the jungle terrain.

"I'll be back," Garret said and then walked into the jungle.

Rebecca sat next to Roland and placed a hand softly onto his head. His fever was very high. "I'm sorry, Roland," she said quietly. "You're going to be okay, I promise." Rebecca laid the notepad onto the dirt next to them and thought, *I should really give Garret a copy of the translation, just in case something happens to this one.* She picked up the notepad again and powered it on. The translation was in the same spot as she left it. Rebecca looked around for Garret but didn't see him anywhere. Her eyes rested onto the notepad screen and onto the words in the translation.

William had finished researching the Voynich manuscript and learned about its history, but he was no closer to answering the question posed: Is what he found in Istanbul and the Voynich manuscript one half of the *Book of Thoth*? William decided that he needed to take his findings back to Benjamin Vermil's place and get everyone's opinion on the matter.

****

My return trip to New York was uneventful, and I decided to completely bypass my apartment and go straight to Tarrytown. Iah Vadimas had video conferenced into Mr. Vermil's study, as did Professor Haggins. I asked Mr. Vermil about Dr. Thatcher and whether they decided if she would be included in any further discussions, because by that point, I felt it best not to include anyone else going forward, especially not Simon Wylde. They, meaning Mr. Vermil,

Iah, and Haggins, agreed. I asked if any of them had contact with Simon over the past week and Mr. Vermil told me, "He has phoned several times. It has become crystal clear that we have shut him out."

"How's he taking it?"

"Not well," said Mr. Vermil.

"Has he confessed anything?"

"No, he has not." Mr. Vermil then coughed up a storm before saying, "William, I don't know if there is anything for him to confess. I haven't discovered any evidence that he was involved with Dr. Theoman or Dr. Horvath"—he saw that I was about to object and raised a hand—"but with that said, we've decided to continue on without him, in favor of your distrust."

"There was an entire brigade of American workers chewing through the Visočica Hill. Who else could have arranged that other than the owner and President of Aeronyte, the sole supplier of Bosnia's military aircraft?"

"No one is saying that Simon isn't suspicious," said Iah through the high-definition screen. "We're just saying that there is no proof."

I didn't need proof at that point; Simon was involved, and I knew it. I was certain he had you killed, Rebecca. I was certain he was jealous and wanted us dead. I was also certain that he wanted the *Book of Thoth* for himself. I was certain of all of this.

"So, what did you learn from Jonas Lundquist?" asked Mr. Vermil.

I laid out what little information he gave me and then explained what I had learned about the Voynich manuscript.

"Yes, that is my assessment as well," declared Professor Haggins. "I too have been looking into the history of the manuscript in-between lab tests on our own Sphinx, and I concluded that the book traveled up to Paris sometime during the Albigensian Crusade."

I was happy to hear some affirmation.

"In 1227, there were two monastic orders competing for young minds, very much like our collegiate Greek societies. There were the Franciscan Friars and there were the Dominicans. Both groups rivaled each other at the universities and were spreading all throughout Europe. But one of these groups, the Dominicans, was chosen by the new Pope, Gregory IX, to be the official prosecutor for the papacy, creating the first Inquisitors. See, Gregory IX had decided that the Cathar Heresy needed to end once and for all and he unleashed his Dogs of God—which Dominican quite literally stands for—onto the Languedoc region. The Franciscan Friars despised the extreme cruelty raining onto the Cathars and preached for a peaceful solution to the conflict. So, it wouldn't surprise my mind to learn that maybe the Franciscan Friars were sympathetic to the Cathars and quite possibly took some into their order, along with their sacred text. And quite naturally, the converted Cathar would seek a young and impressionable mind to carry forth the mission of hiding the text."

"But he failed," declared Iah. "The *Voynich manuscript* was not found in a geometric structure representing a platonic solid."

All of us pondered that conclusion for a moment before Professor Haggins said, "Yes, well, we still need to confirm that the Voynich manuscript is indeed related to our text. I've begun running a computer analysis on a writing sample taken from our text, comparing it to Voynich, but this is not a simple process. There are errors, inconclusive data, conflicting results, et cetera. Is there something else we can do in the meantime?"

I thought about the request for a moment and then said, "Shouldn't there be a symbol on the text, like the one we have?"

No one immediately answered. Professor Haggins then said, "I guess, in theory. But let's assume for a moment that all fourths of the text were detailed with these Platonic symbols, and that each one made its merry way to whomever, and over the years the text began to fade, which we know that they did, and that copies were needed to be made. Would the transcribers be wise enough to include the symbols?"

"Our transcriber was," I pointed out.

"Indeed, but what about the rest? Can we truly trust that the rest of the keepers maintained the integrity of the text?"

"We can't trust anything," I said. "We just have to hope."

"Well I can tell you that no photo I have seen of the Voynich manuscript contained a Platonic Symbol, at least none in recent memory."

"But the ink has greatly faded," I protested. "I read online that there are several words or sentences that have fallen invisible over time and can only be seen using UV rays or some shit. Just like our Declaration of Independence."

Professor Haggins seemed uplifted by this thought. "I haven't seen the results of these tests."

Mr. Vermil cleared his throat and said, "Can we get access to them?"

"That depends," Professor Haggins said.

My mind was already running with a theory. "I imagine that whoever conducted these tests was strictly looking for indication of ownership or words, not something more simplistic, like a rudimentary shape. There might be something on there that everyone has been overlooking."

"Yes," Iah said, "but how do we find out? Do we just stroll on over to Yale and demand access?"

"Demand . . . no," said Professor Haggins. "If one wants access to the manuscript, I'm afraid he or she is required to submit a proposal to the curator of the Beinecke Library. And that person better have a damn good reason to see the manuscript; authorization is rarely given—mainly because of its fragility. The Beinecke has provided very hi-resolution images of each page of the manuscript to be perused online."

"But what we want to do can't be done with those images," I said.

"That is true. . . . I guess it's a good thing I'm friends with Jarvis Reinhart, the Beinecke curator. I'm sure a friendly phone call is all we need."

Smiles and laughter erupted inside the room. Mr. Vermil said, "Good form, Morlan. Why don't you do that."

"I will, gents. How soon shall I request a visit?"

I looked at Mr. Vermil and then to Iah in the monitor. "As soon as possible?"

Professor Haggins hesitated before smiling. "Right. I'll see what I can do. I hope you gents don't mind if I cut communication. . . ."

No one objected and the Professor logged off.

"Who should go to the University?" asked Iah.

Mr. Vermil hacked horribly and staggered away. He wobbled onto a chair and sighed with distress.

"Are you okay?" I asked.

Mr. Vermil removed a handkerchief from his vest's breast pocket and wiped his mouth. "I just needed a seat . . . that's all."

"Is everything alright?" asked Iah.

"I'm fine," Mr. Vermil said more pronounced. "Get on with it. William, you and Morlan should go."

"I would like to attend," added Iah. "I . . . I need to see it in person."

I didn't see any reason to object. I looked over to Mr. Vermil who was still clutching the handkerchief to his mouth. He nodded.

I didn't immediately know it at the time, but Mr. Vermil was growing increasingly ill. He didn't share his ailments with us, choosing to keep his pain to himself, but he was a very sick man. Looking back on it, I understand why he kept quiet, but I do wish he would have exposed his secrets sooner than he did.

Iah eventually signed off the conference call and I told Mr. Vermil I needed to return the rental car. He offered to put me up in one of his guest suites, because going home was not an option, and I agreed to stay.

Upon heading back to the city, I noticed something peculiar in my rearview mirror: a black SUV.

****

There was a crunching sound of footsteps behind Rebecca. She lowered the notepad and turned around just in time to see Garret returning with his arms full of tree branches.

"I'm going to need some help, I reckon," he said and then dropped them to the ground. "In my previous life, I used to work in the Ministry mines, but I've never been much of a woodsman."

Rebecca smiled and nodded. She closed the translation and remembered that she wanted to copy the file. "Oh, do you have a device I can place a file onto?"

Garret gave her a puzzled look and said, "Yeah. What for?"

"I have an extremely important file that my father would really like to have kept safe. It's on this notepad, but I'm afraid if something happens . . ."

"I understand. Sure." Garret removed a small notepad from a side pant pocket and brought it over. "You can put it on here."

Rebecca thanked him, and then she navigated through Simon's notepad, to where the file was stored. It was in that folder that Rebecca noticed another file, one she had completely forgot about. "Oh my God!"

CHAPTER THIRTY-TWO

District 4, Sector 2

"What is it?" Garret asked.

Rebecca read what was on the screen:

****

Candidates for the STAL(KERS) program

STAL(KERS) Bio-Mechanic Blueprints

STAL(KERS) Initiative

STAL(KERS) Operation Status

****

I forgot all about these, she said silently. "When the Wylde's compound was attacked, I broke into the Ministry Database and took some files. The translation I've been reading is one of them—the file I was going to make a copy of—but I also took four other files that deal with Stalkers. And I totally forgot all about it."

Garret came closer. "That's some serious business. How on Earth did you forget that? If my platoon leader knew you had these files, she would have never allowed us to go alone."

"With everything that happened . . . I just forgot."

"Well, what's inside the files? Can you open them?"

"Yes." Rebecca picked *STAL(KERS) Initiative* and it blinked onto the screen.

****

Stealth
Tactical
Attack
Life-forms
Killers
Engineered for
Reconnaissance and
Security

Mission Statement: Identify, Locate, and Terminate.

Overview:

With the growing threat of separatist ideas and rebellious acts, there has been a long-standing need for improved measures of security. The STAL(KERS) Initiative is the answer for this need.

In the year 3502 AFT, Johannes Schlieken had begun research into combining the human brain with a mechanical device. This research led to the first biomechanical bonding, and it opened the gate for further research into the possibility of recreating the human body, but in mechanical form.

Initially, the idea was to help those who had fallen victim to paralyzing accidents or genetic mutations, but our very own Security Chief, Jonas Lundquist, has realized a more useful and rewarding use for this new technology; which has birthed the STAL(KERS) Initiative. It is Jonas Lundquist's vision that solves the two growing problems: threats to the security of the Ministry and the growing population of Misfits.

1. Engineer biomechanical bodies that are far superior to the human body: make them durable, flexible, and agile.

2. Thin the growing number of Misfits and identify those considered most useful, and connect these few to the new bodies through Schlieken's method of neural attachment.

Of course, with all new technology come all new concerns and mishaps—particularly concerning the Misfits gaining of a far more superior body. It is not Jonas Lundquist's desire to have those plaguing the Collective rampage freely. Measures will be put in place that will restrict these Misfits, limiting them to a life we so desire.

In conclusion, the STAL(KERS) Initiative will make the Collective and the Ministry safe by reallocating Misfits from their natural existence, which is to destroy and ruin all that the Ministry has fought for since its inception, to a life of disciplined service aimed at identifying, locating, and terminating all enemies of the Ministry.

****

Rebecca handed the notepad over to Garret so that he could read it too. Her thoughts revolved around Misfits. She knew what they were: the world's murderers, rapists, psychopaths, anarchists, et cetera. Misfits cared only for themselves, hurt whoever and whatever they desired, and were completely incapable of assimilating. Because of this, they were considered worse than the Heretique. *And the Ministry is using them.* Not that it surprised her.

"Unbelievable," Garret said calmly. "I guess none of us should be surprised; those things are wretched—as are Misfits. And it definitely shouldn't surprise us that Jonas Lundquist is behind their creation."

Rebecca took back the notepad and went to another file. *Candidates for the STAL(KERS) program.* Inside was quite a long list of people's names (mostly men). As her eyes scanned through the list, they stopped on one name: *Gregory Hansen.* "I know him," she said.

"You know Gregory Hansen?"

Rebecca started to say, *He killed me in a previous life*, but she refrained. Instead, she said, "It's a long story; but he is definitely a Misfit." She then wondered if Hansen was the Stalker who attacked her six months ago, in her Sector 27 flat. It would have made sense in a terrible, sick way.

"Oh boy," Garret said as he pointed at another name in the list: Morgan Bolling.

"Who's that?"

"He's one of us," Garret declared.

"A member of the Free People was made into a Stalker?"

"No, he still is one of us. . . ."

She looked at the name again: *Morgan Bolling.* She had only met one man in her life named Morgan. . . . "I once met a Morgan down in the Vriezen; he was an ill-looking man who didn't have my best interest in mind."

"That would be Morgan Bolling. He's a Misfit, all right. But there is just enough *human* inside of him to keep within the Free People. But he's watched, and if he ever steps across the line. . . ."

"I wonder why he wasn't made into a Stalker."

"He probably had an inkling that the MSF wanted him, and that is how he came into the service of the Free People. But that's just a guess."

Roland rolled from his left side to his right; he made a light groan and smacked his lips.

Rebecca observed him and said, "I think he needs water."

Garret pulled out his canteen. "It's empty."

Rebecca had consumed all of his water during their walk back—not that it was her fault. "I'll go get some."

Garret shook his head and said, "I'll get it. Why don't you copy those files to my device, like you wanted. Then we'll get started on that stretcher. The sun is full overhead and will be heading down soon. I want to get back to base before nightfall."

Rebecca agreed and took up Garret's device. She was initially going to copy it to Garret's root folder but had a second thought: *It might be better to hide it, just in case he gets curious.* Rebecca went in through several subfolders, to an unassuming folder, and copied the files from Simon's notepad into it. *If something happens, and Garret makes it to the Free People without me, they will eventually find it.* She was sure of it.

Rebecca powered off Garret's device and watched Roland sleep. He was beginning to sweat, which was good sign. She placed her hand onto his head; he still felt hot but not quite as bad. *The antibiotics are working.* Rebecca looked at Simon's notepad and opened up the translation. She glanced around for Garret, but she knew he would be gone for at least fifteen minutes, for that was how long it took her to get Roland water before she left to find help.

In the manuscript, William had met with Benjamin Vermil, Iah, and Morlan Haggins. They decided that they needed to visit the Beinecke Library and inspect the *Vonich Manuscript* personally. William was on his way back into the city to return his rental car when he noticed he was being followed by a black SUV.

****

Now, there are plenty of black SUVs driving around—actually, far more than *plenty*—but this one felt wrong . . . like the one I encountered at the rest stop.

The SUV was closing in on me very quickly—too quickly, if you know what I mean. My initial instinct was to speed up, maneuver around the cars filling all five lanes, and try to lose whoever . . . but I didn't . . . choosing, instead, to maintain my speed. I wanted to see who this person was. I wasn't afraid anymore, and quite frankly, I was tired of the threats.

The black SUV came up on the left side and matched my speed. I looked over to see inside the front passenger window, and to my total lack of surprise, there were two strong-jawed thugs looking at me. The one in the passenger seat pointed a thick finger at me, and then he pointed up to an exit sign high above the road.

Now, again, my instinct was to ignore the *request* and to keep on going, but something about the situation wasn't alarming to me. Maybe it was the fact that the SUV could have very easily ran me off the road, or that the passenger in it could have shot me quite easily through the window without anyone noticing—but none of these things happened. . . .

I exited the highway and pulled over on the Henry Hudson Parkway, across from an apartment building—allowing the SUV to park in front of me. The driver remained inside but the passenger exited the car and walked up to my passenger window. I casually rolled it down. "How can I help you?"

"William Coulee?" asked the man.

"Yeah."

"Simon Wylde would like to speak with you."

That was unexpected. "Simon?"

"Yes, sir."

"Is he with you?" I asked while trying to see in through the SUV's back windshield.

"Yes, sir. Can you please exit your vehicle and follow me?"

Again, this was another moment when I would have normally sped off, leaving this thug in the dust; but I didn't. I got out of the car and walked with him to the SUV's side passenger door. I did, however, dial the last contact in my cell phone, which happened to be Mr. Vermil. I heard his voice come muffling through in my pocket and I pulled the phone out. "Mr. Vermil, I have been approached by two men who are supposed to be taking me to speak with Simon Wylde."

My escort glared at me but said nothing.

"William?" Mr. Vermil said. "Are you okay? Where are you?"

"I'm on the Henry Hudson Parkway, heading west. I'm going to keep you on the line until I feel it is safe to disconnect."

"Simon is there?" he asked.

My escort opened the backseat door. I walked over to see inside and then said into the phone. "Mr. Vermil, I'll have to call you back."

I think he tried to protest but I disconnected the line. "I thought you said he was with you?"

"William," Simon said through the laptop computer monitor, "we need to have a chat."

"See, he's with us," my escort said and then smiled. He pulled out a cigarette and lit it up. The driver of the SUV left the vehicle and joined his companion.

"William," Simon said again, his face making up the majority of the HD screen, "why have I been cut out?"

I was completely taken off guard and didn't know what to say. "Simon, what's going on? Have your—*thugs*—been following me this entire time?"

"I don't know what you mean by 'this entire time.'"

"Since Washington, D.C.?"

Simon looked bothered to have to answer my question. "Yes, I've been trying to get in contact with you—"

"Did your guys break-in and toss my apartment? Sticking a threatening message on my wall?"

"No, absolutely not. I—we had nothing to do with that." His face showed no lie. "I had no way to get a hold of you, and so I had some men from my staff wait for you at your apartment. They followed you to the police station and to Washington, D.C. but then lost you. I then told them to go over to Benjamin Vermil's home and wait for you there."

"Why in the hell are you paying people to follow me?"

Simon looked impatient at this point. "Why do you think? Now can you please answer my question; why have I been cut out?"

"Why do you think?" I practically shouted. "Clearly you're not trustworthy."

"*Not trust . . .*"—he looked like he wanted to shout—"*I'm* not trust worthy? Have *I* lied to anyone? Have *I* been pretending to not know someone?"

It was suddenly clear what he was trying to say. "Is this about Rebecca?"

"You tell me. I'm the one cut out, not you. So why don't you tell me what's happening, since I'm clearly in the dark about everything."

"In the dark? I think you know what's going on, Simon."

He looked incredulous. "How so?"

"Your men in Bosnia—your connection with Dr. Horvath. Come on, don't bullshit me anymore."

"My men in Bosnia?"—he not only looked confused but insulted—"What the *hell* are you talking about? I don't have men in Bosnia. I might have a few sales reps brokering deals . . . my connections with Dr. Horvath? What are you talking about?"

I wasn't sure at that point. Maybe things weren't as I saw them. "All right, forget all of that, you want to know why you are cut out; I'll tell you why . . ." but I didn't know what to say; my reason had just gone up in smoke.

Simon waited to hear the big revelation.

I finally found something to say: "Everyone thinks that you are trying to steal the *Book of Thoth*."

"*How so?* I've done nothing but help them . . . and you!"

"I was almost killed in Bosnia. Everyone knows your connections there. It wasn't hard to figure out who might be involved."

"Why would I want you dead?"

It was time to clear the air. "You know why, *damnit*—Rebecca."

A disgusted smile slithered across his face, as if he just won some gigantic victory. "So, you're admitting it then? You had an affair with her, didn't you?"

I didn't respond. I actually started to feel slightly guilty.

"I knew something was up—she was acting so . . . *unusual* those last couple of months. It was you all along; you were the reason."

"She never told me about you, or anyone else for that matter. I had no idea she was with someone."

My words looked like they slapped him in the face, as if he would have preferred that I knew about your relationship.

"I'm sorry, Simon," I said pretty insincerely.

It took him several seconds to speak; pain was all over his face. My guilty conscience grew. He finally said, "I didn't try to kill you in Bosnia."

This time, I believed him.

"I have nothing to do with Dr. Horvath. I'm just . . ." the words left him. "Excuse me," he said and left the screen.

The next ten or so seconds were as awkward as they come, it was clear that Simon was trying to gather composure. He returned to the screen, completely pulled together, and said, "I want to know everything. I've invested more than my share into this project; I deserve to know."

He was right; he did deserve to know. I realized, finally, that I was the sole proponent of keeping Simon closed out; no one else believed that he was involved. "Okay, you're right. You do deserve to know." I then proceeded to tell him everything. Simon, for his part, sat silently and listened. Like a sponge, he seemed to soak all of it in. When I was finished, Simon looked indifferent. He simply said, "Thank you. I think we're done." And then disconnected from the call. The computer screen refreshed to a connection screen and then I heard a phone ring from where the two men were standing. I looked over and saw the passenger talking into his cell and nodding his head. There was no doubt that Simon had called him with further instruction.

After a moment, the man pocketed his phone. The two of them broke up. The driver returned to the SUV and the passenger walked over to me. He said, "Mr. Wylde wants me to tell you thank you for your time, and he apologizes for the rude manner he went about getting your attention."

I was at a loss for words. I tried to say something along the line of *No problem*, but as soon as I went to speak, the man threw a fierce blow into my gut, completely knocking the wind out of me.

I crumbled to my knees, gasping for air, when a second blow connected across my jaw, literally knocking me silly.

I vaguely recall hearing the man say, "And that is for your affair with Rebecca," before the sound of gravel crunching under tires filled my ears.

I think I had lay on the ground for close to five minutes before standing up and dusting off my pride.

Eventually I called Mr. Vermil back and told him what had just occurred, including the truth about us. I guess I had expected to hear a lecture from him regarding truth and integrity, but he spared me the decency. The truth is, he didn't have much to say other than, "Gather yourself, William; we have much work to do."

I probably should have felt relieved that Mr. Vermil didn't make a big deal out of my conversation with Simon, but there was something about his subtlety that made me feel worse than better. I felt unworthy to be an associate of his, like a child pretending to be an adult. I felt this way the whole rest of the day to the rental car place and then back to Mr. Vermil's. It wasn't until we received another call from Morlan Haggins that the feeling lifted.

****

Rebecca stopped reading; she noticed the familiar crunching noises of Garret walking and looked in the direction of the creek. He was walking toward her with his canteen in hand. Rebecca sat up on her knees and took Roland by the head, tilting it slightly so they could run some water over his mouth. Garret bent down and opened the canteen; he allowed the water to slowly stream out. As it flowed into Roland's mouth, he choked and coughed for a few seconds before opening his eyes slightly, and then shutting them again. "It's okay, Roland," Rebecca said. "It's water. Take a drink."

Roland nodded and Garret ran more water into his mouth. This time Roland gulped some of it before shutting his lips tightly. Garret replaced the cap on the canteen and looked toward Rebecca. "Let's get going on that stretcher."

Garret was worried about nightfall, and for good reasons.

CHAPTER THIRTY-THREE

District 4, Sector 2

The stretcher was shameful looking, but it was the best they could do. It took longer than they had hoped. The biggest challenge Rebecca and Garret faced during its construction was how to bind all of the wood together. They didn't have rope, and neither of them knew that they could make some with the indigenous plant life all around. So instead, Rebecca used Garret's utility knife to cut off the bottom section of her gown, and then she shredded it into individual strands. The cloth was strong enough to bind the joints of the stretcher. They discovered that they needed to create many bindings in order to disperse the weight so not to tear any of the individual joints.

"Alright, let's lift him," said Garret as he took Roland by the shoulders. Rebecca had Roland's legs, and on the count of three, they lifted Roland about a foot from the ground and onto the stretcher. The wood shifted slightly and creaked as Roland's weight settled. "Okay, now here's the real moment of truth. Let's see how it holds up. Are you ready to lift?" Garret asked as he squatted down at the head of the stretcher. Rebecca nodded and squatted at the foot of the stretcher. "On the count of three. . . . One . . . two . . . three!" They lifted Roland and the stretcher maintained.

"Wow," Rebecca said, "it's a lot easier to carry him this way."

"That's why we do it."

Garret transitioned so that he was walking forward and holding Roland behind him. "Are you ready? Let's go." They began walking in the direction that Garret had determined to be the best path to get to the base.

Walking with the stretcher turned out to be a bit more awkward than expected, and they needed to stop often in order to adjust their grip and regain their strength. Rebecca realized it was mainly her fault that they needed to stop so much, and she apologized profusely for the delays. Garret told her to not worry, but she could see that he was growing impatient; he really didn't want to be out there after dark, and Rebecca was scared to ask why. Something told her that the answer would contain more than coyotes. Garret's burn rifle could handle coyotes; there was something more menacing out there that Garret knew could not be easily deterred.

They tried talking to each other in order to take their minds off the physical work. Garret told her about his parents and about his life before and after entering the Free People's Society; Rebecca told him about her parents (Francesca and Francis, not Corbin), and how she was thrust into the grey murky world of being a fugitive and an outcast.

"All right, let's take another break," Garret announced.

Rebecca was glad to lay the stretcher down again.

"We should eat and restore some energy." Garret retrieved a couple of rations and handed one to Rebecca. "I wonder how the operation is going." Garret confessed during the walk that he gave his platoon his direct communication device out of precaution. If he and Rebecca were captured, the MSF would have no way to force them to call for help, thus setting a trap. "They should be infiltrating the depot right now."

"I'm sure it's going well," Rebecca said, wanting to give some kind of assurance.

Garret said nothing more. He scarfed down his ration and then announced that he was going ahead to see what was in front of them. "I'll be back in ten. Rest up."

Rebecca nodded and retrieved Simon's notepad from a pack Garret allowed her to store it inside. She opened the translation and began to read. William had an unpleasant video call with Simon, and he was getting ready to join Iah to journey to the Beinecke Library.

****

Professor Haggins had arranged for us to visit the Beinecke Library in two days time. He said that we would have full access to the manuscript, which was incredible news. He told me that he would meet us at the library since he was coming from Providence, Rhode Island. This information was then immediately relayed to Iah, who flew in from Savannah, Georgia the next day.

When Iah arrived at the mansion, there was a glow radiating from him much like a kid on Christmas morning. I met him in the main foyer, where Rory was collecting Iah's travel bag. "We are on the eve of a momentous day!" Iah said with glee. "Tomorrow, we will confirm where one half of the *Book of Thoth* resides! William, do you see how exciting this is?"

I tried to share in his optimism but there were still so many roadblocks ahead of us, like translating the text.

"It will be done," he said. "Man has understood this wisdom before; therefore, he will understand it again. And as long as we have the will, we'll find the way."

It was hard for me to share his sentiment; I was never one for having faith.

"Faith is believing, William. Believing is seeing. Seeing is understanding. Understanding is knowing. And knowing is achieving. So start believing, my friend, and you will start seeing."

"I take it that you're a proponent of self-fulfilling prophecies."

"Of course. Aren't we all? If we see ourselves eating what is on our fork, don't we eat it? Is that not self-fulfilling?"

I laughed. "I guess it's hard to argue against that. . . . What's your story, Iah? How did you become this man?"

"That is a story best told on a long road."

I resigned to hear it once we were on our way.

Rory provided one of Mr. Vermil's vehicles for us, a silver Audi A3. I had contacted Professor Haggins and told him that we would be there in an hour and a half's time. Mr. Vermil had barely been visible as we made our arrangements. He kept disappearing for long stretches of time, and neither Iah nor myself felt it was our business to poke around and look for him. I think we both realized what was happening. Mr. Vermil was in a terrible weakened state.

We left around eight in the morning the following day. As the road we were on merged onto Interstate 287, Iah said, "Just north of here is Sleepy Hollow. Did you know that?" He then began quoting a line from the short story, "A pleasing land of drowsy head it was, of dreams that wave before the half-shut eye; and of gay castles in the clouds that pass, forever flushing round a summer sky. . . ."

"Washington Irving," I said.

Iah smiled. "His kind of mind is extinct in our day."

"What about your mind," I asked. "What has made it what it is? How did you become—well, *you*?"

"A story I promised to tell you on a long road, and so I guess this one will suit us. It began with my father, Abasi Vadimas. He came to this country when he was twenty-nine. He told me that never in his wildest dreams did he believe there was a land where a simple man, like himself, could earn an honest wage and have an honest living. His life in Egypt—the only life he knew—had been corralled by the government.

"He had known of the United States, of course, and knew that the people living here had a certain level of freedom beyond Egypt's. He came here alone, when he was twenty-three, and briefly took a job driving taxis in New York City. I don't recall how long he worked this job—a few months . . . maybe—but he quickly decided to join the United States Army. His thought was that a country so exceptional, as the United States, was worth fighting and dying for. My father wanted to do his part by serving his new country, and he passed this sentiment down to his children.

"When I was eighteen, I joined the U.S. Army as well. There was no question that my brothers and I would join once graduating high school. I was the middle child of five and the third to go.

"I was sent to Fort Benning for basic training . . . that is where my story really begins.

"Early on in my life, I began to have spells of what we commonly refer to as déjà vu. I would be in certain places, doing certain activities, or having conversations with friends, when suddenly I knew what was going to be said or happen next. It was a five to ten second window into the future. I can still recall the initial feeling I had during my very first 'viewing'—an extreme level of consciousness unlike anything I had ever felt. I could remember everything that had yet to happen. . . . That is what it was like—remembering."

I knew the feeling Iah had described. I had felt it a few times in my life, and it was very much like remembering an event that hadn't happened yet. Confusing, right? I'm sure you know what I'm talking about. I'm sure you have felt it too.

Iah continued, "I tried to tell my mother and father about it, I tried to describe to them what had happened. It was so perplexing—and exciting. I wanted it to happen again, but I couldn't trigger it; the viewing only occurred at random, or so I thought. It wasn't until I was thirteen or fourteen that my father began taking it serious. He told me that the Ancient Egyptians had men who they considered prophets and sages that could control and do what I had described. It was my first introduction into the magical arts—outside the Houdinis in the world. My father told me the story of Djedi, a prophet and magician from the age of the Hyksos."

"Hyksos, meaning the Hebrews?"

Iah nodded.

If you recall, Rebecca, I told you about the Hyksos/Hebrews being the ones who took the *Book of Thoth* out of Egypt.

Iah continued, "The story went like this: An Egyptian prince stood up to speak to his father, the Pharaoh, and said, 'There is someone under Your Majesty and in your own time who can perform such feats that one cannot distinguish truth from falsehood. There is a commoner called Djedi who lives in Djed-Snofru. He is a commoner a hundred and ten years old, who knows how to mend a severed head. He knows how to make a lion walk behind him, with its leash on the ground. He knows the number of lines inside the *Book of Thoth*.' "

Iah said, "At the time of this story, the *Book of Thoth* had been lost, but its legend still existed. The Pharaoh of this tale spent the following day trying to locate the book without success. He then ordered his son to bring Djedi to him. The Prince went to Djed-Snofru and found Djedi. He said, 'Greeting, O blessed one! I have come here to summon you by order of my father, justified.' The Prince and Djedi traveled back to the Pharaoh. The Pharaoh asked Djedi if the stories were true, if he knows how to mend a severed head? And Djedi said, 'Yes.' And so the Pharaoh ordered the execution of a prisoner, whereupon Djedi said, 'But not to a human, my lord!' He explained that doing something like that to the 'noble flock' is not ordained. So the Pharaoh ordered his servants to bring in a procession of animals. And Djedi spoke spells to them, ordered them around, and healed them. Then the Pharaoh said, 'Now, what is said is that you know the number of lines inside the *Book of Thoth*.' And Djedi said, 'I beg your pardon, I don't know the number thereof, my lord, but I know the place where it is kept.' The Pharaoh demanded to know where, and Djedi said, 'There is a casket in a room called the Inventory in Heliopolis; and the book is in that casket.' The Pharaoh ordered Djedi to go and find it and to bring it back. But Djedi said, 'My lord, look, I am not the one who will bring it to you.' He then explained that the eldest of the Pharaoh's three children who've yet to be born would locate and bring it to him."

I asked, "What does all of that mean? How did it relate to you?"

"My father mentioned it because it was an example of the mystical power our ancient people once possessed—a power he said that I might possess. . . . That story was also the first time I had heard of the *Book of Thoth*.

"And so this *gift* I had, it grew as I grew. I developed this ability to know certain things just before these things happened. When a certain person was about to call our house, what someone might say next, or when someone might do something. I could only see a few seconds into the perceived future, but it was enough to astonish my friends and family.

"And so this takes me back to my enlisting into the military and a certain game—or trick, depending on how you per-

ceive it—that I used to play with my fellow enlisted men.
I used to tell them to put something into their hands—
anything. I would look away as they did this and then I
would instruct them to think about what it was that they
were holding. And then I would guess it. And normally, I
guessed correctly the first time.

"As you can imagine, this game drew a lot of attention. One
day, just after PT, I was ordered to the camp's HQ, and was
met by a man named Thomas Kinsella. He worked—"

"For the CIA?" I asked.

Iah looked at me and nodded his head. "I'm impressed.
How did you know this?"

I could barely believe my ears. I filled Iah in on my conversation with Daniel pertaining to PARDUS. Iah said, "Your
friend knows more than you give him credit. Most of what
he told you is accurate. The U.S. Army did have a Psi program, called Project Stargate. It ran from the 1970s to 1995.
It was then taken over by the CIA, publicly evaluated, and
closed—citing that there was little justification to keep the
20 million dollar project running. . . . But that was all on the
surface. The reality of the situation is that PARDUS inherited the entire project, running underneath the NSF bud-
get and completely washed from the government's hands.
When Kinsella recruited me in 1991, at the end of the Gulf
War, I was placed under his command, given a cover within
the Army, and assigned to the PARDUS headquarters in the
middle of the Rocky Mountains, south of Del Norte and
west of Monte Vista.

"When I arrived, they—meaning the scientists at PAR-
DUS—immediately began evaluating my Potential. Everyone's psychic ability was labeled 'Potential.' Some had more
Potential than others, and I had a just enough to be placed
within a team tasked with locating Saddam Hussein."

I think Iah could see my incredulity seeping. He paused in his story to allow questions. I asked, "You're telling me that you once worked for Jonas Lundquist, head of PARDUS?"

He told me flat out, "Yes."

"Why didn't you mention that before . . . ?"

"I didn't want my connection to Jonas known."

"Why?"

Iah hesitated before answering, "You'll understand soon enough."

I remember shaking my head and saying, "So you were pulled from basic training and assigned the task of finding Saddam Hussein . . . by using your *mind?*"

"Yes and no. It didn't exactly happen that cleanly. My basic training was resolved with my reassignment, and when I arrived at PARDUS I was put through a thorough psychic evaluation and several training courses that taught recruits how to harness their mental energy and explode it outward like a radar bouncing waves off everything and returning them, very much like echolocation or biosonar. . . . In short, we were trained to be like dolphins."

"You're losing me," I told him flatly.

"Many animals use echolocation as a form of second sight. They call out and then listen for the echo, which tells them where objects are located. Humans can do the same thing but with their minds instead, utilizing what is called neural oscillation—or more simply put, brain waves."

I must have made a funny face at him because he then said, "You don't believe me? Have you ever heard of the Brain-Computer Interface or Mind Machine Interface? Those are terms used for the direct communication between the brain and a machine. The NSF first funded this research at UCLA in the 1970s before it was wholly consumed by PARDUS, once there was enough evidence demonstrating its capabilities. Different universities developed and tested BCI on several primates, including monkeys, and what they discovered was that a monkey could operate a mechanical arm in order to peel a banana just by thinking about it. They have since used BCI as a new way for humans to interact with their home computers. There is no need for a mouse or keyboard. All one has to do is think about what they want to achieve and it works. . . . You can look this up, William. There are companies out there right now developing this technology. I watched one company give a demonstration of how a user can play World of Warcraft without anything but his mind."

"You're telling me that they just think about moving something and it works?"

"Exactly."

"The person's brain waves just fly out of his head and into the computer, controlling it . . . ?"

"Not exactly like that. The person would have on a headset of sort, kind of like a swimmer's cap. There are sensors connected all around the cap that listen for the pulses, which then transfers them into the computer where they are translated."

"So it's not freeform."

"Not in this instance, no. But there are some things that can be done headset free, which takes me back to Psi program and my Potential. They trained us on how to control specific parts of our neural oscillations, which gives us the ability to perform remote viewing. We all have a certain range we can view before our signals grow too weak. My radius was about twenty feet."

"What do you mean? You could mentally see things up to twenty feet around you?"

"Precisely. . . . Allow me to demonstrate. This is my first time in this car, yes?"

"If you say so."

"And you haven't witnessed me open the glove box, correct?"

"No, I haven't."

"Okay then, I'm going to tell you what is in the glove box without opening it."

"All right, go for it."

Iah closed his eyes and held himself still. I could see an intense level of concentration on his face just before he said, "There's a . . . little cardboard box . . . some papers . . . and . . . a pen—two . . . three pens." He then opened his eyes and blinked hard a few times. "Shall we see?"

"Open it," I said.

Iah unlatched the glove box and there was an unopened juice box—of all things—inside, sitting on top of registration papers, and a few pens. I wanted to accuse him of peeking at some point prior, but I couldn't bring myself to do it. I was blown away. And then it occurred to me. "That's how you're so good at magic."

"I've told you before, magic is science unexplained."

"So then—are you telling me that PARDUS had your team sitting around and thinking about Saddam Hussein's whereabouts? How did that work if your second sight is limited to a twenty foot radius?"

"We used computers to amplify our signal. BCIs, like I just described to you, connected to our brains, feeding our oscillations into the machine and then magnifying their strength before projecting them outward. PARDUS has huge signal dishes that receive the echoes and then transforms them back through the computer and to our minds. It would then be up to us to decipher and filter the visions."

"This is insane," I told him.

"No, it's—"

"Science . . . I know. How long did these sessions last? Based on what you described, I can't imagine that any of this was a simple matter of sending a signal and then sitting back and waiting for a response."

"You're correct in assuming that. A session could last around four to six hours—once that viewer was properly trained and conditioned. Remote viewing isn't a simple thing, William. It is incredibly taxing on the mind. It causes intense levels of stress and anxiety. Part of the reason why PARDUS is up in the Rocky Mountains is because of the serene views over the land. It was relaxing; it had to be relaxing. You might imagine that something so secretive would have to be so buttoned up and tight but the reality is that living at the facility was more like living at a resort. Researchers quickly discovered, early on, that exhausted, stressed out viewers were the least proficient compared to the viewers who were well rested and relaxed."

"If that's the case, then why were the sessions so long?"

"They had to be that long in order to guarantee accurate vision. When you're trying to locate a particular person thousands of miles away, it can be a bit of a task. Sending out signals and receiving echoes for only an hour, when there are quite literally billions of foreign signals scrambling through space at any given second, is a bit futile. We needed to spend large amounts of time plugged-in in order to sort through it all—which is even more the reason why when we weren't plugged-in that we needed to be relaxing and enjoying life. PARDUS understood this and they did all they could to ensure that its viewers were comfortable."

"Dang," was all I could say. I had absolutely no idea these kinds of things were going on. "So, did you ever find him? Saddam?"

"Oh, yes, we found him a few times," Iah admitted.

"Did you, personally?"

Iah nodded his head. "There were more than a couple of times I had caught a vision of him. I remember one instance when he was taking a bath in a large imperial tub, and another time when he was arguing with an adviser inside an armored limousine. . . . But I was only one in a team of viewers looking for and watching him. We worked in shifts, night and day. There was always someone looking for and observing him . . . that is to say until we were given a different target to find."

"Like who?"

"All sorts. Other world leaders, drug lords, terrorists. . . ."

It was a bit unnerving to hear. "Did you ever spy domestically?"

Iah hesitated to answer. "I had not . . . but that's not to say others had not either."

I remember thinking how terrible of a notion it was: men hooked up to machines, seeking out targeted individuals, and watching their whereabouts—but for what? I asked Iah what PARDUS did with their data.

He sighed and said, "The answer to your question is why I left the program. . . . Let me just say that in 2003, when President Bush announced that cruise missiles and precision guided bombs had struck a site near Baghdad, Iraq, which was described as a 'target of opportunity' before the onslaught of war, there was no doubt in my mind that my former team had provided this data to the CIA and they acted."

I was in Iraq when that airstrike occurred. I asked Iah, "How did they know where he was? How does that work? Your second sight?"

"It's complicated. We generally looked for landmarks to identify and then relayed them to a 'map' team who perused every resource they had in order to put a name, address, or coordinate to the location. But the accuracy between our data and theirs was a bit controversial. And there were plenty of times when our CIA sponsors took information that had the chance of being 60-65% accurate and relaying it to whoever in order to carry out an operation. And like I just said, there is no doubt in my mind that the early strike against Saddam was one of these low accuracy scenarios . . . maybe the percentage was a little higher but obviously not 100% . . . not like what we saw this year with the Bin Laden operation."

"You think PARDUS had something to do with that as well?"

"PARDUS has something to do with everything, William."

I then thought about some of the other things Daniel had mentioned, the more absurd ideas he had that were now appearing not so absurd. "Has PARDUS assassinated anyone by using psychic energy?" I then told him about the hilarity of what Daniel had theorized.

Iah didn't find it so funny. "There were occasions when the CIA needed to carry out an operation under the highest level of cover, a level that indisputably disconnected the United States government from any involvement whatsoever. These operations were so air tight that we referred to them as the 'Black Hole Operations' because anything that came too close was immediately sucked in and crushed, never to be seen again."

I said to him, "You probably shouldn't be telling a journalist these things."

Iah grinned. "You're not a journalist anymore; you're a member of Project Renew Our History . . . and I think you know it."

He was right.

"Do you want me to continue . . . ?"

"By all means."

"These Black Hole Operations didn't happen very often, and when they did, you didn't know it; black holes can't be seen. I can think of only one during my tenure at PARDUS. It began after an assassination attempt on President George H. W. Bush by Saddam Hussein's Iraqi Intelligence Service, which involved a car bomb that was to detonate within the vicinity of the President during his visit to Kuwait. The plot was foiled by border security and sixteen men were arrested. My team was redirected from Saddam surveillance to Owais Al-Shamari, the Director of IIS. There was an unusual amount of pressure from our sponsors to get this man's location correct and maintain a constant watch. Our sponsors didn't want to lose him. But what really made the operation unusual was that our data was being pushed to another team within PARDUS, not the U.S. military. . . . Anyway, a few days or so passed and we were redirected from Owais Al-Shamari to another target. And I don't recall if it happened that day or the next, but a news report came out that an agent working within the IIS had gone berserk and killed Owais Al-Shamari along with three others before being gunned down by soldiers. . . . At the time, I don't recall how much thought I had put into it other than, 'Well that was a coincidence.' But not too much later I realized the full Potential of other members within PARDUS and just how dangerous they could be. I then put one and one together and . . . well . . .'"

"Damn," was all I said.

"Precisely."

"Was there a man named Saño Wining involved?"

"Oh yes. This takes me back to Jonas Lundquist. Saño was considered the Supreme Being inside PARDUS. Together with Jonas, Saño pushed the boundary of what can be accomplished with the mind. They discovered all kinds of things, and quite literally wrote the handbook for all incoming recruits."

"This included how to control people—how to drive them to kill?"

Iah sighed. "It's not that simple, William. No, their intentions were not to control and kill, at least not in the beginning. But time, pressure, and turmoil can change one's perspective. . . . Saño Wining was a brilliant—admittedly eccentric—man. His early intentions with mind control were telepathy and speaking to animals, particularly his dog. Saño believed he could communicate with his dog nonverbally, and he dedicated his time to researching and understanding how—not if, never if—it could happen. His work led him to PARDUS and to Jonas Lundquist. Jonas cultivated Saño's brilliance and together they expanded the psychic field. But like I said, turmoil and pressure had pushed them into using psychic power for espionage and eventually warfare. And like most of us, Saño lost his luster and bowed out of the program."

"Where is he now?"

"I have no idea."

"And Lundquist? Is he still involved?"

"Again, I have no idea. Once you're out, you're out. PARDUS disappears, and if you go looking for it again, you disappear too."

I told Iah about the folder on Jonas's desk.

Iah considered it for a moment before saying, "Who knows what his level of involvement is these days. Jonas isn't exactly a power sharing man. Saño learned that the hard way."

"What do you mean?"

"Saño was more interested in using psychic powers as a means of communication. Jonas wanted to do far more than that . . . and Jonas won."

"Okay, but what do you mean regarding whether or not he is still involved?"

"The Intelligence Community wanted more control over PARDUS's activities. Jonas didn't like their meddling. I'm sure that he eventually was forced out or forced to take a reduced role."

I was pondering that thought when I began to see exit signs for Yale University.

We were there.

CHAPTER THIRTY-FOUR

District 4, Sector 2

"What are you reading?"

Rebecca was startled to see Garret standing near her. "I didn't notice you returned; I'm reading a translation of a manuscript."

Garret walked over and sat down. He picked up his canteen and took a drink. He then looked up at the sky and pointed. "We're losing daylight."

"I know," Rebecca said. "Are you ready to go?"

Garret nodded and looked at her, as if to say, *Are you ready?* "We have some troubling terrain just ahead of us. There's a small hill, and its surface is anything but smooth. The sides of the hill are broken open and rock covered; it will be difficult to carry Roland and maintain our footing."

"There's no way around?"

"No way that doesn't take us far off course. We have roughly three more miles to hike; I'm not interested in having that number grow."

"Neither am I," Rebecca said and then stood up. Garret matched her movement. They both grabbed their respective end of the stretcher and hoisted Roland.

The jerky movement stirred Roland and his eyes opened for the first time. "What's happening?" he asked quietly.

Rebecca looked at Garret, and they silently agreed to set the stretcher back down. She then said, "You've been out for hours. We built a stretcher so that we could move you along. How are you feeling?"

Roland looked at her, confused, and then looked at his surroundings; he particularly took notice of Garret, seeing him for the first time. "Who are you?"

Garret introduced himself and Rebecca explained how they met.

Roland sat up and said, "The two of you have been carrying me the entire time?" His expression was of embarrassment. "I'm sorry. . . . I . . ."

"Don't apologize," Rebecca said assuring. "I would be dead if it wasn't for you. This is the least I can do."

Garret took Roland's arm and inspected the bandage. "Can you walk?"

Roland nodded. "I think so, yeah. I just need to get a drink."

"Sure," Garret said and retrieved his canteen as well as a ration. "Have something to eat, too."

Roland did not hesitate to open the ration.

Garret smiled and said, "That's the last of the rations. We're on our own from here. We've got only a few more miles to travel." He gestured to the ration in Roland's hands. "Eat up, but don't make yourself sick. We need to get moving soon, and you'll need energy."

Rebecca checked Roland's forehead and said, "Your fever is still there, but it seems a little lighter. I was worried about you."

Roland looked into her eyes and saw she was being genuine. He looked like he wanted to say something witty or charismatic, but settled on an awkward smile. Rebecca left him alone to gather himself and picked up Simon's notepad; the translation was still on the screen.

"Have you made it any further?" asked Roland.

"I have," but she left it at that. Rebecca knew she could trust Garret, but she felt a responsibility to not unnecessarily share the contents of William's manuscript.

Roland continued eating while Garret meandered around. Rebecca could see that Garret was doing his best to patiently wait. *At least we won't have to carry Roland any farther*, thought Rebecca. It was a good thought that made her entire body celebrate. She asked Roland, "How long do you need?"

Roland took a small bite of dehydrated vegetables and said, "Just a few minutes, guys. I need to gather my strength."

Rebecca smiled and sat down next to him.

Garret announced that he was going to patrol the perimeter, to see if there was anything lurking.

"I just need ten minutes," Roland said.

Garret nodded and walked away.

Rebecca watched him leave and then began reading the translation again.

William and Iah had arrived at Yale University, where the Beinecke Library resided.

****

Iah and I ended our conversation as we navigated through New Haven. I pulled onto the narrow Wall Street and parked.

The Beinecke Library was terribly unusual looking. It reminded me of a plastic milk crate on legs. I know that means little to you but I don't know how else to explain its exterior.

Iah and I went inside and I can tell you that the interior was by far more impressive than the exterior. The walls were translucent, there were glass display cases around the perimeter that held extremely rare and valuable books; and in the center, making up the core, was a sealed off tower comprised of columns and rows of countless books—which was our ultimate destination. But in order to gain access we had to check in with the front desk, which was down a short flight of stairs, underground. I informed the man working it that we were scheduled to meet Professor Haggins and to view the Voynich manuscript. He told us that the Professor had already arrived and was inside a private viewing room. We had to relinquish any electronic devices before he led us inside to where Morlan was waiting with a female librarian.

"Gentlemen!" he said gleefully, "It's about time. I was growing entirely too anxious to wait any longer! My friend, Jarvis, won't be joining us today, but he assured me that Holly will be able to aid us in any way."

Holly then left to retrieve the Voynich manuscript while Professor Haggins began setting up his equipment: a florescent black light, his netbook computer, and a pair of magnifying glasses.

"How did you get those things in here?" I asked. "The man at the front desk made us surrender our phones."

Professor Haggins winked. "It pays to be a scholar, gents."

Holly returned wearing latex gloves and with the ancient book in her possession. It was a lot thicker than I anticipated and ill cared for. The years had not been kind. The book looked like it had been dipped in coffee, but it was still intact nonetheless. The ink was very faint on each page and I could now see why a UV light was needed.

Holly placed the book onto the table next to a box of latex gloves and then stepped out of the room. Professor Haggins pulled out a pair and squeezed his fingers inside them. "Let's see what we have here." He lifted the front cover and revealed the inside cover and first page. The inside cover had flaps folded in with a piece of white paper, or possibly cardboard, making up the body. Tucked tightly inside the innermost flap was a little identification card that bore Yale's crest and read, YALE UNIVERSITY LIBRARY Gift of HANS P. KRAUS. There were penciled notations on several areas, but nothing of significance.

The first page of the manuscript had the familiar looking

writing in what looked like brown ink (which could have very well been black at some point in time). A painted image on the reverse side of the page had bled its green pigment through, creating a faint backdrop of oval shaped leaves.

Professor Haggins placed on his head a pair of magnifying glasses. He clicked on his black light and asked us to dim the overhead lighting. Iah walked over to a panel and did as requested. The room went from a bright candescent to near blackness, save the little blue florescent light. Professor Haggins carefully held the black light over the first page of the manuscript, revealing a whole different side not seen in normal lighting. It was the difference between the living and the dead. Professor Haggins slowly glided the light down the page, examining everything the light exposed. It was at the bottom of the page that he saw the most action. There was definitely something written . . . but what?

"I see some letters," he announced. "They look like . . . an 'S' 'A' 'T' . . . and maybe another 'A', but I'm not sure."

"Professor," Iah said, "do you mind if I look?"

Professor Haggins looked over to Iah and then stepped away. "Be my guest." He lifted up his glasses and handed over the UV light. Iah took the light and leaned in rather close. He said, "Yes, I see what you're talking about. I see an 'SAT' but I'm not sure about the rest. However, it looks like there is a whole sentence written here. There appears to be more characters." He moved the light along the page and toward its outer edge. "Oh, did you see this? There might be writing on the right margin."

"Yes, I saw it, but it could be only scratches."

I then remembered something from my research on the book. "Isn't there supposed to be someone's name at the bottom of this page? *Jacobus Horcicky de Tepenecz?*

The two men looked at me before the Professor said, "Is that right? I suppose that could be what we're seeing. The second letter is very much like an 'A' and the fourth letter could be an 'O' rather than an 'A.' And a 'J' could possibly be mistaken for an 'S'. And that is a long name. Jacobus Horcicky de Tepenecz. That could possibly make up all of the characters we are seeing at the bottom of the page."

But something told me he wasn't happy about it . . . and I knew why. There was nothing on the page that represented a geometric symbol.

Iah eventually handed the light back over to the Professor once he was satisfied, but no one said what I was thinking. Instead, Professor Haggins suggested, "Maybe we should examine some of the inside pages."

I asked, "Does that make sense?"

"I don't think it will hurt."

Iah remained silent before taking in a deep breath and releasing it. "Guys, I don't think there will be anything further inside that will indicate what we're looking for. It should have been on this page or on the cover."

The room fell silent for a moment. I said, "We didn't check the cover."

Professor Haggins said, "There's nothing on the cover, William. All of the writing is inside."

"Do you know that? You didn't use your UV light on it. Maybe there is something hidden. Like you said before. It doesn't hurt to check."

Professor Haggins saw no use in arguing with me about it; he walked over to the book and closed the cover. He then took the light and slowly waved it over its surface. "I'm not seeing anything other than its rugged texture. There are some worn marks along the top and bottom of the cover . . . they make up parallel lines . . . and I think the top line actually forms a corner that faintly goes down the side and into oblivion. . . . That's it."

I looked over the Professor's shoulder and could see what he was describing; however, I didn't see it as discouraging as he did. "Those lines could be making up a square, don't you think?"

"They're pretty faint, William. I'm not sure."

Iah slid over to take a look as well. He said, "I see what you're talking about . . . but . . ." he didn't finish his sentence, nor was he going to get the chance to say anything more on the matter.

An unexpected visitor had opened the door and slid into the dark room.

"Hello?" I said.

Professor Haggins and Iah turned around to see who it was. Professor Haggins waved the light in front of him but it was too faint to see more than a human form.

I went to turn the overhead light on but was stopped short by a female voice that said, "Don't you dare. . . ."

The woman's words came out awkwardly forceful and a bit nervous sounding.

"Who are you?" I said.

The woman said, "No one move, understand? I don't want to see any movements whatsoever. I have a gun."

At that moment, all I could think was, *Are you kidding me?*

"A *gun?*" Professor Haggins said, astounded. "Who are you?"

"I'm taking the manuscript," the woman said. "I'm taking it and I wouldn't dare mess with me. This isn't a game and I'm dead serious. . . ."

I felt her walk past me, her scent was familiar; and from the faint UV light I could see the contours of her face—she was Dr. Caroline Thatcher.

Iah and the Professor also discovered who she was. Professor Haggins said, "Caroline? Is that truly you?"

"Don't talk to me, Morlan," she said. "I'm taking it."

"But, why? I don't understand."

She quickly grabbed the book and then stepped back. "You can't understand. None of you can."

"Understand what?" asked Iah.

Dr. Thatcher said with shaky words in a loud hush, "The danger you're putting the world in! What you're trying to discover, what you're trying to learn, is not for YOU. It isn't! All of those stories—Iah—all of the legends, all of the history, has it taught you nothing? This book is destructive! It will ruin our world and bring about The End. Nothing good has come to those who possessed it. It killed the ancient Egyptians who read it; it killed many when it was inside the Ark; it brought down Jerusalem; it killed the Cathars; and if you try to take it from me, it will kill you!"

"You mean you will kill us," I said.

"It won't be me," she said hysterically. "It won't be *my* fault."

"And what will happen to you," asked Iah, "now that you have it?"

Dr. Thatcher backed toward the door. "It will kill me. . . . I
know it will. But I have to take it—I have to!"

"Why, Caroline?" Professor Haggins said, pleadingly. "Why
do you have to do any of this? Who is making you?"

"GOD IS MAKING ME! I heard His voice, I felt His touch,
He is here on Earth, and He is demanding His book back!
He says it's not ours to own. It was stolen from Him and He
wants it back. . . ."

I now knew what was going on. "You're working with
Bertók. He is the one who told you to do this."

"You're misguided," she told me. "You think He's a luna-
tic who killed those people in Bosnia, who killed Charles
Theoman, but He's not; He is God."

Professor Haggins said, "Caroline . . . *you* are misguided.
Whatever he told you, he is filling your mind with falsities.
The man is delusional."

"You would think that! You don't know! None of you know!
I felt His presence, and I heard His word. He was with
Charles, and now He is with Bertók. He is who he chooses
to be. And He has told me . . . He has told me what is right
and what I must do. I will be rewarded—if not in this lifetime then in the next."

"*Caroline*," Professor Haggins said, "you can't possibly believe this; you're a woman of science."

I wanted to grab her and try to disarm her, but it was so
dark in the room and I couldn't make out where she was
holding the gun. There was too much room for error and
mishap.

"I still am!" she practically shouted out. "I was there, Morlan—I was in Bosnia when Charles showed me His true

self. I was there and I listened to His explanation, His un-believable knowledge about the past and about all things, and I witnessed His transmigration from one mortal body to the next. . . ."

"To Bertók," I said.

"Yes. This was no performance designed to bedazzle me. This was a true demonstration of transmigration, William. He has shown me so many things that go beyond our scientific comprehension. He is God on Earth."

"God doesn't impale people," I said.

There was a pause before she said, "All things have purpose. It isn't my place to understand all that He does. I have a job to do."

"What are you going to do, Caroline?" Professor Haggins asked.

"I'm going to return this manuscript to Him. We aren't capable of comprehending its message, nor should we try."

"You're mad," Professor Haggins said. "You won't get two cities from here. And that manuscript, every page is documented on the web."

"Not for long. I'm not the only one serving our Lord. Very soon, this will be the only copy. His servants will bring the documents down and destroy all of the files."

"Did you not hear me? You won't get a chance to return that book to your *Lord*. You will be caught and it will be taken."

Caroline sputtered, "I'm not taking it anywhere. I'm going to destroy it."

"*What?*"

"I will do exactly what Pope Innocent III couldn't do. I will destroy this text. And if it destroys me in return, then so be it; for I did the Lord's bidding and I will be rewarded."

"Caroline, don't do this," Professor Haggins pleaded. He took a step toward her, his hand outstretched.

"DON'T!" she shouted. The room lit up and there was an ear piercing pop.

I instinctively dropped to a crouch. Caroline Thatcher found the door and carelessly flung it open before running away. The light that spilled into the reading room revealed a horrible sight. Iah had Professor Haggins by the armpits and was slowly lowering him to the ground; a stain of blood was quickly filling the shirt covering Professor Haggins' chest. The Professor gasped a few times but there was nothing that could be done. He was gone before Iah could get his hands over the wound.

I ran out into the main lobby, shouting wildly for help. The librarians had already responded; they had the few visitors take cover and had called the police.

There was nothing anyone could do for Professor Morlan Haggins. Paramedics arrived shortly after the New Haven Police secured the building, but Morlan had long been dead by that point. An autopsy later showed, the bullet went right through his heart, which was why he died so quickly.

Iah and I were taken into custody for questioning and eventually released later that evening. The police put out an alert for Caroline Thatcher's personal vehicle. She managed to disappear for two days before a few people discovered her car parked on a dirt path right by Judges Cave inside West Rock Ridge State Park, just northwest of New Haven. Caroline's body was found shortly after inside the cave made famous by Edward Whalley and William Goffe. Caroline had been dead for many days by apparent suicide via the handgun in her possession. Beside her body were the ashes of the Voynich manuscript, which inspectors later said were dissolving from the wet soil caused by the heavy rainfall that had recently saturated the land.

As for the online versions of the manuscript, we were too late to save them. By the time the police took down our testimony and warning, passed it along to the proper authorities (Yale security, the Curator of the Beinecke Library, and the FBI) all digital copies had been either infected or trashed. A few images of the book remained in random websites, but no copies of the text in its entirety could be located outside of the backup servers. The overall scale of digital destruction was quite impressive, actually. It was the single largest demonstration of virtual vandalism to date.

Despite Iah and mine's attempt at keeping the details of our conversation with Caroline discreet (particularly the parts that concerned our intentions), much was leaked and within hours of our release, the whole world knew a skewed version of the truth. The national news was all over Yale's campus, sensational headlines blanketed covers of newspapers and online media; primetime investigative programs delved deep into the New Haven/Bosnia connection and into Caroline Thatcher's involvement with Charles Theoman as well as the disappearance of Bertók Horvath. Literally within hours, the whole thing became a conspiracy circus, further ignited with the discovery of Caroline's body. Tales of impaled people made its way around, whispers of an underground cult worshipping the devil were heard, and a renewed curiosity into archeological mysteries was felt. We (meaning Project Renew Our History) realized that every move we made was going to be under a gigantic microscope, and that the next time we decided to make a public move we needed to be über cautious not to draw any attention. However, the one good thing that came from all of the media focus was that everyone was now looking for Dr. Bertók Horvath—if only for questioning. They wanted to know what part he played. The authorities and the media were unsure if he was a mastermind or another victim of something sinister. And of course Iah and I withheld the complete truth. We knew what he was and we did all that we could to paint him not as a victim but as the leader of evil.

A private funeral was held for Professor Morlan Haggins. None of the members of Project Renew Our History attended. We steered clear of each other for several weeks, hoping that the spotlight would be directed to something else; and eventually it was.

I didn't return to my apartment—other than to gather some possessions—and I took residence in a hotel just outside New York City; Mr. Vermil had set it up for me/. He felt responsible for my situation and decided to extend financial aid for my living expenses until things settled—if things ever settled—which I can tell you things did not.

Three days after Professor Haggins' murder, I was in my hotel room when a knock came at the door. I had been spending my time trying to figure out what I should do next. I was far too deep into this whole *Book of Thoth* thing to back out, and yet I hadn't a clue on what to do next. Fortunately, for me, the person waiting at my hotel room door provided the new path I needed to take.

I went over to the door and looked through the peephole; there was a bald-headed man with squinty, serious eyes waiting on the other side. I asked, "Who is it?"

The man held up what looked like identification and a badge and said, "Mr. Coulee? My name is Corbin Byrne; I'm with the federal government. Can we talk?"

****

"*Ehm.*" Roland and Garret were impatiently waiting.

Against Rebecca's strong desire to continue reading, she powered off the notepad and apologized. "I'm ready." She stood up and joined her companions.

All three of them looked back toward the makeshift stretcher. Rebecca asked, "Do we just leave it?"

Garret said, "I don't see a need to take it with us, and I don't see any harm of leaving it intact."

Rebecca agreed but felt a strange attachment to the rickety tool they constructed—guilt for walking away from the first thing she practically created out of nothing. And then, in an equally strange moment, she had a new thought—a new feeling—one that could not be explained nor could its genesis be remotely discovered; right there in the middle of a struggle to survive in the jungle, Rebecca thought, *I want to have a baby some day.*

"Let's go," Garret ordered.

The three of them began walking, symbolically leaving the stretcher behind, and started a new journey to their new life inside the Free People's Society. . . .

CHAPTER THIRTY-FIVE

The Dead Sands – Kaacital

Kaacital was no city, as William quickly realized.

Kaacital was nothing more than twelve or fifteen traveling caravans, much like the one William was traveling within. There were elephants harnessed to hold canvases, camels carrying men, women, and children; there were small one-person huts bridging the gap between larger camels, and larger huts bridging the gaps between elephants. William had never seen anything like it before. The sight was so strange and perplexing that if someone had told him that people lived in this manner, he would not have believed it, and yet there it was, right before his eyes.

They had arrived just before sundown and the enormous traveling camp was breaking down in preparation for the night. The elephants and camels were relieved of their duties and were watered and fed, the small and large huts were placed on the sand, cooks pulled out their cauldrons and lit fires, children chased each other on their endlessly energetic legs, women chased the children and prepared bedding on the ground and inside the huts, and the men were either cleaning their kills from the day's hunt, their rifles, or were tending to the animals and the canvas structures. William wondered what it was that he was supposed to do; there was no instructional handbook for how to live with the Desert Demons.

During the long ride through the hot sands, William found driving his camel rather easy to master. It wasn't too long before he felt comfortable enough to depart from the others leading him and venture on his own. By the time they reached Kaacital, William was a confidant rider.

William rode toward the old woman he briefly met when he and the warriors first arrived at the traveling caravan. She was in the process of getting off her camel when he said, "So, now what?"

The woman groaned as she slid off the kneeling animal and said, "We sleep."

"That's great, but what do I do? Where do I sleep? Am I to meet the Kaa? What am I—"

The woman hushed him; she was visibly agitated. "You talk too much." She waved a hand at him and said, "You cost too much and you talk too much. Go and be silent. Go and sleep. Someone will find you in the morning."

Thanks, old hag. William was tired of her impudence. "You speak to me as if I'm some damn burden that was thrust onto you. I want to be here as much as you want me here. So how about we help each other? You tell me where I can find some bedding and maybe some food, and I'll shut my mouth for the remainder of the night."

The woman stared at him for an uncomfortable moment, but before she could give a reply, three men approached her and began speaking in their native tongue. All three men watched William as they waited for the old woman's reply.

"They've come for you," she said to William.

Great, he thought. "What do they want?"

"To fulfill your wants."

One of the men, a thin, muscular man much like Saño, walked over and clicked his tongue while tapping William's camel on its front left leg. The camel lowered to the sand and William slipped off. The pain he felt in his legs and back was enormous.

"You are weak, William Coulee," the old woman said. "You groan and bitch like me, but I am old and I am a woman."

"Don't sell yourself short," William said.

The man standing before him said, "*Confrom. Bas confrom.*"

"He wants you to go with him," the old woman translated.

William asked, "What's his name?"

"Ballo-cel."

William looked at Ballo-cel and said, "Where are we going?"

The man didn't speak, he simply led William from the camel and into the dense population of Kaacital.

The people they passed between were busily building tents and rolling out sleeping bags. Some men laughed in the distance, and the children continued to play. William witnessed several people digging holes in the sand and saw an old man relieving himself in one already dug. *Savages,* he thought, unable to contain his discrimination.

The further William and Ballo-cel went into Kaacital the larger the huts and tents became. William looked to his right and saw what could only be described as an unusual sight for the crowd: a fair-haired, fair-skinned man building a tent. Even though William was certain he had never met the man, there was something familiar about his face. William wanted to ask Ballo-cel who the man was but knew it would be pointless.

It wasn't a moment later that Ballo-cel stopped them at the largest hut. William looked at its ornately patterned cloth walls, which stretched upward, making a trapezoidal shape. The hut was large enough to fit possibly seven to ten people. Ballo-cel walked up to the entrance and then stopped; he raised a hand toward William as if to signal "wait here" and went inside. William wiggled his sore toes inside his boots and watched a beautiful woman with defined facial features walk outside a smaller hut while carrying a clay jug. Her eyes had met his and she quickly turned her attention to the jug and walked through the maze of huts and tents. *They do have attractive women.* Ballo-cel returned through the opening of the hut and waved for William to come inside.

Before he entered, William could already smell the sweet incense burning inside. The hut had bouquets of wonderful smelling sticks inside ceramic jugs, burning slowly and creating lightly shaded, multi-colored clouds of smoke.

A shiny cloth completely covered the sand. It reflected the low light coming from what William recognized as a solar powered lamp. *I wonder where they stole that.* There were other cloths hanging from the ceiling and breaking up the hut into multiple rooms.

Ballo-cel said something to William and then pointed down at William's feet. William looked down at his boots and asked, "What? Do you want me to take my boots off?"

Ballo-cel pointed at William's boots again and imitated taking them off.

William sat down on the ground and quite painfully removed each shoe. He then struggled to stand on his blistered feet. Ballo-cel went ahead and drew back one of the hanging clothes before them. He gestured for William to walk through. William took careful steps as he passed into the next room.

This room was slightly larger than the first and a lot more comfortable looking with a ring of plush pillows circling another solar powered lantern. Already sitting on one of the plush pillows was a narrow-eyed man with a thin mustache just above his upper lip and bushy hair surrounding his face. He was grandly dressed, and he was holding some kind of wooden pipe just short of the length of his forearm. The man gave a clean, toothy smile and said, "Come, sit."

William walked further inside and stepped over and into the ring of pillows. He looked back and saw that Ballo-cel was not joining them. He then said to the man, "You speak my language?"

"Yes, very much so. Please, sit."

William tried to carefully lower his body onto the pillows but ended up crashing.

"You are very tired. Yes, I see this. You've made a long journey."

William nodded his head as he pulled each leg in for a better cross-legged sitting position.

The man said, "I am Kaa."

William wasn't surprised to hear this, but he did have higher expectations for the elected leader of the Desert Demons. "My name is William Coulee."

"Yes, I know this. It was I who sent Saño, The Seeker, to find you."

"Then it should trouble you to know that your seeker perished on his return trip."

Kaa nodded his head. "I was told such."

"And yet you are not sad?"

"I am sad that another lifetime must pass before I see him again."

"Are you speaking of the afterlife?"

"I know not of this afterlife; I speak of the next life."

William was tired of enigmatic talk. "What do you mean by 'next life'?"

Kaa looked unsure of the reason behind William's confusion. "I do not know your people's word for 'next life.'"

"We don't have a term for it; when you die, you die. Only Zius lives on."

Kaa stared emotionlessly before saying, "You speak of *Demozi*, the Dream Maker."

"I've never heard of Demozi. I'm speaking of the fabled leader of my people."

"Yes, you speak of Demozi. That is the name we know him as, Demozi means Dream Maker. He took our lands, killed our people, and he traps us in our dreams."

"You must be confused. Zius doesn't trap people in their dreams; he supposedly lives on, indefinitely. When the world is filled with war and death, Zius returns to set things right. Many believe he will return again, soon."

Kaa smiled and raised a finger. "Ah, you see, we are talking about the same person. Demozi never dies; he takes another body and lives on, trapping his host in forever dream. They become sleepwalkers."

The debate was irritating William. "Okay, fine. Why did you send Saño to find me? Why am I here?"

"Yes, these are important questions, for you know not your destiny, and you do not know that Demozi is everything. The Sleepwalker leads your people, and you must stop him."

"You're mistaken," William said rather curtly. *I have no idea who is leading my people now.*

Kaa smiled and nodded his head. "It is known that you would have trouble. Saño feared as much. You still have amnesia; it is true. We will help you remember."

I'm sure you will. William scanned the room, searching for a weapon.

"You have great fear and anger within you; I know this. Don't let it guide you; control your emotions and accept your fate."

"And what is that?"

"You will be our guest until the time comes when you will no longer be called 'guest.'"

"You plan on holding me prisoner?"

"We keep no prisoners, William Coulee."

"Then you'll let me leave?"

"When you are no longer our guest."

William observed the post holding the overhead solar-powered lamp. *I wonder how heavy that is.*

"Your fear is driving you, William Coulee."

It's not fear, Kaa; it's anger; it's survival. "Why am I here?

"We brought you here so that you will remember your former self. You have forgotten, William Coulee, who you are and where you come from."

"You're still mistaken. I know exactly who I am and where I come—" William leaped up with all his remaining strength and grabbed the lamppost.

Like a jungle cat, Kaa met him every step of the way.

The two struggled for the post, but Kaa was too much for the weary William to handle. William released and fell back to the ground, grimacing in pain and cursing out of frustration. "You can't keep me prisoner! There is nothing for me to remember!"

Kaa stood over William with the lamppost in hand. Three men entered the tent and immediately grabbed William's arms. Kaa held out his hand and said, "*Shite com zeet!*"

The men refrained from yanking William to his feet but stood close by.

"William Coulee, you have much to learn, you have much to remember, but first, you have much rest to get." All of the pleasantness that was once in Kaa's voice had left, leaving the stern tone of a fearless leader. "You will be taken to a tent prepared for you by my people. Rest. Do not trouble yourself with the worries plaguing your mind. Your answers will come and you will soon see that we are not your enemies but your friends."

Kaa looked at the three men and nodded his head.

The three warriors helped William to his feet and led him out of the tent. William wanted to fight, but the Kaa was right, he was too tired to do anything but rest.

The three men led William past a crowd of onlookers, all of whom seemed interested in the strange new *guest*. They passed several tents and came upon a modest one that had two men flanking the entrance flap. The men were larger than the average Desert Demon, and they were holding solid wood staffs.

The three men warriors escorting William stopped at the entrance. One said, "*Yamiz. Bas yamiz.*" He had thrust an open hand toward the entrance flap, indicating that he wanted William to enter.

"All right, all right." William bent as low as his achy body would allow and stepped through the flap.

Inside the tent was a small solar-powered lamp resting on top of a small woven table. There were cloths covering the sand and several satin-covered pillows making up a half-circle in the center of the tight space. *Comfy*, William thought sardonically. He crumbled into the half-circle of pillows and melted into their softness. A few moments later, William's shoes found their way to their new home inside the tent. William had completely forgotten that he had left them inside the Kaa's tent. "Thanks," he called out to the anonymous pair of hands that dropped the shoes inside. He then allowed his head to fall back into the pillows and remained that way for the duration of the night.

Outside the tent stood Kaa. He ordered his men to be alert just in case William Coulee found a hidden reserve of energy and determination. The two large men with staffs assured him that they would not allow anyone in or out of his tent. Kaa knew their word was as good as gold. *Rest up, William Coulee; tomorrow will be a big day.*

CHAPTER THIRTY-SIX

District 4, Sector 2

The sun was barely above the horizon when the three companions arrived just outside the Free People base perimeter. Garret halted them and stood silently. He then said quietly, "Listen."

Rebecca and Roland listened as ordered. The life surrounding them was agitated. There were screeches, howls, cries, and rustling; all of it was much louder than either of them had noticed before. "What's going on?" Rebecca said in a hush tone.

"Something's wrong," Garret announced. "They're never like this. Something is stirring them."

"Maybe it's us?" suggested Roland.

Garret didn't seem to think so. "We come in and out of here all of the time, I've never heard the animals sound like this."

Rebecca's achy, exhausted body filled with adrenaline as her heart began to race. Her senses were at an acute level. Even Roland, who looked more dead than alive, was suddenly filled with an energy that had been missing since he suffered the coyote bite. "What do we do?" Rebecca asked. According to Garret, the base was less than a hundred yards away. "Can't we just go for it?"

Garret was hesitant in answering. "I'm worried about what we'll find."

No, no, no, thought Rebecca, *this can't be happening. We've come so far; we're finally going to be safe.*

Roland said what she was feeling. "I don't think I can handle anything else right now."

Garret observed them and said, "Wait here; get low and hide behind some trees; I'll go ahead and see what's causing the disturbance." He slipped his burn rifle from his shoulder and began charging it.

"Can you use your communicator?" asked Rebecca.

"No. I told you before . . ."

Rebecca nodded and did as he ordered; so did Roland.

Garret went carefully through the brush and past the trees until he was no longer in sight. The sounds all around them continued with the whoops and wails. Roland wiped the sweat from his brow and said, "I hope he's wrong . . . I hope everything is okay. . . ." Rebecca wanted to say something encouraging but couldn't; she just looked at him and forced a phony smile.

Garret was gone now for at least five minutes. Rebecca's legs, particularly her calves, were beginning to cramp. Her feet and ankles were itching badly, and the rash on her arm had grown worse. *We're so close*, she thought. *Please let everything be okay, just for this once. Please!*

Another five or so minutes passed. Roland rotated around and sat onto the ground with his back against the tree. He looked absolutely exhausted. Their adrenaline had worn off and was replaced by impatience and discouragement. "This is taking too long," Roland said weakly.

Rebecca was thinking the same thing. She had sprung several droplets of blood on her ankles from her persistent scratching. "How much longer do we wait?" she asked.

"I don't know. Someone will eventually come for us, either Garret or . . . whoever."

The *whoever* part was not appealing.

More time passed, maybe ten or twelve minutes. They remained behind their respective trees, waiting, just waiting; it was all they could do. Rebecca eventually looked over to Roland and said, "Maybe we should go."

Roland's head was slumped, as if he was sleeping. "Go where?"

She had nowhere particular in mind, just anywhere. "Maybe I should go ahead and see what's happening, see if I can find out where Garret is, what has happened to him—if anything—and then I'll come back for you."

Roland turned his head, "You're leaving?"

"Do you want to come with me? We can go together."

Roland looked like he wanted to join her, to get up and leave that spot behind the tree, to take his fate into his own hands, but he couldn't. He was too weak and tired. "I'll wait for you."

Rebecca looked into Roland's bloodshot eyes and felt a level of guilt rise. She was about to leave him for a second time. But the sitting and waiting for who knew what to come and get them was more than she could handle; she was able-bodied and so she needed to try to do something. But as Rebecca stood, using the tree to shift her weight off of her sore feet and ankles, the world around them became more audible. She slid the pack that was carrying Simon's notepad off her shoulder and walked to another tree where there was a heavy amount of greenery and slid the pack inside; it was completely out of sight. She then went back to Roland and said, "If something happens to me, and if you are capable, go get the notepad and take it to my father. He'll know what to do with it."

"Nothing is going to happen," Roland said faintly. "I'll be waiting here—resting—for you to come back. Just don't take too long."

Rebecca agreed and then hesitated another moment before deciding now or never; she took in a deep breath, released it, and started to walk when suddenly her intuition told her to not move. She stopped immediately and stood completely still. Her senses heightened. . . .

Something was coming . . . many things were coming.

"Roland," she whispered, "get up. Get up right now! We have to get out of here!"

Roland looked up at her, and all at once his senses snapped awake, too. Roland looked around and stood as Rebecca did while wincing in pain. But there was no more time.

The surrounding jungle took the form of twenty humans, each converging on Rebecca and Roland. Rebecca recognized the sight. They looked just like Garret's platoon of Free People dressed in light bending camouflage suits. And like her encounter with that platoon, these figures had their weapons pointing directly at her.

"Arms out!" ordered one of the figures—a man.

Rebecca did as told. Roland had a bit of a tougher time extending his wounded arm but managed to suffice. Rebecca wasn't sure if they were in trouble or if they were rescued. She wanted to tell the man—whichever one spoke to them—that she was a friend of Garret's, but deep down she knew to keep her mouth shut until the time was right.

The figures surrounding them cautiously closed in. Rebecca felt both of her arms get detained and pulled around her back as she stared at the figure directly ahead. Laserlocks were placed onto her wrists. The same was done to Roland, who screamed out in pain.

"Who are you?" Rebecca demanded.

The man in front of her removed his camouflaged mask, revealing an unattractive face wearing a stern glare. He said, "You two are to be detained under Ministry Order 211."

Rebecca thought, *Order 211?* But then she remembered what it stood for; it was a decree that allowed the MSF to detain anyone suspected of rebellious activity. Rebecca quickly said, "Sir, we're not rebels, we were—"

The man put his finger to his lips and shushed. "Don't speak."

Another agent took her left arm and ran a scanner over it. Rebecca thought, *This is it. Now they know who I am. . . . I'm dead.*

The agent took the scanner over to the lead agent and showed him the screen. The lead agent looked at it and gave a modest smile. "Not rebels, eh?" he said to Rebecca. "But not born within the Collective, either. Don't you know that all Free Born are rebels?"

Free Born? She thought. *What is he talking about?* Rebecca was not free born. She had a chip in her arm like everyone else in the Collective and it revealed everything about her identity. Free Borns had no chip, thus no identity. Rebecca went to argue but then held her tongue for she had an epiphany. *They don't know who I am. My chip isn't working. The chip scanner didn't work!*

"Check the other one," the lead agent ordered.

The man with the device walked over to Roland and took his left arm. "This man's arm is mangled. . . . It looks infected."

The lead agent asked, "What happened to you?"

Roland cried out through the pain. "I was attacked by a coyote."

The lead agent looked to the man with the scanner who seemed to agree. The man with the scanner said, "Looks like bite marks. It's pretty bad."

Rebecca said, "We came across a group of people who gave us medicine. It should be healing soon."

The lead agent said, "Scan him."

The man with the scanner did so and then looked up to the lead agent and shook his head.

This confirmed it for Rebecca. *They can't read Roland's chip either. I don't understand why, but they can't read our chips. We might live!*

The lead agent grunted and said, "Take his arm off."

The agents holding Roland released the laser locks before either Roland or Rebecca had realized what was just ordered.

"Wait a second!" Roland finally cried out as one of the agents extended his arm.

"What are you doing!" shouted Rebecca.

Another agent with a burn rifle already charged, ignited it and very swiftly slashed down and through Roland's arm.

Roland screamed out in pain.

"NO!" Rebecca cried.

Roland fell limp and was immediately helped up by the agents who detached his arm.

Rebecca immediately began to sob. *"Why did you do that!?"*

The lead agent walked over to Roland and pointed to where the agent had severed it. "See, just above the infected area. We just saved his life. You're welcome."

The wound that was once Roland's left arm was smoking from the burn.

The lead agent continued, "The good thing about lasers is that they help seal wounds."

Rebecca burst out in anger, *"You didn't have to do that! He had medicine! He was going to be okay!"*

The lead agent had no care in his eyes. He casually walked over to her and said, "You are both to be detained, and you both will be processed. Load them up with the other."

Rebecca looked at Roland, who was pale white and in complete shock, as agents forcefully jerked them into a march. *"I'm sorry,"* she sobbed to Roland. *"I'm sorry."*

They walked for a few minutes, long enough for Rebecca to regain her wits, and she realized again, *They don't know who we are.* In a strange way, it was almost a blessing. Rebecca knew it could give them a little bit of time, that maybe they wouldn't be executed. As long as the MSF didn't know her name was Rebecca Badeau, anything was possible. She looked over at Roland who was in a complete daze and thought *I need Roland to realize what's going on.* Under no circumstance could they reveal their real names or their lives would surely be over.

CHAPTER THIRTY-SEVEN

District 4, Sector 2

As swiftly as they were captured, Rebecca and Roland were taken to a loading zone where several hovercrafts waited, just outside the smoldering ruins of a Free People's base.

Roland didn't speak the entire time; the look of shock never left his face, even after the MSF medics finished bandaging what remained of his left arm. Rebecca didn't speak either. She disconnected herself from the situation and merely observed what was happening. She wasn't able to learn much from the men escorting her; they said very little outside of what their duties required.

The MSF agents secured them inside one of the three hovercrafts where a third person was already sitting, laserlocked, and with a hood over his head. Rebecca looked at the man's clothes and recognized him to be Garret. He was a bit bloodied, possibly from being beaten, but wholly looked intact—far more than Roland.

A moment later, Rebecca and Roland had hoods pulled over their heads as well.

She finally allowed her mind to speak. *We're in so much trouble.* How much so was yet to be determined.

The hovercraft's engines revved and squealed as it prepared to lift upward.

Rebecca didn't dare talk to anyone, but she knew that she needed to communicate with Roland somehow. She needed to make sure that he would not accidentally reveal who they are. Rebecca wasn't positive whether he had processed their situation appropriately. She thought about what she had read inside William's manuscript, how Iah was able to communicate with others just by using his mind: *telepathy.* With nothing to see past the blankness brought on by the hood, Rebecca focused her thoughts on a single thing: *Give them a fake name, Roland. Give them a fake name. Give them a fake name. . . .*

Unfortunately there was no way for her to determine if the message was received.

Rebecca mentally played out the upcoming scenario. *When we land, they will take us into the detention center and question us who we are. I have to speak first. I have to give a false name . . . but what name? . . .* She pondered that for a moment. *It must be real sounding and yet far different from my own.* Rebecca thought about the people she had known in her life, girls she went to the Academy with, women she worked with when life was normal and simple . . . *Mary,* she decided, the first name of a childhood friend.

She thought more about her Academy years, but more about her acquaintances from class, not friends . . . there was a boy—a man now—named John Macyntire . . . *Macyntire—Mary Macyntire.*

And just like that, her identity was set.

The hovercraft had risen over the jungle at this point.

They'll want to know what we were doing in the middle of the jungle. There was no easy explanation for that. Time passed before anything plausible came into her mind. *I can tell them that we were relocating . . . that we were looking for a new place to live, a new village. . . . But why?* Rebecca tossed a few more ideas. *We are lovers and we . . . tradition has it that . . .* Rebecca then remembered the Coctavians; she remembered a tradition of theirs. *I can tell them that tradition forces new lovers to leave their home village and find new land to settle in. We were looking for a new place to call home when coyotes attacked us.* She realized she couldn't lie about Garret. *We stumbled upon him along the way. He helped us with medicine, that is all.*

For the rest of the flight, Rebecca tried to come up with a few more supporting lies to help sell her story. The flight, however, wasn't long, and so she had little time to come up with anything else that was truly compelling.

When they touched down at the Sector 2 – 17th District's MSF detention center. The agents brought Rebecca, Roland, and Garret to their feet and escorted them inside the low-lying, single story, steel walled compound.

The first-floor interior of the detention center was a labyrinth of medium height walls that segregated desks and conference tables. The perimeter of the floor was lined with offices and interrogation rooms.

Rebecca, Roland, and Garret were led directly down the main alleyway, which was known as Rebel Row (because everyone who was escorted down it was arrested for being some form of a rebel). Rebel Row had several scanners posted parallel to each other that the rebels were led through. The first pairing tagged the rebels' identification chips in their arms, which immediately updated Ministry databases with the arrest; and the second pairing scanned them for anything foreign: a surgically hidden bomb, weapons, electronic devices, et cetera.

It was this second set of scanners that sounded off when Rebecca walked through.

Almost instantaneously, there were agents pointing laser tubes or burn rifles at her. She was ordered to extend her arms straight out and kneel onto the ground.

Roland and Garret, who were still standing at the start of Rebel Row, were ordered to do the same. An agent with a handheld scanner walked up to Rebecca and waved it all across her body, stopping at her left arm. Rebecca knew instantly what was happening. *My identification chip. For some reason it is reading as a foreign electronic device.* She then knew that the same thing would happen to Roland when he passed through.

The agent with the scanner adjusted its settings before allowing her to continue, but not before she gained the attention of the entire MSF force stationed there, including the attention of an older, higher-ranked agent who slowly passed through the serpentine of desk walls and into the center of Rebel Row, where Rebecca now stood.

"What's your name?" he asked after examining a digital report posted on a d-reader handed to him by another agent.

Rebecca carefully and very loudly responded, "Mary Macintyre."

The agent's eyebrows lifted as he looked at the d-reader again, and then he said, "How is it that you have an identification chip in your arm with no profile associated with it?"

This answer required more careful, yet quick, thought. She said loudly, again, "It is a failed experiment conducted by the Free People when I was first born. They tried to replicate the Ministry's process of chipping babies."

The man scoffed, "I'm sure." He looked toward the agent escorting Rebecca. "Place her in IR-3." Then he yelled down Rebel Row, "Next!"

Rebecca tried to watch as Roland was escorted down the alleyway; she hoped with every ounce of her soul that Roland overheard her responses and knew he needed to lie. She continued trying to transmit a single thought to him. *Give them a fake name.*

An agent carrying Roland's severed arm inside a plastic bag waved it in front of both scanners. The second scanner's alarm sounded off just as it did with her. Roland received the same treatment, lasers aimed and a scan of his body, but before Rebecca could hear how he answered the questions asked by the supervising agent, she was stuffed inside Interrogation Room 3.

There she remained in the small barren room—with only a single metallic chair bolted to the floor—for almost an hour before the door opened again and the supervising agent walked inside. He was carrying a d-reader and was wearing an unpleasant scowl. "So, *Mary*," he said sullenly, "we need to have a little chat." He then closed the door.

CHAPTER THIRTY-EIGHT

District 17, Sector 2

The name he gave Rebecca was Archibald Moore. "I'm District 17's Senior Inquisitor." He licked his lips quickly and then tapped something on his d-reader. "Your identification chip appears to be operational, and we have assigned it your name and detainment code." He paused for no apparent reason. "Are you familiar with our operation?"

Rebecca was unsure how to respond. She knew some things—like the fact that detention centers existed and that they served as short-term locations for newly detained criminals, but that was it; and the real question was whether Mary Macintyre would know. So she played dumb and shook her head.

"Your stay here will be temporary. We will question you, judge you, and process you. From there you will be someone else's problem. Is that clear?"

Rebecca nodded.

"Speak your answers. You had no problem talking loudly before."

"Yes," she said, "that is clear."

"Good." He then walked back to the door and left her alone.

And alone she remained.

She thought, *Roland must have played along, thank God! Otherwise we would be dealt with already.* But she didn't know for sure what Roland said, or what had happened to him—or Garret. The laserlocks on her wrists were dreadfully tight, and her arms—bound behind her back—had repeating patterns of pins-and-needles pass through them. She tried sitting on the metal chair bolted to the floor, in the center of the room, but with her arms as they were, she couldn't find a position that was comfortable. Knots had formed in the muscles in her back. All of this left Rebecca completely incapable of relaxing, which she assumed was the point.

Another hour passed and she felt the inconvenient pain of needing to use the restroom. When the pain peaked, Rebecca went to the door and called out for help. She did this for nearly ten minutes; all the while she paced the floor anxiously, trying to fight off the urge. It was after ten minutes, and to the point of her soiling herself, that an agent finally opened the door and slid in a metallic bowl that he clearly intended her to use. Rebecca looked at it and refused the idea for only a brief moment—long enough to realize they weren't kidding—and then struggled to pull down her underwear with her hands bound behind her. Miraculously, she managed the feat.

Another half-an-hour passed by, one filled with embarrassment, before the door opened once again. Archibald Moore entered and gazed at Rebecca standing miserably by the chair. He simply said, "Why were you in the jungle?"

Rebecca lifted her weary eyes and looked at him through the sheet of exhaustion that shielded her from reality. "As I told your agents before, we were walking to the base. We're not freedom fighters."

"But you don't live within the Collective, right?"

"No, I don't."

"So then you are fighting the system, yes?"

Rebecca heaved a heavy sigh. "Then, yes."

"So you are a freedom fighter."

"I meant *no*, I'm not a soldier."

"But that is not what I asked you."

Unnoticed by her, Rebecca's head slowly bobbed up and down from the weakness of her neck.

"I'll take your silence as a yes." He cleared his throat and then moved on. "From your condition, it is clear something more had happened these past few days than you have lead us to believe. Please explain."

Rebecca felt her frustration bubble within as she tried to come up with a story that made sense. *All I have to do is not tell them that I'm Rebecca Badeau.* "We were traveling from one village to another—"

"Who?" demanded Archibald.

"My companion and I. We were leaving one village for another—"

"Why?"

Rebecca sighed; her level of frustration had risen. "Because we wanted to. It is tradition."

"Clearly," Archibald said, almost humorously, "but every tradition has a reason."

"Because it's what my people have done for many years."

"Yes, but why?"

Rebecca's exhausted mind struggled to answer. "Because, that is how my people spread."

Archibald noted something and then said, "You're wearing a peculiar traveling outfit." He walked over to her and tugged lightly on her tattered and dirtied nightgown. "My wife sleeps in something similar to this. . . . Where did you get it?"

"My mother gave it to me. I don't know where she got it from."

"We've brought many *Free People* in here and none of them were ever dressed as you are. How about you tell me the truth."

"I am," Rebecca said through a tired breath. "I'm telling you everything."

Archibald noted her answer and smiled. "Alright, now then, when did you leave?"

"Two . . . or maybe three days ago."

"You don't know?"

"We were attacked by coyotes along the way. My companion was bitten rather severely. We lost all of our things in the attack, and he grew very ill. I got very little rest from that point on. . . . So I'm sorry, I'm not sure how long we've been traveling."

"But it seems you had medicine . . . am I right?"

Rebecca shook her head, her hair was getting into her eyes. "We didn't have medicine. Garret had the medicine. He found us along the way and was taking us back to his base."

"And about how many days had you been walking when you came across Garret?"

"Two, maybe?" *But has it been two?* Rebecca couldn't remember. She didn't even know how many hours had passed since their arrival at the detention center; it felt like forever.

Archibald noted her answer in his d-reader and asked, "Why were you traveling on foot?"

"Walking was our only means of transportation."

"Walking," he repeated and noted. "And so, then, tell me where you were walking to?"

Rebecca thought, *Didn't I already answer this question?* And so she gave him the same answer as before. The repeating of questions—worded differently—became the overall theme of their conversation for the next hour. Rebecca did her best to be discreet with her responses, and it seemed Archibald was growing agitated that she wasn't giving him what he wanted. Eventually the questioning stopped and he left her alone again. Then it seemed to Rebecca that another hour passed before a different agent walked inside the room. His name was Carlz Rudolph. And the questioning began all over again; the same questions as before, worded differently. Rebecca tried to give him as consistent of a response as she gave Archibald, but her mind was so very weary, which made it difficult to organize her thoughts and recall the specifics of what she had already said.

Eventually Carlz was satisfied and left her alone for another hour before returning and asking the questions all over again. However, this time he added a few new ones. He asked about her childhood, who her friends were, her age, and about her parents. Rebecca gave him more lies; she told him that her father's name was Markus, her mother's was Maurine—keeping them similar to her own—that she was of thirty years, and that her companion— meaning Roland—was a childhood friend who played Scatter-O-Maze with her (which was a made up game). Carlz asked her if she was married to her companion, to which she answered, "Yes." She said it without realizing the gamble. Carlz gave her no indication whether she passed this line of questioning or not, he simply left and locked the door, again.

The next time Carlz came in the room, Rebecca was crashed in the corner. Her legs were tucked underneath her so that she was sitting on her right thigh, and the wall served as a pillow for her right shoulder and head. Somehow she was asleep; or at least to him, she appeared to be sleeping. Carlz walked over to her and bent down. He asked very calmly, "What is your companion's name?"

It was the one question she couldn't answer; and apparently they knew this now, too.

"Mary," he said louder, "what is your companion's name?"

Rebecca wasn't asleep, but she didn't open her eyes, either; Rebecca was concentrating intensely on Roland. *What is the name you gave them?*

"WAKE UP!" yelled Carlz.

What is the name you gave them?

Carlz stood and walked to the door; he yelled out for assistance and then returned with two other men. The three of them hoisted Rebecca—to which she realized she needed to keep the charade going—and they took her out of Interrogation Room 3. Rebecca heard the men's footfalls echo, indicating a much larger room. There was a more noticeable ambiance of people talking, walking, and moving things. She realized she was inside the main floor but passing through it rather quickly. All the while, Rebecca continued the stream of thought directed at Roland. *What is the name you gave them?*

The men carried her into an elevator and it seemed to Rebecca that they went down. She struggled with keeping her eyes shut at this point. The fear inside of her had taken hold and she wanted to see where she was going, what danger lay before her, and who might also be around her.

When the doors opened, the agents quickly left the elevator and carried her far away from it. Rebecca felt them make several turns: right, then left, then left again, and then another right. She was dropped onto the ground, rather carelessly, before the agents walked away from her and the door was slammed shut.

The floor was cold and not as pleasant as the previous room's. There were noticeable cracks, pebbles, and moisture. Rebecca deeply desired to open her eyes and to see her new environment, but she continued pretending and concentrating. *Roland, what is the name you gave them? Please hear me! What name are you using?* She did this for an unmeasured amount of time before she finally resigned to open her eyes.

At first she thought she was inside a cave again. The floor, which her face was pressed against, was unrefined and dirty, much like the cave she and Roland stayed in when the coyotes attacked; but the walls were industrial and not as kind as the walls making up Interrogation Room 3.

"You're awake," declared an unseen voice through a speaker—Carlz's voice.

Rebecca slowly looked around—the room was an impenetrable enclosure with a row of holes, it seemed, wrapping around each wall except for the one containing the only door, which appeared air tight, and the floor had four circular areas that resembled drains—but she didn't see a camera or the source of Carlz voice. The air was rather cold against her bare skin.

"Your level of cooperation has not met our requirements; therefore, we feel that further measures need to be taken."

Dread shrouded Rebecca. She stood in the center of the room—shifting from one cold barefoot to the other—and looked anxiously around for what might be coming.

Carlz voice returned. "What is the name of your companion?"

Rebecca had nothing to give him. Her mind was blank, which unfortunately was taken as intentional resistance. Suddenly there was a creaking sound coming through the walls, and water sprouted from each hole. Rebecca's initial response was of curiosity; but as the water pressure increased—and roared into the room—the floor turned into a shallow pool of icy water; and Rebecca's curiosity turned into terror.

Carlz said, "I want to know your companion's name."

Rebecca was frozen stiff from indecision. She had to tell him something, but nothing she came up with seemed logical or helpful. If she gave him Roland's name, then she would be dead for sure; but if she gave him a false name that didn't align with what Roland said, then Carlz might drown her.

The water crept above her ankles.

Rebecca sloshed toward the door, but there was no handle for her to turn. She pushed up against it anyway, but it gave her no indication of opening.

Carlz said, "The temperature of the water is just above freezing. It will fill the entire room quickly. So, if I were you, I would give me an answer."

The water was freezing; there was no doubt about that. The level rose above Rebecca's knees. The bottom of her tattered nightgown became soaked as it dragged through the water's surface.

Rebecca sloshed back toward the center of the room; already she was beginning to lose feeling in her feet, which was making it difficult to move. *Roland!* She cried out in her mind. *What name did you give them?*

Still nothing came to her.

Carlz said no more as the water continued to rise; it was up to Rebecca's waist before she knew it. *I'm going to drown*, she thought.

Rebecca reconsidered coming clean, telling them Roland's real name. *I'm dead no matter what. Maybe they will kill me more humanely if I tell them Roland's name. He might already be dead for all I know. What further harm will come?* She tried hard to rationalize it. *But they don't know my real name*, she reminded herself. *Therefore, Roland didn't give me away despite whatever they did to him.* Her allegiance to Roland returned as the water reached below her chest. Her nightgown looked like pedals from a flower—and she was the stem—as it floated along the water's surface.

Her whole body was so very cold.

Her teeth began to chatter while she tried to bounce around and keep the blood flowing. *Roland, what name did you give them!? Please hear me! What name!?*

There was no response.

Rebecca tried treading to keep her head above the water surface. All of her limbs were numb and slow to react. She had little to no strength. She silently cried out, *Please, help! I can't do this any longer!* But even her pleas were weak and feeble.

Her face dropped below surface and she took in a mouthful of cold, dirty water. With a limited, renewed energy, Rebecca had thrust her head back through and sprayed out the water. Her cry this time was louder and direr. "HELP! I'M GOING TO DROWN!"

Her thoughts of Roland had all but disappeared. One last plea entered her mind. *ROLAND, TELL ME YOUR NAME SO I CAN SHOUT IT OUT!*

Her face went below the surface, again.

Water pushed into her nasal cavities and into her lungs before one final push allowed her to explode upward and eject what she inhaled.

In one final moment of flail, Rebecca cried out words that she was unconscious of, and then she was submerged. She tried to swim, to tread; but she couldn't feel anymore. All she could do was hold what breath she had with what little energy was left.

It wasn't long before she succumbed.

CHAPTER THIRTY-NINE

District 17, Sector 2

Rebecca awoke to the sound of coughing—her own coughing. Someone had rolled her onto her stomach and was heavily slapping her upper back.

The coughing was now combined with vomiting.

She struggled to take a breath.

Pain became noticeable in her chest as tears flowed freely down her cheeks. This episode lasted several minutes before all of the water was expelled.

Rebecca was rolled onto her side by the pair of unknown hands and then left alone on the floor. A door opened, several people passed through, and then it shut. Rebecca uttered several nonsensical words as she struggled to keep consciousness.

Sensation in her body returned. She was freezing cold. She folded her legs up to her chest, tucked her arms in, and trembled uncontrollably.

There she remained for the duration of an hour, slipping in and out of consciousness. Eventually she made the decision to move; Rebecca lifted her head and looked around. She was still in the same room as before, when the water filled it, but now it was drained and devoid of any indication that the space was once filled with the freezing cold liquid. The only sign that anything had happened was her sopping wet clothes, hair, and the puddle of water vomit.

I'm so cold, she thought.

In a way, she wished she had died, then she could rest comfortably, her mind would be at ease, and she wouldn't have any further pain to suffer. But, of course, she wasn't dead. Her life continued on, somehow.

Rebecca rested her head back onto the floor and thought, *I want to sleep. . . . I just want this over so I can sleep.*

The door opened and several people walked inside the room. Rebecca braced herself and lifted her head to see who it was. She didn't recognize two of the agents but did recognize Archibald Moore. The two agents rolled Rebecca onto her stomach and bound her hands behind her back again— like before—and then lifted her limp body until her two feet took position underneath.

Archibald casually walked over to Rebecca and said, "Mary Macintyre, you have been found guilty of aiding and assisting Heretique forces, and thereby are subject to the maximum penalty associated with such offense."

Rebecca could barely comprehend what was being said.

"You will be transferred to the CS Processing Compound in Sector 12 until a decision on your fate can be decided."

Rebecca had nothing to say; she lifted her head just high enough to see Archibald's dispassionate face and then lowered it.

"Take her away."

The two agents supporting her began to walk out of the room, dragging Rebecca's powerless legs along the way. They said nothing to each other as they carried her through the sparse hall and into an elevator. It then seemed they went further into the ground and not up as expected. Rebecca tried to regain her footing, but once the elevator doors opened, and the agents started walking again, her strength was not enough to keep the pace and she fell limp.

The agents took her inside a large hangar that somewhat reminded Rebecca of the Free People city down in the Vriezen. Loud noises filled her ears: turbines from hovercrafts, motor vehicles zipping to and fro, shouts from other agents, bangs and clanks, and hydraulic presses loading things onto large transports. The agents led Rebecca up the ramp of one of those transports and inside its hold. Another agent, who seemed overly pleased with his job, took Rebecca's left arm and ran a scanner over it. It beeped and then the agent said, "All right, drop her off."

The two agents walked Rebecca over to a seat that was bolted into the side of the hull and forcefully placed her down. Rebecca's head snapped back and banged against the metal wall. She tried to cry out in pain, but no sound escaped her mouth.

The agents buckled her in and another agent—a female—came over with an injection gun. Rebecca noticed clumps of hair on the ground across the way, in front of a row of chairs, and someone sweeping it up. The female agent placed the injection gun against Rebecca's right arm and pulled the trigger, sounding off compressed air and piercing Rebecca's skin with five little needles. Fortunately the pain was minimal. The woman retracted the gun and walked away without saying a word.

Rebecca looked down at the five little piercings in her arm and saw blood droplets ooze. She then looked up to the man sweeping and saw him collect the hair into a dustbin. The man, who looked like he was in his sixties, took pause and noticed her. There was no feeling coming from his face; his eyes merely observed and then he returned to his work of cleaning up hair. And just as Rebecca began to wonder why there was hair on the ground, her sight grew fuzzy. Not a minute later, Rebecca was asleep.

CHAPTER FORTY

The Dead Sands – Kaacital

"*Gaez! Umpta Gaez!*"

William awoke to Ballo-cel vigorously shaking him.

"*Simbatoo, Umpta Gaez!*"

"What's the matter?" William said as he pushed Ballo-cel's hands away.

"*Thera um ziffen, bas.*"

William had no idea what the man was saying to him; his body hurt as he tried to move. "I'm getting up! Give me a second . . ." William rose to his knees and Ballo-cel left the tent. Sunlight blasted through as the tent flap swung. William cursed as every muscle reminded him of what he had been through the past couple of days. *What in the Minister's name is going on?*

As he left the tent, William saw that he was one of the last few to wake; almost all of the tents were broken down and packed up. The elephants that made up the perimeter already had their harnesses attached and the canvas covering was raised. William looked toward the Kaa's tent and saw that it too was broken down and packed. Kaa was mounted on a camel and staring back at William.

Ballo-cel, who was packing up William's tent, barked out a few more indiscernible things to William. In reply, William said, "I don't know what you're saying."

"He's telling you that you're lazy," said an old woman's voice.

William turned around and saw the old woman from the day before mounted on her camel.

"He's agitated because you are making everyone late."

William had never been called lazy in his entire life. Anger quickly rose within him. "You can tell *Ballo* that . . ." but then William thought better of what he was going to say and he resisted finishing.

"I see that you're learning," said a new voice.

William turned around again and saw that Kaa had rode up behind him. "This is good, William Coulee."

William didn't know what to say.

"We are leaving," Kaa said. "It is time for us to move, once again."

William observed the people hoisting their packs and covering their waste holes. "Time to make more circles in the desert?"

Kaa smiled and said, "Not this time." He then rode off.

William turned to the old woman. "What did he mean?"

"What you probably think he meant."

"We're leaving the Dead Sands?"

"Kaa leads the way. We ask no questions."

So much blind faith, William thought. It reminded him of how the people of the Collective had blindly followed the Minister. *And look how that is turning out.* "Maybe you and your people should start asking questions. The Dead Sands is where you are safe; outside, the Ministry controls everything, and they are not tolerant of outsiders."

The old woman didn't look concerned. "Fate is more powerful than your Ministry. Kaa will lead us through harm."

Ballo-cel finished neatly packing the tent into a large tanned-skin pack. He handed the pack to William and then walked over to one of the pair of camels remaining riderless. William saw that the pack had straps and observed others who were wearing packs on their backs.

"You need to mount up," the old woman advised. "We are leaving."

The traveling city was already in motion.

Not knowing where in the desert he was located, William reluctantly walked over to the remaining camel and mounted it.

As the camel stood upright, it seemed that all that William had learned the day before had left his memory, and he nearly lost his balance. Ballo-cel steadied William as he regained his composure. The old woman merely laughed and rode ahead. *Such hospitality*, William thought.

Ballo-cel rode on and William chased after him and the old woman. When he caught up to them, William said to the woman, "I still don't know your name."

"The woman merely glanced at him and said, "Cjella."

William repeated it back to her and she shook her head. "You need to say it from the bottom of your throat, like a man: *Cjel*-la."

William said it more correctly the second time.

"Good."

"Tell me then, Cjella, how far of a ride do you believe we have before leaving the Dead Sands?"

"I cannot tell you. It will be long, that I do know. These sands run for many countries. They confuse the lonely traveler and they swallow the weak. We ride in packs so that we are never alone nor are we ever weak."

"Saño was traveling alone."

Cjella looked away before speaking. "That was of his choosing. Saño was not weak, even when alone." There was a hint of a tear in her left eye, which William could see.

"You loved him."

"Of course I loved him. Saño was my husband."

Cjella's admission was a knife in William's heart. *And he's dead because of me.* It took him a moment before finally saying, "I'm sorry for your loss."

"Sorrow is for the blind. I need none of it." Cjella's tears were gone.

The three of them rode on for quite a while underneath Kaacital's canvas without speaking another word. It wasn't until a young female rider joined them that the silence broke. Cjella spoke in their native tongue to the girl who then passed in front of them. William had recognized her beauty as the girl he saw the night before carrying a clay jug.

"Who is that?"

"My daughter," Cjella said quickly.

"Yours and Saño's daughter?"

"Yes, that is what I said."

William looked at her and was amazed that something so perfect could come from the wrinkly beaten woman next to him and the gap-toothed Saño.

"I have not always looked the manner I do now, if that is what you are wondering."

William felt a bit embarrassed; it seemed his thoughts had betrayed him. "I wasn't thinking that; I was merely thinking of how beautiful your daughter is and how proud you must be of her."

"Proud of her beauty? I will be proud when she proves to be a powerful leader like her father and her brother now."

Her brother now? William thought about it for a second before asking, "Kaa is her brother?"

Cjella nodded.

"Then Saño was Kaa's father?"

"Yes."

Well then I'll be damned for sure. "Saño mentioned none of this to me; I had no idea."

"Saño told you exactly what you needed to know. Your mind was not prepared, and Saño knew this. It is unfortunate that he is no longer here to teach you your purpose. There was much he wanted to show you."

"What exactly?"

"It is not my place to share such things. Saño and only Saño can be the one."

"So then, are you telling me that I will never know?"

"I am telling you that only Saño will let you know."

"But Saño is dead."

"Yes, so I have heard."

"Then how is he going to teach me anything?"

Cjella gave a smug grin. "Saño was right about you." She then pulled her camel away from William and their conversation.

Thanks for nothing, he thought. And for the next three hours, all William thought about was how he was going to get away from the old woman, the Kaa, and the this traveling band of bizarre riders.

It was past midday when Kaacital took its first rest. William brought his camel to a halt behind a group of male warriors, both young and old. He had learned that all of the camels had been walking for three days in the intense heat without water. "They can go four, maybe five days without it. We never take them past four. Today, we will break for water." Cjella had pointed out several water troughs being carried by a multitude of camels, two by two. "We have just enough water for today and then we must find a new source."

So, we'll be stopping, William had thought as he conspired. He had been carefully watching how the people of Kaacital rode; they formed a diamond pattern and rotated positions, similar to how birds took turns leading the flock. Each rider seemed nimble and an expert driver of his or her own camel. He had realized that breaking away from the traveling citadel would be difficult when they were on the move, so he had conspired an escape for when they halted. *I'll lead my camel over to the water trough, like everyone, but before they can give their camels a drink, I'll make my move.* He had also realized that not giving his camel water would be a risky move, especially considering William had no idea how long it could run for before completely tiring out or dying of thirst. *That's a risk I'll have to take.*

It was at that moment that William had noticed Cjella's daughter again, riding out and in front of the pack. She had strayed off from the others and headed over a dune and out of sight. He had looked around to see if anyone was concerned, but no one took notice. He had thought about asking Cjella why her daughter had broken away but then refrained. *I don't want to come across overtly interested in her.* So he continued with their conversation. "Is finding a water source difficult?"

"For outsiders, yes. For us, no. My people have been in this desert for well over a thousand years. This is our home. We know everything about it." She had pointed to the sky "*Bashi* brings us heat and light, she brings us life." Cjella had pointed to the ground. "*Velliumo* brings us grit and makes us tough, gives us a place to rest our feet and a path to travel." She had then patted her camel and said, "*Garzellas* give us legs and lift us to greatness; they carry our bodies, our food, our water; they are our home when we have no time for home. Garzellas are special and they are sacred."

Sacred camels, William had thought. *I better not tell her that they only live in zoos within the Collective.*

"Galloz bas! Umptu nierda muno!" Ballo-cel said.

William, standing on the ground now, took the man's words as orders to lead his camel over to the water trough. Ballo-cel fell in line with the other riders walking their camels over, and William decided that now was his opportunity.

He momentarily considered going for a weapon but then thought better of it. *They've done me no harm; besides, they have excellent marksmen. I would be dead before I reached the horizon.* Instead, William quietly walked next to his camel's head and gave it the order to kneel.

The camel slowly lowered down and William very quickly took a few steps back and threw his leg over its back. He then ordered the camel to rise. The animal grunted and moaned and stood.

A couple of warriors following Ballo-cel turned and took notice of William mounting the camel. Once William began riding away from the line, they stopped walking and called out to Ballo-cel.

William ordered his camel to run, just as the Desert Demons had taught him, and he was out from under Kaacital's canvas in no time. He looked back to see who was following him; a couple of warriors had mounted their camels, but Ballo-cel had yelled an order to them and the group didn't proceed. *I hope that is a good sign.*

William had been paying attention to the sun all day and knew that he was riding west. *My outpost is west of here. If I can get back there, maybe I can get my hoverbike and find a place of refuge in Sector 32.* His parents were all he could think about now. *I have to get back to them. I have to make sure they are okay.*

The sun was hot that day, and after William felt confident enough that his escape was temporarily successful, he allowed his camel to travel more leisurely.

Damn it's hot. Sweat dripped all down his face, chest, and back. He didn't have much with him in regards of supplies, food, and water. He did have the tent on his back, and he did have half a jug of water and some of their dried out food they called *minjo*, but none of that would last him past the next day. *I knew this would be a risk*, he told himself. *I have to keep trying. . . . I just hope I'm not too far out.*

When the sun began to lower itself, William halted his camel and decided to make camp for the night. He unpacked his tent and fumbled with it until he found a logical way to construct it, like Ballo-cel did before him. All of his water was gone, and he had only a quarter of his food left.

By the time he had finished, William was exhausted. His camel looked exhausted too. "Hang in there, buddy," he told his camel. "Get some sleep. Tomorrow will hopefully be a better day." William crawled into his sparse tent and rolled over onto his back. He stripped off all of his clothes and was lying there nude.

As it became nighttime, the temperature dropped and William found it easier to sleep. He fell into a deep sleep, deeper than he had slept in a long time. He dreamed a simple dream: He was back in his post within the MSF and was still pursuing Corbin Byrne, except he had a new partner, Rebecca Badeau. She was beautiful and lusty and everything he had ever imagined a woman to be. She had told him that all she wanted to do was to bring her biological father to justice and to help bring the Collective back into order. William found that he was madly in love with her and vowed to do anything and everything to see her dream come true; however, he noticed something peculiar about her personality that didn't make sense. It seemed that maybe she was holding something back, that maybe she was hiding something from him.

The dream continued on that way, William and Rebecca working together, looking for Corbin Byrne, William lusting for her but never making a move, Rebecca pretending that all was on the up and up but hinting that she was hiding something. Eventually it came to an end as sunlight leaked into the tent through the improperly sealed flap.

William was surprised to feel cold that morning. He quickly began putting on his stink-filled, dirty clothes. After he dressed, William slipped out of the tent and was shocked to see that his camel was not where he left it.

Panicked, William quickly walked around the tent in search for his missing camel. It took him only a second or two to discover where the animal had gone. . . .

"William Coulee!" shouted down a voice from a top of a sand dune to the east.

William shaded his eyes as he looked up at the silhouettes of four riders and a fifth camel with no rider. "*Shit*," was all he could muster.

CHAPTER FORTY-ONE

The Dead Sands

"William Coulee!" shouted the voice again, a female voice. "We have your garzella! Come up here so we can head back!"

William sighed and sat down in the sand. "How about you come down here and get me!"

The four riders conversed amongst themselves before one rider headed down the dune alone. As the rider drew closer, William recognized her to be Cjella's daughter. She was nothing like the shy girl he had mistakenly thought two days before; she was riding tall, her hair flowed through the quickening breeze, and the sun highlighted her muscular arms and legs.

She said in a proud voice, "We have come to return you to Kaacital."

"I'm not going back," William said, defiantly. *If they want me to fight, then I'll fight.*

"Stand up, William Coulee, and walk with me. This is a fight you cannot win."

"*Oh yeah?*" he said, standing. "Try me."

"It is not our wish to hurt you, William Coulee. You are important to our people. You must come back with us."

"I'm not going back. And as a matter of fact, I'm going to have whatever supplies you are carrying so that I can return to *my* home."

The young woman slid out a short club, about the length of William's forearm. "Then you will be made to come." She clicked her tongue and had her camel break into a jog around William's right side.

William backed up and braced for the attack, but the woman slid off the camel's opposite side. As the camel passed around, William saw the woman standing in a fighting position with her right hand extended toward him and her left holding the club back and above her head.

William had never seen this type of defensive stance before so he refrained from attacking. The two of them stood idle, facing one another. William saw underneath her fierce glare the same blue eyes her father once had. It was difficult for him to take her threat seriously; *she's too beautiful.*

"Make your move, William Coulee, or give up and join us."

"I'm just waiting for you, sweetheart."

The other riders began to trot down the sand dune, splitting apart. *Great, I'm going to be surrounded.* "Are you too afraid to attack me alone? You're the one with the weapon."

"Your time is running out," was all she said.

The three men on their camels—including Ballo-cel—had surrounded William and were now slowly closing in.

I need a weapon. William looked at the woman's club and realized he would have to settle for that.

"That is right," she taunted. "Come get it."

"You're too confi—" and then William shot forward, lunging toward her left arm, trying to get in close in order to decrease the power of her blow.

The woman anticipated William's move and had completely spun free of his hands. Her movement was so quick that William didn't see her backhanded swing of the club, which connected with the side of his head, dropping him to the sand.

The fight was over within a single blow.

The remaining three men had pounced on William before he had a chance to regain his composer and launch a second attack. Ballo-cel bound William's hands and then lifted him to his feet. The warrior shouted several things, which William took as insults and/or complaints. "You got lucky," he said to the woman. "I'm weak."

"I see that you are weak," she said, stone-faced.

"On a better day I would have taken that club from you." But he didn't necessarily believe those words—the woman was fast.

"If you like, on a better day we will try it again."

The warriors marched William up the sand dune and toward his camel. With his hands bound, they had to help him mount it. "We have a two full-day ride to get back," the woman told him. She and her warriors mounted their camels and began leading William back east. The woman then said, "Your garzella needs water."

I know, but William didn't respond.

"We do not have water for it."

William observed that all four riders had extra pouches with them to the point of being excessive. "Then what is in those pouches?"

"Salt," the woman said.

"Salt?" *Why did you bring salt?* But William kept quiet.

They traveled until evening, until William's camel decided to walk no further. "Come on," he said to it.

The camel looked exhausted.

The woman looked back to William and then said, "Humptoy bas."

All of the warriors stopped and lowered the camels. William's camel staggered and lowered itself without being commanded. "I think he's done for the day."

The woman dismounted her camel and walked over to William. She looked at his camel's face and into its eyes . . . tears then formed in her own.

"What's the matter?"

"Get off, please," she ordered.

William struggled to do as told with his hands still bound. He feared what might be coming next. "What's wrong?"

"Your garzella will go no further."

William nodded his head and said, "He might just need the night to rest."

The woman walked over to her camel and retrieved a small device. William moved away from the camel and looked at the device more closely, realizing then that she was carrying some sort of weapon. "What are you doing?"

The woman went right up to the camel and pointed the weapon at its head. The bang that followed startled William and the other camels.

William's camel slumped and died right there in the sand.

Damnit . . . damnit to everything, was what William thought.

The other riders dismounted and began removing the excess pouches. They each dropped their pouches to the ground next to the dead camel and then returned to their own. Ballo-cel extracted his ballistic rifle from his camel and loaded it.

William was unsure of what was to come.

The woman walked back to her camel and removed an eight-inch knife. She then walked to William and ordered him to turn around. Silently nervous, William did as ordered. The woman placed the blade between his wrists and sliced the rope.

With his hands free, William turned around and saw that the woman had walked away and dropped the knife by the dead camel. She said to him, "You brought death, and so now you will bring life."

The statement baffled William. "How will I do that?"

"You will remove the garzella's meat and place it in each pouch. This meat will feed our people, giving them life."

William looked at the dead camel and then at the knife. He saw that Ballo-cel was aiming the rifle at him. *Shit.* "I haven't carved an animal since my training."

"Then this should be a good reminder for you. Take everything, including the liver and the heart."

William sighed and walked over to the dead animal. *Good thing I don't get squeamish.* "Sorry, old buddy," he said as he knelt down next to the carcass. William lifted up the knife and then planned his attack.

That night, William slept terribly. No dreams for him.

When William finished gutting the camel, he was forced to dig a grave for it. It took him into nightfall. His bloodied hands were then rebound and his tent was built for him. The warriors each took a turn watching him as he tried to sleep.

Everyone awoke early the following day. One of the warriors had gone out and scouted. When he returned, he brought news that Kaacital was a day's ride away. The woman ordered everyone to mount up. William was told to ride with Ballo-cel.

Very little conversation occurred that day. When it did happen, it was mainly between the warriors and the woman. William stayed silent. He was exhausted and a bit defeated. Gutting the camel had been a humbling experience for him.

It wasn't until nighttime that they had finally caught up with Kaacital, which William observed was moving south now. Ballo-cel took William back to the spot close to Kaa's tent so that he could prepare for sleep. By this point, all of the tents had been erected and the people were bedding down for the night.

William's hands were unbound, as when he had first arrived days before, but he was left to erect his tent alone. When he had finished, he crawled inside and crashed onto the ground. A few moments later, a pair of hands holding pillows appeared through his tent flap, dropping them onto the ground. William was too tired and defeated to say thank you. Another moment later, a second pair of hands entered his tent. William sat up to say he didn't need anything else but held his tongue when he recognized Cjella's daughter was the owner of the hands. "May I enter, William Coulee?"

"Yeah, sure."

The woman crawled into his tent and then sat down. She reached back outside it and grabbed a bundle of something—*paper* William eventually realized—and placed it in her lap.

"You don't have a club hiding out there as well, do you?"

The woman gave a small smile, indicating that she was human after all, and said, "That is for another day."

William said, "Then what brings you to my humble tent? I was half expecting Kaa to pay me visit."

"I have come on his behalf. He is very unhappy about your leaving us. He thinks I will be better at talking sense into you."

William grabbed a pillow and leaned back. "I don't even know your name."

The woman nodded and said, "My name is *Vweenu.*"

"Well, Vweenu, I wish I could have met you under better circumstances."

"These are the best circumstances available."

William thought, *If you say so.*

"You are at the point most suitable to speak with right now. Until now, there was no point in talking."

William didn't know how to respond. "Okay, what do you want to talk about?"

Vweenu held out the stack of paper. "This comes from my father. It is for you."

William took the paper and placed it down next to him. He saw that it was covered in handwriting. "What is this?"

"My father was a seer and a seeker. He wrote down everything he saw and knew. He did this in preparation for your arrival and in case something were to happen to him. It was his belief that you are a powerful person who will lift our people out of the clutches of despair. He had been watching and waiting for you. When you came to the desert, he went looking for you."

Puzzled, William picked up the first piece of paper, and read the first few lines.

****

He is pacing the floor. He is alone, like always.

He is very hot and angry.

He cleans his desk. Third time today. He isn't doing much more.

There is a picture of an older man on the wall—I think it is Demozi.

****

"What is this?" William asked.

"This was you. My father was observing you. Those are the last notes he took down of you before he went out to meet you." Vweenu pointed at the bottom of the stack. "He wrote some things specifically for you. They are at the bottom."

William pulled out the sheet at the bottom and saw that it was definitely written more like a letter rather than notes. "I don't understand."

"Read them, William Coulee, and then you will understand. You and my father are connected. But I can say no more."

"Why? I mean, why can you say no more? Your mother says the same to me. Why can no one talk about it?"

Vweenu pointed at the stack again and said definitively, "Read, William Coulee, and you will see why."

And with that, she backed out of the tent, shutting the flap along the way.

William stared at the flap for a long moment in disbelief. *Why would Sańo think we're connected?* He looked at the papers, at Sańo's mind written out. *Well, I guess there is only one thing to do—the Minister knows I'm not doing anything else tonight.*

William rolled onto his back with the bottom sheet in hand, and he began to read.

CHAPTER FORTY-TWO

District 19, Sector 12 – CS Processing Compound

Rebecca awoke to the sight of another woman's face: a round, soft face with caring eyes. The woman said, "Good, you're waking up." Rebecca was groggy and still numb from the effects of whatever drug was injected into her arm. She looked past the woman and toward their surroundings. They were inside a small, dark cinderblock room. There were other women as well—about eleven if she were to count—of all ages. The older ones looked nervous, the younger ones looked scared, and the middle-aged ones looked collected but tense. The thing that truly caught Rebecca's attention was that all of the women were nude. . . . *And so am I*, she realized instantly.

The second thing Rebecca noticed was that all of the women had their heads shaved—or better stated—butchered. Their scalps were covered with less than an inch of patchy hair.

The third thing Rebecca noticed was that she was laying on straw instead of the grass she initially thought was covering the ground.

"What's your name?" asked the woman squatting next to her.

"Rebecca," she said without thinking. "*I mean*, Mary."

The woman looked at her. "Mary, or Rebecca?"

"My name is Mary. I used Rebecca as a cover. It didn't work."

"Yeah," the woman said, smiling somehow, "I can see that."

Rebecca found some strength and sat upward. If all of the women were once asleep, as she was, then Rebecca was the last to wake. The woman next to her helped Rebecca to her feet. "My name is Isla. I remember seeing you unconscious while they boarded me onto the transport."

Rebecca reached up and carefully felt for her own hair, which seemed no different than the others.

"They had already cut you before I came on board. I'm sorry."

Rebecca looked into Isla's eyes and saw true sorrow. "They cut you too," she said.

Isla smiled halfheartedly and nodded; tears filled her eyes. "I never had a haircut before. . . ."

No more words followed. All of the women shifted uncomfortably inside the dark enclosure, waiting for what was to come, tortured by their imagination. Rebecca asked Isla, "Did they drug you too?"

"Yes. They drugged all of us. When I woke up, almost all of the women were still asleep. Cherrilee over there"—Isla pointed out a fuller figured woman with jet black, frizzy hair—"was already awake."

Rebecca looked at the head of the room, where there stood a single door, where none of the women were huddled, either by chance or out of fear of what might come through. "Has anyone tried opening the door?"

Isla looked at her and then at the door. "I don't know. I don't—I don't know."

To Rebecca, it seemed like a logical thing to do, but she understood why no one had done so. Rebecca's eyes scanned the room for something else, some kind of indication that might give a clue as to what could be next. *Are there cameras?* She saw a little black box in the upper-corner, opposite of the door, and judged it to be something watching them. And as if they read her mind, there was a loud clank coming from the door, indicating a lock being reversed, and it swung wipe open, spilling what seemed like an enormous amount of light into the room, which thoroughly devoured the darkness.

All of the women—including Rebecca—covered their eyes and staggered away; some even turned their backs toward the door, and others shrieked with terror.

A large figure stepped through the door and blotted out some of the sunlight. A booming voice, one that could easily be mistaken for a man's, bellowed out, "All of you file through the door in a single line. Only stop when you are handed your assigned clothes and then immediately continue onward. If any of you violate this order you will be immediately punished. Now MOOOVE!"

Rebecca's eyes adjusted just enough to see that the large figure was a woman with her hair pulled up into a taut bun; she was wearing an unidentifiable Ministry uniform.

There was no time to waste on thought as the large woman grabbed the closest girl—maybe in her teens—and yanked her through the door, effortlessly. That act of brute force started all of the women to follow behind, including Rebecca.

All of the women took short awkward steps forward and into the pitiless sunlight that exposed their naked bodies to all of creation. Some women tried to maintain a level of modesty by covering what they could with their hands, while others kept their hands free in case they would be needed for a different kind of protection. Rebecca chose to keep her hands free.

When it was her turn to cross the threshold, she saw for the first time the enormity of their situation and just how *not alone* they truly were. Nude backs obscured her view forward, but she could see a procession of tables and women in the same unidentifiable Ministry uniforms manning those stations. There was a chalky white cloud engulfing some of the women closer to the front of the line. To her left side, where more could be seen, Rebecca witnessed a similar sight but with men staggering out of a cinderblock cell, nude, and being pushed through a similar procession of Ministry men manning tables. There was also a chalky cloud engulfing the men hitting the first station. Rebecca witnessed a Ministry man standing at the table, wearing rubber gloves, reach into a bucket and pull out a powdery substance before flinging it onto the next nude man in line, where it exploded against his chest and formed the white cloud. Rebecca's eyes then focused beyond the line of men and to the other cinderblock cells far off and facing another wall of the building they were all hurriedly walking— and in some instances running—toward. She then focused her attention more onto the building that made up the nucleus of the entire operation and saw that it was not shaped like a rectangle or a pyramid—as commonly seen inside Ministry cities—but more like a pentagon or a hexagon. She quickly deduced that each face of the structure had two columns that led directly to two cinderblock cells, much like the one they were trotting from.

Poof—without her notice, a female manning the first station exploded a handful of the powdery substance against Rebecca's bare chest. The white chalky cloud enveloped her and even made its way into her eyes and mouth—instantly burning in both cases.

From that point forward, Rebecca didn't witness much.

She continued staggering forward; her pace fell to a walk. A woman behind her, apparently blinded too, or possibly more anxious to continue forward, collided into Rebecca's back, knocking her down. On her hands and knees, Rebecca tried spitting the chalky powder out of her mouth. She used the back of her left hand to wipe worthlessly at her eyes.

A pair of strong hands gripped Rebecca under her armpits and hoisted her up. "GET MOVING!" the woman screamed into Rebecca's face and then shoved her back into the line of other blinded women.

Someone steadied Rebecca and guided her forward—another prisoner, she later suspected. Rebecca wiped furiously at her eyes until someone had thrust an arm full of folded clothes into her stomach. She caught them despite her ineptness and then walked into another woman in front of her who was bent over trying to pick up some article she had dropped. The woman fell onto her face and Rebecca staggered aside, apologizing. She heard the beastly guard from before moan at the sight of a prisoner lying on the ground. "ON YOUR FEET, SCUM!" Rebecca felt awful for the accident—as if she wasn't feeling awful enough.

The next station had someone shoving a pair of shoes into their arms, which stirred another round of fumbling and confusion amongst the females trying to stay in line. Rebecca only managed to secure one shoe and dropped the other, which tumbled against her right foot. Luckily, she was able to scoop it up with little stall.

Something not too far ahead was causing a pileup. Rebecca slowed her pace; her vision came back ever so slightly, and she saw women struggling to regain articles they had dropped, and a guard grabbing new arrivals by the arm and running a scanner over their identification chips. The guard wasn't gentle or careful and seemed to be purposely causing articles to fall from their grasps. And the same was for Rebecca when she reached her turn. The woman—who would probably be considered pretty if it weren't for the scowl she wore—grabbed Rebecca's left arm and yanked it free from what she was holding. Everything went spilling to the ground. The guard scanned Rebecca's chip and then flung her arm back. Rebecca lost her balance, tripped over her new shoes, and fell to one knee.

"GET UP AND MOVE IT!" shouted another woman guard from somewhere unseen. Rebecca did her best to recover everything she dropped; she forced her eyes open despite the burning pain and quickly gathered two shoes and a pile of clothes. Another woman kicked her in the backside and Rebecca fell forward, only saving herself from a complete spill with a single free hand.

She had everything collected and stood up. With her eyes somewhat cleared, she saw that the door into the building was just ahead, which symbolized a temporary end to the humiliation. Rebecca found her balance on two wobbly legs and hurried through.

The inside of the building was a far cry from the outside. It was dark, cold, and quiet. It was more like an interchange than an actual room. There was a door opposite of the one Rebecca came through, and a single guard stood watch. The guard simply said, "Dress, ladies. Don't waste time." Her demeanor was calm and cruelly relaxed—giving a false hope that the aggressive nature of the place was merely a facade.

Rebecca found a free area from the other nude, partially nude, and hysterical women who struggled to piece together an outfit from the articles they had dropped outside. There were cries from some that they did not have a shirt, while others cried about having two right shoes or having two shirts and no pants. And then there were some who bartered to get what they needed. Rebecca witnessed this and took stock of what she came inside with: a shirt, two shoes—a right and a left (of undetermined size)—and pants. She had everything; and apparently she was one of the few lucky ones.

Rebecca dressed in the drab oversize outfit and slid on the pair of shoes that were entirely too large for her feet.

"Let's go, ladies; time is wasting," the smiling guard reminded them.

Rebecca watched one girl, who was perfectly dressed, hurry to the closed door and open it wide enough to slip through. Rebecca followed behind her. Because almost all of the women were still trying to get their outfits oriented, there wasn't much room to open the door. Like the girl before, Rebecca created a narrow passageway and slipped through.

She was now inside a stubby hall just large enough for all of the women to assemble. There were only four others and a guard waiting. The guard, like the one who started the rat race, was tall and large. She had puffy cheeks, hard squinty eyes, fat lips, and a protruding lower jaw. The other prisoners—the teen she saw go first from the cinderblock cell, the woman she knew as Isla, a skinny woman who appeared to be mildly hyperventilating, and very young girl no older than ten—were all hastily dressed and gathered together. Rebecca joined them in front of the guard, who silently studied them, and took a place next to Isla.

Rebecca observed the younger girl—the one who looked comical in the adult clothes—and marveled at the strength displayed on her face. She looked neither scared nor upset. The young girl behaved as if it were another day in her life—which caused a thought to stir inside Rebecca's mind. *This isn't her first time through.* She couldn't imagine how that could be, but the little girl demonstrated a control that seemed impossible.

A fifth prisoner joined them through the door, and then a sixth and seventh. The trickle of women coming through turned into a stream until all twelve women were amassed. Only the first seven were properly dressed; the last four to come through were missing something: a shirt, a shoe, or pants. Rebecca observed what a terrible and humiliating sight these women were; she easily imagined how it would feel to stand there with no pants or shirt on, with her bare bottom or chest exposed to everyone. Having only one shoe was not as critical in Rebecca's mind—there was no loss of modesty with that—but having one's private areas uncovered at all times was outrageous.

The large guard walked along all of the women, scanning their attire, and then went to the door from which they came through. She opened it and said something inaudible before closing it again. "All right," she bellowed at them, "each of you that is not properly dressed, stand to the left!"

Each woman scanned her neighbor while sorting herself according to instruction. The large guard walked to the front of the group and said, "You will call me Master Brenna. Anything else will result in punishment. You are here because the Ministry found you guilty of a treasonous act, and you are no longer fit to live within the Collective. But since the Ministry is kind and concerned about all of the Minister's creatures—including you scum— this facility is designed and instructed to rehabilitate each one of you until it is determined whether or not you can return to the Collective and live a noble life. Is that understood?"

Some women said, "Yes," while others nodded their head. Brenna walked over to the teen girl, who nodded but didn't speak, and smacked her face. "PEOPLE USE WORDS INSIDE THE COLLECTIVE!" She then addressed everyone, "And if ANY of you ever respond to me again without addressing me as Master Brenna, you will be punished! IS THAT UNDERSTOOD!"

Everyone responded, "Yes, Master Brenna."

The guard from the previous room entered the hall, still smiling as before, and joined Master Brenna. "All of you who have properly dressed in the issued attire, follow me!"

Master Brenna led the seven dressed women, including Rebecca, through the next door and into a much larger, multi-floor hall that ran horizontal. Its official name, Rebecca learned later, was the gallery. The inner side of the hall was an open view to the courtyard nucleus of the facility. The hall ceiling only covered half, while the other half of the hall ceiling was two stories higher. As Master Brenna brought them closer to the viewing wall, Rebecca looked up and saw connected balconies for the two stories above and what appeared to be offices connected to those balconies.

Suddenly, Isla grabbed Rebecca's arm. Rebecca, in return, almost said, *What are you doing*, but the words stopped in her throat, instead, coming out as several squeamish gasps. Master Brenna pointed past the glass wall and toward what all of the women were now gaping at. "The first thing you waste-of-time need to understand is that we do not tolerate conspiring."

Rebecca's hand found Isla's and squeezed it hard.

Out in front of them, and in the center of the courtyard, was the wretched sight of three impaled decomposed bodies.

Master Brenna continued, "Those three were caught plotting an escape, and this is how they ended up. So, take a long look and let it be a lesson to all of you! No one leaves here until WE let them leave!"

Rebecca could feel the acid in her stomach rise and she looked away. Others had a tougher time; they began to gag, covering their mouths and bending toward the ground. Rebecca looked at Master Brenna, who showed no expression, and then to the other sparse few men and women walking about on the several different floors. Rebecca thought, *How could they do this to someone?* Corbin, Iah, and Morlan had tried to tell her six months ago; she had read about it in William's manuscript; but all of the forewarnings had failed. The good nature of Rebecca's soul refused to allow the possibility that people were capable of skewering living humans and leaving them to die.

At that moment, a door further down the hall opened and a large man, much like Master Brenna, led a group of men into the gallery. Rebecca eyed them, hoping to see Roland's familiar face. All of the men looked exhausted and humiliated. One man was terribly overweight and had three sad looking chins patched with hair. Another man was his opposite, sallow and bone thin. There were two sockets were his eyes should have been.

All of the men's attention turned toward the guard. Rebecca could hear only the warble of the security guard's bellows as he guided the men to the looking glass. Then a young, almost innocent looking face appeared within the mix of the defeated men. His face was yellow and unshaven— much more so than the last time Rebecca had seen him—nonetheless, it was Roland.

Rebecca's heart rejoiced. *He's alive!*

All hope was not lost, and she was not alone.

Master Brenna shouted in Rebecca's ear—"Looking for a lover!"—before jabbing something cylindrical and hard into her gut. Rebecca gasped, doubled over, and fell to her knees. Her hollow stomach filled with burning pain. Master Brenna reached down and took a fist full of what was left of Rebecca's blond hair. The brute yanked upward, forcing Rebecca to grasp for Master Brenna's arm. "STAND UP, WHORE!"

Rebecca's face streamed with tears as she gasped for air.

"See her face!" Master Brenna yelled at the rest of the women. "If I ever catch you little rats looking at those pathetic cocks over yonder, I will give it to you twice as bad." Master Brenna had let go of Rebecca's hair and shoved her into the line of girls. Isla caught Rebecca as she fell, supporting her weight until Rebecca gained enough composure to stand.

"I see you two are going to be lovers," Master Brenna said with a smirk. "But don't get too close. You might find yourselves spiked out there in the courtyard." She then turned to the group. "Get into a single file line and follow me!"

Rebecca tried to wipe the tears away but was overwhelmed. She found Isla's back and followed behind with her head hung low. She wanted desperately to look over toward Roland; his face was the closest connection she had to home. However, Rebecca did not dare. Her stomach burned and ached from the blow it received.

Master Brenna led the women through the gallery and to a sealed doorway where she stopped. "Listen up! Through here is where some of you will spend your days!" She placed her palm on a sensor pad and the door unlocked. Master Brenna pulled a large handle upright and opened the door inward, revealing the courtyard beyond. "File through!"

Rebecca and the women did as ordered, but she didn't care where she would be spending her days; she just wanted the journey to be over with so she could lie down and sleep—forever if possible.

"Stop there!" ordered Master Brenna. "And look about you!"

Thinking that it was another cruel jape, Rebecca lifted her head but kept her tear filled eyes looking downward at the cement path. She didn't want to look at the impaled bodies again. However, she didn't need to in order to smell their decay.

"This courtyard has ten acres of garden! This complex has five houses filled with you social rejects! Each house has close to a thousand people! Each house has its own two acres of garden! Two acres of garden can feed roughly five hundred people! Am I getting through to you knuckle heads!?"

All of the women murmured a response.

Rebecca lifted her gaze and briefly looked about. She saw the gardens, each divided by a cement path just like the one she was standing on, and each path conjoined in the center where the impaled bodies resided.

"These gardens are your primary food source! We will only supply you with protein substitute and water! The rest is up to you and this garden! Am I getting through to you!?"

Before the women could respond, Master Brenna continued, "Some of you will tend to this garden! I cannot express the importance of this task! The food you grow is the food you and everyone else in your house will eat! If it dies, then you will die! Does that make sense!?"

The women's response was more in unison, "Yes, Master Brenna."

Rebecca was paying closer attention now. She looked at the garden to her right and saw that some of the plants were unhealthy looking and that even a few were already dead. The implications of this sight wouldn't hit her until much later.

Master Brenna shouted, "Back through the door!"

Rebecca turned around and followed the order. She looked toward another garden and saw that it was healthier, but it had some ill looking plants as well. Rebecca then thought, *Each house has a thousand people and each garden feeds five hundred. . . .* Of course, the numbers didn't add up. *Does that mean five hundred people do not eat?* At that moment, while the women stood in the gallery waiting for Master Brenna, a door opened down a ways, and a frail looking woman came stepping through. There couldn't have been more or less a year or two age difference between her and Rebecca; but the woman was so gaunt that anyone could have mistaken her for someone in their sixties. At that point, the answer to Rebecca's question was pretty clear, *They eat only half of what they need. Everyone is starving.*

"All right you scum!" Master Brenna bellowed. "Stay in a single file line and follow me! If any of you step out of line"—she began tapping her foot onto the ground—"I will smash your face into this nice shiny floor! Is that clear?!"

In unison this time, "Yes, Master Brenna."

The women walked through the gallery and past the gaunt woman, who began to mop up some liquid mess over by the seeing window. Rebecca locked eyes with her just long enough to feel the woman's guttural sadness and defeat. There was a strange sort of apology that passed from the woman to Rebecca as well, as if the woman's eyes said, *I'm sorry for what is going to happen to you.*

Rebecca broke eye contact out of fear and crossed her arms. *How did I end up here?* That was all she could think. The last three—or however many days—had been whirlwinds, each uprooting her and tossing her to a new and far worse situation. Her only solace was the knowledge that her friend, Roland, was stuck there too. However, that thought was a selfish one, and whatever comfort it brought, also came guilt and shame.

Master Brenna led the women out of the gallery and down three flights of stairs. They passed into another long hall that had no doors or windows. It led into the nucleus of the building where a pentagonal room resided. Inside there were four gigantic women who wore matching scowls and had their hair pulled into taut buns. They nodded toward Master Brenna and then scrutinized each girl who passed through the door. The room had a single doorway on each of the five walls that appeared to lead into another long hall just as the one they passed through.

"Halt!" ordered Master Brenna. "Make a single line in front of these women!"

Rebecca stepped further into the room and eyed where the line was taking form. She looked toward her neighbors and then took position in between them. The four gigantic brutes separated and began inspecting each woman as they walked down the line from opposite ends. One of these four—a woman with jet black hair lined with wisps of grey and an unpleasant scar running across her bottom lip—stopped in front of Rebecca. For her part, Rebecca didn't know if she should look the woman in the eye or not at all. Her eyes danced from the ugly brute to the floor and then back again. The ugly woman grunted something that resembled a laugh or a sneer and then continued down the line.

Another brute with auburn hair and pockmarked skin, stopped in front of Rebecca. She stuck out a meaty index finger and jabbed Rebecca once in the stomach and then once in the breast. In both instances, Rebecca covered herself but tried not to shrink away. This brute, too, sneered before moving on to another.

The other two women passed by without giving pause, and then all four regrouped with Master Brenna in front of the line. "All right you dead meat, this here is our recruiting room! These four other women, like me, will be your mama and your papa! Each of these women are the Masters of the five houses!" Master Brenna pointed at the brute furthest to her right, the most pleasant looking of the group (if any of them could be considered pleasant). "This is Master Carmen! She runs Water House!" Master Brenna's finger pointed to the next woman, the one with the scarred bottom lip. "This is Master Vikki! She runs Earth House!" The next woman was a brunette too, whose eyes were far apart across the vast space of her face. "This is Master Kristoffa! She runs Air House!" Master Brenna pointed to her far left, toward the pock-faced woman with auburn hair. "And this is Master Katie! She runs Fire House!" Master Brenna pointed a fat thumb into her own chest. "As for me, I run Ether House! Each of you will be divided up into one of these five houses, which will serve as your new home until you are rehabilitated or dead!"

After Master Brenna finished speaking, the five brutes conjoined into a circle and discussed something in hushed tones. Rebecca saw Master Kristoffa hold up four fingers and nod her head. She also saw that Master Vikki was doing a lot of talking. Master Brenna started shaking her head and said something with finality. Then all five women broke and returned to their position in front of the women. "All right, listen up! When a Master selects you, you go to the wall of your new house! Is that understood?!"

All of the women said, "Yes, Master Brenna."

Master Vikki started the selection process. She walked over to a fair shaped woman with pretty eyes and wrenched her arm toward the wall furthest from the line. And so it went for all of them. The teenage girl was taken by Master Carmen, Isla was taken by Master Kristoffa, and all of the other women were divided up and taken except for Rebecca, the little girl comically dressed in the adult clothes, and a heavy set woman with a gritty glare that was on par with the masters of the houses; they now belonged to the Ether House and Master Brenna.

After the selection process ended, each master shouted out orders to their recruits—including Master Brenna. "Turn around, you pukes! Go back through the door before I stick one in your stomach!"

Rebecca, the little girl, and the bigger woman did as ordered and hurriedly walked back into the plain, long hall, which evidently led to Ether House. Rebecca watched as the little girl in front of her wrestled with the oversized pants and shoes. She wanted to scoop the little girl up and carry her the rest of the way, but she knew it would only cause the poor thing more harm than good.

When they reached the doorway, Master Brenna shouted, "Halt!" The three women stood in place as Master Brenna walked before them. She shouted, "We're about to enter my house! You three holes are my guests! Do not forget your manners!" She then led the three of them down a flight of stairs and through another heavily sealed door. Beyond was another hall completely unlike the last. It had at least thirty doors lining one side and thirty more lining the other.

"This is where you little bitches will bunk down each day and night!" Master Brenna continued walking. Rebecca and the other two followed close behind her. With each door they passed, Rebecca could see through its thick glass-viewing window and into the dismal space beyond; the *guests* inside were all drawn and miserable looking. Some were lying on hard looking benches with their limbs draped over the sides, others were standing or pacing, and a few were caught talking or were in the process of doing whatever. Each room had three guests, which quickly led Rebecca to assume that the little girl and the large one were going to accompany her beyond the walk.

After they passed three quarters of the length of the hall, Master Brenna stopped at an empty room and confirmed Rebecca's suspicion. "This will be your living quarters! It once belonged to three women. Two of them graduated and the other hangs in the courtyard!" There was a terrible smirk on Master Brenna's face, which spoke volumes.

Rebecca and the other two went inside the room that was more fit for one than three. Master Brenna slammed the door shut. A clank sound followed, indicating that she locked the door.

The larger woman of the group immediately spoke up, "I'm taking the bunk furthest from the crapper."

Rebecca looked toward what she was referring and saw indeed that there was a toilet in the corner of the room, just in between the ends of two bunks. *I don't want to sleep next to the toilet.*

The little girl looked up at Rebecca's face and then to the two remaining beds.

"Take your pick," Rebecca told her.

The little girl nodded her head; and for the first time, her eyes turned red and welled up.

Rebecca knelt next to her and said, "You are a very strong little girl. What's your name?"

The little girl tugged uncomfortably at the adult size shirt and sniffled. "Birdie. I'm sorry I cry. I'm sorry."

"Don't be sorry. I've cried, too. We've all cried."

Birdie looked toward the large woman sitting on the opposite bed. "She don't cry."

The large woman realized that they were looking at her and shifted uncomfortably. "We all cry, little bird."

It pleased Rebecca to see that this woman wasn't as hard as she initially appeared.

Birdie said, "What are your name?"

"My name is Rebecca." She then looked toward the larger woman who said, "My name is Meeshell." Meeshell stood from the bunk, pressed the palms and fingers of her hands together, and brought the sides of her index fingers to her lips; she then lowered her hands in an arching motion that indicated some kind of greeting. Birdie must have recognized it because she mimicked the motion and smiled shyly.

Meeshell asked, "Are you from the Shoreline Peoples, little Bird?"

Birdie shook her head and said, "I'm from the Wetlands, north of you Shoreliners."

Rebecca had no idea what they were referring; she had not heard of either.

Meeshell asked, "Your Ma and Pa still there?"

Birdie shook her head, "They was taken, like most of the Wetlanders."

"How did you get separated?"

"We was together—in the beginning—but they separated us at one of them processors-*thingys*."

Rebecca had a brief flashback of drowning inside the tank room. She quickly shook her head and asked, "Where are the Shoreline and Wetlands located? I've never heard of either."

Meeshell and Birdie looked at her; Meeshell was more forthcoming with her surprise. "You never heard of the Shoreline or the Wetlands? I thought all Free Peoples knew of these places."

Rebecca confessed, "I'm not really a free-person. I've spent my entire life inside the Collective."

This surprised both of them. Meeshell said, "Dang on! How did you end up here?"

It was a good question . . . Rebecca gave an exhausted sigh. She laid out her tale, omitting a few key points and anything involving William's manuscript.

"You must be jesting," Meeshell said in earnest—almost agitated. "You can't be Corbin Byrne's daughter."

Rebecca said, "I told you the truth. The people here cannot know these secrets—because if they do, they will terminate me."

Meeshell shook her head. "Tell me something about him that others might not know."

It was tough for Rebecca to tell her anything about him; she had only just met him six months ago. Rebecca told what she could but none of it seemed satisfactory. "Anyone knows that. Tell me something no one knows."

"I told you already, I don't know him very well."

Meeshell seemed far from convinced. "Sure, okay. So Corbin Byrne—the leader of the resistance—had a daughter living inside the Collective, the one place he would be caught dead inside."

"I don't ask that you believe me, all I ask is that you keep the secret safe . . . please."

"Oh, don't you worry, I'm not tellin nothin. That secret can stay with you."

Birdie said, "I believe you."

Rebecca looked down at the little girl's face, which was clear of tears now. "Thank you. But I ask the same from you."

"I won't tell no one. I promise."

Meeshell said, "The Shoreline is mostly west of here—maybe a bit north, too. The Wetlands is directly atop of the Shoreline—if you lookin at a map."

Rebecca imagined a world map and thought, *Sectors 16 and 14 are over there.* She voiced her thought, and Meeshell said, "Yeah, I know it. Them damn sectors are everywhere."

"But then, how can the Shoreline and Wetlands exist there? That area is inside the Collective."

"Boy, you Collies are thick—the Ministry don't control every inch of the land, you know. There are some places they know nothin about. Inch by inch, we been taken the land back. The Shoreline and Wetlands were once technically Collective lands, but we took them about twenty years ago." She then looked down toward Birdie who was listening. "Although it seems we lost the Wetlands, if what the little Bird says is true."

"It's true enough," Birdie confirmed.

Suddenly, a rapping sound came from the door. The three of them looked toward the window but nothing immediately noticeable. Meeshell grumbled, "What now?" and walked over to the window. She peered through and then turned back to Rebecca and Birdie. "Just some klutzy fellow bangin the door with his broom handle. I can't believe they let the men clean the floors on this floor."

Curious, Rebecca walked over to the window and waited her turn to look through. Meeshell said, "Ain't much to see. I guess you can say he's a fine lookin fellow, if you like that type of thing." Meeshell then walked away and allowed Rebecca to peer through; and as she did, a jolt of excitement careened through her body.

Through the window, across the hall, and pretending to be mopping was a man she had not expected to see in such a horrid place: *Iah Vadimas!*

His sharp eyes looked into hers, and then he tapped a finger against his right temple. Rebecca tried to understand the message. *Does he want me to think? . . . Think about what?* She wanted to yell through the glass but knew it wouldn't be prudent to do so. Iah continued to sweep and moved further down the hall. He looked at her one final time and winked. And then he was out of sight.

Rebecca remained at the door for a short while as she tried to figure out what message he was attempting to pass. Regardless, Rebecca knew two things for sure: she wasn't alone, and it was okay to hope.

CHAPTER FORTY-THREE

District 19, Sector 12 – CS Processing Compound

Rebecca and her two cellmates were not allowed out of their room for the remainder of the day. Someone had delivered a single tray of food that barely had enough to feed Meeshell let alone all three of them—thankfully Birdie was very young and didn't need much to eat. The lights went out at an unknown time and the three cellmates took to their bunks. Meeshell's demeanor eased with each passing hour and she even offered up her bunk away from the toilet after admitting that it was rude of her to claim it without any discussion. "It's just that, I'm rather large—as I'm sure you've noticed—and these bunks are pretty small . . . anyhow, I tend to dangle, and being next to the toilet just seemed . . . you know what I mean?"

Rebecca and Birdie had told her not to worry; she could keep the bunk. Both Rebecca and Birdie slept with their feet facing the toilet and that satisfied them enough. Rebecca had trouble sleeping, however. Nighttime was the worst; that was when all of her worries and fears reappeared and taunted her about things she could do nothing about; and this night in particular, Iah's message was tormenting her. *What did he mean by tapping his temple?* Outside of "think," Iah's message was obscure, and Rebecca didn't want to accept "think" as the only answer to what he was trying to tell her; she wanted to believe that there was a much larger meaning eluding her, something that will help set her free when the time came. However, she felt uneasy; even though she was certain that the man she saw was Iah Vadimas, he didn't look exactly like the man she had first met; meaning, his hair was shaved down, just like hers, he was very thin and a bit beat up looking. Therefore, it was obvious that he had been living within the CS Processing Compound for an immeasurable amount of time. *But maybe that was Corbin's—I mean, my father's—plan.* Rebecca wasn't above thinking that her biological father was some sort of puppet master pulling everyone's strings in order to get what he wanted. She allowed herself to believe that Corbin *knew* she would end up there inside the CS Processing Compound, and that he was indirectly guiding her along some sort of spiritual journey that he *knew* she needed to take. *Iah being here with me is just another waypoint along this journey. Iah is going to help me grow inside of here, and then we will escape.* Unfortunately, without actually talking to Iah, there was no way for Rebecca to put her uneasiness to rest.

Morning came with a thunderous roar at the cell door. Rebecca popped up before her brain had time to wake, and she looked around at the confusing setting. Meeshell, who truly did dangle from her bunk, rolled onto her side and looked at the door with tired eyes. Birdie at some point during the night had tucked her head and arms inside her oversized shirt and used it as a sleeping bag; she pulled the collar of the shirt just low enough for her eyes to peer through and see what was the source of the commotion.

The source was Master Brenna. She had opened their door and was using some sort of metal stick—which Rebecca suspected was the same stick Master Brenna had jabbed into her stomach the day before—to bang the three metallic sides of the door frame. "WAKE UP! WAKE UP! WAKE UP!"

While still numb from being half asleep, Rebecca was the first to rise from her bunk. Birdie soon followed, as did Meeshell. The three of them stood idle inside their cell as Master Brenna moved further down the hall, banging on a few more doorframes of other sleepy *guests*.

And so this is how it's going to be every morning, thought Rebecca as she wiped sleep from her eyes.

"Form up!"

All of the women stepped into the hallway. There were roughly 250 to 300 women standing in the hall. One could easily and falsely think that if all 300 women were to organize, even with the simplest plot, that they could overtake Master Brenna and the Ether House; but Master Brenna wasn't the lone force this morning. There were 50 or more armed female guards with her, and each of those guards looked beefy and muscly; and, of course, there was also the factor that the great majority of the female guests were suffering from malnutrition and were feeble looking.

Almost at once, all 50 of the guards began shouting orders at select groups of women; the female guard standing before Rebecca's small group ordered them to turn to their right and raise their arms above their heads. Everyone did as ordered. Rebecca looked down at little Birdie and saw that each time she raised her arms, her pants dropped. *This is ridiculous*, she thought. *Give the girl some fitting clothes.*

And as if her thoughts were heard, the guard said, "You! Little girl! Get out of line!"

Birdie was very hesitant to stand alone, but what could she do? The little girl picked up her pants and stepped out of the line.

"These clothes make you worthless!" the guard shouted. "Go back into your room and wait for my return! This will be the only time I make this exception! Do you hear?!"

Birdie shouted out, "Yes, Master—"

"Then go!"

Holding her oversized pants, Birdie walked back into their room.

"The rest of you waste of human skin, march your asses toward the door! Stop when you get there! If I catch any of you pukes passing through, I will personally slay your ass!" And as if to make her point more thorough, the guard charged up her half-sized burn rifle.

Other guards in front of other groups made similar demands and threats.

All of the shouting and the congested marching made for a very disorienting start to the day. *Is it really going to be like this every morning?* It was a terrifying thought.

Rebecca and the women marched down the hall and toward the

doorway, stopping every so often as a group in front waited for their guard to allow them through. As Rebecca drew closer, she saw Master Brenna was at the doorway and holding a scanner, which she used on each woman that passed through into the stairwell.

"Good morning, lover," Master Brenna said to Rebecca while scanning her arm. The woman wore a terrible grin that suggested several foul things inside Rebecca's mind.

"Keep walking!" shouted the guard responsible for Rebecca's group. She had her burn rifle pointed right at Rebecca's chest.

Rebecca came into the stairwell and stopped next to the other two women who went before her. Rebecca watched the aggressiveness of their guard with her burn rifle and wondered if this doorway had been a previous point of defiance by former guests. *She acts as if all of us might rush through at once and make a run for it.* More questions she was sure would not be answered.

After Meeshell and a few others passed through, the guard led them up to the gallery and toward the doorway that led out to the gardens. "Today, you worms are responsible for the garden! You will pick the fruit and vegetables, and you will do so in a careful fashion! Is that clear?!"

The march to the courtyard was shorter this time. The three deteriorating bodies were still dangling from their poles. Rebecca had not a clue how to garden and assumed that someone would lead her, but when they stood on the central path dividing Ether House's garden, the guard said nothing more other than, "You have two hours!"

Two hours to do what? Rebecca's small group of women looked at each other and it seemed that only one had any experience with this task. Surprisingly, it was a younger woman—maybe in her twentieth year of age—who broke away from the group and went to a solid aluminum box, which was roughly the size of a human, and flipped open a lid. She pulled out some bags and tossed them to the ground, and she pulled out a metal watering can that had rust patches all over it. The young woman looked at Rebecca and company and said, "Come on, two hours isn't much time."

Rebecca was the first to start walking; Meeshell was right behind her. Rebecca asked in a hush tone, "What do we do? I've never gardened before." But before the woman could answer, Meeshell took up one of the bags and said, "We pick em. Boy, you sure did grow up in the Collective."

Rebecca grabbed a bag too and then watched all of the other woman grab bags before following the group into the rows of plants. Meeshell wasted no time; she walked right up to the first plant in the row, stuck her hand inside, and plucked out a fist full of green beans, stuffed them into the bag and went on to the next. Rebecca watched for a few seconds longer and then observed that the other women were doing similar actions, each was in her own row. *I guess do as they do.* She walked along the path, away from the first row Meeshell was inside, and into one of her own. The young woman who initiated today's work was already ahead of Meeshell; she was working vigorously. Rebecca initially took that as some sort of *good behavior* act, but by the end of their two hours, Rebecca would understand that haste was absolutely necessary in order to gather enough food for the day.

She bent down next to the prickly little plant and stuck her hands inside with little precaution. Her fingers grasped a two or three beans—she couldn't see exactly how many—and then plucked them free. Rebecca stuffed them into her bag and peered into the plant again. There were only a few more visible. She plucked those out as well and then observed the other woman already making their way down the line. *I need to move faster.* Rebecca went on to the next plant, sticking her hands inside, grabbing a few beans, and then placing them into the bag. She did this act again and witnessed a long-legged spider rush out of the plant and up her arm. She jerked her hands free and swatted the spider away, which then sent chills all through her body. *I didn't think there would be spiders inside.* The next time she stuck her hands inside, Rebecca was a lot more cautious, thus slower.

By the time Rebecca reached the halfway point, the other women were either near the end of their row or starting a new row.

"One hour!" shouted the observing guard.

At some point in time, and without Rebecca's notice, other houses had led their guests into the courtyard for gardening. Rebecca saw that every garden had bodies in it now, working just as her group was working. In some gardens, there were men as well as women working. Rebecca looked for Iah or Roland but found neither. Sighing, Rebecca went back to plucking beans.

She had eventually matched the other women's pace, but it was strenuous and difficult work. After an hour in, Rebecca's lower back was aching from the awkward squatting position. She thought that being in good physical shape should have prevented these back pains, but this position and movement was new to Rebecca's body, therefore, it was very hard on her.

She moved from plant to plant, each time seeming to find more and more beans and realizing that maybe she missed a few on the first quarter of the row.

Rebecca was almost a quarter into her second row when the guard yelled out, "Time's up!"

All of the women in Ether House's garden stood in their spots. Meeshell, who was at the end of her second row, used her dirty right hand to wipe the sweat seeping from her brow. She looked disappointed to be done so soon. Rebecca looked into her own bag and saw that it was halfway filled. *This isn't very much food.* She then noticed that the young woman from earlier had walked back to the aluminum container and extracted an armful of dirty red stakes. She walked to each row they worked inside and placed a stake at the heads of the rows. *So others know where we worked*, Rebecca figured. The remaining women gathered back at the aluminum container, as did Rebecca. When she arrived, she saw that their bags were full of beans, even more so than hers would have been had she been further along. *I didn't do a very good job.*

"Let's go!" the guard shouted.

Rebecca and the other women carried their bags to the door and into the gallery. The guard led them through the wide hall, passing several lines of women led by their masters, and into a large kitchen filled with different assortments of cooking appliances, machinery, pots and pans. Men and women in white clothes working diligently filled half of the room. Most of them were cleaning, but some of them were prepping for possibly the first meal of the day, Rebecca couldn't be sure—the only thing she was positive of was that she had yet to eat.

A sallow woman who looked too young for the gray hair on her head walked over to them and collected the bags. She said thank you with each bag she collected until she reached Rebecca. The woman felt the weight of the bag and looked despairingly into Rebecca's eyes.

"I'm sorry," was all Rebecca could utter.

The woman said nothing. She took the bags over to the counter and emptied their contents into a large mesh bin.

"Move it!" the guard screamed into Rebecca's ear. The rest of the women were already waiting outside the kitchen; Rebecca read caution on Meeshell's face. She quickly scuttled out of the kitchen and into the line. "That's your only warning, blondie! All right, you sorry sacks of estrogen, move out! Back to your rooms!"

The women walked hastily back toward the doorway they originally passed through (not too fast, but cautiously fast). Each of them returned to their respective rooms and the guard locked the doors behind them. Rebecca and Meeshell found Birdie standing suddenly from her bed. She said, "Where did you go?"

"To the courtyard," Meeshell answered. "We were gardening."

"If you can call what I did as gardening," Rebecca chimed.

Meeshell looked as if she wanted to say something critical in regards to Rebecca's poor results, but she withheld. Rebecca issued her a silent *thank you*; the last thing she needed was to hear criticism.

Breakfast (or lunch for that matter) came about an hour later. There were three trays delivered by a different group of women whose daily job was obviously that. The portions of food on the plastic plates were so small that it appeared comical. Meeshell laughed and then muttered curses as she ate hers with no effort. Rebecca did her best to extend the meal as long as possible in hope that the act would trick her stomach into thinking there was more. Her mind, during all of this—and during their gardening hours—was completely occupied by Iah's cryptic message: his tapping an index finger against his temple. *He clearly wants me to think, but about what?* Every possibility seemed as unlikely as the previous. The only thing that had any level of tangibility with her is that he wanted her to concentrate on something—to think.

"Well that was a real treat," Meeshell complained after licking her plate clean. She then looked at Birdie and Rebecca's nearly finished food and said, "Don't think I'm above licking yours too."

Birdie said, "You can have the rest of mine; I'm not very hungry."

Meeshell's eyes revealed how powerful the temptation was, but she said, "No, you need to eat, little bird. I'll live."

Rebecca handed her plate over to Meeshell and said, "Take mine."

Meeshell tried to refuse Rebecca's too but failed. "Thank you. Maybe after I lose a few pounds I will be able to handle such small portions.

Rebecca hoped they wouldn't be there long enough to find out. She then returned her attention to the message. *Maybe I'm approaching this all wrong. Maybe I need to consider William's manuscript.* Iah had played an integral role in the last bit she read, and Rebecca figured it was safe to assume that William included their conversation for a reason. She considered the telepathic power Iah had described, how we was capable of communication with people by thinking; and then she considered her failure at the MSF holding center, her almost drowning. *It didn't work,* she told herself. *I tried and I heard nothing. . . . Or maybe it did work, except Roland didn't hear me, but Iah did.* Rebecca also considered that maybe Roland did hear her but didn't know how to respond. This prospect energized her enough to throw away discouragement and try again.

She lay back onto her bed and closed her eyes. Rebecca concentrated as intensely as possible. *Iah, I'm here . . . hear me . . . I'm here.* She repeated this several times before eventually allowing peace to return to her mind. *It doesn't work.* Rebecca began picturing Iah in his room, pacing. She visualized him stopping and then silently saying, "There is nothing to fear. I'm here too. We will get out together." *But why can't you hear me? You're supposed to have this ability.* "We all have that ability. Haven't you considered that maybe it is working and that you aren't just imagining this?" *But I am just imagining it,* Rebecca thought. *I can make you do whatever I want.* She visualized Iah walking over to his door and looking through the window; she then saw Roland in the hall, standing there with some giant man in uniform yelling at him. She imagined Roland looking healthy, or at least healthier, and then she heard Iah say, "See, he's okay, for now. Our time here will be brief, I promise." But, of course, Rebecca believed none of it. *This is all imaginary. I'm going to lose my mind if I'm not careful.* She visualized Iah turning toward her, his words: "You can believe what you like. Either I am really having this conversation with you, or you are imagining it; regardless, it will only be what you make of it. So, I suggest making good from it and not madness." *It's mad either way. . . .* She sighed. *What am I doing?*

Outside their room came a low murmur of something scraping against either the floor or wall. Rebecca changed her vision from Iah to Master Brenna, slowly walking down the hall, dragging her stick along the wall, and wearing the smuggest grin she had ever seen. *Someone is going to be impaled today,* Rebecca realized or imagined; she was not sure which. Visions of Roland standing in the hall with a giant guard now abusing him filled her mind. Roland was healthy, but he was scared. *Not you*, Rebecca suddenly thought. *You can't be the one.* His face was so scared. "Don't make yourself mad," Iah's words echoed in her thoughts. *I won't.* Rebecca cleared the vision of Roland and thought of something entirely new. She imagined an entire city's worth of people amassing somewhere distant, under some large covering, in a desert. There were thousands of tents set up, yet only a single one had a light on. Rebecca visualized inside the tent and saw a man, unlike those of who surrounded him, reading a stack of papers. A scowl of concern was on his handsome face—or maybe it was a scowl of concentration or curiosity . . . Rebecca was unsure. She was, however, sure that the man was the one who haunted her thoughts almost daily, that the man was William Coulee. Rebecca wanted to reach out to him, call his name, but all he did was read and make concerned faces.

And then William, the tents, and the desert—all of it—vanished. Iah's words echoed in Rebecca's thoughts—her words in Iah's voice, she thought—"We're not alone." *Who else is here?* Someone she knew . . . but whom. And a new vision filled her mind: An older man—not too old, but older—was sitting on a bed just like Rebecca's, like everyone's inside the CS Processing Center. Rebecca's vision rotated so that she could see his face. His eyes were gazing at the floor but simultaneously appeared to be looking at her. Rebecca knew those eyes. "They've fooled all of us, haven't they?" the man said. "But we know, don't we. My stay here is temporary, and when the time is right, I will get out, and there will be hell to pay. . . . Are you familiar with that term—that place? Are you, Rebecca? I will bring it—I will bring Hell right here and there will be nowhere to hide. I will start with them and then I will find you, my sweet. Oh how I tried to let you live, oh how I tried. But no longer. You and your lover, your family, and even those bitches in the room with you, all of you will pay the toll. This world is mine! Do you hear me?! THIS WORLD IS MINE!"

Rebecca cleared her mind and she opened her eyes.

"Are you all right?" Birdie asked from her bed.

Rebecca looked to Birdie and then to Meeshell; both of them were looking back at her. "Yeah, I'm fine."

"We thought you fell asleep."

Rebecca swung her legs over the edge and sat up. "No, I was just thinking."

"Happy thoughts, I hope."

Rebecca forced a weak smile. "Yeah . . . happy thoughts."

EPILOGUE

District 1, Sector 1

Tension filled the MSF Situation Room. Originally constructed to be an amphitheater by the forty-seventh Minister, the building had since been converted it into a high-tech monitoring system that played host to the Security Chief and his MSF officers whenever a conflict had arisen. And there were many conflicts these days.

Jonas Lundquist stood in the center of the room; his hands folded behind his back. His eyes glazed over the seventy-one faces that stared anxiously back at him. There were supposed to be ninety-six pairs of eyes staring at him, not seventy-one. "Am I to assume this is all?"

A few officers quickly looked at each other, then toward the main doorway that remained open for last minute stragglers, and then back to the newly declared Lord. Another officer quietly cleared his throat before the room fell back into total silence.

"Well, then, maybe I should assume that these missing twenty-five are being deliberately insubordinate. I can read on some of your faces that these twenty-five officers had made it clear that they were 'uncomfortable' with my detainment of Minister Theoman, that maybe their absence from our mandatory meeting is not only an act of defiance but possibly an act of . . . war?"

Some of the officers shuffled their feet while others cleared their throats or tugged at their constrictive collars.

A man in the middle of the room stood up and said, "I think your assessment, Lord Lunquist, is dead on."

Every single face in the room turned to look at Amon Walkure.

"And based on your assessment," Lord Lundquist said, "what would you have me do with these insubordinate officers?"

Walkure grinned slightly and said very casually, "I would execute them, sir, in the same manner used for traitors and members of the Heretique. I would then send their subordinate officers, their family members, and even their friends to me, at one of my many CS compounds."

"And you would have me be that lenient?"

Lenient? thought Yarmen Cassell, who sat seven rows back from Lord Lundquist. He wasn't shocked by the things Walkure had said or by the fact that Lord Lundquist wanted these traitors dead; he was shocked that Lord Lundquist had used the word "lenient" to describe the brutal impaling those twenty-five seceding officers would receive.

"Very well," Lord Lundquist continued. "You may have your way, Director Walkure. I do feel that it is imperative that we send a strong message to those who feel defiant. The lenient and forgiving days of Minister Theoman's reign have ended; a strong, tightly gripped Collective is the future. Leniency brings forth insubordination, insubordination brings forth chaos, chaos brings forth insurrection, and I think we all know what insurrection brings forth. . . ."

The third coming of Ziusudra, thought Yarmen Cassell. No one in the room wanted that. It would mean reform, which would mean terminations and displacements, *if one believes in such lore.* Yarmen Cassell was not a theological man, but living within the Collective forced him and everyone else to acknowledge the traditions of the Ministry and its supposed mystical elements.

"*Ehm,*" coughed Amon Walkure.

Lord Lundquist's disingenuously kind eyes focused on the man.

"Director Walkure, you wish to speak?"

"Yes, my Lord. I was just pondering the possibility of putting the disgraced Minister to death. His execution may extinguish any hope that the seceding sectors have in reinstating the old Ministry. Or we could possibly make his death less public with a silent assassination that appears 'natural' in its cause. Either way, the termination of the Minister may be good for the Collective's step to move beyond the Minister's broken policies."

You just want to kill a leader, thought Cassell. *You drip with a thirst for blood. Lord Lundquist must see past this. Killing the Minister will only prove to be—*

"I understand your concern and resolve, Director Walkure," said Lord Lundquist, "however, I do believe that the Minister's death will merely accelerate the situation. Eliminating Theoman will eliminate the seceding sector's hope. Hope will make the seceding officers and sectors weak. We want them to hope. We want them to be cautious. Their hope and caution will allow our forces to overrun them. If we kill their hope, then we kill their caution, and there is nothing more dangerous than a quarry that has no caution."

Wise words, thought Cassell.

"But, with that stated, I want Theoman completely cut off from any human contact. Keep him locked tight, Director Walkure. I do not want a repeat of the previous Director's mistakes made with Benjamin Vermil."

Interesting comparison, thought Cassell. Benjamin Vermil's manipulation of Jillian Heddington had completely escaped his mind. *His converting of that caretaker is what sparked all of this turmoil. They feared Vermil, and yet they kept him alive, just like Lord Lundquist is keeping Theoman alive. Why? What is this fear?*

"Minister Theoman is safely contained inside your custom-made cell at our main processing center in Sector 12," Walkure assured. "There are four main vents that will pass a sleep agent inside the room, incapacitating the former Minister and allowing our caretakers to enter without any possible threat of . . . mental manipulation."

"Good, Director. Ensure that it stays that way."

"Excuse me, my Lord," said a stern-faced man, thin and proud.

"Officer Martin, you may speak."

"Thank you, my Lord. I am wondering what your plans are for our detained former directors. Each of my sector's directors surrendered without challenge. Am I to assume that we will be transferring them to one of Director Walkure's facilities?"

Lord Lundquist paced about the room. "Thank you for your question, Officer Martin; and no, you will not be transferring your detained directors. I'm afraid that reformation is not in order for these corrupted souls; they're too engrained with the former Minister's ideology, his philosophy. While they promised the Collective liberty, they are servants of corruption. 'For of whom a man is overcome, of the same is he brought in bondage.' I would rather have these disgraced directors disappear. Their authority is still too hot. We need to smother these souls and bury their influence."

I'm not surprised, thought Cassell. *It would be a dangerous game, allowing these directors to live on.*

"My Lord," said a stouter, demonstrative man, "are you asking us to terminate these former directors?"

A creased grin formed on Lord Lundquist's face. "Asking . . . ? No. Telling, yes. And before another of you can ask another question with an obvious answer, I want these men and women terminated in silence. I want their bodies immediately disposed of, as if they had never existed. Not buried. Not casketed. Gone. Is that clear?"

The stout officer gulped, nodded, and said, "Yes, my Lord," as did all of the officers in the room, including Yarmen Cassell. *This will not be pleasant business.*

"Now," Lord Lundquist said in a deceivingly pleasant tone, "are there any more questions that I can answer?"

The room remained silent.

"Then you are dismissed." Lord Lundquist's eyes found Yarmen Cassell and Officer Carrie Gutherie's eyes. "All, but you two, we have further business to discuss."

As expected, thought Yarmen Cassell, who had stood and straightened his MSF uniform. Officer Gutherie stood too, Cassell noticed as he glanced over in her direction. Officer Gutherie wasn't a comely woman, but she was also not an ugly one. *She is not my Penelope*, Cassell compared, as he often did when seeing a woman. No woman but one had ever compared to his Penelope. *And undoubtedly, this woman's fate is what we're going to discuss.*

After all of the officers had exited the room, including Director Walkure, who seemed reluctant to leave, the main doorway closed and Lord Lundquist immediately turned to Yarmen Cassell and said, "I want a status update."

The vagueness of the question was not as it seemed; Yarmen Cassell knew what Lord Lundquist wanted. "My men had located the stolen hovercar at a crash site just north of the Wylde's compound in Sector 2." Cassell opened some images on his digital notepad and showed them to Lord Lundquist while Officer Gutherie stood anxiously by. "As you can see, my Lord, there was hardly anything left when we had arrived."

Lord Lundquist looked at the charred remains of the stolen Sector 18 hovercar and even saw what he believed to be the fragments of a human skull. "And its passengers?"

"All three were deceased upon arrival. I ordered my men to take samples to be tested and all three passengers' remains—Roland Weymouth, Simon Wylde, and Rebecca Wylde—were confirmed. Their identities had been wiped from the Ministry database, just as you had ordered. My men then had the remains of the car dismantled and sent the salvageable pieces to the scrapping center in Sector 3."

Lord Lundquist returned the digital notepad to Yarmen Cassell and said, "I had ordered you to personally oversee the executions of Simon and Rebecca Wylde, not clean up the ashes of your mistake."

Yarmen Cassell remained calm. "Yes, my Lord. The operation did not go well, nonetheless, Simon and Rebecca Wylde were terminated, as you desired. I take full responsibility for the failure of the operation and will oblige to whatever discipline you seem fit."

Lord Lundquist smiled and said, "I know you will, Officer." He then looked toward Officer Gutherie and said, "What is the status of your operation?"

Officer Gutherie's eyes danced from Lord Lundquist's to Yarmen Cassell's in what appeared to be an appeal for courage. "My Lord, the operation had a similar fate as Officer Cassell's. I had ordered my tactical unit to the outer perimeter of Outpost 6. We needed to confirm Agent Coulee's direct whereabouts, and so I had ordered an early delivery of supplies to the outpost, which confirmed Agent Coulee's location. And as you had suggested, my Lord, I had my tactical team deploy a stalker into the outpost, but Agent Coulee and another, unidentified man neutralized it. Agent Coulee and the unidentified man escaped on foot—"

"I had suggested," Lord Lundquist interrupted, "that you send in a stalker and have your tactical team *surround* the outpost so that Agent Coulee could not escape."

Officer Guthrie stammered, "Yes, my Lord, that was my intention, but the tactical unit's hovercraft malfunctioned and had to make an emergency landing during the operation. A replacement hovercraft picked the unit up, but by that point Agent Coulee and the other man had escaped the outpost. However, my unit did locate Agent Coulee and neutralized the unidentified man."

"And yet, Agent Coulee escaped once again?"

"My tactical unit was ambushed, my Lord. Our post-mortem unit estimated that the ambush was carried out by four or five nomadic soldiers armed with ballistic rifles. It is assumed that Agent Coulee was either taken prisoner by these men or is dead."

What a colossal failure, thought Yarmen Cassell.

Lord Lundquist stared long and hard at Officer Guthrie in chilling silence. He finally said, "Taken prisoner or dead."

Officer Guthrie nodded quickly. "Yes, my Lord."

"Tell me that you sent a second unit into the Dead Sands to locate these . . . nomads."

"I did, my Lord. However, they failed to locate Agent Coulee or the nomads, which reinforces my theory that Agent Coulee is—"

"I don't want to hear *theories*," Lord Lundquist hissed; his anger showed itself for the first time. "I want resolve. I want success"—he then snapped an awful glare at Yarmen Cassell—"not *failure*."

Yarmen Cassell nodded his head and said almost synchronously with Officer Guthrie, "Yes, my Lord."

"What am I to think when two of my most competent officers prove themselves to be *incompetent*? What does that say about the MSF and its leadership?"

When neither Yarmen Cassell nor Officer Guthrie responded, Lord Lundquist said, "Officer Guthrie, you are relieved of your duty as Chief Officer of Sector 32. You will return to your post and await my word for who will be replacing you. And I do pray that you are right about Agent Coulee's death in the desert, because if he is found alive, you will not be. Understood?"

Officer Guthrie nodded her head nervously and said shakily, "Yes, my Lord."

"As for you, Officer Cassell, the same can be said. If you are certain that both Simon and Rebecca Wylde are dead, then so be it. But if you are wrong . . ."

"I understand, my Lord," Yarmen Cassell said with confidence.

Lord Lundquist stared at him for a slight moment before saying, "You two are dismissed."

Yarmen Cassell and Officer Guthrie left with considerable haste. Yarmen Cassell waited until they were safely away from the Situation Room before saying to Officer Guthrie, "How did your second unit manage to not locate Agent Coulee?"

Officer Guthrie, who still looked shaken from the meeting, managed to fire back, "How is it that your dozen or so agents failed to kill a spoiled sot and his pretty little wife?"

Yarmen Cassell smiled. *You dumb bitch. You know so little.* "Simon and Rebecca Wylde were killed, therefore, the objective was achieved, no matter how the manner. Your failure, however, will be your undoing."

"You should keep your thoughts to yourself," Officer Guthrie huffed and continued to walk.

"Tell me, was it Agent Coulee's admirable good looks that caused you to flub the mission, or was it simply your incompetence?"

Officer Guthrie's face flushed as she said, "Maybe I failed at killing Agent Coulee, but I will not fail at killing you if you don't shut your mouth."

"Careful, *Agent* Guthrie; you're threatening an officer."

Officer Guthrie glared at Yarmen Cassell as she turned the corner at the hallway's t-junction and continued walking with haste.

That is why the Ministry should not have granted women the authority of being MSF officers, thought Yarmen Cassell. *They have their places in this world, but an MSF officer is not one of them. I do hope that Jonas Lundquist sees this and undoes its mess.* He turned the other corner and thought, *But then again, it may not matter if he ever discovers what I did.* The act he was referring to was the falsification of Rebecca Wylde and Roland Weymouth's deaths. *He was right about the Ministry being corrupt.* It wasn't difficult for Yarmen Cassell to get access to Rebecca Wylde and Roland Weymouth's files in the database and wipe their identification numbers clean. *Even if they are picked up by the MSF, no one will know their true identities, unless they tell them, which would be a grievous situation for both them and me.* Sticking his neck out for the daughter of the enemy's leader was not something Yarmen Cassell felt wonderful about doing. *But I pay my debts. No matter what she does from here on out, I hope she never surfaces again. I paid my debt, but I will not pay it twice.*

Twenty miles away, and gaining further distance, sat Director Amon Walkure inside his hovercar. He was in the midst of returning to his office at the CS Main Processing Center when he pulled out his digital notepad and ordered up the most recent list of newly arrived "guests." The names that filed down the left side of the screen were organized by the house each was assigned. Accompanying each name was an MSF-taken profile picture. Walkure took a mild level of pleasure in perusing the sad faces of each new guest. Since his relatively recent appointment, Walkure had recognized several faces inside previous incoming waves: an academic-aged and troubled son of a former instructor of his, an older man he had seen often at one of the food markets in District 14 of Sector 6 eight years prior, when Walkure was working as an undercover agent ousting Heretique sympathizers. Walkure had even seen the face of an estranged aunt on his mother's side. He had heard several months later that she had died in her cell from some bacteria infection that liquefied her internal organs. "One less to pity," he had told his aid who had delivered the news.

With the new wave of incoming guests listed before him, Walkure scanned through the faces before stopping on one. *Wait a second . . .*

Walkure expanded the photo of the tired, dirt-smudged female face. She had bags under her green eyes, and her soiled blond hair was draped slightly over her freckled cheeks, but Amon Walkure was positive he had seen this blond beauty before. He looked at the name associated with the face but didn't recognize it. *Mary Macyntire? . . . No, no, no . . .* he thought; Amon Walkure was not a man who forgot a face. He looked closer at the female's green eyes and thought, *I know you, Beauty,* and then fell into a fit of laughter.

Walkure's driver briefly looked into the mirror to see what the commotion was about.

"Oh ho! This is too good, too good to be true. You are not Mary

Macyntire . . . no, no no. You have a different name, my Beauty." *And how sweet it will be when I expose her . . . and when I expose him, Cassell . . . you've been a bad boy, Yarmen Cassell.* Walkure's devious mind settled for a moment and his eyes returned to Mary Macyntire's photo. *All in due time, all in due time. But for now, you're mine, my Beauty . . . you're mine.* "Driver, pick up the speed. I am needed back at the office." *Rebecca Badeau is waiting for me, and I will not keep her waiting much longer.*

COMING SOON

The Sinner King:
BOOK OF AIR

Visit
www.TheSinnerKing.com
to discover more.

Born in 1979. Donald Ray Crislip is the author of *The Sinner King* series. He attended Kent State University and the University of Toledo where he studied English, screenwriting, and filmmaking. He was a nominee for the Dean's Award for Outstanding Achievements in the College of Arts and Sciences. He spent many years working in the film and web industries before becoming a novelist.